Acclaim for Cormac McCarthy's

THE ROAD

"Illuminated by extraordinary tenderness. . . . Simple yet mysterious, simultaneously cryptic and crystal clear. *The Road* offers nothing in the way of escape or comfort. But its fearless wisdom is more indelible than reassurance could ever be." —*The New York Times*

"No American writer since Faulkner has wandered so willingly into the swamp waters of deviltry and redemption. . . . [McCarthy] has written this last waltz with enough elegant reserve to capture what matters most." —*The Boston Globe*

"There is an urgency to each page, and a raw emotional pull . . . making [*The Road*] easily one of the most harrowing books you'll ever encounter. . . . Once opened, [it is] nearly impossible to put down; it is as if you must keep reading in order for the characters to stay alive. . . . *The Road* is a deeply imagined work and harrowing no matter what your politics." —*Bookforum*

Cormac McCarthy

THE ROAD

Cormac McCarthy is the author of ten previous novels. Among his honors are the National Book Award and the National Book Critics Circle Award.

INTERNATIONAL

THE ROAD

THE ROAD

Cormac McCarthy

Vintage International

VINTAGE BOOKS

A DIVISION OF RANDOM HOUSE, INC.

NEW YORK

FIRST VINTAGE INTERNATIONAL EDITION

Copyright © 2006 by M-71, Ltd.

The Library of Congress has cataloged the Knopf edition as follows:
McCarthy, Cormac, [date]
The road / by Cormac McCarthy.— 1st ed.
p. cm.
1. Fathers and sons—Fiction.   2. Voyages and travels—United States—Fiction.   3. Regression (Civilization)—Fiction.
4. Survival skills—Fiction.   I. Title.
PS3563.C337R63   2006
813'.54—dc22
2006023629

VINTAGE ISBN: 978-0-307-27792-3

www.vintagebooks.com

Book design by Peter A. Andersen
Manufactured in the United States of America
30 29 28

This book is dedicated to

JOHN FRANCIS McCARTHY

THE ROAD

When he woke in the woods in the dark and the cold of the night he'd reach out to touch the child sleeping beside him. Nights dark beyond darkness and the days more gray each one than what had gone before. Like the onset of some cold glaucoma dimming away the world. His hand rose and fell softly with each precious breath. He pushed away the plastic tarpaulin and raised himself in the stinking robes and blankets and looked toward the east for any light but there was none. In the dream from which he'd wakened he had wandered in a cave where the child led him by the hand. Their light playing over the wet flowstone walls. Like pilgrims in a fable swallowed up and lost among the inward parts of some granitic beast. Deep stone flues where the water dripped and sang. Tolling in the silence the minutes of the earth and the hours and the days of it and the years without cease. Until they stood in a great stone room where lay a black and ancient lake. And on the far shore a creature that raised its dripping mouth from the rimstone pool and stared into the light with eyes dead white and sightless as the eggs of spiders. It swung its head low over the water as if to take the scent of what it could not see. Crouching there pale and naked and translucent, its alabaster bones cast up in shadow on the rocks behind it. Its bowels, its beating heart. The brain that pulsed in a dull glass bell. It swung its head from side to side and then gave out a low moan and turned and lurched away and loped soundlessly into the dark.

With the first gray light he rose and left the boy sleeping and walked out to the road and squatted and studied the country to the south. Barren, silent, godless. He thought the month was October but he wasnt sure. He hadnt kept a calendar for years. They were moving south. There'd be no surviving another winter here.

When it was light enough to use the binoculars he glassed the valley below. Everything paling away into the murk. The soft ash blowing in loose swirls over the blacktop. He studied what he could see. The segments of road down there among the dead trees. Looking for anything of color. Any movement. Any trace of standing smoke. He lowered the glasses and pulled down the cotton mask from his face and wiped his nose on the back of his wrist and then

glassed the country again. Then he just sat there holding
the binoculars and watching the ashen daylight congeal
over the land. He knew only that the child was his warrant.
He said: If he is not the word of God God never spoke.

When he got back the boy was still asleep. He pulled the
blue plastic tarp off of him and folded it and carried it out
to the grocery cart and packed it and came back with their
plates and some cornmeal cakes in a plastic bag and a plastic bottle of syrup. He spread the small tarp they used for a
table on the ground and laid everything out and he took
the pistol from his belt and laid it on the cloth and then he
just sat watching the boy sleep. He'd pulled away his mask
in the night and it was buried somewhere in the blankets.
He watched the boy and he looked out through the trees
toward the road. This was not a safe place. They could be
seen from the road now it was day. The boy turned in the
blankets. Then he opened his eyes. Hi, Papa, he said.

I'm right here.

I know.

An hour later they were on the road. He pushed the cart
and both he and the boy carried knapsacks. In the knapsacks were essential things. In case they had to abandon

the cart and make a run for it. Clamped to the handle of the cart was a chrome motorcycle mirror that he used to watch the road behind them. He shifted the pack higher on his shoulders and looked out over the wasted country. The road was empty. Below in the little valley the still gray serpentine of a river. Motionless and precise. Along the shore a burden of dead reeds. Are you okay? he said. The boy nodded. Then they set out along the blacktop in the gunmetal light, shuffling through the ash, each the other's world entire.

They crossed the river by an old concrete bridge and a few miles on they came upon a roadside gas station. They stood in the road and studied it. I think we should check it out, the man said. Take a look. The weeds they forded fell to dust about them. They crossed the broken asphalt apron and found the tank for the pumps. The cap was gone and the man dropped to his elbows to smell the pipe but the odor of gas was only a rumor, faint and stale. He stood and looked over the building. The pumps standing with their hoses oddly still in place. The windows intact. The door to the service bay was open and he went in. A standing metal toolbox against one wall. He went through the drawers but there was nothing there that he could use. Good half-inch drive sockets. A ratchet. He stood looking around the garage. A metal barrel full of trash. He went into the office. Dust and ash everywhere. The boy stood in the door. A metal desk, a cashregister. Some old automotive manuals, swollen and sodden. The linoleum was stained and curling from the leaking roof. He crossed to the desk and stood there. Then he picked up the phone and dialed the number of his father's house in that long ago. The boy watched him. What are you doing? he said.

A quarter mile down the road he stopped and looked back. We're not thinking, he said. We have to go back. He pushed the cart off the road and tilted it over where it could not be seen and they left their packs and went back to the station. In the service bay he dragged out the steel trashdrum and tipped it over and pawed out all the quart plastic oilbottles. Then they sat in the floor decanting them of their dregs one by one, leaving the bottles to stand upside down draining into a pan until at the end they had almost a half quart of motor oil. He screwed down the plastic cap and wiped the bottle off with a rag and hefted it in his hand. Oil for their little slutlamp to light the long gray dusks, the long gray dawns. You can read me a story, the boy said. Cant you, Papa? Yes, he said. I can.

. . .

On the far side of the river valley the road passed through a stark black burn. Charred and limbless trunks of trees stretching away on every side. Ash moving over the road and the sagging hands of blind wire strung from the blackened lightpoles whining thinly in the wind. A burned house in a clearing and beyond that a reach of meadowlands stark and gray and a raw red mudbank where a roadworks lay abandoned. Farther along were billboards advertising motels. Everything as it once had been save faded and weathered. At the top of the hill they stood in the cold and the wind, getting their breath. He looked at the boy. I'm all right, the boy said. The man put his hand on his shoulder and nodded toward the open country below them. He got the binoculars out of the cart and stood in the road and glassed the plain down there where the shape of a city stood in the grayness like a charcoal drawing sketched across the waste. Nothing to see. No smoke. Can I see? the boy said. Yes. Of course you can. The boy leaned on the cart and adjusted the wheel. What do you see? the man said. Nothing. He lowered the glasses. It's raining. Yes, the man said. I know.

They left the cart in a gully covered with the tarp and made their way up the slope through the dark poles of the standing trees to where he'd seen a running ledge of rock and they sat under the rock overhang and watched the gray sheets of rain blow across the valley. It was very cold. They sat huddled together wrapped each in a blanket over their coats and after a while the rain stopped and there was just the dripping in the woods.

When it had cleared they went down to the cart and pulled away the tarp and got their blankets and the things they would need for the night. They went back up the hill and made their camp in the dry dirt under the rocks and the man sat with his arms around the boy trying to warm him. Wrapped in the blankets, watching the nameless dark come to enshroud them. The gray shape of the city vanished in the night's onset like an apparition and he lit the little lamp and set it back out of the wind. Then they walked out to the road and he took the boy's hand and they went to the top of the hill where the road crested and where they could see out over the darkening country to the south, standing there in the wind, wrapped in their blankets, watching for any sign of a fire or a lamp. There was nothing. The lamp in the rocks on the side of the hill was little more than a mote of light and after a while they walked back. Everything too wet to make a fire. They ate their poor meal cold and lay down in their bedding with the lamp between them. He'd brought the boy's book but the boy was too tired for reading. Can we leave the lamp on till I'm asleep? he said. Yes. Of course we can.

He was a long time going to sleep. After a while he turned and looked at the man. His face in the small light streaked with black from the rain like some old world thespian. Can I ask you something? he said.

Yes. Of course.

Are we going to die?

Sometime. Not now.

And we're still going south.

Yes.

So we'll be warm.

Yes.

Okay.

Okay what?

Nothing. Just okay.

Go to sleep.

Okay.

I'm going to blow out the lamp. Is that okay?

Yes. That's okay.

And then later in the darkness: Can I ask you something?

Yes. Of course you can.

What would you do if I died?

If you died I would want to die too.

So you could be with me?

Yes. So I could be with you.

Okay.

He lay listening to the water drip in the woods. Bedrock, this. The cold and the silence. The ashes of the late world carried on the bleak and temporal winds to and fro in the void. Carried forth and scattered and carried forth again. Everything uncoupled from its shoring. Unsupported in the ashen air. Sustained by a breath, trembling and brief. If only my heart were stone.

He woke before dawn and watched the gray day break. Slow and half opaque. He rose while the boy slept and pulled on his shoes and wrapped in his blanket he walked out through the trees. He descended into a gryke in the stone and there he crouched coughing and he coughed for a long time. Then he just knelt in the ashes. He raised his face to the paling day. Are you there? he whispered. Will I see you at the last? Have you a neck by which to throttle you? Have you a heart? Damn you eternally have you a soul? Oh God, he whispered. Oh God.

They passed through the city at noon of the day following. He kept the pistol to hand on the folded tarp on top of the cart. He kept the boy close to his side. The city was mostly burned. No sign of life. Cars in the street caked with ash, everything covered with ash and dust. Fossil tracks in the dried sludge. A corpse in a doorway dried to leather. Grimacing at the day. He pulled the boy closer. Just remember that the things you put into your head are there forever, he said. You might want to think about that.

You forget some things, dont you?

Yes. You forget what you want to remember and you remember what you want to forget.

There was a lake a mile from his uncle's farm where he and his uncle used to go in the fall for firewood. He sat in the back of the rowboat trailing his hand in the cold wake while his uncle bent to the oars. The old man's feet in their black kid shoes braced against the uprights. His straw hat. His cob pipe in his teeth and a thin drool swinging from the pipebowl. He turned to take a sight on the far shore, cradling the oarhandles, taking the pipe from his mouth to wipe his chin with the back of his hand. The shore was lined with birchtrees that stood bone pale against the dark of the evergreens beyond. The edge of the lake a riprap of twisted stumps, gray and weathered, the windfall trees of a hurricane years past. The trees themselves had long been sawed for firewood and carried away. His uncle turned the boat and shipped the oars and they drifted over the sandy shallows until the transom grated in the sand. A dead perch lolling belly up in the clear water. Yellow leaves. They left their shoes on the warm painted boards and dragged the boat up onto the beach and set out the anchor at the end of its rope. A lardcan poured with concrete with an eyebolt in the center. They walked along the shore while his uncle studied the treestumps, puffing at his pipe, a manila rope coiled over his shoulder. He picked one out and they turned it over, using the roots for leverage, until they got it half floating in the water. Trousers rolled to the knee but still they got wet. They tied the rope to a cleat at the rear of the boat and rowed back across the lake, jerking the stump slowly behind them. By then it was already evening. Just the slow periodic rack and shuffle of the oarlocks. The lake dark glass and windowlights coming on along the shore. A radio somewhere. Neither of them had spoken a word. This was the perfect day of his childhood. This the day to shape the days upon.

· · ·

They bore on south in the days and weeks to follow. Solitary and dogged. A raw hill country. Aluminum houses. At times they could see stretches of the interstate highway below them through the bare stands of secondgrowth timber. Cold and growing colder. Just beyond the high gap in the mountains they stood and looked out over the great gulf to the south where the country as far as they could see was burned away, the blackened shapes of rock standing out of the shoals of ash and billows of ash rising up and blowing downcountry through the waste. The track of the dull sun moving unseen beyond the murk.

They were days fording that cauterized terrain. The boy had found some crayons and painted his facemask with fangs and he trudged on uncomplaining. One of the front wheels of the cart had gone wonky. What to do about it? Nothing. Where all was burnt to ash before them no fires were to be had and the nights were long and dark and cold beyond anything they'd yet encountered. Cold to crack the stones. To take your life. He held the boy shivering against him and counted each frail breath in the blackness.

. . .

He woke to the sound of distant thunder and sat up. The faint light all about, quivering and sourceless, refracted in the rain of drifting soot. He pulled the tarp about them and he lay awake a long time listening. If they got wet there'd be no fires to dry by. If they got wet they would probably die.

The blackness he woke to on those nights was sightless and impenetrable. A blackness to hurt your ears with listening. Often he had to get up. No sound but the wind in the bare and blackened trees. He rose and stood tottering in that cold autistic dark with his arms outheld for balance while the vestibular calculations in his skull cranked out their reckonings. An old chronicle. To seek out the upright. No fall but preceded by a declination. He took great marching steps into the nothingness, counting them against his return. Eyes closed, arms oaring. Upright to what? Something nameless in the night, lode or matrix. To which he and the stars were common satellite. Like the great pendulum in its rotunda scribing through the long day movements of the universe of which you may say it knows nothing and yet know it must.

· · ·

It took two days to cross that ashen scabland. The road beyond ran along the crest of a ridge where the barren woodland fell away on every side. It's snowing, the boy said. He looked at the sky. A single gray flake sifting down. He caught it in his hand and watched it expire there like the last host of christendom.

They pushed on together with the tarp pulled over them. The wet gray flakes twisting and falling out of nothing. Gray slush by the roadside. Black water running from under the sodden drifts of ash. No more balefires on the distant ridges. He thought the bloodcults must have all consumed one another. No one traveled this road. No road-agents, no marauders. After a while they came to a road-side garage and they stood within the open door and looked out at the gray sleet gusting down out of the high country.

They collected some old boxes and built a fire in the floor and he found some tools and emptied out the cart and sat working on the wheel. He pulled the bolt and bored out the collet with a hand drill and resleeved it with a section of pipe he'd cut to length with a hacksaw. Then he bolted it all back together and stood the cart upright and wheeled it around the floor. It ran fairly true. The boy sat watching everything.

In the morning they went on. Desolate country. A boarhide nailed to a barndoor. Ratty. Wisp of a tail. Inside the barn three bodies hanging from the rafters, dried and dusty among the wan slats of light. There could be something here, the boy said. There could be some corn or something. Let's go, the man said.

Mostly he worried about their shoes. That and food. Always food. In an old batboard smokehouse they found a ham gambreled up in a high corner. It looked like something fetched from a tomb, so dried and drawn. He cut into it with his knife. Deep red and salty meat inside. Rich and good. They fried it that night over their fire, thick slices of it, and put the slices to simmer with a tin of beans. Later he woke in the dark and he thought that he'd heard bulldrums beating somewhere in the low dark hills. Then the wind shifted and there was just the silence.

. . .

In dreams his pale bride came to him out of a green and leafy canopy. Her nipples pipeclayed and her rib bones painted white. She wore a dress of gauze and her dark hair was carried up in combs of ivory, combs of shell. Her smile, her downturned eyes. In the morning it was snowing again. Beads of small gray ice strung along the lightwires overhead.

He mistrusted all of that. He said the right dreams for a man in peril were dreams of peril and all else was the call of languor and of death. He slept little and he slept poorly. He dreamt of walking in a flowering wood where birds flew before them he and the child and the sky was aching blue but he was learning how to wake himself from just such siren worlds. Lying there in the dark with the uncanny taste of a peach from some phantom orchard fading in his mouth. He thought if he lived long enough the world at last would all be lost. Like the dying world the newly blind inhabit, all of it slowly fading from memory.

From daydreams on the road there was no waking. He plodded on. He could remember everything of her save her scent. Seated in a theatre with her beside him leaning forward listening to the music. Gold scrollwork and sconces and the tall columnar folds of the drapes at either side of the stage. She held his hand in her lap and he could feel the tops of her stockings through the thin stuff of her summer dress. Freeze this frame. Now call down your dark and your cold and be damned.

He fashioned sweeps from two old brooms he'd found and wired them to the cart to clear the limbs from the road in front of the wheels and he put the boy in the basket and stood on the rear rail like a dogmusher and they set off down the hills, guiding the cart on the curves with their bodies in the manner of bobsledders. It was the first that he'd seen the boy smile in a long time.

At the crest of the hill was a curve and a pullout in the road. An old trail that led off through the woods. They walked out and sat on a bench and looked out over the valley where the land rolled away into the gritty fog. A lake down there. Cold and gray and heavy in the scavenged bowl of the countryside.

What is that, Papa?

It's a dam.

What's it for?

It made the lake. Before they built the dam that was

just a river down there. The dam used the water that ran through it to turn big fans called turbines that would generate electricity.

To make lights.

Yes. To make lights.

Can we go down there and see it?

I think it's too far.

Will the dam be there for a long time?

I think so. It's made out of concrete. It will probably be there for hundreds of years. Thousands, even.

Do you think there could be fish in the lake?

No. There's nothing in the lake.

In that long ago somewhere very near this place he'd watched a falcon fall down the long blue wall of the mountain and break with the keel of its breastbone the midmost from a flight of cranes and take it to the river below all gangly and wrecked and trailing its loose and blowsy plumage in the still autumn air.

The grainy air. The taste of it never left your mouth. They stood in the rain like farm animals. Then they went on, holding the tarp over them in the dull drizzle. Their feet were wet and cold and their shoes were being ruined.

On the hillsides old crops dead and flattened. The barren ridgeline trees raw and black in the rain.

And the dreams so rich in color. How else would death call you? Waking in the cold dawn it all turned to ash instantly. Like certain ancient frescoes entombed for centuries suddenly exposed to the day.

The weather lifted and the cold and they came at last into the broad lowland river valley, the pieced farmland still visible, everything dead to the root along the barren bottomlands. They trucked on along the blacktop. Tall clapboard houses. Machinerolled metal roofs. A log barn in a field with an advertisement in faded ten-foot letters across the roofslope. See Rock City.

The roadside hedges were gone to rows of black and twisted brambles. No sign of life. He left the boy standing in the road holding the pistol while he climbed an old set of limestone steps and walked down the porch of the farmhouse shading his eyes and peering in the windows. He let himself in through the kitchen. Trash in the floor, old newsprint. China in a breakfront, cups hanging from their hooks. He went down the hallway and stood in the door to the parlor. There was an antique pumporgan in the corner. A television set. Cheap stuffed furniture together with an old handmade cherrywood chifforobe. He climbed the stairs and walked through the bedrooms. Everything covered with ash. A child's room with a stuffed dog on the windowsill looking out at the garden. He went through the closets. He stripped back the beds and came away with two good woolen blankets and went back down the stairs. In the pantry were three jars of homecanned tomatoes. He blew the dust from the lids and studied them. Someone before him had not trusted them and in the end neither did he and he walked out with the blankets over his shoulder and they set off along the road again.

On the outskirts of the city they came to a supermarket. A few old cars in the trashstrewn parking lot. They left the cart in the lot and walked the littered aisles. In the produce section in the bottom of the bins they found a few ancient runner beans and what looked to have once been apricots, long dried to wrinkled effigies of themselves. The boy followed behind. They pushed out through the rear door. In the alleyway behind the store a few shopping carts, all badly rusted. They went back through the store again looking for another cart but there were none. By the door were two softdrink machines that had been tilted over into the floor and opened with a prybar. Coins everywhere in the ash. He sat and ran his hand around in the works of the gutted machines and in the second one it closed over a cold metal cylinder. He withdrew his hand slowly and sat looking at a Coca Cola.

What is it, Papa?

It's a treat. For you.

What is it?

Here. Sit down.

He slipped the boy's knapsack straps loose and set the pack on the floor behind him and he put his thumbnail under the aluminum clip on the top of the can and opened it. He leaned his nose to the slight fizz coming from the can and then handed it to the boy. Go ahead, he said.

The boy took the can. It's bubbly, he said.

Go ahead.

He looked at his father and then tilted the can and drank. He sat there thinking about it. It's really good, he said.

Yes. It is.

You have some, Papa.

I want you to drink it.

You have some.

He took the can and sipped it and handed it back. You drink it, he said. Let's just sit here.

It's because I wont ever get to drink another one, isnt it?

Ever's a long time.

Okay, the boy said.

By dusk of the day following they were at the city. The long concrete sweeps of the interstate exchanges like the ruins of a vast funhouse against the distant murk. He carried the revolver in his belt at the front and wore his parka unzipped. The mummied dead everywhere. The flesh cloven along the bones, the ligaments dried to tug and taut as wires. Shriveled and drawn like latterday bogfolk, their faces of boiled sheeting, the yellowed palings of their teeth. They were discalced to a man like pilgrims of some common order for all their shoes were long since stolen.

They went on. He kept constant watch behind him in the mirror. The only thing that moved in the streets was the blowing ash. They crossed the high concrete bridge over the river. A dock below. Small pleasureboats half sunken in the gray water. Tall stacks downriver dim in the soot.

The day following some few miles south of the city at a bend in the road and half lost in the dead brambles they came upon an old frame house with chimneys and gables and a stone wall. The man stopped. Then he pushed the cart up the drive.

What is this place, Papa?

It's the house where I grew up.

The boy stood looking at it. The peeling wooden clapboards were largely gone from the lower walls for firewood leaving the studs and the insulation exposed. The rotted screening from the back porch lay on the concrete terrace.

Are we going in?

Why not?

I'm scared.

Dont you want to see where I used to live?

No.

It'll be okay.

There could be somebody here.

I dont think so.

But suppose there is?

He stood looking up at the gable to his old room. He looked at the boy. Do you want to wait here?

No. You always say that.

I'm sorry.

I know. But you do.

. . .

They slipped out of their backpacks and left them on the terrace and kicked their way through the trash on the porch and pushed into the kitchen. The boy held on to his hand. All much as he'd remembered it. The rooms empty. In the small room off the diningroom there was a bare iron cot, a metal foldingtable. The same castiron coalgrate in the small fireplace. The pine paneling was gone from the walls leaving just the furring strips. He stood there. He felt with his thumb in the painted wood of the mantle the pinholes from tacks that had held stockings forty years ago. This is where we used to have Christmas when I was a boy. He turned and looked out at the waste of the yard. A tangle of dead lilac. The shape of a hedge. On cold winter nights when the electricity was out in a storm we would sit at the fire here, me and my sisters, doing our homework. The boy watched him. Watched shapes claiming him he could not see. We should go, Papa, he said. Yes, the man said. But he didnt.

They walked through the diningroom where the firebrick in the hearth was as yellow as the day it was laid because his mother could not bear to see it blackened. The floor buckled from the rainwater. In the livingroom the bones of a small animal dismembered and placed in a pile. Possibly a cat. A glass tumbler by the door. The boy gripped his hand. They went up the stairs and turned and went down the hallway. Small cones of damp plaster standing in the floor. The wooden lathes of the ceiling exposed. He stood in the doorway to his room. A small space under the eaves. This is where I used to sleep. My cot was against this wall. In the nights in their thousands to dream the dreams of a child's imaginings, worlds rich or fearful such as might offer themselves but never the one to be. He pushed open the closet door half expecting to find his childhood things. Raw cold daylight fell through from the roof. Gray as his heart.

We should go, Papa. Can we go?

Yes. We can go.

I'm scared.

I know. I'm sorry.

I'm really scared.

It's all right. We shouldnt have come.

Three nights later in the foothills of the eastern mountains he woke in the darkness to hear something coming. He lay with his hands at either side of him. The ground was trembling. It was coming toward them.

Papa? The boy said. Papa?

Shh. It's okay.

What is it, Papa?

It neared, growing louder. Everything trembling. Then it passed beneath them like an underground train and drew away into the night and was gone. The boy clung to him crying, his head buried against his chest. Shh. It's all right.

I'm so scared.

I know. It's all right. It's gone.

What was it, Papa?

It was an earthquake. It's gone now. We're all right. Shh.

In those first years the roads were peopled with refugees shrouded up in their clothing. Wearing masks and goggles, sitting in their rags by the side of the road like ruined aviators. Their barrows heaped with shoddy. Towing wagons or carts. Their eyes bright in their skulls. Creedless shells of men tottering down the causeways like migrants in a feverland. The frailty of everything revealed at last. Old and troubling issues resolved into nothingness and night. The last instance of a thing takes the class with it. Turns out the light and is gone. Look around you. Ever is a long time. But the boy knew what he knew. That ever is no time at all.

He sat by a gray window in the gray light in an abandoned house in the late afternoon and read old newspapers while the boy slept. The curious news. The quaint concerns. At

eight the primrose closes. He watched the boy sleeping.
Can you do it? When the time comes? Can you?

They squatted in the road and ate cold rice and cold beans
that they'd cooked days ago. Already beginning to fer-
ment. No place to make a fire that would not be seen. They
slept huddled together in the rank quilts in the dark and
the cold. He held the boy close to him. So thin. My heart,
he said. My heart. But he knew that if he were a good
father still it might well be as she had said. That the boy
was all that stood between him and death.

Late in the year. He hardly knew the month. He thought
they had enough food to get through the mountains but
there was no way to tell. The pass at the watershed was five
thousand feet and it was going to be very cold. He said that
everything depended on reaching the coast, yet waking in
the night he knew that all of this was empty and no sub-
stance to it. There was a good chance they would die in the
mountains and that would be that.

They passed through the ruins of a resort town and took
the road south. Burnt forests for miles along the slopes

and snow sooner than he would have thought. No tracks in the road, nothing living anywhere. The fireblackened boulders like the shapes of bears on the starkly wooded slopes. He stood on a stone bridge where the waters slurried into a pool and turned slowly in a gray foam. Where once he'd watched trout swaying in the current, tracking their perfect shadows on the stones beneath. They went on, the boy trudging in his track. Leaning into the cart, winding slowly upward through the switchbacks. There were fires still burning high in the mountains and at night they could see the light from them deep orange in the soot-fall. It was getting colder but they had campfires all night and left them burning behind them when they set out again in the morning. He'd wrapped their feet in sacking tied with cord and so far the snow was only a few inches deep but he knew that if it got much deeper they would have to leave the cart. Already it was hard going and he stopped often to rest. Slogging to the edge of the road with his back to the child where he stood bent with his hands on his knees, coughing. He raised up and stood with weeping eyes. On the gray snow a fine mist of blood.

They camped against a boulder and he made a shelter of poles with the tarp. He got a fire going and they set about dragging up a great brushpile of wood to see them through the night. They'd piled a mat of dead hemlock boughs over the snow and they sat wrapped in their blankets watching the fire and drinking the last of the cocoa scavenged weeks before. It was snowing again, soft flakes drifting down out of the blackness. He dozed in the wonderful warmth. The boy's shadow crossed over him. Carrying an armload of wood. He watched him stoke the flames. God's own firedrake. The sparks rushed upward and died in the starless dark. Not all dying words are true and this blessing is no less real for being shorn of its ground.

He woke toward the morning with the fire down to coals and walked out to the road. Everything was alight. As if the lost sun were returning at last. The snow orange and quivering. A forest fire was making its way along the tinderbox ridges above them, flaring and shimmering against the overcast like the northern lights. Cold as it was he stood there a long time. The color of it moved something in him long forgotten. Make a list. Recite a litany. Remember.

It was colder. Nothing moved in that high world. A rich smell of woodsmoke hung over the road. He pushed the cart on through the snow. A few miles each day. He'd no notion how far the summit might be. They ate sparely and they were hungry all the time. He stood looking out over the country. A river far below. How far had they come?

In his dream she was sick and he cared for her. The dream bore the look of sacrifice but he thought differently. He did not take care of her and she died alone somewhere in the dark and there is no other dream nor other waking world and there is no other tale to tell.

On this road there are no godspoke men. They are gone and I am left and they have taken with them the world. Query: How does the never to be differ from what never was?

Dark of the invisible moon. The nights now only slightly less black. By day the banished sun circles the earth like a grieving mother with a lamp.

People sitting on the sidewalk in the dawn half immolate and smoking in their clothes. Like failed sectarian suicides. Others would come to help them. Within a year there were fires on the ridges and deranged chanting. The screams of the murdered. By day the dead impaled on spikes along the road. What had they done? He thought that in the history of the world it might even be that there was more punishment than crime but he took small comfort from it.

The air grew thin and he thought the summit could not be far. Perhaps tomorrow. Tomorrow came and went. It didnt snow again but the snow in the road was six inches deep and pushing the cart up those grades was exhausting work. He thought they would have to leave it. How much could they carry? He stood and looked out over the barren slopes. The ash fell on the snow till it was all but black.

At every curve it looked as though the pass lay just ahead and then one evening he stopped and looked all about and he recognized it. He unsnapped the throat of his parka and lowered the hood and stood listening. The wind in the dead black stands of hemlock. The empty parking lot at the overlook. The boy stood beside him. Where he'd stood once with his own father in a winter long ago. What is it, Papa? the boy said.

It's the gap. This is it.

. . .

In the morning they pressed on. It was very cold. Toward the afternoon it began to snow again and they made camp early and crouched under the leanto of the tarp and watched the snow fall in the fire. By morning there was several inches of new snow on the ground but the snow had stopped and it was so quiet they could all but hear their hearts. He piled wood on the coals and fanned the fire to life and trudged out through the drifts to dig out the cart. He sorted through the cans and went back and they sat by the fire and ate the last of their crackers and a tin of sausage. In a pocket of his knapsack he'd found a last half packet of cocoa and he fixed it for the boy and then poured his own cup with hot water and sat blowing at the rim.

You promised not to do that, the boy said.

What?

You know what, Papa.

He poured the hot water back into the pan and took the boy's cup and poured some of the cocoa into his own and then handed it back.

I have to watch you all the time, the boy said.

I know.

If you break little promises you'll break big ones. That's what you said.

I know. But I wont.

· · ·

They slogged all day down the southfacing slope of the watershed. In the deeper drifts the cart wouldnt push at all and he had to drag it behind him with one hand while he broke trail. Anywhere but in the mountains they might have found something to use for a sled. An old metal sign or a sheet of roofingtin. The wrappings on their feet had soaked through and they were cold and wet all day. He leaned on the cart to get his breath while the boy waited. There was a sharp crack from somewhere on the mountain. Then another. It's just a tree falling, he said. It's okay. The boy was looking at the dead roadside trees. It's okay, the man said. All the trees in the world are going to fall sooner or later. But not on us.

How do you know?

I just know.

Still they came to trees across the road where they were forced to unload the cart and carry everything over the trunks and then repack it all on the far side. The boy found toys he'd forgot he had. He kept out a yellow truck and they went on with it sitting on top of the tarp.

They camped in a bench of land on the far side of a frozen roadside creek. The wind had blown the ash from the ice and the ice was black and the creek looked like a path of basalt winding through the woods. They collected firewood from the north side of the slope where it was not so wet, pushing over whole trees and dragging them into camp. They got the fire going and spread their tarp and hung their wet clothes on poles to steam and stink and they sat wrapped in the quilts naked while the man held the boy's feet against his stomach to warm them.

He woke whimpering in the night and the man held him. Shh, he said. Shh. It's okay.

I had a bad dream.

I know.

Should I tell you what it was?

If you want to.

I had this penguin that you wound up and it would waddle and flap its flippers. And we were in that house that we used to live in and it came around the corner but nobody had wound it up and it was really scary.

Okay.

It was a lot scarier in the dream.

I know. Dreams can be really scary.

Why did I have that scary dream?

I dont know. But it's okay now. I'm going to put some wood on the fire. You go to sleep.

The boy didnt answer. Then he said: The winder wasnt turning.

It took four more days to come down out of the snow and even then there were patches of snow in certain bends of the road and the road was black and wet from the up-country runoff even beyond that. They came out along the rim of a deep gorge and far down in the darkness a river. They stood listening.

High rock bluffs on the far side of the canyon with thin black trees clinging to the escarpment. The sound of the river faded. Then it returned. A cold wind blowing up from the country below. They were all day reaching the river.

They left the cart in a parking area and walked out through the woods. A low thunder coming from the river. It was a waterfall dropping off a high shelf of rock and falling eighty feet through a gray shroud of mist into the pool below. They could smell the water and they could feel the cold coming off of it. A bench of wet river gravel. He stood and watched the boy. Wow, the boy said. He couldnt take his eyes off it.

He squatted and scooped up a handful of stones and smelled them and let them fall clattering. Polished round and smooth as marbles or lozenges of stone veined and striped. Black disclets and bits of polished quartz all bright from the mist off the river. The boy walked out and squatted and laved up the dark water.

The waterfall fell into the pool almost at its center. A gray curd circled. They stood side by side calling to each other over the din.

Is it cold?

Yes. It's freezing.

Do you want to go in?

I dont know.

Sure you do.

Is it okay?

Come on.

He unzipped his parka and let it fall to the gravel and the boy stood up and they undressed and walked out into the water. Ghostly pale and shivering. The boy so thin it stopped his heart. He dove headlong and came up gasping and turned and stood, beating his arms.

Is it over my head? the boy called.

No. Come on.

He turned and swam out to the falls and let the water beat upon him. The boy was standing in the pool to his waist, holding his shoulders and hopping up and down. The man went back and got him. He held him and floated him about, the boy gasping and chopping at the water. You're doing good, the man said. You're doing good.

They dressed shivering and then climbed the trail to the upper river. They walked out along the rocks to where the river seemed to end in space and he held the boy while he ventured out to the last ledge of rock. The river went sucking over the rim and fell straight down into the pool below. The entire river. He clung to the man's arm.

It's really far, he said.

It's pretty far.

Would you die if you fell?

You'd get hurt. It's a long way.

It's really scary.

They walked out through the woods. The light was failing. They followed the flats along the upper river among huge dead trees. A rich southern wood that once held may-apple and pipsissewa. Ginseng. The raw dead limbs of the rhododendron twisted and knotted and black. He stopped. Something in the mulch and ash. He stooped and cleared it away. A small colony of them, shrunken, dried and wrinkled. He picked one and held it up and sniffed it. He bit a piece from the edge and chewed.

What is it, Papa?

Morels. It's morels.

What's morels?

They're a kind of mushroom.

Can you eat them?

Yes. Take a bite.

Are they good?

Take a bite.

The boy smelled the mushroom and bit into it and stood chewing. He looked at his father. These are pretty good, he said.

They pulled the morels from the ground, small alien-looking things that he piled in the hood of the boy's parka. They hiked back out to the road and down to where they'd left the cart and they made camp by the river pool at the falls and washed the earth and ash from the morels and put them to soak in a pan of water. By the time he had the fire going it was dark and he sliced a handful of the mushrooms on a log for their dinner and scooped them into the frying pan along with the fat pork from a can of beans and set them in the coals to simmer. The boy watched him. This is a good place Papa, he said.

They ate the little mushrooms together with the beans and drank tea and had tinned pears for their dessert. He banked the fire against the seam of rock where he'd built it and he strung the tarp behind them to reflect the heat and they sat warm in their refuge while he told the boy stories. Old stories of courage and justice as he remembered them until the boy was asleep in his blankets and then he stoked the fire and lay down warm and full and listened to the low thunder of the falls beyond them in that dark and threadbare wood.

He walked out in the morning and took the river path downstream. The boy was right that it was a good place and he wanted to check for any sign of other visitors. He found nothing. He stood watching the river where it swung loping into a pool and curled and eddied. He dropped a white stone into the water but it vanished as suddenly as if it had been eaten. He'd stood at such a river once and watched the flash of trout deep in a pool, invisible to see in the teacolored water except as they turned on their sides to feed. Reflecting back the sun deep in the darkness like a flash of knives in a cave.

We cant stay, he said. It's getting colder every day. And the waterfall is an attraction. It was for us and it will be for others and we dont know who they will be and we cant hear them coming. It's not safe.

We could stay one more day.

It's not safe.

Well maybe we could find some other place on the river.

We have to keep moving. We have to keep heading south.

Doesnt the river go south?

No. It doesnt.

Can I see it on the map?

Yes. Let me get it.

The tattered oilcompany roadmap had once been taped together but now it was just sorted into leaves and numbered with crayon in the corners for their assembly. He sorted through the limp pages and spread out those that answered to their location.

We cross a bridge here. It looks to be about eight miles or so. This is the river. Going east. We follow the road here along the eastern slope of the mountains. These are our roads, the black lines on the map. The state roads.

Why are they the state roads?

Because they used to belong to the states. What used to be called the states.

But there's not any more states?

No.

What happened to them?

I dont know exactly. That's a good question.

But the roads are still there.

Yes. For a while.

How long a while?

I dont know. Maybe quite a while. There's nothing to uproot them so they should be okay for a while.

But there wont be any cars or trucks on them.

No.

Okay.

Are you ready?

The boy nodded. He wiped his nose on his sleeve and shouldered up his small pack and the man folded away the map sections and rose and the boy followed him out through the gray palings of the trees to the road.

When the bridge came in sight below them there was a tractor-trailer jackknifed sideways across it and wedged into the buckled iron railings. It was raining again and they stood there with the rain pattering softly on the tarp. Peering out from under the blue gloom beneath the plastic.

Can we get around it? the boy said.

I dont think so. We can probably get under it. We may have to unload the cart.

The bridge spanned the river above a rapids. They could hear the noise of it as they came around the curve in the road. A wind was coming down the gorge and they pulled the corners of the tarp about them and pushed the cart out onto the bridge. They could see the river through the ironwork. Below the rapids was a railroad bridge laid on limestone piers. The stones of the piers were stained well above the river from the high water and the bend of the river was choked with great windrows of black limbs and brush and the trunks of trees.

The truck had been there for years, the tires flat and crumpled under the rims. The front of the tractor was jammed against the railing of the bridge and the trailer had sheared forward off the top plate and jammed up against the back of the cab. The rear of the trailer had swung out and buckled the rail on the other side of the bridge and it hung several feet out over the river gorge. He pushed the cart up under the trailer but the handle wouldnt clear. They'd have to slide it under sideways. He left it sitting in the rain with the tarp over it and they duckwalked under the trailer and he left the boy crouched there in the dry while he climbed up on the gastank step and wiped the water from the glass and peered inside the cab. He stepped back down and reached up and opened the door and then climbed in and pulled the door shut behind him. He sat looking around. An old doghouse sleeper behind the seats. Papers in the floor. The glovebox was open but it was empty. He climbed back between the seats. There was a raw damp mattress on the bunk and a small refrigerator with the door standing open. A fold-down table. Old magazines in the floor. He went through the plywood lockers overhead but they were empty. There were drawers under the bunk and he pulled them out and looked through the trash. He climbed forward into the cab again and sat in the driver's seat and looked out down the river through the slow trickle of water on the glass. The thin drum of rain on the metal roof and the slow darkness falling over everything.

They slept that night in the truck and in the morning the rain had stopped and they unloaded the cart and passed everything under the truck to the other side and reloaded it. Down the bridge a hundred feet or so were the blackened remains of tires that had been burned there. He stood looking at the trailer. What do you think is in there? he said.

I dont know.

We're not the first ones here. So probably nothing.

There's no way to get in.

He put his ear to the side of the trailer and whacked the sheetmetal with the flat of his hand. It sounds empty, he said. You can probably get in from the roof. Somebody would have cut a hole in the side of it by now.

What would they cut it with?

They'd find something.

He took off his parka and laid it across the top of the cart and climbed on to the fender of the tractor and on to the hood and clambered up over the windscreen to the roof of the cab. He stood and turned and looked down at the river. Wet metal underfoot. He looked down at the boy. The boy looked worried. He turned and reached and got a grip on the front of the trailer and slowly pulled himself up. It was all he could do and there was a lot less of him to pull. He got one leg up over the edge and hung there resting. Then he pulled himself up and rolled over and sat up.

. . .

There was a skylight about a third of the way down the roof and he made his way to it in a walking crouch. The cover was gone and the inside of the trailer smelled of wet plywood and that sour smell he'd come to know. He had a magazine in his hip pocket and he took it out and tore some pages from it and wadded them and got out his lighter and lit the papers and dropped them into the darkness. A faint whooshing. He wafted away the smoke and looked down into the trailer. The small fire burning in the floor seemed a long way down. He shielded the glare of it with his hand and when he did he could see almost to the rear of the box. Human bodies. Sprawled in every attitude. Dried and shrunken in their rotted clothes. The small wad of burning paper drew down to a wisp of flame and then died out leaving a faint pattern for just a moment in the incandescence like the shape of a flower, a molten rose. Then all was dark again.

They camped that night in the woods on a ridge overlooking the broad piedmont plain where it stretched away to the south. He built a cookfire against a rock and they ate the last of the morels and a can of spinach. In the night a storm broke in the mountains above them and came cannonading downcountry cracking and booming and the stark gray world appeared again and again out of the night in the shrouded flare of the lightning. The boy clung to him. It all passed on. A brief rattle of hail and then the slow cold rain.

When he woke again it was still dark but the rain had stopped. A smoky light out there in the valley. He rose and walked out along the ridge. A haze of fire that stretched for miles. He squatted and watched it. He could smell the smoke. He wet his finger and held it to the wind. When he rose and turned to go back the tarp was lit from within where the boy had wakened. Sited there in the darkness the frail blue shape of it looked like the pitch of some last venture at the edge of the world. Something all but unaccountable. And so it was.

All the day following they traveled through the drifting haze of woodsmoke. In the draws the smoke coming off the ground like mist and the thin black trees burning on the slopes like stands of heathen candles. Late in the day they came to a place where the fire had crossed the road and the macadam was still warm and further on it began to soften underfoot. The hot black mastic sucking at their shoes and stretching in thin bands as they stepped. They stopped. We'll have to wait, he said.

. . .

They backtracked and camped in the actual road and when they went on in the morning the macadam had cooled. Bye and bye they came to a set of tracks cooked into the tar. They just suddenly appeared. He squatted and studied them. Someone had come out of the woods in the night and continued down the melted roadway.

Who is it? said the boy.

I dont know. Who is anybody?

They came upon him shuffling along the road before them, dragging one leg slightly and stopping from time to time to stand stooped and uncertain before setting out again.

What should we do, Papa?

We're all right. Let's just follow and watch.

Take a look, the boy said.

Yes. Take a look.

They followed him a good ways but at his pace they were losing the day and finally he just sat in the road and did not get up again. The boy hung on to his father's coat. No one spoke. He was as burntlooking as the country, his clothing scorched and black. One of his eyes was burnt shut and his hair was but a nitty wig of ash upon his blackened skull. As they passed he looked down. As if he'd done something wrong. His shoes were bound up with wire and coated with roadtar and he sat there in silence, bent over in his rags. The boy kept looking back. Papa? he whispered. What is wrong with the man?

He's been struck by lightning.

Cant we help him? Papa?

No. We cant help him.

The boy kept pulling at his coat. Papa? he said.

Stop it.

Cant we help him Papa?

No. We cant help him. There's nothing to be done for him.

They went on. The boy was crying. He kept looking back. When they got to the bottom of the hill the man stopped and looked at him and looked back up the road. The burned man had fallen over and at that distance you couldnt even tell what it was. I'm sorry, he said. But we have nothing to give him. We have no way to help him. I'm sorry for what happened to him but we cant fix it. You know that, dont you? The boy stood looking down. He nodded his head. Then they went on and he didnt look back again.

. . .

At evening a dull sulphur light from the fires. The standing water in the roadside ditches black with the runoff. The mountains shrouded away. They crossed a river by a concrete bridge where skeins of ash and slurry moved slowly in the current. Charred bits of wood. In the end they stopped and turned back and camped under the bridge.

He'd carried his billfold about till it wore a cornershaped hole in his trousers. Then one day he sat by the roadside and took it out and went through the contents. Some money, credit cards. His driver's license. A picture of his wife. He spread everything out on the blacktop. Like gaming cards. He pitched the sweatblackened piece of leather into the woods and sat holding the photograph. Then he laid it down in the road also and then he stood and they went on.

In the morning he lay looking up at the clay nests that swallows had built in the corners under the bridge. He looked at the boy but the boy had turned away and lay staring out at the river.

There's nothing we could have done.

He didnt answer.

He's going to die. We cant share what we have or we'll die too.

I know.

So when are you going to talk to me again?

I'm talking now.

Are you sure?

Yes.

Okay.

Okay.

They stood on the far shore of a river and called to him. Tattered gods slouching in their rags across the waste. Trekking the dried floor of a mineral sea where it lay cracked and broken like a fallen plate. Paths of feral fire in the coagulate sands. The figures faded in the distance. He woke and lay in the dark.

The clocks stopped at 1:17. A long shear of light and then a series of low concussions. He got up and went to the window. What is it? she said. He didnt answer. He went into the bathroom and threw the lightswitch but the power was already gone. A dull rose glow in the windowglass. He dropped to one knee and raised the lever to stop the tub and then turned on both taps as far as they would go. She was standing in the doorway in her nightwear, clutching the jamb, cradling her belly in one hand. What is it? she said. What is happening?

I dont know.

Why are you taking a bath?

I'm not.

Once in those early years he'd wakened in a barren wood and lay listening to flocks of migratory birds overhead in that bitter dark. Their half muted crankings miles above where they circled the earth as senselessly as insects trooping the rim of a bowl. He wished them godspeed till they were gone. He never heard them again.

He'd a deck of cards he found in a bureau drawer in a house and the cards were worn and spindled and the two of clubs was missing but still they played sometimes by firelight wrapped in their blankets. He tried to remember the rules of childhood games. Old Maid. Some version of Whist. He was sure he had them mostly wrong and he made up new games and gave them made up names. Abnormal Fescue or Catbarf. Sometimes the child would ask him questions about the world that for him was not even a memory. He thought hard how to answer. There is no past. What would you like? But he stopped making things up because those things were not true either and the telling made him feel bad. The child had his own fantasies. How things would be in the south. Other children. He tried to keep a rein on this but his heart was not in it. Whose would be?

No lists of things to be done. The day providential to itself. The hour. There is no later. This is later. All things of grace and beauty such that one holds them to one's heart have a common provenance in pain. Their birth in grief and ashes. So, he whispered to the sleeping boy. I have you.

He thought about the picture in the road and he thought that he should have tried to keep her in their lives in some way but he didnt know how. He woke coughing and walked out so as not to wake the child. Following a stone wall in the dark, wrapped in his blanket, kneeling in the ashes like a penitent. He coughed till he could taste the blood and he said her name aloud. He thought perhaps he'd said it in his sleep. When he got back the boy was awake. I'm sorry, he said.

It's okay.

Go to sleep.

I wish I was with my mom.

He didnt answer. He sat beside the small figure wrapped in the quilts and blankets. After a while he said: You mean you wish that you were dead.

Yes.

You musnt say that.

But I do.

Dont say it. It's a bad thing to say.

I cant help it.

I know. But you have to.

How do I do it?

I dont know.

We're survivors he told her across the flame of the lamp.

Survivors? she said.

Yes.

What in God's name are you talking about? We're not survivors. We're the walking dead in a horror film.

I'm begging you.

I dont care. I dont care if you cry. It doesnt mean anything to me.

Please.

Stop it.

I am begging you. I'll do anything.

Such as what? I should have done it a long time ago. When there were three bullets in the gun instead of two. I was stupid. We've been over all of this. I didnt bring myself to this. I was brought. And now I'm done. I thought about not even telling you. That would probably have been best. You have two bullets and then what? You cant protect us. You say you would die for us but what good is that? I'd take him with me if it werent for you. You know I would. It's the right thing to do.

You're talking crazy.

No, I'm speaking the truth. Sooner or later they will catch us and they will kill us. They will rape me. They'll rape him. They are going to rape us and kill us and eat us and you wont face it. You'd rather wait for it to happen. But I cant. I cant. She sat there smoking a slender length of dried grapevine as if it were some rare cheroot. Holding it with a certain elegance, her other hand across her knees where she'd drawn them up. She watched him across the small flame. We used to talk about death, she said. We dont any more. Why is that?

I dont know.

It's because it's here. There's nothing left to talk about.

I wouldnt leave you.

I dont care. It's meaningless. You can think of me as a

faithless slut if you like. I've taken a new lover. He can give me what you cannot.

Death is not a lover.

Oh yes he is.

Please dont do this.

I'm sorry.

I cant do it alone.

Then dont. I cant help you. They say that women dream of danger to those in their care and men of danger to themselves. But I dont dream at all. You say you cant? Then dont do it. That's all. Because I am done with my own whorish heart and I have been for a long time. You talk about taking a stand but there is no stand to take. My heart was ripped out of me the night he was born so dont ask for sorrow now. There is none. Maybe you'll be good at this. I doubt it, but who knows. The one thing I can tell you is that you wont survive for yourself. I know because I would never have come this far. A person who had no one would be well advised to cobble together some passable ghost. Breathe it into being and coax it along with words of love. Offer it each phantom crumb and shield it from harm with your body. As for me my only hope is for eternal nothingness and I hope it with all my heart.

He didnt answer.

You have no argument because there is none.

Will you tell him goodbye?

No. I will not.

Just wait till morning. Please.

I have to go.

She had already stood up.

For the love of God, woman. What am I to tell him?

I cant help you.

Where are you going to go? You cant even see.

I dont have to.

He stood up. I'm begging you, he said.

No. I will not. I cannot.

She was gone and the coldness of it was her final gift. She would do it with a flake of obsidian. He'd taught her himself. Sharper than steel. The edge an atom thick. And she was right. There was no argument. The hundred nights they'd sat up debating the pros and cons of self destruction with the earnestness of philosophers chained to a madhouse wall. In the morning the boy said nothing at all and when they were packed and ready to set out upon the road he turned and looked back at their campsite and he said: She's gone isn't she? And he said: Yes, she is.

. . .

Always so deliberate, hardly surprised by the most outlandish advents. A creation perfectly evolved to meet its own end. They sat at the window and ate in their robes by candlelight a midnight supper and watched distant cities burn. A few nights later she gave birth in their bed by the light of a drycell lamp. Gloves meant for dishwashing. The improbable appearance of the small crown of the head. Streaked with blood and lank black hair. The rank meconium. Her cries meant nothing to him. Beyond the window just the gathering cold, the fires on the horizon. He held aloft the scrawny red body so raw and naked and cut the cord with kitchen shears and wrapped his son in a towel.

Did you have any friends?
Yes. I did.
Lots of them?
Yes.
Do you remember them?
Yes. I remember them.
What happened to them?
They died.
All of them?
Yes. All of them.

Do you miss them?
Yes. I do.
Where are we going?
We're going south.
Okay.

They were all day on the long black road, stopping in the afternoon to eat sparingly from their meager supplies. The boy took his truck from the pack and shaped roads in the ash with a stick. The truck tooled along slowly. He made truck noises. The day seemed almost warm and they slept in the leaves with their packs under their heads.

Something woke him. He turned on his side and lay listening. He raised his head slowly, the pistol in his hand. He looked down at the boy and when he looked back toward the road the first of them were already coming into view. God, he whispered. He reached and shook the boy, keeping his eyes on the road. They came shuffling through the ash casting their hooded heads from side to side. Some of them wearing canister masks. One in a biohazard suit. Stained and filthy. Slouching along with clubs in their hands, lengths of pipe. Coughing. Then he heard on the road behind them what sounded like a diesel truck. Quick, he whispered. Quick. He shoved the pistol in his belt and grabbed the boy by the hand and he dragged the cart through the trees and tilted it over where it would not so easily be seen. The boy was frozen with fear. He pulled him to him. It's all right, he said. We have to run. Dont look back. Come on.

He slung their knapsacks over his shoulder and they tore through the crumbling bracken. The boy was terrified. Run, he whispered. Run. He looked back. The truck had rumbled into view. Men standing in the bed looking out. The boy fell and he pulled him up. It's all right, he said. Come on.

He could see a break through the trees that he thought was a ditch or a cut and they came out through the weeds into an old roadway. Plates of cracked macadam showing through the drifts of ash. He pulled the boy down and they crouched under the bank listening, gasping for breath. They could hear the diesel engine out on the road, running on God knows what. When he raised up to look he could just see the top of the truck moving along the road. Men standing in the stakebed, some of them holding rifles.

The truck passed on and the black diesel smoke coiled through the woods. The motor sounded ropy. Missing and puttering. Then it quit.

He sank down and put his hand on top of his head. God, he said. They could hear the thing rattle and flap to a halt. Then just the silence. He had the pistol in his hand, he couldnt even remember taking it from his belt. They could hear the men talking. Hear them unlatch and raise the hood. He sat with his arm around the boy. Shh, he said. Shh. After a while they heard the truck begin to roll. Lumbering and creaking like a ship. They'd have no other way to start it save to push it and they couldnt get it fast enough to start on that slope. After a few minutes it coughed and bucked and stopped again. He raised his head to look and coming through the weeds twenty feet away was one of their number unbuckling his belt. They both froze.

He cocked the pistol and held it on the man and the man stood with one hand out at his side, the dirty crumpled paintmask that he wore sucking in and out.

Just keep coming.

He looked at the road.

Dont look back there. Look at me. If you call out you're dead.

He came forward, holding his belt by one hand. The holes in it marked the progress of his emaciation and the leather at one side had a lacquered look to it where he was used to stropping the blade of his knife. He stepped down into the roadcut and he looked at the gun and he looked at the boy. Eyes collared in cups of grime and deeply sunk. Like an animal inside a skull looking out the eyeholes. He wore a beard that had been cut square across the bottom with shears and he had a tattoo of a bird on his neck done by someone with an illformed notion of their appearance. He was lean, wiry, rachitic. Dressed in a pair of filthy blue coveralls and a black billcap with the logo of some vanished enterprise embroidered across the front of it.

Where are you going?

I was going to take a crap.

Where are you going with the truck.

I dont know.

What do you mean you dont know? Take the mask off.

He pulled the mask off over his head and stood holding it.

I mean I dont know, he said.

You dont know where you're going?

No.

What's the truck running on.

Diesel fuel.

How much do you have.

There's three fifty-five gallon drums in the bed.

Do you have ammunition for those guns?

He looked back toward the road.

I told you not to look back there.

Yeah. We got ammunition.

Where did you get it?

Found it.

That's a lie. What are you eating.

Whatever we can find.

Whatever you can find.

Yeah. He looked at the boy. You wont shoot, he said.

That's what you think.

You aint got but two shells. Maybe just one. And they'll hear the shot.

Yes they will. But you wont.

How do you figure that?

Because the bullet travels faster than sound. It will be in your brain before you can hear it. To hear it you will need a frontal lobe and things with names like colliculus and temporal gyrus and you wont have them anymore. They'll just be soup.

Are you a doctor?

I'm not anything.

We got a man hurt. It'd be worth your while.

Do I look like an imbecile to you?

I dont know what you look like.

Why are you looking at him?

I can look where I want to.

No you cant. If you look at him again I'll shoot you.

The boy was sitting with both hands on top of his head and looking out between his forearms.

I'll bet that boy is hungry. Why dont you all just come on to the truck? Get something to eat. Aint no need to be such a hard-ass.

You dont have anything to eat. Let's go.

Go where?

Let's go.

I aint goin nowheres.

You're not?

No. I aint.

You think I wont kill you but you're wrong. But what I'd rather do is take you up this road a mile or so and then turn you loose. That's all the head start we need. You wont find us. You wont even know which way we went.

You know what I think?

What do you think.

I think you're chickenshit.

He let go of the belt and it fell in the roadway with the gear hanging from it. A canteen. An old canvas army pouch. A leather sheath for a knife. When he looked up the roadrat was holding the knife in his hand. He'd only taken two steps but he was almost between him and the child.

What do you think you're going to do with that?

He didnt answer. He was a big man but he was very quick. He dove and grabbed the boy and rolled and came up holding him against his chest with the knife at his throat. The man had already dropped to the ground and he swung with him and leveled the pistol and fired from a two-handed position balanced on both knees at a distance of six feet. The man fell back instantly and lay with blood bubbling from the hole in his forehead. The boy was lying in his lap with no expression on his face at all. He shoved the pistol in his belt and slung the knapsack over his shoulder and picked up the boy and turned him around and lifted him over his head and set him on his shoulders and set off up the old roadway at a dead run, holding the boy's knees, the boy clutching his forehead, covered with gore and mute as a stone.

They came to an old iron bridge in the woods where the vanished road had crossed an all but vanished stream. He was starting to cough and he'd hardly breath to do it with. He dropped down out of the roadway and into the woods. He turned and stood gasping, trying to listen. He heard nothing. He staggered on another half mile or so and finally dropped to his knees and put the boy down in the ashes and leaves. He wiped the blood from his face and held him. It's okay, he said. It's okay.

In the long cold evening with the darkness dropping down he heard them only once. He held the boy close. There was a cough in his throat that never left. The boy so frail and thin through his coat, shivering like a dog. The footsteps in the leaves stopped. Then they moved on. They neither spoke nor called to each other, the more sinister for that. With the final onset of dark the iron cold locked down and the boy by now was shuddering violently. No moon rose beyond the murk and there was nowhere to go. They had a single blanket in the pack and he got it out and covered the boy with it and he unzipped his parka and held the boy against him. They lay there for a long time but they were freezing and finally he sat up. We've got to move, he said. We cant just lie here. He looked around but there was nothing to see. He spoke into a blackness without depth or dimension.

He held the boy's hand as they stumbled through the woods. The other hand he held out before him. He could see no worse with his eyes shut. The boy was wrapped in the blanket and he told him not to drop it because they would never find it again. He wanted to be carried but the man told him that he had to keep moving. They stumbled and fell through the woods the night long and long before dawn the boy fell and would not get up again. He wrapped him in his own parka and wrapped him in the blanket and sat holding him, rocking back and forth. A single round left in the revolver. You will not face the truth. You will not.

In the grudging light that passed for day he put the boy in the leaves and sat studying the woods. When it was a bit lighter he rose and walked out and cut a perimeter about their siwash camp looking for sign but other than their own faint track through the ash he saw nothing. He went back and gathered the boy up. We have to go, he said. The boy sat slumped, his face blank. The filth dried in his hair and his face streaked with it. Talk to me, he said, but he would not.

They moved on east through the standing dead trees. They passed an old frame house and crossed a dirt road. A cleared plot of ground perhaps once a truckgarden. Stopping from time to time to listen. The unseen sun cast no shadow. They came upon the road unexpectedly and he stopped the boy with one hand and they crouched in the roadside ditch like lepers and listened. No wind. Dead silence. After a while he rose and walked out into the road. He looked back at the boy. Come on, he said. The boy came out and the man pointed out the tracks in the ash where the truck had gone. The boy stood wrapped in the blanket looking down at the road.

He'd no way to know if they'd got the truck running again. No way to know how long they might be willing to lie in ambush. He thumbed the pack down off his shoulder and sat and opened it. We need to eat, he said. Are you hungry?

The boy shook his head.

No. Of course not. He took out the plastic bottle of water and unscrewed the cap and held it out and the boy took it and stood drinking. He lowered the bottle and got his breath and he sat in the road and crossed his legs and drank again. Then he handed the bottle back and the man drank and screwed the cap back on and rummaged through the pack. They ate a can of white beans, passing it between them, and he threw the empty tin into the woods. Then they set out down the road again.

. . .

The truck people had camped in the road itself. They'd built a fire there and charred billets of wood lay stuck in the melted tar together with ash and bones. He squatted and held his hand over the tar. A faint warmth coming off of it. He stood and looked down the road. Then he took the boy with him into the woods. I want you to wait here, he said. I wont be far away. I'll be able to hear you if you call.

Take me with you, the boy said. He looked as if he was going to cry.

No. I want you to wait here.

Please, Papa.

Stop it. I want you to do what I say. Take the gun.

I dont want the gun.

I didnt ask you if you wanted it. Take it.

He walked out through the woods to where they'd left the cart. It was still lying there but it had been plundered. The few things they hadnt taken scattered in the leaves. Some books and toys belonging to the boy. His old shoes and some rags of clothing. He righted the cart and put the boy's things in it and wheeled it out to the road. Then he went back. There was nothing there. Dried blood dark in the leaves. The boy's knapsack was gone. Coming back he found the bones and the skin piled together with rocks over them. A pool of guts. He pushed at the bones with the toe of his shoe. They looked to have been boiled. No pieces of clothing. Dark was coming on again and it was already very cold and he turned and went out to where he'd left the boy and knelt and put his arms around him and held him.

They pushed the cart through the woods as far as the old road and left it there and headed south along the road hurrying against the dark. The boy was stumbling he was so tired and the man picked him up and swung him onto his shoulders and they went on. By the time they got to the bridge there was scarcely light at all. He put the boy down and they felt their way down the embankment. Under the bridge he got out his lighter and lit it and swept the ground with the flickering light. Sand and gravel washed up from the creek. He set down the knapsack and put away the lighter and took hold of the boy by the shoulders. He could just make him out in the darkness. I want you to wait here, he said. I'm going for wood. We have to have a fire.

I'm scared.

I know. But I'll just be a little ways and I'll be able to hear you so if you get scared you call me and I'll come right away.

I'm really scared.

The sooner I go the sooner I'll be back and we'll have a fire and then you wont be scared anymore. Dont lie down. If you lie down you'll fall asleep and then if I call you you wont answer and I wont be able to find you. Do you understand?

The boy didnt answer. He was close to losing his temper with him and then he realized that he was shaking his head in the dark. Okay, he said. Okay.

He scrambled up the bank and into the woods, holding his hands out in front of him. There was wood everywhere, dead limbs and branches scattered over the ground. He shuffled along kicking them into a pile and when he had an armful he stooped and gathered them up and called the boy and the boy answered and talked him back to the bridge. They sat in the darkness while he shaved sticks into a pile with his knife and broke up the small branches with his hands. He took the lighter from his pocket and struck the wheel with his thumb. He used gasoline in the lighter and it burned with a frail blue flame and he bent and set the tinder alight and watched the fire climb upward through the wicker of limbs. He piled on more wood and bent and blew gently at the base of the little blaze and arranged the wood with his hands, shaping the fire just so.

. . .

He made two more trips into the woods, dragging arm-loads of brush and limbs to the bridge and pushing them over the side. He could see the glow of the fire from some distance but he didnt think it could be seen from the other road. Below the bridge he could make out a dark pool of standing water among the rocks. A rim of shelving ice. He stood on the bridge and shoved the last pile of wood over, his breath white in the glow of the firelight.

He sat in the sand and inventoried the contents of the knap-sack. The binoculars. A half pint bottle of gasoline almost full. The bottle of water. A pair of pliers. Two spoons. He set everything out in a row. There were five small tins of food and he chose a can of sausages and one of corn and he opened these with the little army can opener and set them at the edge of the fire and they sat watching the labels char and curl. When the corn began to steam he took the cans from the fire with the pliers and they sat bent over them with their spoons, eating slowly. The boy was nodding with sleep.

When they'd eaten he took the boy out on the gravelbar below the bridge and he pushed away the thin shore ice with a stick and they knelt there while he washed the boy's face and his hair. The water was so cold the boy was crying. They moved down the gravel to find fresh water and he washed his hair again as well as he could and finally stopped because the boy was moaning with the cold of it. He dried him with the blanket, kneeling there in the glow of the light with the shadow of the bridge's understructure broken across the palisade of treetrunks beyond the creek. This is my child, he said. I wash a dead man's brains out of his hair. That is my job. Then he wrapped him in the blanket and carried him to the fire.

The boy sat tottering. The man watched him that he not topple into the flames. He kicked holes in the sand for the boy's hips and shoulders where he would sleep and he sat holding him while he tousled his hair before the fire to dry it. All of this like some ancient anointing. So be it. Evoke the forms. Where you've nothing else construct ceremonies out of the air and breathe upon them.

He woke in the night with the cold and rose and broke up more wood for the fire. The shapes of the small treelimbs burning incandescent orange in the coals. He blew the flames to life and piled on the wood and sat with his legs crossed, leaning against the stone pier of the bridge. Heavy limestone blocks laid up without mortar. Overhead the ironwork brown with rust, the hammered rivets, the wooden sleepers and crossplanks. The sand where he sat was warm to the touch but the night beyond the fire was sharp with the cold. He got up and dragged fresh wood in under the bridge. He stood listening. The boy didnt stir. He sat beside him and stroked his pale and tangled hair. Golden chalice, good to house a god. Please dont tell me how the story ends. When he looked out again at the darkness beyond the bridge it was snowing.

All the wood they had to burn was small wood and the fire was good for no more than an hour or perhaps a bit more. He dragged the rest of the brush in under the bridge and broke it up, standing on the limbs and cracking them to length. He thought the noise would wake the boy but it didnt. The wet wood hissed in the flames, the snow continued to fall. In the morning they would see if there were tracks in the road or not. This was the first human being other than the boy that he'd spoken to in more than a year. My brother at last. The reptilian calculations in those cold and shifting eyes. The gray and rotting teeth. Claggy with human flesh. Who has made of the world a lie every word. When he woke again the snow had stopped and the grainy dawn was shaping out the naked woodlands beyond the bridge, the trees black against the snow. He was lying curled up with his hands between his knees and he sat up and got the fire going and he set a can of beets in the embers. The boy lay huddled on the ground watching him.

The new snow lay in skifts all through the woods, along the limbs and cupped in the leaves, all of it already gray with ash. They hiked out to where they'd left the cart and he put the knapsack in and pushed it out to the road. No tracks. They stood listening in the utter silence. Then they set out along the road through the gray slush, the boy at his side with his hands in his pockets.

They trudged all day, the boy in silence. By afternoon the slush had melted off the road and by evening it was dry. They didnt stop. How many miles? Ten, twelve. They used to play quoits in the road with four big steel washers they'd found in a hardware store but these were gone with everything else. That night they camped in a ravine and built a fire against a small stone bluff and ate their last tin of food. He'd put it by because it was the boy's favorite, pork and beans. They watched it bubble slowly in the coals and he retrieved the tin with the pliers and they ate in silence. He rinsed the empty tin with water and gave it to the child to drink and that was that. I should have been more careful, he said.

The boy didnt answer.

You have to talk to me.

Okay.

You wanted to know what the bad guys looked like. Now you know. It may happen again. My job is to take care of you. I was appointed to do that by God. I will kill anyone who touches you. Do you understand?

Yes.

He sat there cowled in the blanket. After a while he looked up. Are we still the good guys? he said.

Yes. We're still the good guys.

And we always will be.

Yes. We always will be.

Okay.

In the morning they came up out of the ravine and took to the road again. He'd carved the boy a flute from a piece of roadside cane and he took it from his coat and gave it to him. The boy took it wordlessly. After a while he fell back and after a while the man could hear him playing. A formless music for the age to come. Or perhaps the last music on earth called up from out of the ashes of its ruin. The man turned and looked back at him. He was lost in concentration. The man thought he seemed some sad and solitary changeling child announcing the arrival of a traveling spectacle in shire and village who does not know that behind him the players have all been carried off by wolves.

He sat crosslegged in the leaves at the crest of a ridge and glassed the valley below them with the binoculars. The still poured shape of a river. The dark brick stacks of a mill. Slate roofs. An old wooden watertower bound with iron hoops. No smoke, no movement of life. He lowered the glasses and sat watching.

What do you see? the boy said.

Nothing.

He handed the binoculars across. The boy slung the strap over his neck and put them to his eyes and adjusted the wheel. Everything about them so still.

I see smoke, he said.

Where.

Past those buildings.

What buildings?

The boy handed the glasses back and he refocused them. The palest wisp. Yes, he said. I see it.

What should we do, Papa?

I think we should take a look. We just have to be careful.

If it's a commune they'll have barricades. But it may just be refugees.

Like us.

Yes. Like us.

What if it's the bad guys?

We'll have to take a risk. We need to find something to eat.

They left the cart in the woods and crossed a railroad track and came down a steep bank through dead black ivy. He carried the pistol in his hand. Stay close, he said. He did. They moved through the streets like sappers. One block at a time. A faint smell of woodsmoke on the air. They waited in a store and watched the street but nothing moved. They went through the trash and rubble. Cabinet drawers pulled out into the floor, paper and bloated cardboard boxes. They found nothing. All the stores were rifled years ago, the glass mostly gone from the windows. Inside it was all but too dark to see. They climbed the ribbed steel stairs of an escalator, the boy holding on to his hand. A few dusty suits hanging on a rack. They looked for shoes but there were none. They shuffled through the trash but there was nothing there of any use to them. When they came back he slipped the suitcoats from their hangers and shook them out and folded them across his arm. Let's go, he said.

He thought there had to be something overlooked but there wasnt. They kicked through the trash in the aisles of a foodmarket. Old packaging and papers and the eternal ash. He scoured the shelves looking for vitamins. He opened the door of a walk-in cooler but the sour rank smell of the dead washed out of the darkness and he quickly closed it again. They stood in the street. He looked at the gray sky. Faint plume of their breath. The boy was exhausted. He took him by the hand. We have to look some more, he said. We have to keep looking.

The houses at the edge of the town offered little more. They climbed the back steps into a kitchen and began to go through the cabinets. The cabinet doors all standing open. A can of bakingpowder. He stood there looking at it. They went through the drawers of a sideboard in the diningroom. They walked into the livingroom. Scrolls of fallen wallpaper lying in the floor like ancient documents. He left the boy sitting on the stairs holding the coats while he went up.

Everything smelled of damp and rot. In the first bedroom a dried corpse with the covers about its neck. Rem-

nants of rotted hair on the pillow. He took hold of the
lower hem of the blanket and towed it off the bed and
shook it out and folded it under his arm. He went through
the bureaus and the closets. A summer dress on a wire
hanger. Nothing. He went back down the stairs. It was getting dark. He took the boy by the hand and they went out
the front door to the street.

At the top of the hill he turned and studied the town.
Darkness coming fast. Darkness and cold. He put two
of the coats over the boy's shoulders, swallowing him up
parka and all.

I'm really hungry, Papa.

I know.

Will we be able to find our stuff?

Yes. I know where it is.

What if somebody finds it?

They wont find it.

I hope they dont.

They wont. Come on.

What was that?

I didnt hear anything.

Listen.

I dont hear anything.

They listened. Then in the distance he heard a dog bark. He turned and looked toward the darkening town. It's a dog, he said.

A dog?

Yes.

Where did it come from?

I dont know.

We're not going to kill it, are we Papa?

No. We're not going to kill it.

He looked down at the boy. Shivering in his coats. He bent over and kissed him on his gritty brow. We wont hurt the dog, he said. I promise.

They slept in a parked car beneath an overpass with the suitcoats and the blanket piled over them. In the darkness and the silence he could see bits of light that appeared random on the night grid. The higher floors of the buildings were all dark. You'd have to carry up water. You could be smoked out. What were they eating? God knows. They sat wrapped in the coats looking out the window. Who are they, Papa?

I dont know.

.   .   .

He woke in the night and lay listening. He couldnt remember where he was. The thought made him smile. Where are we? he said.

What is it, Papa?

Nothing. We're okay. Go to sleep.

We're going to be okay, arent we Papa?

Yes. We are.

And nothing bad is going to happen to us.

That's right.

Because we're carrying the fire.

Yes. Because we're carrying the fire.

In the morning a cold rain was falling. It gusted over the car even under the overpass and it danced in the road beyond. They sat and watched through the water on the glass. By the time it had slacked a good part of the day was gone. They left the coats and the blanket in the floor of the back seat and went up the road to search through more of the houses. Woodsmoke on the damp air. They never heard the dog again.

They found some utensils and a few pieces of clothing. A sweatshirt. Some plastic they could use for a tarp. He was sure they were being watched but he saw no one. In a pantry they came upon part of a sack of cornmeal that rats had been at in the long ago. He sifted the meal through a section of windowscreen and collected a small handful of dried turds and they built a fire on the concrete porch of the house and made cakes of the meal and cooked them over a piece of tin. Then they ate them slowly one by one. He wrapped the few remaining in a paper and put them in the knapsack.

The boy was sitting on the steps when he saw something move at the rear of the house across the road. A face was looking at him. A boy, about his age, wrapped in an out-sized wool coat with the sleeves turned back. He stood up. He ran across the road and up the drive. No one there. He looked toward the house and then he ran to the bottom of the yard through the dead weeds to a still black creek. Come back, he called. I wont hurt you. He was standing there crying when his father came sprinting across the road and seized him by the arm.

What are you doing? he hissed. What are you doing?

There's a little boy, Papa. There's a little boy.

There's no little boy. What are you doing?

Yes there is. I saw him.

I told you to stay put. Didnt I tell you? Now we've got to go. Come on.

I just wanted to see him, Papa. I just wanted to see him.

The man took him by the arm and they went back up through the yard. The boy would not stop crying and he would not stop looking back. Come on, the man said. We've got to go.

I want to see him, Papa.

There's no one to see. Do you want to die? Is that what you want?

I dont care, the boy said, sobbing. I dont care.

The man stopped. He stopped and squatted and held him. I'm sorry, he said. Dont say that. You musnt say that.

They made their way back through the wet streets to the viaduct and collected the coats and the blanket from the car and went on to the railway embankment where they climbed up and crossed the tracks into the woods and got the cart and headed out to the highway.

What if that little boy doesnt have anybody to take care of him? he said. What if he doesnt have a papa?

There are people there. They were just hiding.

He pushed the cart out into the road and stood there. He could see the tracks of the truck through the wet ash, faint and washed out, but there. He thought that he could smell them. The boy was pulling at his coat. Papa, he said.

What?

I'm afraid for that little boy.

I know. But he'll be all right.

We should go get him, Papa. We could get him and take him with us. We could take him and we could take the dog. The dog could catch something to eat.

We cant.

And I'd give that little boy half of my food.

Stop it. We cant.

He was crying again. What about the little boy? he sobbed. What about the little boy?

At a crossroads they sat in the dusk and he spread out the pieces of the map in the road and studied them. He put his finger down. This is us, he said. Right here. The boy wouldnt look. He sat studying the twisted matrix of routes in red and black with his finger at the junction where he thought that they might be. As if he'd see their small selves crouching there. We could go back, the boy said softly. It's not so far. It's not too late.

They made a dry camp in a woodlot not far from the road. They could find no sheltered place to make a fire that would not be seen so they made none. They ate each of them two of the cornmeal cakes and they slept together huddled on the ground in the coats and blankets. He held the child and after a while the child stopped shivering and after a while he slept.

The dog that he remembers followed us for two days. I tried to coax it to come but it would not. I made a noose of wire to catch it. There were three cartridges in the pistol. None to spare. She walked away down the road. The boy looked after her and then he looked at me and then he looked at the dog and he began to cry and to beg for the dog's life and I promised I would not hurt the dog. A trellis of a dog with the hide stretched over it. The next day it was gone. That is the dog he remembers. He doesnt remember any little boys.

He'd put a handful of dried raisins in a cloth in his pocket and at noon they sat in the dead grass by the side of the road and ate them. The boy looked at him. That's all there is, isnt it? he said.

Yes.

Are we going to die now?

No.

What are we going to do?

We're going to drink some water. Then we're going to keep going down the road.

Okay.

In the evening they tramped out across a field trying to find a place where their fire would not be seen. Dragging the cart behind them over the ground. So little of promise in that country. Tomorrow they would find something to eat. Night overtook them on a muddy road. They crossed into a field and plodded on toward a distant stand of trees skylighted stark and black against the last of the visible world. By the time they got there it was dark of night. He held the boy's hand and kicked up limbs and brush and got a fire going. The wood was damp but he shaved the dead bark off with his knife and he stacked brush and sticks all about to dry in the heat. Then he spread the sheet of plastic on the ground and got the coats and blankets from the cart and he took off their damp and muddy shoes and they sat there in silence with their hands outheld to the flames. He tried to think of something to say but he could not. He'd had this feeling before, beyond the numbness and the dull despair. The world shrinking down about a raw core of parsible entities. The names of things slowly following those things into oblivion. Colors.

The names of birds. Things to eat. Finally the names of things one believed to be true. More fragile than he would have thought. How much was gone already? The sacred idiom shorn of its referents and so of its reality. Drawing down like something trying to preserve heat. In time to wink out forever.

They slept through the night in their exhaustion and in the morning the fire was dead and black on the ground. He pulled on his muddy shoes and went to gather wood, blowing on his cupped hands. So cold. It could be November. It could be later. He got a fire going and walked out to the edge of the woodlot and stood looking over the countryside. The dead fields. A barn in the distance.

They hiked out along the dirt road and along a hill where a house had once stood. It had burned long ago. The rusted shape of a furnace standing in the black water of the cellar. Sheets of charred metal roofing crumpled in the fields where the wind had blown it. In the barn they scavenged a few handfuls of some grain he did not recognize out of the dusty floor of a metal hopper and stood eating it dust and all. Then they set out across the fields toward the road.

They followed a stone wall past the remains of an orchard. The trees in their ordered rows gnarled and black and the fallen limbs thick on the ground. He stopped and looked across the fields. Wind in the east. The soft ash moving in the furrows. Stopping. Moving again. He'd seen it all before. Shapes of dried blood in the stubble grass and gray coils of viscera where the slain had been field-dressed and hauled away. The wall beyond held a frieze of human heads, all faced alike, dried and caved with their taut grins and shrunken eyes. They wore gold rings in their leather ears and in the wind their sparse and ratty hair twisted about on their skulls. The teeth in their sockets like dental molds, the crude tattoos etched in some homebrewed woad faded in the beggared sunlight. Spiders, swords, targets. A dragon. Runic slogans, creeds misspelled. Old scars with old motifs stitched along their borders. The heads not truncheoned shapeless had been flayed of their skins and the raw skulls painted and signed across the forehead in a scrawl and one white bone skull had the plate sutures etched carefully in ink like a blueprint for assembly. He looked back at the boy. Standing by the cart in the wind. He looked at the dry grass where it moved and at the dark and twisted trees in their rows. A few shreds of clothing blown against the wall, everything gray in the ash. He walked along the wall passing the masks in a last review and through a stile and out to where the boy was waiting. He put his arm around his shoulder. Okay, he said. Let's go.

He'd come to see a message in each such late history, a message and a warning, and so this tableau of the slain and the devoured did prove to be. He woke in the morning and turned over in the blanket and looked back down the road through the trees the way they'd come in time to see the marchers appear four abreast. Dressed in clothing of every description, all wearing red scarves at their necks. Red or orange, as close to red as they could find. He put his hand on the boy's head. Shh, he said.

What is it, Papa?

People on the road. Keep your face down. Dont look.

No smoke from the dead fire. Nothing to be seen of the cart. He wallowed into the ground and lay watching across his forearm. An army in tennis shoes, tramping. Carrying three-foot lengths of pipe with leather wrappings. Lanyards at the wrist. Some of the pipes were threaded through with lengths of chain fitted at their ends with every manner of bludgeon. They clanked past, marching with a swaying gait like wind-up toys. Bearded, their breath smoking through their masks. Shh, he said. Shh. The phalanx following carried spears or lances tasseled with ribbons, the long blades hammered out of trucksprings in some crude forge up-country. The boy lay with his face in his arms, terrified. They passed two hundred feet away, the ground shuddering lightly. Tramping. Behind them came wagons drawn by slaves in harness and piled with goods of war and after that the women, perhaps a dozen in number, some of them pregnant, and lastly a supplementary consort of catamites illclothed against the cold and fitted in dogcollars and yoked each to each. All passed on. They lay listening.

Are they gone, Papa?

Yes, they're gone.

Did you see them?

Yes.

Were they the bad guys?

Yes, they were the bad guys.

There's a lot of them, those bad guys.

Yes there are. But they're gone.

They stood and brushed themselves off, listening to the silence in the distance.

Where are they going, Papa?

I dont know. They're on the move. It's not a good sign.

Why isnt it a good sign?

It just isnt. We need to get the map and take a look.

. . .

They pulled the cart from the brush with which they'd covered it and he raised it up and piled the blankets in and the coats and they pushed on out to the road and stood looking where the last of that ragged horde seemed to hang like an afterimage in the disturbed air.

In the afternoon it started to snow again. They stood watching the pale gray flakes sift down out of the sullen murk. They trudged on. A frail slush forming over the dark surface of the road. The boy kept falling behind and he stopped and waited for him. Stay with me, he said.

You walk too fast.

I'll go slower.

They went on.

You're not talking again.

I'm talking.

You want to stop?

I always want to stop.

We have to be more careful. I have to be more careful.

I know.

We'll stop. Okay?

Okay.

We just have to find a place.

Okay.

The falling snow curtained them about. There was no way to see anything at either side of the road. He was coughing again and the boy was shivering, the two of them side by side under the sheet of plastic, pushing the grocery cart through the snow. Finally he stopped. The boy was shaking uncontrollably.

We have to stop, he said.

It's really cold.

I know.

Where are we?

Where are we?

Yes.

I dont know.

If we were going to die would you tell me?

I dont know. We're not going to die.

They left the cart overturned in a field of sedge and he took the coats and the blankets wrapped in the plastic tarp and they set out. Hold on to my coat, he said. Dont let go. They crossed through the sedge to a fence and climbed through, holding down the wire for each other with their hands. The wire was cold and it creaked in the staples. It was darkening fast. They went on. What they came to was a cedar wood, the trees dead and black but still full enough to hold the snow. Beneath each one a precious circle of dark earth and cedar duff.

They settled under a tree and piled the blankets and coats on the ground and he wrapped the boy in one of the blankets and set to raking up the dead needles in a pile. He kicked a cleared place in the snow out where the fire wouldnt set the tree alight and he carried wood from the other trees, breaking off the limbs and shaking away the snow. When he struck the lighter to the rich tinder the fire crackled instantly and he knew that it would not last long. He looked at the boy. I've got to go for more wood, he said. I'll be in the neighborhood. Okay?

Where's the neighborhood?

It just means I wont be far.

Okay.

The snow by now was half a foot on the ground. He floundered out through the trees pulling up the fallen branches where they stuck out of the snow and by the time he had an armload and made his way back to the fire it had burned down to a nest of quaking embers. He threw the branches on the fire and set out again. Hard to stay ahead. The woods were getting dark and the firelight did not reach far. If he hurried he only grew faint. When he looked behind him the boy was trudging through snow half way to his knees gathering limbs and piling them in his arms.

The snow fell nor did it cease to fall. He woke all night and got up and coaxed the fire to life again. He'd unfolded the tarp and propped one end of it up beneath the tree to try and reflect back the heat from the fire. He looked at the boy's face sleeping in the orange light. The sunken cheeks streaked with black. He fought back the rage. Useless. He didnt think the boy could travel much more. Even if it stopped snowing the road would be all but impassable. The snow whispered down in the stillness and the sparks rose and dimmed and died in the eternal blackness.

He was half asleep when he heard a crashing in the woods. Then another. He sat up. The fire was down to scattered flames among the embers. He listened. The long dry crack of shearing limbs. Then another crash. He reached and shook the boy. Wake up, he said. We have to go.

He rubbed the sleep from his eyes with the backs of his hands. What is it? he said. What is it, Papa?

Come on. We have to move.

What is it?

It's the trees. They're falling down.

The boy sat up and looked about wildly.

It's all right, the man said. Come on. We need to hurry.

He scooped up the bedding and he folded it and wrapped the tarp around it. He looked up. The snow drifted into his eyes. The fire was little more than coals and it gave no light and the wood was nearly gone and the trees were falling all about them in the blackness. The boy clung to him. They moved away and he tried to find a clear space in the darkness but finally he put down the tarp and they just sat and pulled the blankets over them and he held the boy against him. The whump of the falling trees and the low boom of the loads of snow exploding on the ground set the woods to shuddering. He held the boy and told him it would be all right and that it would stop soon and after a while it did. The dull bedlam dying in the distance. And again, solitary and far away. Then nothing. There, he said. I think that's it. He dug a tunnel under one of the fallen trees, scooping away the snow with his arms, his frozen hands clawed inside his sleeves. They dragged in their bedding and the tarp and after a while they slept again for all the bitter cold.

When day broke he pushed his way out of their den, the tarp heavy with snow. He stood and looked about. It had stopped snowing and the cedar trees lay about in hillocks of snow and broken limbs and a few standing trunks that stood stripped and burntlooking in that graying landscape. He trudged out through the drifts leaving the boy to sleep under the tree like some hibernating animal. The snow was almost to his knees. In the field the dead sedge was drifted nearly out of sight and the snow stood in razor kerfs atop the fencewires and the silence was breathless. He stood leaning on a post coughing. He'd little idea where the cart was and he thought that he was getting stupid and that his head wasnt working right. Concentrate, he said. You have to think. When he turned to go back the boy was calling him.

We have to go, he said. We cant stay here.
The boy stared bleakly at the gray drifts.
Come on.
They made their way out to the fence.

Where are we going? the boy said.

We have to find the cart.

He just stood there, his hands in the armpits of his parka.

Come on, the man said. You have to come on.

He waded out across the drifted fields. The snow lay deep and gray. Already there was a fresh fall of ash on it. He struggled on a few more feet and then turned and looked back. The boy had fallen. He dropped the armload of blankets and the tarp and went back and picked him up. He was already shivering. He picked him up and held him. I'm sorry, he said. I'm sorry.

They were a long time finding the cart. He pulled it upright out of the drifts and dug out the knapsack and shook it out and opened it and stuffed in one of the blankets. He put the pack and the other blankets and the coats in the basket and picked up the boy and set him on top and unlaced his shoes and pulled them off. Then he got out his knife and set about cutting up one of the coats and wrapping the boy's feet. He used the entire coat and then he cut big squares of plastic out of the tarp and gathered them up from underneath and wrapped and tied them at the boy's ankles with the lining from the coatsleeves. He stood back.

The boy looked down. Now you, Papa, he said. He wrapped one of the coats around the boy and then he sat on the tarp in the snow and wrapped his own feet. He stood and warmed his hands inside his parka and then packed their shoes into the knapsack along with the binoculars and the boy's truck. He shook out the tarp and folded it and tied it with the other blankets on top of the pack and shouldered it up and then took a last look through the basket but that was it. Let's go, he said. The boy took one last look back at the cart and then followed him out to the road.

It was harder going even than he would have guessed. In an hour they'd made perhaps a mile. He stopped and looked back at the boy. The boy stopped and waited.

You think we're going to die, dont you?

I dont know.

We're not going to die.

Okay.

But you dont believe me.

I dont know.

Why do you think we're going to die?

I dont know.

Stop saying I dont know.

Okay.

Why do you think we're going to die?

We dont have anything to eat.

We'll find something.

Okay.

How long do you think people can go without food?

I dont know.

But how long do you think?

Maybe a few days.

And then what? You fall over dead?

Yes.

Well you dont. It takes a long time. We have water. That's the most important thing. You dont last very long without water.

Okay.

But you dont believe me.

I dont know.

He studied him. Standing there with his hands in the pockets of the outsized pinstriped suitcoat.

Do you think I lie to you?

No.

But you think I might lie to you about dying.

Yes.

Okay. I might. But we're not dying.

Okay.

. . .

He studied the sky. There were days when the ashen over-cast thinned and now the standing trees along the road made the faintest of shadows over the snow. They went on. The boy wasnt doing well. He stopped and checked his feet and retied the plastic. When the snow started to melt it was going to be hard to keep their feet dry. They stopped often to rest. He'd no strength to carry the child. They sat on the pack and ate handfuls of the dirty snow. By afternoon it was beginning to melt. They passed a burned house, just the brick chimney standing in the yard. They were on the road all day, such day as there was. Such few hours. They might have covered three miles.

He thought the road would be so bad that no one would be on it but he was wrong. They camped almost in the road itself and built a great fire, dragging dead limbs out of the snow and piling them on the flames to hiss and steam. There was no help for it. The few blankets they had would not keep them warm. He tried to stay awake. He would jerk upright out of his sleep and slap about him looking for the pistol. The boy was so thin. He watched him while he slept. Taut face and hollow eyes. A strange beauty. He got up and dragged more wood onto the fire.

. . .

They walked out to the road and stood. There were tracks in the snow. A wagon. Some sort of wheeled vehicle. Something with rubber tires by the narrow treadmarks. Bootprints between the wheels. Someone had passed in the dark going south. In the early dawn at latest. Running the road in the night. He stood thinking about that. He walked the tracks carefully. They'd passed within fifty feet of the fire and had not even slowed to look. He stood looking back up the road. The boy watched him.

We need to get out of the road.

Why, Papa?

Someone's coming.

Is it bad guys?

Yes. I'm afraid so.

They could be good guys. Couldnt they?

He didnt answer. He looked at the sky out of old habit but there was nothing to see.

What are we going to do, Papa?

Let's go.

Can we go back to the fire?

No. Come on. We probably dont have much time.

I'm really hungry.

I know.

What are we going to do?

We have to hole up. Get off the road.

Will they see our tracks?

Yes.

What can we do about it?

I dont know.

Will they know what we are?

What?

If they see our tracks. Will they know what we are?

He looked back at their great round tracks in the snow.

They'll figure it out, he said.

Then he stopped.

We need to think about this. Let's go back to the fire.

He'd thought to find some place in the road where the snow had melted off completely but then he thought that since their tracks would not reappear on the far side it would be no help. They kicked snow over the fire and went on through the trees and circled and came back. They hurried, leaving a maze of tracks and then they set out back north through the woods keeping the road in view.

The site they picked was simply the highest ground they came to and it gave views north along the road and over-looked their backtrack. He spread the tarp in the wet snow and wrapped the boy in the blankets. You're going to be cold, he said. But maybe we wont be here long. Within the hour two men came down the road almost at a lope. When they had passed he stood up to watch them. And when he did they stopped and one of them looked back. He froze. He was wrapped in one of the gray blankets and he would have been hard to see but not impossible. But he thought probably they had smelled the smoke. They stood talking. Then they went on. He sat down. It's okay, he said. We just have to wait. But I think it's okay.

They'd had no food and little sleep in five days and in this condition on the outskirts of a small town they came upon a once grand house sited on a rise above the road. The boy stood holding his hand. The snow was largely melted on the macadam and in the southfacing fields and woods. They stood there. The plastic bags over their feet had long since worn through and their feet were wet and cold. The house was tall and stately with white doric columns across the front. A port cochere at the side. A gravel drive that curved up through a field of dead grass. The windows were oddly intact.

What is this place, Papa?

Shh. Let's just stand here and listen.

There was nothing. The wind rustling the dead roadside bracken. A distant creaking. Door or shutter.

I think we should take a look.

Papa let's not go up there.

It's okay.

I dont think we should go up there.

It's okay. We have to take a look.

They approached slowly up the drive. No tracks in the random patches of melting snow. A tall hedge of dead privet. An ancient birdsnest lodged in the dark wicker of it. They stood in the yard studying the facade. The hand-made brick of the house kilned out of the dirt it stood on. The peeling paint hanging in long dry sleavings down the columns and from the buckled soffits. A lamp that hung from a long chain overhead. The boy clung to him as they climbed the steps. One of the windows was slightly open and a cord ran from it and across the porch to vanish in the grass. He held the boy's hand and they crossed the porch. Chattel slaves had once trod those boards bearing food and drink on silver trays. They went to the window and looked in.

What if there's someone here, Papa?

There's no one here.

We should go, Papa.

We've got to find something to eat. We have no choice.

We could find something somewhere else.

It's going to be all right. Come on.

. . .

He took the pistol from his belt and tried the door. It swung slowly in on its great brass hinges. They stood listening. Then they stepped into a broad foyer floored in a domino of black and white marble tiles. A broad staircase ascending. Fine Morris paper on the walls, waterstained and sagging. The plaster ceiling was bellied in great swags and the yellowed dentil molding was bowed and sprung from the upper walls. To the left through the doorway stood a large walnut buffet in what must have been the diningroom. The doors and the drawers were gone but the rest of it was too large to burn. They stood in the doorway. Piled in a windrow in one corner of the room was a great heap of clothing. Clothes and shoes. Belts. Coats. Blankets and old sleeping bags. He would have ample time later to think about that. The boy hung on to his hand. He was terrified. They crossed the foyer to the room on the far side and walked in and stood. A great hall of a room with ceilings twice the height of the doors. A fireplace with raw brick showing where the wooden mantel and surround had been pried away and burned. There were mattresses and bedding arranged on the floor in front of the hearth. Papa, the boy whispered. Shh, he said.

. . .

The ashes were cold. Some blackened pots stood about. He squatted on his heels and picked one up and smelled it and put it back. He stood and looked out the window. Gray trampled grass. Gray snow. The cord that came through the window was tied to a brass bell and the bell was fixed in a rough wooden jig that had been nailed to the window molding. He held the boy's hand and they went down a narrow back hallway into the kitchen. Trash piled everywhere. A ruststained sink. Smell of mold and excrement. They went on into the adjoining small room, perhaps a pantry.

In the floor of this room was a door or hatch and it was locked with a large padlock made of stacked steel plates. He stood looking at it.

Papa, the boy said. We should go. Papa.

There's a reason this is locked.

The boy pulled at his hand. He was almost in tears. Papa? he said.

We've got to eat.

I'm not hungry, Papa. I'm not.

We need to find a prybar or something.

. . .

They pushed out through the back door, the boy hanging on to him. He shoved the pistol in his belt and stood looking out over the yard. There was a brick walkway and the twisted and wiry shape of what once had been a row of boxwoods. In the yard was an old iron harrow propped up on piers of stacked brick and someone had wedged between the rails of it a forty gallon castiron cauldron of the kind once used for rendering hogs. Underneath were the ashes of a fire and blackened billets of wood. Off to one side a small wagon with rubber tires. All these things he saw and did not see. At the far side of the yard was an old wooden smokehouse and a toolshed. He crossed half dragging the child and went sorting through tools standing in a barrel under the shed roof. He came up with a longhandled spade and hefted it in his hand. Come on, he said.

Back in the house he chopped at the wood around the haspstaple and finally jammed the blade under the staple and pried it up. It was bolted through the wood and the whole thing came up lock and all. He kicked the blade of the shovel under the edge of the boards and stopped and got his lighter out. Then he stood on the tang of the shovel and raised the edge of the hatch and leaned and got hold of it. Papa, the boy whispered.

He stopped. Listen to me, he said. Just stop it. We're starving. Do you understand? Then he raised the hatch door and swung it over and let it down on the floor behind.

Just wait here, he said.

I'm going with you.

I thought you were scared.

I am scared.

Okay. Just stay close behind me.

He started down the rough wooden steps. He ducked his head and then flicked the lighter and swung the flame out over the darkness like an offering. Coldness and damp. An ungodly stench. The boy clutched at his coat. He could see part of a stone wall. Clay floor. An old mattress darkly stained. He crouched and stepped down again and held out the light. Huddled against the back wall were naked people, male and female, all trying to hide, shielding their faces with their hands. On the mattress lay a man with his legs gone to the hip and the stumps of them blackened and burnt. The smell was hideous.

Jesus, he whispered.

Then one by one they turned and blinked in the pitiful light. Help us, they whispered. Please help us.

Christ, he said. Oh Christ.

He turned and grabbed the boy. Hurry, he said. Hurry.

He'd dropped the lighter. No time to look. He pushed the boy up the stairs. Help us, they called.

Hurry.

A bearded face appeared blinking at the foot of the stairs. Please, he called. Please.

Hurry. For God's sake hurry.

He shoved the boy through the hatch and sent him sprawling. He stood and got hold of the door and swung it over and let it slam down and he turned to grab the boy but the boy had gotten up and was doing his little dance of terror. For the love of God will you come on, he hissed. But the boy was pointing out the window and when he looked he went cold all over. Coming across the field toward the house were four bearded men and two women. He grabbed the boy by the hand. Christ, he said. Run. Run.

They tore through the house to the front door and down the steps. Half way down the drive he dragged the boy into the field. He looked back. They were partly screened by the ruins of the privet but he knew they had minutes at most and maybe no minutes at all. At the bottom of the field they crashed through a stand of dead cane and out into the road and crossed into the woods on the far side. He redoubled his grip on the boy's wrist. Run, he whispered. We have to run. He looked toward the house but he could see nothing. If they came down the drive they would see him running through the trees with the boy. This is the moment. This is the moment. He fell to the ground and pulled the boy to him. Shh, he said. Shh.

Are they going to kill us? Papa?

Shh.

They lay in the leaves and the ash with their hearts pounding. He was going to start coughing. He'd have put his hand over his mouth but the boy was holding on to it and would not let go and in the other hand he was holding the pistol. He had to concentrate to stifle the cough and at the same time he was trying to listen. He swung his chin through the leaves, trying to see. Keep your head down, he whispered.

Are they coming?

No.

They crawled slowly through the leaves toward what looked like lower ground. He lay listening, holding the boy. He could hear them in the road talking. Voice of a woman. Then he heard them in the dry leaves. He took the boy's hand and pushed the revolver into it. Take it, he whispered. Take it. The boy was terrified. He put his arm around him and held him. His body so thin. Dont be afraid,

he said. If they find you you are going to have to do it. Do
you understand? Shh. No crying. Do you hear me? You
know how to do it. You put it in your mouth and point it
up. Do it quick and hard. Do you understand? Stop crying. Do you understand?

I think so.

No. Do you understand?

Yes.

Say yes I do Papa.

Yes I do Papa.

He looked down at him. All he saw was terror. He took
the gun from him. No you dont, he said.

I dont know what to do, Papa. I dont know what to do.
Where will you be?

It's okay.

I dont know what to do.

Shh. I'm right here. I wont leave you.

You promise.

Yes. I promise. I was going to run. To try and lead them
away. But I cant leave you.

Papa?

Shh. Stay down.

I'm so scared.

Shh.

· · ·

They lay listening. Can you do it? When the time comes? When the time comes there will be no time. Now is the time. Curse God and die. What if it doesnt fire? It has to fire. What if it doesnt fire? Could you crush that beloved skull with a rock? Is there such a being within you of which you know nothing? Can there be? Hold him in your arms. Just so. The soul is quick. Pull him toward you. Kiss him. Quickly.

He waited. The small nickelplated revolver in his hand. He was going to cough. He put his whole mind to holding it back. He tried to listen but he could hear nothing. I wont leave you, he whispered. I wont ever leave you. Do you understand? He lay in the leaves holding the trembling child. Clutching the revolver. All through the long dusk and into the dark. Cold and starless. Blessed. He began to believe they had a chance. We just have to wait, he whispered. So cold. He tried to think but his mind swam. He was so weak. All his talk about running. He couldnt run. When it was truly black about them he unfastened the straps on the backpack and pulled out the blankets and spread them over the boy and soon the boy was sleeping.

. . .

In the night he heard hideous shrieks coming from the house and he tried to put his hands over the boy's ears and after a while the screaming stopped. He lay listening. Coming through the canebrake into the road he'd seen a box. A thing like a child's playhouse. He realized it was where they lay watching the road. Lying in wait and ringing the bell in the house for their companions to come. He dozed and woke. What is coming? Footsteps in the leaves. No. Just the wind. Nothing. He sat up and looked toward the house but he could see only darkness. He shook the boy awake. Come on, he said. We have to go. The boy didnt answer but he knew he was awake. He pulled the blankets free and strapped them onto the knapsack. Come on, he whispered.

They set out through the dark woods. There was a moon somewhere beyond the ashen overcast and they could just make out the trees. They staggered on like drunks. If they find us they'll kill us, wont they Papa.

Shh. No more talking.

Wont they Papa.

Shh. Yes. Yes they will.

He'd no idea what direction they might have taken and his fear was that they might circle and return to the house. He tried to remember if he knew anything about that or if it were only a fable. In what direction did lost men veer? Perhaps it changed with hemispheres. Or handedness. Finally he put it out of his mind. The notion that there could be anything to correct for. His mind was betraying him. Phantoms not heard from in a thousand years rousing slowly from their sleep. Correct for that. The boy was tottering on his feet. He asked to be carried, stumbling and slurring his words, and the man did carry him and he fell asleep on his shoulder instantly. He knew he couldnt carry him far.

He woke in the dark of the woods in the leaves shivering violently. He sat up and felt about for the boy. He held his hand to the thin ribs. Warmth and movement. Heartbeat.

When he woke again it was almost light enough to see. He threw back the blanket and stood and almost fell. He steadied himself and tried to see about him in the gray woods. How far had they come? He walked to the top of a rise and crouched and watched the day accrue. The chary dawn, the cold illucid world. In the distance what looked to be a pine wood, raw and black. A colorless world of wire and crepe. He went back and got the boy and made him sit up. His head kept slumping forward. We have to go, he said. We have to go.

He carried him across the field, stopping to rest each fifty counted steps. When he got to the pines he knelt and laid him in the gritty duff and covered him with the blankets and sat watching him. He looked like something out of a deathcamp. Starved, exhausted, sick with fear. He leaned and kissed him and got up and walked out to the edge of the woods and then he walked the perimeter round to see if they were safe.

Across the fields to the south he could see the shape of a house and a barn. Beyond the trees the curve of a road. A long drive with dead grass. Dead ivy along a stone wall and a mailbox and a fence along the road and the dead trees beyond. Cold and silent. Shrouded in the carbon fog. He walked back and sat beside the boy. It was desperation that had led him to such carelessness and he knew that he could not do that again. No matter what.

The boy wouldnt wake for hours. Still if he did he'd be terrified. It had happened before. He thought about waking him but he knew that he wouldnt remember anything if he did. He'd trained him to lie in the woods like a fawn. For how long? In the end he took the pistol from his belt and laid it alongside him under the blankets and rose and set out.

He came upon the barn from the hill above it, stopping to watch and to listen. He made his way down through the ruins of an old apple orchard, black and gnarly stumps, dead grass to his knees. He stood in the door of the barn and listened. Pale slatted light. He walked along the dusty stalls. He stood in the center of the barn bay and listened but there was nothing. He climbed the ladder to the loft and he was so weak he wasnt sure he was going to make it to the top. He walked down to the end of the loft and looked out the high gable window at the country below, the pieced land dead and gray, the fence, the road.

There were bales of hay in the loft floor and he squatted and sorted a handful of seeds from them and sat chewing. Coarse and dry and dusty. They had to contain some nutrition. He rose and rolled two of the bales across the floor and let them fall into the bay below. Two dusty thumps. He went back to the gable and stood studying what he could see of the house beyond the corner of the barn. Then he climbed back down the ladder.

The grass between the house and the barn looked untrodden. He crossed to the porch. The porch screening rotted and falling away. A child's bicycle. The kitchen door stood open and he crossed the porch and stood in the doorway. Cheap plywood paneling curled with damp. Collapsing into the room. A red formica table. He crossed the room and opened the refrigerator door. Something sat on one of the racks in a coat of gray fur. He shut the door. Trash everywhere. He took a broom from the corner and poked about with the handle. He climbed onto the counter and felt his way through the dust on top of the cabinets. A mousetrap. A packet of something. He blew away the dust. It was a grape flavored powder to make drinks with. He put it in the pocket of his coat.

He went through the house room by room. He found nothing. A spoon in a bedside drawer. He put that in his pocket. He thought there might be some clothes in a closet or some bedding but there wasnt. He went back out and crossed to the garage. He sorted through tools. Rakes. A shovel. Jars of nails and bolts on a shelf. A boxcutter. He held it to the light and looked at the rusty blade and put it back. Then he picked it up again. He took a screwdriver from a coffee can and opened the handle. Inside were four new blades. He took out the old blade and laid it on the shelf and put in one of the new ones and screwed the handle back together and retracted the blade and put the cutter in his pocket. Then he picked up the screwdriver and put that in his pocket as well.

He walked back out to the barn. He had a piece of cloth that he intended to use to collect seeds from the haybales but when he got to the barn he stopped and stood listening to the wind. A creaking of tin somewhere high in the roof above him. There was yet a lingering odor of cows in the barn and he stood there thinking about cows and he realized they were extinct. Was that true? There could be a cow somewhere being fed and cared for. Could there? Fed what? Saved for what? Beyond the open door the dead grass rasped dryly in the wind. He walked out and stood looking across the fields toward the pine wood where the boy lay sleeping. He walked up through the orchard and then he stopped again. He'd stepped on something. He took a step back and knelt and parted the grass with his hands. It was an apple. He picked it up and held it to the light. Hard and brown and shriveled. He wiped it with the cloth and bit into it. Dry and almost tasteless. But an apple. He ate it entire, seeds and all. He held the stem between his thumb and forefinger and let it drop. Then he went treading softly through the grass. His feet were still wrapped in the remnants of the coat and the shreds of tarp and he sat and untied them and stuffed the wrappings in his pocket and went down the rows barefoot. By the time he got to the bottom of the orchard he had four more apples and he put them in his pocket and came back. He went row by row till he'd trod a puzzle in the grass. He'd more apples than he could carry. He felt out the spaces about the trunks and filled his pockets full and he piled apples in the hood of his parka behind his head and carried apples stacked along his forearm against his chest. He dumped them in a pile at the door of the barn and sat there and wrapped up his numb feet.

In the mudroom off the kitchen he'd seen an old wicker basket full of masonjars. He dragged the basket out into the floor and set the jars out of it and then tipped over the basket and tapped out the dirt. Then he stopped. What had he seen? A drainpipe. A trellis. The dark serpentine of a dead vine running down it like the track of some enterprise upon a graph. He stood up and walked back through the kitchen and out into the yard and stood looking at the house. The windows giving back the gray and nameless day. The drainpipe ran down the corner of the porch. He was still holding the basket and he set it down in the grass and climbed the steps again. The pipe came down the corner post and into a concrete tank. He brushed away the trash and rotted bits of screening from the cover. He went back into the kitchen and got the broom and came out and swept the cover clean and set the broom in the corner and lifted the cover from the tank. Inside was a tray filled with a wet gray sludge from the roof mixed with a compost of dead leaves and twigs. He lifted out the tray and set it in the floor. Underneath was white gravel. He scooped back the gravel with his hand. The tank beneath was filled with charcoal, pieces burned out of whole sticks and limbs in carbon effigies of the trees themselves. He put the tray back. In the floor was a green brass ringpull. He reached and got the broom and swept away the ash. There were sawlines in the boards. He swept the boards clean and knelt and hooked his fingers in the ring and lifted the trap door and swung it open. Down there in the darkness was a cistern filled with water so sweet that he could smell it. He lay in the floor on his stomach and reached down. He could just touch the water. He scooted forward and reached again and laved up a handful of it and smelled and tasted it and then drank. He lay there a long time, lifting up the water to

his mouth a palmful at a time. Nothing in his memory anywhere of anything so good.

He went back to the mudroom and returned with two of
the jars and an old blue enameled pan. He wiped out the
pan and dipped it full of water and used it to clean the jars.
Then he reached down and sank one of the jars till it was
full and raised it up dripping. The water was so clear. He
held it to the light. A single bit of sediment coiling in the
jar on some slow hydraulic axis. He tipped the jar and
drank and he drank slowly but still he drank nearly the
whole jar. He sat there with his stomach bloated. He could
have drunk more but he didnt. He poured the remaining
water into the other jar and rinsed it out and he filled both
jars and then let down the wooden cover over the cistern
and rose and with his pockets full of apples and carrying
the jars of water he set out across the fields toward the pine
wood.

He was gone longer than he'd meant to be and he hurried
his steps the best he could, the water swinging and gurgling in the shrunken swag of his gut. He stopped to rest
and began again. When he got to the woods the boy did
not look as if he'd even stirred and he knelt and set the jars

carefully in the duff and picked up the pistol and put it in
his belt and then he just sat there watching him.

They spent the afternoon sitting wrapped in the blankets
and eating apples. Sipping the water from the jars. He
took the packet of grape flavor from his pocket and opened
it and poured it into the jar and stirred it and gave it to the
boy. You did good Papa, he said. He slept while the boy
kept watch and in the evening they got out their shoes
and put them on and went down to the farmhouse and collected the rest of the apples. They filled three jars with
water and screwed on the two-piece caps from a box of
them he'd found on a shelf in the mudroom. Then he
wrapped everything in one of the blankets and packed
it into the knapsack and tied the other blankets across
the top of the knapsack and shouldered it up. They stood
in the door watching the light draw down over the world
to the west. Then they went down the drive and set out
upon the road again.

The boy hung on to his coat and he kept to the edge of the
road and tried to feel out the pavement under his feet in
the dark. In the distance he could hear thunder and after a
while there were dim shudderings of light ahead of them.

He got out the plastic sheeting from the knapsack but there was hardly enough of it left to cover them and after a while it began to rain. They stumbled along side by side. There was nowhere to go. They had the hoods of their coats up but the coats were getting wet and heavy from the rain. He stopped in the road and tried to rearrange the tarp. The boy was shaking badly.

You're freezing, arent you?

Yes.

If we stop we'll get really cold.

I'm really cold now.

What do you want to do?

Can we stop?

Yes. Okay. We can stop.

It was as long a night as he could remember out of a great plenty of such nights. They lay on the wet ground by the side of the road under the blankets with the rain rattling on the tarp and he held the boy and after a while the boy stopped shaking and after a while he slept. The thunder trundled away to the north and ceased and there was just the rain. He slept and woke and the rain slackened and after a while it stopped. He wondered if it was even midnight. He was coughing and it got worse and it woke the child. The dawn was a long time coming. He raised up from time to time to look to the east and after a while it was day.

He wrapped their coats each in turn around the trunk of a small tree and twisted out the water. He had the boy take off his clothes and he wrapped him in one of the blankets and while he stood shivering he wrung the water out of his clothes and passed them back. The ground where they'd slept was dry and they sat there with the blankets draped over them and ate apples and drank water. Then they set out upon the road again, slumped and cowled and shivering in their rags like mendicant friars sent forth to find their keep.

By evening they at least were dry. They studied the pieces of map but he'd little notion of where they were. He stood at a rise in the road and tried to take his bearings in the twilight. They left the pike and took a narrow road through the country and came at last upon a bridge and a dry creek and they crawled down the bank and huddled underneath.

Can we have a fire? the boy said.

We dont have a lighter.

The boy looked away.

I'm sorry. I dropped it. I didnt want to tell you.

That's okay.

I'll find us some flint. I've been looking. And we've still got the little bottle of gasoline.

Okay.

Are you very cold?

I'm okay.

The boy lay with his head in the man's lap. After a while he said: They're going to kill those people, arent they?

Yes.

Why do they have to do that?

I dont know.

Are they going to eat them?

I dont know.

They're going to eat them, arent they?

Yes.

And we couldnt help them because then they'd eat us too.

Yes.

And that's why we couldnt help them.

Yes.

Okay.

They passed through towns that warned people away with messages scrawled on the billboards. The billboards had been whited out with thin coats of paint in order to write on them and through the paint could be seen a pale palimpsest of advertisements for goods which no longer existed. They sat by the side of the road and ate the last of the apples.

What is it? the man said.

Nothing.

We'll find something to eat. We always do.

The boy didnt answer. The man watched him.

That's not it, is it?

It's okay.

Tell me.

The boy looked away down the road.

I want you to tell me. It's okay.

He shook his head.

Look at me, the man said.

He turned and looked. He looked like he'd been crying.

Just tell me.

We wouldnt ever eat anybody, would we?

No. Of course not.

Even if we were starving?

We're starving now.

You said we werent.

I said we werent dying. I didnt say we werent starving.

But we wouldnt.

No. We wouldnt.

No matter what.

No. No matter what.

Because we're the good guys.

Yes.

And we're carrying the fire.

And we're carrying the fire. Yes.

Okay.

He found pieces of flint or chert in a ditch but in the end it was easier to rake the pliers down the side of a rock at the bottom of which he'd made a small pile of tinder soaked in gas. Two more days. Then three. They were starving right enough. The country was looted, ransacked, ravaged. Rifled of every crumb. The nights were blinding cold and casket black and the long reach of the morning had a terrible silence to it. Like a dawn before battle. The boy's candlecolored skin was all but translucent. With his great staring eyes he'd the look of an alien.

He was beginning to think that death was finally upon them and that they should find some place to hide where they would not be found. There were times when he sat watching the boy sleep that he would begin to sob uncontrollably but it wasnt about death. He wasnt sure what it was about but he thought it was about beauty or about goodness. Things that he'd no longer any way to think about at all. They squatted in a bleak wood and drank ditchwater strained through a rag. He'd seen the boy in a dream laid out upon a coolingboard and woke in horror. What he could bear in the waking world he could not by night and he sat awake for fear the dream would return.

They scrabbled through the charred ruins of houses they would not have entered before. A corpse floating in the black water of a basement among the trash and rusting ductwork. He stood in a livingroom partly burned and open to the sky. The waterbuckled boards sloping away into the yard. Soggy volumes in a bookcase. He took one down and opened it and then put it back. Everything damp. Rotting. In a drawer he found a candle. No way to light it. He put it in his pocket. He walked out in the gray light and stood and he saw for a brief moment the absolute truth of the world. The cold relentless circling of the intestate earth. Darkness implacable. The blind dogs of the sun in their running. The crushing black vacuum of the universe. And somewhere two hunted animals trembling like groundfoxes in their cover. Borrowed time and borrowed world and borrowed eyes with which to sorrow it.

· · ·

At the edge of a small town they sat in the cab of a truck to rest, staring out a glass washed clean by the recent rains. A light dusting of ash. Exhausted. By the roadside stood another sign that warned of death, the letters faded with the years. He almost smiled. Can you read that? he said.

Yes.

Dont pay any attention. There's no one here.

Are they dead?

I think so.

I wish that little boy was with us.

Let's go, he said.

Rich dreams now which he was loathe to wake from. Things no longer known in the world. The cold drove him forth to mend the fire. Memory of her crossing the lawn toward the house in the early morning in a thin rose gown that clung to her breasts. He thought each memory recalled must do some violence to its origins. As in a party game. Say the word and pass it on. So be sparing. What you alter in the remembering has yet a reality, known or not.

They walked through the streets wrapped in the filthy blankets. He held the pistol at his waist and held the boy by the hand. At the farther edge of the town they came upon a solitary house in a field and they crossed and entered and walked through the rooms. They came upon themselves in a mirror and he almost raised the pistol. It's us, Papa, the boy whispered. It's us.

He stood in the back door and looked out at the fields and the road beyond and the bleak country beyond the road. On the patio was a barbeque pit made from a fifty-five gallon drum slit endways with a torch and set in a welded iron frame. A few dead trees in the yard. A fence. A metal tool shed. He shrugged off the blanket and wrapped it around the boy's shoulder.

I want you to wait here.

I want to go with you.

I'm only going over there to take a look. Just sit here. You'll be able to see me the whole time. I promise.

He crossed the yard and pushed open the door, still holding the gun. It was a sort of garden shed. Dirt floor. Metal shelves with some plastic flowerpots. Everything covered with ash. There were garden tools standing in the corner. A lawnmower. A wooden bench under the window and beside it a metal cabinet. He opened the cabinet. Old catalogs. Packets of seed. Begonia. Morning glory. He stuck them in his pocket. For what? On the top shelf were two cans of motor oil and he put the pistol in his belt and reached and got them and set them on the bench. They were very old, made of cardboard with metal endcaps. The oil had soaked through the cardboard but still they seemed full. He stepped back and looked out the door. The boy was sitting on the back steps of the house wrapped in the blankets watching him. When he turned he saw a gascan in the corner behind the door. He knew it couldnt have gas in it yet when he tilted it with his foot and let it fall back again there was a gentle slosh. He picked it up and carried it to the bench and tried to unscrew the cap but he could not. He got the pliers out of his coat pocket and extended the jaws and tried it. It would just fit and he twisted off the cap and laid it on the bench and sniffed the can. Rank odor. Years old. But it was gasoline and it would burn. He screwed the cap back on and put the pliers in his pocket. He looked around for some smaller container but there wasnt one. He shouldnt have thrown away the bottle. Check the house.

Crossing the grass he felt half faint and he had to stop. He wondered if it was from smelling the gasoline. The boy was watching him. How many days to death? Ten? Not so many more than that. He couldnt think. Why had he stopped? He turned and looked down at the grass. He walked back. Testing the ground with his feet. He stopped and turned again. Then he went back to the shed. He returned with a garden spade and in the place where he'd stood he chucked the blade into the ground. It sank to half its length and stopped with a hollow wooden sound. He began to shovel away the dirt.

Slow going. God he was tired. He leaned on the spade. He raised his head and looked at the boy. The boy sat as before. He bent to his work again. Before long he was resting between each shovelful. What he finally unburied was a piece of plywood covered with roofingfelt. He shoveled out along the edges. It was a door perhaps three feet by six. At one end was a hasp with a padlock taped up in a plastic bag. He rested, holding on to the handle of the spade, his forehead in the crook of his arm. When he looked up again the boy was standing in the yard just a few feet from him. He was very scared. Dont open it, Papa, he whispered.

It's okay.

Please, Papa. Please.

It's okay.

No it's not.

He had his fists clutched at his chest and he was bobbing up and down with fear. The man dropped the shovel and put his arms around him. Come on, he said. Let's just go sit on the porch and rest a while.

Then can we go?

Let's just sit for a while.

Okay.

They sat wrapped in the blankets and looked out at the yard. They sat for a long time. He tried to explain to the boy that there was no one buried in the yard but the boy just started crying. After a while he even thought that maybe the child was right.

Let's just sit, he said. We wont even talk.

Okay.

They walked through the house again. He found a beer bottle and an old rag of a curtain and he tore an edge from the cloth and stuffed it down the neck of the bottle with a coathanger. This is our new lamp, he said.

How can we light it?

I found some gasoline in the shed. And some oil. I'll show you.

Okay.

Come on, the man said. Everything's okay. I promise.

But when he bent to see into the boy's face under the hood of the blanket he very much feared that something was gone that could not be put right again.

They went out and crossed the yard to the shed. He set the bottle on the bench and he took a screwdriver and punched a hole in one of the cans of oil and then punched a smaller one to help it drain. He pulled the wick out of the bottle and poured the bottle about half full, old straight weight oil thick and gelid with the cold and a long time pouring. He twisted the cap off the gascan and he made a small paper spill from one of the seedpackets and poured gas into the bottle and put his thumb over the mouth and shook it. Then he poured some out into a clay dish and took the rag and stuffed it back into the bottle with the screwdriver. He took a piece of flint from his pocket and got the pair of pliers and struck the flint against the serrated jaw. He tried it a couple of times and then he stopped and poured more gasoline into the dish. This may flare up, he said. The boy nodded. He raked sparks into the dish and it bloomed into flame with a low whoosh. He reached and got the bottle and tilted it and lit the wick and blew out the flame in the dish and handed the smoking bottle to the boy. Here, he said. Take it.

What are we going to do?

Hold your hand in front of the flame. Dont let it go out.

He rose and took the pistol from his belt. This door looks like the other door, he said. But it's not. I know you're scared. That's okay. I think there may be things in there and we have to take a look. There's no place else to go. This is it. I want you to help me. If you dont want to hold the lamp you'll have to take the pistol.

I'll hold the lamp.

Okay. This is what the good guys do. They keep trying. They dont give up.

Okay.

He led the boy out into the yard trailing the black smoke from the lamp. He put the pistol in his belt and picked up the spade and began to chop the hasp out of the plywood. He wedged the corner of the blade under it and pried it up and then knelt and took hold of the lock and twisted the whole thing loose and pitched it into the grass. He pried the blade under the door and got his fingers under it and then stood and raised it up. Dirt went rattling down the boards. He looked at the boy. Are you all right? he said. The boy nodded mutely, holding the lamp in front of him. The man swung the door over and let it fall in the grass. Rough stairs carpentered out of two by tens leading down into the darkness. He reached and took the lamp from the boy. He started to descend the stairs but then he turned and leaned and kissed the child on the forehead.

The bunker was walled with concrete block. A poured concrete floor laid over with kitchen tile. There were a couple of iron cots with bare springs, one against either wall, the mattress pads rolled up at the foot of them in army fashion. He turned and looked at the boy crouched above him blinking in the smoke rising up from the lamp and then he descended to the lower steps and sat and held the lamp out. Oh my God, he whispered. Oh my God.

What is it Papa?

Come down. Oh my God. Come down.

Crate upon crate of canned goods. Tomatoes, peaches, beans, apricots. Canned hams. Corned beef. Hundreds of gallons of water in ten gallon plastic jerry jugs. Paper towels, toiletpaper, paper plates. Plastic trashbags stuffed with blankets. He held his forehead in his hand. Oh my God, he said. He looked back at the boy. It's all right, he said. Come down.

Papa?

Come down. Come down and see.

He stood the lamp on the step and went up and took the boy by the hand. Come on, he said. It's all right.

What did you find?

I found everything. Everything. Wait till you see. He led him down the stairs and picked up the bottle and held the flame aloft. Can you see? he said. Can you see?

What is all this stuff, Papa?

It's food. Can you read it?

Pears. That says pears.

Yes. Yes it does. Oh yes it does.

There was just headroom for him to stand. He ducked under a lantern with a green metal shade hanging from a hook. He held the boy by the hand and they went along the rows of stenciled cartons. Chile, corn, stew, soup, spaghetti sauce. The richness of a vanished world. Why is this here? the boy said. Is it real?

Oh yes. It's real.

He pulled one of the boxes down and clawed it open and held up a can of peaches. It's here because someone thought it might be needed.

But they didnt get to use it.

No. They didnt.

They died.

Yes.

Is it okay for us to take it?

Yes. It is. They would want us to. Just like we would want them to.

They were the good guys?

Yes. They were.

Like us.

Like us. Yes.

So it's okay.

Yes. It's okay.

There were knives and plastic utensils and silverware and kitchen tools in a plastic box. A can opener. There were electric torches that didnt work. He found a box of batteries and drycells and went through them. Mostly corroded and leaking an acid goo but some of them looked okay. He finally got one of the lanterns to work and he set it on the table and blew out the smoky flame of the lamp. He tore a flap from the opened cardboard box and chased out the smoke with it and then he climbed up and lowered the trap door and turned and looked at the boy. What would you like for supper? he said.

Pears.

Good choice. Pears it is.

He took two paperware bowls from a stack of them wrapped in plastic and set them out on the table. He unrolled the mattress pads on the bunks for them to sit on and he opened the carton of pears and took out a can and set it on the table and clamped the lid with the can opener and began to turn the wheel. He looked at the boy. The boy was sitting quietly on the bunk, still wrapped in the blanket, watching. The man thought he had probably not fully committed himself to any of this. You could wake in the dark wet woods at any time. These will be the best pears you ever tasted, he said. The best. Just you wait.

They sat side by side and ate the can of pears. Then they ate a can of peaches. They licked the spoons and tipped the bowls and drank the rich sweet syrup. They looked at each other.

One more.

I dont want you to get sick.

I wont get sick.

You havent eaten in a long time.

I know.

Okay.

He put the boy to bed in the bunk and smoothed his filthy hair on the pillow and covered him with blankets. When he climbed up and lifted the door it was almost dark out. He went to the garage and got the knapsack and came back and took a last look around and then went down the steps and pulled the door shut and jammed one of the handles of the pliers through the heavy inside hasp. The electric lantern was already beginning to dim and he looked through the stores until he found some cases of white gas in gallon cans. He got one of the cans out and set it on the table and unscrewed the cap and punched out the metal seal with a screwdriver. Then he took down the lamp from the hook overhead and filled it. He'd already found a plastic box of butane lighters and he lit the lamp with one of them and adjusted the flame and hung it back up. Then he just sat on the bunk.

While the boy slept he began to go methodically through the stores. Clothes, sweaters, socks. A stainless steel basin and sponges and bars of soap. Toothpaste and toothbrushes. In the bottom of a big plastic jar of bolts and screws and miscellaneous hardware he found a double handful of gold krugerrands in a cloth sack. He dumped them out and kneaded them in his hand and looked at them and then scooped them back into the jar along with the hardware and put the jar back on the shelf.

He sorted through everything, shifting boxes and crates from one side of the room to the other. There was a small steel door that led into a second room where bottles of gas

were stored. In the corner a chemical toilet. There were
vent pipes in the walls covered with wire mesh and there
were drains in the floor. It was getting warm in the bunker
and he'd taken off his coat. He went through everything.
He found a box of .45 ACP cartridges and three boxes of
.30-30 rifle shells. What he didnt find was a gun. He took
the battery lantern and walked over the floor and he
checked the walls for any hidden compartment. After a
while he just sat on the bunk eating a bar of chocolate.
There was no gun and there wasnt going to be one.

When he woke the gaslamp overhead was hissing softly.
The bunker walls were there in the light and the boxes and
crates. He didnt know where he was. He was lying with his
coat over him. He sat up and looked at the boy asleep on the
other bunk. He'd taken off his shoes but he didnt remember
that either and he got them from under the bunk and pulled
them on and climbed the stairs and pulled the pliers from
the hasp and lifted the door and peered out. Early morning. He looked at the house and he looked out toward the
road and he was about to lower the hatch door again when
he stopped. The vague gray light was in the west. They'd
slept the night through and the day that followed. He lowered the door and secured it again and climbed back down
and sat on the bunk. He looked around at the supplies.

He'd been ready to die and now he wasnt going to and he had to think about that. Anyone could see the hatch lying in the yard and they would know at once what it was. He had to think about what to do. This was not hiding in the woods. This was the last thing from that. Finally he rose and went to the table and hooked up the little two burner gas stove and lit it and got out a frying pan and a kettle and opened the plastic box of kitchen implements.

What woke the boy was him grinding coffee in a small hand grinder. He sat up and stared all around. Papa? he said.

Hi. Are you hungry?

I have to go to the bathroom. I have to pee.

He pointed with the spatula toward the low steel door. He didnt know how to use the toilet but they would use it anyway. They werent going to be here that long and he wasnt going to be opening and closing the hatch any more than they had to. The boy went past, his hair matted with sweat. What is that? he said.

Coffee. Ham. Biscuits.

Wow, the boy said.

. . .

He dragged a footlocker across the floor between the bunks and covered it with a towel and set out the plates and cups and plastic utensils. He set out a bowl of biscuits covered with a handtowel and a plate of butter and a can of condensed milk. Salt and pepper. He looked at the boy. The boy looked drugged. He brought the frying pan from the stove and forked a piece of browned ham onto the boy's plate and scooped scrambled eggs from the other pan and ladled out spoonfuls of baked beans and poured coffee into their cups. The boy looked up at him.

Go ahead, he said. Dont let it get cold.

What do I eat first?

Whatever you like.

Is this coffee?

Yes. Here. You put the butter on your biscuits. Like this.

Okay.

Are you all right?

I dont know.

Do you feel okay?

Yes.

What is it?

Do you think we should thank the people?

The people?

The people who gave us all this.

Well. Yes, I guess we could do that.

Will you do it?

Why dont you?

I dont know how.

Yes you do. You know how to say thank you.

The boy sat staring at his plate. He seemed lost. The man was about to speak when he said: Dear people, thank you for all this food and stuff. We know that you saved it for yourself and if you were here we wouldnt eat it no matter how hungry we were and we're sorry that you didnt get to eat it and we hope that you're safe in heaven with God.

He looked up. Is that okay? he said.

Yes. I think that's okay.

He wouldnt stay in the bunker by himself. He followed the man back and forth across the lawn while he carried the plastic jugs of water to the bathroom at the rear of the house. They took the little stove with them and a couple of pans and he heated water and poured it into the tub and poured in water from the plastic jugs. It took a long time but he wanted it to be good and warm. When the tub was almost full the boy got undressed and stepped shivering into the water and sat. Scrawny and filthy and naked. Holding his shoulders. The only light was from the ring of blue teeth in the burner of the stove. What do you think? the man said.

Warm at last.

Warm at last?

Yes.

Where did you get that?

I dont know.

Okay. Warm at last.

He washed his dirty matted hair and bathed him with the soap and sponges. He drained away the filthy water he sat in and laved fresh warm water over him from the pan and wrapped him shivering in a towel and wrapped him again in a blanket. He combed his hair and looked at him. Steam was coming off of him like smoke. Are you okay? he said.

My feet are cold.

You'll have to wait for me.

Hurry.

He bathed and then climbed out and poured detergent into the bathwater and shoved their stinking jeans down into the water with a toilet plunger. Are you ready? he said.

Yes.

He turned down the burner until it sputtered and went out and then he turned on the flashlight and laid it in the floor. They sat on the edge of the tub and pulled their shoes on and then he handed the boy the pan and soap and he took the stove and the little bottle of gas and the pistol and wrapped in their blankets they went back across the yard to the bunker.

They sat on the cot with a checkerboard between them, wearing new sweaters and socks and swaddled in the new blankets. He'd hooked up a small gas heater and they drank Coca Cola out of plastic mugs and after a while he went back to the house and wrung the water out of the jeans and brought them back and hung them to dry.

How long can we stay here Papa?

Not long.

How long is that?

I dont know. Maybe one more day. Two.

Because it's dangerous.

Yes.

Do you think they'll find us?

No. They wont find us.

They might find us.

No they wont. They wont find us.

Later when the boy was asleep he went to the house and dragged some of the furniture out onto the lawn. Then he dragged out a mattress and laid it over the hatch and from inside he pulled it up over the plywood and carefully lowered the door so that the mattress covered it completely. It wasnt much of a ruse but it was better than nothing. While the boy slept he sat on the bunk and by the light of the lantern he whittled fake bullets from a treebranch with his knife, fitting them carefully into the empty bores of the cylinder and then whittling again. He shaped the ends with the knife and sanded them smooth with salt and he stained them with soot until they were the color of lead. When he had all five of them done he fitted them to the bores and snapped the cylinder shut and turned the gun and looked at it. Even this close the gun looked as if it were loaded and he laid it by and got up to feel the legs of the jeans steaming above the heater.

He'd saved the small handful of empty cartridge casings for the pistol but they were gone with everything else. He should have kept them in his pocket. He'd even lost the last one. He thought he might have been able to reload them out of the .45 cartridges. The primers would probably fit if he could get them out without ruining them. Shave the bullets to size with the boxcutter. He got up and made a last tour of the stores. Then he turned down the lamp until the flame puttered out and he kissed the boy and crawled into the other bunk under the clean blankets and gazed one more time at this tiny paradise trembling in the orange light from the heater and then he fell asleep.

The town had been abandoned years ago but they walked the littered streets carefully, the boy holding on to his hand. They passed a metal trashdump where someone had once tried to burn bodies. The charred meat and bones under the damp ash might have been anonymous save for the shapes of the skulls. No longer any smell. There was a market at the end of the street and in one of the aisles piled with empty boxes there were three metal grocery carts. He looked them over and pulled one of them free and squatted and turned the wheels and then stood and pushed it up the aisle and back again.

We could take two of them, the boy said.

No.

I could push one.

You're the scout. I need you to be our lookout.

What are we going to do with all the stuff?

We'll just have to take what we can.

Do you think somebody is coming?

Yes. Sometime.

You said nobody was coming.

I didnt mean ever.

I wish we could live here.

I know.

We could be on the lookout.

We are on the lookout.

What if some good guys came?

Well, I dont think we're likely to meet any good guys on the road.

We're on the road.

I know.

If you're on the lookout all the time does that mean that you're scared all the time?

Well. I suppose you have to be scared enough to be on the lookout in the first place. To be cautious. Watchful.

But the rest of the time you're not scared?

The rest of the time.

Yeah.

I dont know. Maybe you should always be on the lookout. If trouble comes when you least expect it then maybe the thing to do is to always expect it.

Do you always expect it? Papa?

I do. But sometimes I might forget to be on the lookout.

He sat the boy on the footlocker under the gaslamp and with a plastic comb and a pair of scissors he set about cutting his hair. He tried to do a good job and it took some time. When he was done he took the towel from around the boy's shoulders and he scooped the golden hair from the floor and wiped the boy's face and shoulders with a damp cloth and held a mirror for him to see.

You did a good job, Papa.

Good.

I look really skinny.

You are really skinny.

He cut his own hair but it didnt come out so good. He trimmed his beard with the scissors while a pan of water heated and then he shaved himself with a plastic safety razor. The boy watched. When he was done he regarded himself in the mirror. He seemed to have no chin. He turned to the boy. How do I look? The boy cocked his head. I dont know, he said. Will you be cold?

They ate a sumptuous meal by candlelight. Ham and green beans and mashed potatoes with biscuits and gravy. He'd found four quarts of bonded whiskey still in the paper bags in which they'd been purchased and he drank a little of it in a glass with water. It made him dizzy before he'd even finished it and he drank no more. They ate peaches and cream over biscuits for dessert and drank coffee. The paper plates and plastic tableware he dumped in a trash-

bag. Then they played checkers and then he put the boy
to bed.

In the night he was wakened by the muted patter of rain on
the mattress over the door above them. He thought it must
be raining pretty hard for him to hear it. He got up with
the flashlight and climbed the stairs and raised the hatch
and played the light across the yard. The yard was already
flooded and the rain was slashing down. He closed the
hatch. Water had leaked in and dripped down the stairs
but he thought the bunker itself seemed pretty watertight.
He went to see about the boy. He was damp with sweat and
the man pulled back one of the blankets and fanned his face
and then turned down the heater and went back to bed.

When he woke again he thought the rain had stopped. But
that wasnt what woke him. He'd been visited in a dream by
creatures of a kind he'd never seen before. They did not
speak. He thought that they'd been crouching by the side
of his cot as he slept and then had skulked away on his
awakening. He turned and looked at the boy. Maybe he
understood for the first time that to the boy he was himself
an alien. A being from a planet that no longer existed. The

tales of which were suspect. He could not construct for the child's pleasure the world he'd lost without constructing the loss as well and he thought perhaps the child had known this better than he. He tried to remember the dream but he could not. All that was left was the feeling of it. He thought perhaps they'd come to warn him. Of what? That he could not enkindle in the heart of the child what was ashes in his own. Even now some part of him wished they'd never found this refuge. Some part of him always wished it to be over.

He checked the valve on the tank that it was turned off and swung the little stove around on the footlocker and sat and went to work dismantling it. He unscrewed the bottom panel and he removed the burner assembly and disconnected the two burners with a small crescent wrench. He tipped out the plastic jar of hardware and sorted out a bolt to thread into the fitting of the junction and then tightened it down. He connected the hose from the tank and held the little potmetal burner up in his hand, small and lightweight. He set it on the locker and carried the sheetmetal over and put it in the trash and went to the stairs to check the weather. The mattress on top of the hatch had soaked up a good deal of water and the door was hard to lift. He stood with it resting on his shoulders and looked out at the day. A light drizzle falling. Impossible to tell what time of the day he was looking at. He looked at the house and he looked out over the dripping countryside and then let the door back down and descended the steps and set about making breakfast.

They spent the day eating and sleeping. He'd planned to leave but the rain was justification enough to stay. The grocery cart was in the shed. Not likely that anyone would travel the road today. They sorted through the stores and set out what they could take, making of it a measured cube in the corner of the shelter. The day was brief, hardly a day at all. By dark the rain had ceased and they opened the hatch and began to carry boxes and parcels and plastic bags across the wet yard to the shed and to pack the cart. The faintly lit hatchway lay in the dark of the yard like a grave yawning at judgment day in some old apocalyptic painting. When the cart was loaded with all that it could hold he tied a plastic tarp down over it and fastened the grommets to the wire with short bungee cords and they stood back and looked at it with the flashlight. He thought that he should have gotten a couple of extra sets of wheels from the other carts in the store but it was too late now. He should have saved the motorcycle mirror off their old cart too. They ate dinner and slept till morning and then bathed again with sponges and washed their hair in basins of warm water. They ate breakfast and by first light they were on the road, wearing fresh masks cut from sheeting, the boy going ahead with a broom and clearing the way of sticks and branches and the man bent over the handle of the cart watching the road fall away before them.

The cart was too heavy to push into the wet woods and they nooned in the middle of the road and fixed hot tea and ate the last of the canned ham with crackers and with mustard and applesauce. Sitting back to back and watching the road. Do you know where we are Papa? the boy said.

Sort of.

How sort of?

Well. I think we're about two hundred miles from the coast. As the crow flies.

As the crow flies?

Yes. It means going in a straight line.

Are we going to get there soon?

Not real soon. Pretty soon. We're not going as the crow flies.

Because crows dont have to follow roads?

Yes.

They can go wherever they want.

Yes.

Do you think there might be crows somewhere?

I dont know.

But what do you think?

I think it's unlikely.

Could they fly to Mars or someplace?

No. They couldnt.

Because it's too far?

Yes.

Even if they wanted to.

Even if they wanted to.

What if they tried and they just got half way or something and then they were too tired. Would they fall back down?

Well. They really couldnt get half way because they'd be in space and there's not any air in space so they wouldnt be able to fly and besides it would be too cold and they'd freeze to death.

Oh.

Anyway they wouldnt know where Mars was.

Do we know where Mars is?

Sort of.

If we had a spaceship could we go there?

Well. If you had a really good spaceship and you had people to help you I suppose you could go.

Would there be food and stuff when you got there?

No. There's nothing there.

Oh.

They sat for a long time. They sat on their folded blankets and watched the road in both directions. No wind. Nothing. After a while the boy said: There's not any crows. Are there?

No.

Just in books.

Yes. Just in books.

I didnt think so.

Are you ready?

Yes.

They rose and put away their cups and the rest of the crackers. The man piled the blankets on top of the cart and fastened the tarp down and then he stood looking at the boy. What? the boy said.

I know you thought we were going to die.

Yeah.

But we didnt.

No.

Okay.

Can I ask you something?

Sure.

If you were a crow could you fly up high enough to see the sun?

Yes. You could.

I thought so. That would be really neat.

Yes it would. Are you ready?

Yes.

He stopped. What happened to your flute?

I threw it away.

You threw it away?

Yes.

Okay.

Okay.

In the long gray dusk they crossed a river and stopped and looked down from the concrete balustrade at the slow dead water passing underneath. Sketched upon the pall of soot downstream the outline of a burnt city like a black paper scrim. They saw it again just at dark pushing the heavy cart up a long hill and they stopped to rest and he turned the cart sideways in the road against it rolling. Their masks were already gray at the mouth and their eyes darkly cupped. They sat in the ashes by the side of the road and looked out to the east where the shape of the city was darkening into the coming night. They saw no lights.

Do you think there's anyone there, Papa?

I dont know.

How soon can we stop?

We can stop now.

On the hill?

We can get the cart down to those rocks and cover it with limbs.

Is this a good place to stop?

Well, people dont like to stop on hills. And we dont like for people to stop.

So it's a good place for us.

I think so.

Because we're smart.

Well, let's not get too smart.

Okay.

Are you ready?

Yes.

The boy stood up and got his broom and put it over his shoulder. He looked at his father. What are our long term goals? he said.

What?

Our long term goals.

Where did you hear that?

I dont know.

No, where did you?

You said it.

When?

A long time ago.

What was the answer?

I dont know.

Well. I dont either. Come on. It's getting dark.

Late in the day following as they rounded a bend in the road the boy stopped and put his hand on the carriage. Papa, he whispered. The man looked up. A small figure distant on the road, bent and shuffling.

He stood leaning on the handle of the grocery cart. Well, he said. Who's this?

What should we do, Papa?

It could be a decoy.

What are we going to do?

Let's just follow. We'll see if he turns around.

Okay.

The traveler was not one for looking back. They followed him for a while and then they overtook him. An old man, small and bent. He carried on his back an old army rucksack with a blanket roll tied across the top of it and he tapped along with a peeled stick for a cane. When he saw them he veered to the side of the road and turned and stood warily. He had a filthy towel tied under his jaw as if he suffered from toothache and even by their new world standards he smelled terrible.

I dont have anything, he said. You can look if you want. We're not robbers.

He leaned one ear forward. What? he called.

I said we're not robbers.

What are you?

They'd no way to answer the question. He wiped his nose with the back of his wrist and stood waiting. He had no shoes at all and his feet were wrapped in rags and cardboard tied with green twine and any number of layers of vile clothing showed through the tears and holes in it. Of a sudden he seemed to wilt even further. He leaned on his cane and lowered himself into the road where he sat among the ashes with one hand over his head. He looked like a pile of rags fallen off a cart. They came forward and stood looking down at him. Sir? the man said. Sir?

The boy squatted and put a hand on his shoulder. He's scared, Papa. The man is scared.

He looked up the road and down. If this is an ambush he goes first, he said.

He's just scared, Papa.

Tell him we wont hurt him.

The old man shook his head from side to side, his fingers laced in his filthy hair. The boy looked up at his father.

Maybe he thinks we're not real.

What does he think we are?

I dont know.

We cant stay here. We have to go.

He's scared, Papa.

I dont think you should touch him.

Maybe we could give him something to eat.

He stood looking off down the road. Damn, he whispered. He looked down at the old man. Perhaps he'd turn into a god and they to trees. All right, he said.

He untied the tarp and folded it back and rummaged through the canned goods and came up with a tin of fruit cocktail and took the can opener from his pocket and opened the tin and folded back the lid and walked over and squatted and handed it to the boy.

What about a spoon?

He's not getting a spoon.

The boy took the tin and handed it to the old man. Take it, he whispered. Here.

The old man raised his eyes and looked at the boy. The boy gestured at him with the tin. He looked like someone trying to feed a vulture broken in the road. It's okay, he said.

The old man lowered his hand from his head. He blinked. Grayblue eyes half buried in the thin and sooty creases of his skin.

Take it, the boy said.

He reached with his scrawny claws and took it and held it to his chest.

Eat it, the boy said. It's good. He made tipping motions with his hands. The old man looked down at the tin. He took a fresh grip and lifted it, his nose wrinkling. His long and yellowed claws scrabbled at the metal. Then he tipped it and drank. The juice ran down his filthy beard. He lowered the can, chewing with difficulty. He jerked his head when he swallowed. Look, Papa, the boy whispered.

I see, the man said.

The boy turned and looked at him.

I know what the question is, the man said. The answer is no.

What's the question?

Can we keep him. We cant.

I know.

You know.

Yeah.

All right.

Can we give him something else?

Let's see how he does with this.

They watched him eat. When he was done he sat holding the empty tin and looking down into it as if more might appear.

What do you want to give him?

What do you think he should have?

I dont think he should have anything. What do you want to give him?

We could cook something on the stove. He could eat with us.

You're talking about stopping. For the night.

Yeah.

He looked down at the old man and he looked at the road. All right, he said. But then tomorrow we go on.

The boy didnt answer.

That's the best deal you're going to get.

Okay.

Okay means okay. It doesnt mean we negotiate another deal tomorrow.

What's negotiate?

It means talk about it some more and come up with some other deal. There is no other deal. This is it.

Okay.

Okay.

They helped the old man to his feet and handed him his cane. He didnt weigh a hundred pounds. He stood looking about uncertainly. The man took the tin from him and slung it into the woods. The old man tried to hand him the cane but he pushed it away. When did you eat last? he said.

I dont know.

You dont remember.

I ate just now.

Do you want to eat with us?

I dont know.

You dont know?

Eat what?

Maybe some beef stew. With crackers. And coffee.

What do I have to do?

Tell us where the world went.

What?

You dont have to do anything. Can you walk okay?

I can walk.

He looked down at the boy. Are you a little boy? he said.

The boy looked at his father.

What does he look like? his father said.

I dont know. I cant see good.

Can you see me?

I can tell someone's there.

Good. We need to get going. He looked at the boy. Dont hold his hand, he said.

He cant see.

Dont hold his hand. Let's go.

Where are we going? the old man said.

We're going to eat.

He nodded and reached out with his cane and tapped
tentatively at the road.

How old are you?

I'm ninety.

No you're not.

Okay.

Is that what you tell people?

What people?

Any people.

I guess so.

So they wont hurt you?

Yes.

Does that work?

No.

What's in your pack?

Nothing. You can look.

I know I can look. What's in there?

Nothing. Just some stuff.

Nothing to eat.

No.

What's your name?

Ely.

Ely what?

What's wrong with Ely?

Nothing. Let's go.

· · ·

They bivouacked in the woods much nearer to the road than he would have liked. He had to drag the cart while the boy steered from behind and they built a fire for the old man to warm himself though he didnt much like that either. They ate and the old man sat wrapped in his solitary quilt and gripped his spoon like a child. They had only two cups and he drank his coffee from the bowl he'd eaten from, his thumbs hooked over the rim. Sitting like a starved and threadbare buddha, staring into the coals.

You cant go with us, you know, the man said.

He nodded.

How long have you been on the road?

I was always on the road. You cant stay in one place.

How do you live?

I just keep going. I knew this was coming.

You knew it was coming?

Yeah. This or something like it. I always believed in it.

Did you try to get ready for it?

No. What would you do?

I dont know.

People were always getting ready for tomorrow. I didnt believe in that. Tomorrow wasnt getting ready for them. It didnt even know they were there.

I guess not.

Even if you knew what to do you wouldnt know what to do. You wouldnt know if you wanted to do it or not. Suppose you were the last one left? Suppose you did that to yourself?

Do you wish you would die?

No. But I might wish I had died. When you're alive you've always got that ahead of you.

Or you might wish you'd never been born.

Well. Beggars cant be choosers.

You think that would be asking too much.

What's done is done. Anyway, it's foolish to ask for luxuries in times like these.

I guess so.

Nobody wants to be here and nobody wants to leave. He lifted his head and looked across the fire at the boy. Then he looked at the man. The man could see his small eyes watching him in the firelight. God knows what those eyes saw. He got up to pile more wood on the fire and he raked the coals back from the dead leaves. The red sparks rose in a shudder and died in the blackness overhead. The old man drank the last of his coffee and set the bowl before him and leaned toward the heat with his hands out. The man watched him. How would you know if you were the last man on earth? he said.

I dont guess you would know it. You'd just be it.

Nobody would know it.

It wouldnt make any difference. When you die it's the same as if everybody else did too.

I guess God would know it. Is that it?

There is no God.

No?

There is no God and we are his prophets.

I dont understand how you're still alive. How do you eat?

I dont know.

You dont know?

People give you things.

People give you things.

Yes.

To eat.

To eat. Yes.

No they dont.

You did.

No I didnt. The boy did.

There's other people on the road. You're not the only ones.

Are you the only one?

The old man peered warily. What do you mean? he said.

Are there people with you?

What people?

Any people.

There's not any people. What are you talking about?

I'm talking about you. About what line of work you might be in.

The old man didnt answer.

I suppose you want to go with us.

Go with you.

Yes.

You wont take me with you.

You dont want to go.

I wouldnt have even come this far but I was hungry.

The people that gave you food. Where are they?

There's not any people. I just made that up.

What else did you make up?

I'm just on the road the same as you. No different.

Is your name really Ely?

No.

You dont want to say your name.

I dont want to say it.

Why?

I couldnt trust you with it. To do something with it. I dont want anybody talking about me. To say where I was or what I said when I was there. I mean, you could talk about me maybe. But nobody could say that it was me. I could be anybody. I think in times like these the less said the better. If something had happened and we were survivors and we met on the road then we'd have something to talk about. But we're not. So we dont.

Maybe not.

You just dont want to say in front of the boy.

You're not a shill for a pack of roadagents?

I'm not anything. I'll leave if you want me to. I can find the road.

You dont have to leave.

I've not seen a fire in a long time, that's all. I live like an animal. You dont want to know the things I've eaten. When I saw that boy I thought that I had died.

You thought he was an angel?

I didnt know what he was. I never thought to see a child again. I didnt know that would happen.

What if I said that he's a god?

The old man shook his head. I'm past all that now. Have been for years. Where men cant live gods fare no better. You'll see. It's better to be alone. So I hope that's not true what you said because to be on the road with the last god would be a terrible thing so I hope it's not true. Things will be better when everybody's gone.

They will?

Sure they will.

Better for who?

Everybody.

Everybody.

Sure. We'll all be better off. We'll all breathe easier.

That's good to know.

Yes it is. When we're all gone at last then there'll be nobody here but death and his days will be numbered too. He'll be out in the road there with nothing to do and nobody to do it to. He'll say: Where did everybody go? And that's how it will be. What's wrong with that?

In the morning they stood in the road and he and the boy argued about what to give the old man. In the end he didnt get much. Some cans of vegetables and of fruit. Finally the boy just went over to the edge of the road and sat in the ashes. The old man fitted the tins into his knapsack and fastened the straps. You should thank him you know, the man said. I wouldnt have given you anything.

Maybe I should and maybe I shouldnt.

Why wouldnt you?

I wouldnt have given him mine.

You dont care if it hurts his feelings?

Will it hurt his feelings?

No. That's not why he did it.

Why did he do it?

He looked over at the boy and he looked at the old man. You wouldnt understand, he said. I'm not sure I do.

Maybe he believes in God.

I dont know what he believes in.

He'll get over it.

No he wont.

The old man didnt answer. He looked around at the day.

You wont wish us luck either, will you? the man said.

I dont know what that would mean. What luck would look like. Who would know such a thing?

Then all went on. When he looked back the old man had set out with his cane, tapping his way, dwindling slowly on the road behind them like some storybook peddler from an antique time, dark and bent and spider thin and soon to vanish forever. The boy never looked back at all.

In the early afternoon they spread their tarp on the road and sat and ate a cold lunch. The man watched him. Are you talking? he said.

Yes.

But you're not happy.

I'm okay.

When we're out of food you'll have more time to think about it.

The boy didnt answer. They ate. He looked back up the road. After a while he said: I know. But I wont remember it the way you do.

Probably not.

I didnt say you were wrong.

Even if you thought it.

It's okay.

Yeah, the man said. Well. There's not a lot of good news on the road. In times like these.

You shouldnt make fun of him.

Okay.

He's going to die.

I know.

Can we go now?

Yeah, the man said. We can go.

In the night he woke in the cold dark coughing and he coughed till his chest was raw. He leaned to the fire and blew on the coals and he put on more wood and rose and walked away from the camp as far as the light would carry him. He knelt in the dry leaves and ash with the blanket wrapped about his shoulders and after a while the coughing began to subside. He thought about the old man out there somewhere. He looked back at the camp through the black palings of the trees. He hoped the boy had gone back to sleep. He knelt there wheezing softly, his hands on his knees. I am going to die, he said. Tell me how I am to do that.

. . .

The day following they trekked on till almost dark. He could find no safe place to make a fire. When he lifted the tank from the cart he thought that it felt light. He sat and turned the valve but the valve was already on. He turned the little knob on the burner. Nothing. He leaned and listened. He tried both valves again in their combinations. The tank was empty. He squatted there with his hands folded into a fist against his forehead, his eyes closed. After a while he raised his head and just sat there staring out at the cold and darkening woods.

They ate a cold supper of cornbread and beans and franks from a tin. The boy asked him how the tank had gone empty so soon but he said that it just had.

You said it would last for weeks.

I know.

But it's just been a few days.

I was wrong.

They ate in silence. After a while the boy said: I forgot to turn off the valve, didnt I?

It's not your fault. I should have checked.

The boy set his plate down on the tarp. He looked away.

It's not your fault. You have to turn off both valves. The

threads were supposed to be sealed with teflon tape or it would leak and I didnt do it. It's my fault. I didnt tell you.

There wasnt any tape though, was there?

It's not your fault.

They plodded on, thin and filthy as street addicts. Cowled in their blankets against the cold and their breath smoking, shuffling through the black and silky drifts. They were crossing the broad coastal plain where the secular winds drove them in howling clouds of ash to find shelter where they could. Houses or barns or under the bank of a roadside ditch with the blankets pulled over their heads and the noon sky black as the cellars of hell. He held the boy against him, cold to the bone. Dont lose heart, he said. We'll be all right.

The land was gullied and eroded and barren. The bones of dead creatures sprawled in the washes. Middens of anonymous trash. Farmhouses in the fields scoured of their paint and the clapboards spooned and sprung from the wallstuds. All of it shadowless and without feature. The road descended through a jungle of dead kudzu. A marsh where the dead reeds lay over the water. Beyond the edge of the fields the sullen haze hung over earth and sky alike. By late afternoon it had begun to snow and they went on with the tarp over them and the wet snow hissing on the plastic.

He'd slept little in weeks. When he woke in the morning the boy was not there and he sat up with the pistol in his hand and then stood and looked for him but he was not in sight. He pulled on his shoes and walked out to the edge of the trees. Bleak dawn in the east. The alien sun commencing its cold transit. He saw the boy coming at a run across the fields. Papa, he called. There's a train in the woods.

A train?

Yes.

A real train?

Yes. Come on.

You didnt go up to it did you?

No. Just a little. Come on.

There's nobody there?

No. I dont think so. I came to get you.

Is there an engine?

Yes. A big diesel.

They crossed the field and entered the woods on the far side. The tracks came down out of the country on a banked rise and ran through the woods. The locomotive was a diesel electric and there were eight stainless steel passenger coaches behind it. He took hold of the boy's hand. Let's just sit and watch, he said.

They sat on the embankment and waited. Nothing moved. He handed the pistol to the boy. You take it, Papa, the boy said.

No. That's not the deal. Take it.

He took the pistol and sat with it in his lap and the man went down the right of way and stood looking at the train. He crossed the tracks to the other side and walked down the length of the cars. When he came out from behind the last coach he waved for the boy to come and the boy rose and put the pistol in his belt.

Everything was covered in ash. The aisles littered. Suitcases stood open in the seats where they'd been lifted down from the overhead racks and rifled long ago. In the club car he found a stack of paper plates and he blew the dust from them and put them inside his parka and that was all.

How did it get here, Papa?

I dont know. I guess someone was taking it south. A group of people. This is probably where they ran out of fuel.

Has it been here for a long time?

Yes. I think so. A pretty long time.

They went through the last of the cars and then walked up the track to the locomotive and climbed up to the catwalk. Rust and scaling paint. They pushed into the cab and he blew away the ash from the engineer's seat and put the boy at the controls. The controls were very simple. Little to do but push the throttle lever forward. He made train noises and diesel horn noises but he wasnt sure what these might mean to the boy. After a while they just looked out through the silted glass to where the track curved away in the waste of weeds. If they saw different worlds what they knew was the same. That the train would sit there slowly decomposing for all eternity and that no train would ever run again.

Can we go, Papa?

Yes. Of course we can.

They began to come upon from time to time small cairns of rock by the roadside. They were signs in gypsy language, lost patterans. The first he'd seen in some while, common in the north, leading out of the looted and exhausted cities, hopeless messages to loved ones lost and dead. By then all stores of food had given out and murder was everywhere upon the land. The world soon to be largely populated by men who would eat your children in front of your eyes and the cities themselves held by cores of blackened looters who tunneled among the ruins and crawled from the rubble white of tooth and eye carrying charred and anonymous tins of food in nylon nets like shoppers in the commissaries of hell. The soft black talc blew through the streets like squid ink uncoiling along a sea floor and the cold crept down and the dark came early and the scavengers passing down the steep canyons with their torches trod silky holes in the drifted ash that closed behind them silently as eyes. Out on the roads the pilgrims sank down and fell over and died and the bleak and shrouded earth went trundling past the sun and returned again as trackless and as unremarked as the path of any nameless sisterworld in the ancient dark beyond.

Long before they reached the coast their stores were all but gone. The country was stripped and plundered years ago and they found nothing in the houses and buildings by the roadside. He found a telephone directory in a filling station and he wrote the name of the town on their map with a pencil. They sat on the curb in front of the building and ate crackers and looked for the town but they couldnt find it. He sorted through the sections and looked again. Finally he showed the boy. They were some fifty miles west of where he'd thought. He drew stick figures on the map. This is us, he said. The boy traced the route to the sea with his finger. How long will it take us to get there? he said.

Two weeks. Three.

Is it blue?

The sea? I dont know. It used to be.

The boy nodded. He sat looking at the map. The man watched him. He thought he knew what that was about. He'd pored over maps as a child, keeping one finger on the town where he lived. Just as he would look up his family in the phone directory. Themselves among others, everything in its place. Justified in the world. Come on, he said. We should go.

In the late afternoon it began to rain. They left the road and took a dirt drive through a field and spent the night in a shed. The shed had a concrete floor and at the far end stood some empty steel drums. He blocked the doors with the drums and built a fire in the floor and he made beds out of some flattened cardboard boxes. The rain drummed all night on the steel roof overhead. When he woke the fire had burned down and it was very cold. The boy was sitting up wrapped in his blanket.

What is it?

Nothing. I had a bad dream.

What did you dream about?

Nothing.

Are you okay?

No.

He put his arms around him and held him. It's okay, he said.

I was crying. But you didnt wake up.

I'm sorry. I was just so tired.

I meant in the dream.

In the morning when he woke the rain had stopped. He listened to the slack drip of water. He shifted his hips on the hard concrete and looked out through the boards at the gray country. The boy was still sleeping. Water dripped in puddles in the floor. Small bubbles appeared and skated and vanished again. In a town in the piedmont they'd slept in a place like this and listened to the rain. There was an oldfashioned drugstore there with a black marble counter and chrome stools with tattered plastic seats patched with electrical tape. The pharmacy was looted but the store itself was oddly intact. Expensive electronic equipment sat unmolested on the shelves. He stood looking the place over. Sundries. Notions. What are these? He took the boy's hand and led him out but the boy had already seen it. A human head beneath a cakebell at the end of the counter. Dessicated. Wearing a ballcap. Dried eyes turned sadly inward. Did he dream this? He did not. He rose and knelt and blew at the coals and dragged up the burned board ends and got the fire going.

There are other good guys. You said so.

Yes.

So where are they?

They're hiding.

Who are they hiding from?

From each other.

Are there lots of them?

We dont know.

But some.

Some. Yes.

Is that true?

Yes. That's true.

But it might not be true.

I think it's true.

Okay.

You dont believe me.

I believe you.

Okay.

I always believe you.

I dont think so.

Yes I do. I have to.

They hiked back down to the highway through the mud. Smell of earth and wet ash in the rain. Dark water in the roadside ditch. Sucking out of an iron culvert into a pool. In a yard a plastic deer. Late the day following they entered a small town where three men stepped from behind a truck and stood in the road before them. Emaciated, clothed in rags. Holding lengths of pipe. What have you got in the basket? He leveled the pistol at them. They stood. The boy clung to his coat. No one spoke. He set the cart forward again and they moved to the side of the road. He had the boy take the cart and he walked backwards keeping the pistol on them. He tried to look like any common migratory killer but his heart was hammering and he knew he was going to start coughing. They drifted back into the road and stood watching. He put the pistol in his belt and turned and took the cart. At the top of the rise when he looked back they were still standing there. He told the boy to push the cart and he walked out through a yard to where he could see back down the road but now they were gone. The boy was very scared. He laid the gun on top of the tarp and took the cart and they went on.

They lay in a field until dark watching the road but no one came. It was very cold. When it was too dark to see they got the cart and stumbled back to the road and he got the blankets out and they wrapped themselves up and went on. Feeling out the paving under their feet. One wheel on the cart had developed a periodic squeak but there was nothing to be done about it. They struggled on for some hours and then floundered off through the roadside brush and lay shivering and exhausted on the cold ground and slept till day. When he woke he was sick.

He'd come down with a fever and they lay in the woods like fugitives. Nowhere to build a fire. Nowhere safe. The boy sat in the leaves watching him. His eyes brimming. Are you going to die, Papa? he said. Are you going to die?

No. I'm just sick.

I'm really scared.

I know. It's all right. I'm going to get better. You'll see.

. . .

His dreams brightened. The vanished world returned. Kin long dead washed up and cast fey sidewise looks upon him. None spoke. He thought of his life. So long ago. A gray day in a foreign city where he stood in a window and watched the street below. Behind him on a wooden table a small lamp burned. On the table books and papers. It had begun to rain and a cat at the corner turned and crossed the sidewalk and sat beneath the cafe awning. There was a woman at a table there with her head in her hands. Years later he'd stood in the charred ruins of a library where blackened books lay in pools of water. Shelves tipped over. Some rage at the lies arranged in their thousands row on row. He picked up one of the books and thumbed through the heavy bloated pages. He'd not have thought the value of the smallest thing predicated on a world to come. It surprised him. That the space which these things occupied was itself an expectation. He let the book fall and took a last look around and made his way out into the cold gray light.

Three days. Four. He slept poorly. The racking cough woke him. Rasping suck of air. I'm sorry, he said to the pitiless dark. It's okay said the boy.

.   .   .

He got the little oillamp lit and left it sitting on a rock and he rose and shuffled out through the leaves wrapped in his blankets. The boy whispered for him not to go. Just a little ways, he said. Not far. I'll hear you if you call. If the lamp should blow out he could not find his way back. He sat in the leaves at the top of the hill and looked into the blackness. Nothing to see. No wind. In the past when he walked out like that and sat looking over the country lying in just the faintest visible shape where the lost moon tracked the caustic waste he'd sometimes see a light. Dim and shapeless in the murk. Across a river or deep in the blackened quadrants of a burned city. In the morning sometimes he'd return with the binoculars and glass the countryside for any sign of smoke but he never saw any.

Standing at the edge of a winter field among rough men. The boy's age. A little older. Watching while they opened up the rocky hillside ground with pick and mattock and brought to light a great bolus of serpents perhaps a hundred in number. Collected there for a common warmth. The dull tubes of them beginning to move sluggishly in the cold hard light. Like the bowels of some great beast exposed to the day. The men poured gasoline on them and burned them alive, having no remedy for evil but only for the image of it as they conceived it to be. The burning snakes twisted horribly and some crawled burning across the floor of the grotto to illuminate its darker recesses. As they were mute there were no screams of pain and the men watched them burn and writhe and blacken in just such silence themselves and they disbanded in silence in the winter dusk each with his own thoughts to go home to their suppers.

One night the boy woke from a dream and would not tell him what it was.

You dont have to tell me, the man said. It's all right.

I'm scared.

It's all right.

No it's not.

It's just a dream.

I'm really scared.

I know.

The boy turned away. The man held him. Listen to me, he said.

What.

When your dreams are of some world that never was or of some world that never will be and you are happy again then you will have given up. Do you understand? And you cant give up. I wont let you.

. . .

When they set out again he was very weak and for all his speeches he'd become more faint of heart than he had been in years. Filthy with diarrhea, leaning on the bar handle of the shopping cart. He looked at the boy out of his sunken haggard eyes. Some new distance between them. He could feel it. In two day's time they came upon a country where firestorms had passed leaving mile on mile of burn. A cake of ash in the roadway inches deep and hard going with the cart. The blacktop underneath had buckled in the heat and then set back again. He leaned on the handle and looked down the long straight of way. The thin trees down. The waterways a gray sludge. A blackened jackstraw land.

Beyond a crossroads in that wilderness they began to come upon the possessions of travelers abandoned in the road years ago. Boxes and bags. Everything melted and black. Old plastic suitcases curled shapeless in the heat. Here and there the imprint of things wrested out of the tar by scavengers. A mile on and they began to come upon the dead. Figures half mired in the blacktop, clutching themselves, mouths howling. He put his hand on the boy's shoulder. Take my hand, he said. I dont think you should see this.

What you put in your head is there forever?

Yes.

It's okay Papa.

It's okay?

They're already there.

I dont want you to look.

They'll still be there.

He stopped and leaned on the cart. He looked down the road and he looked at the boy. So strangely untroubled.

Why dont we just go on, the boy said.

Yes. Okay.

They were trying to get away werent they Papa?

Yes. They were.

Why didnt they leave the road?

They couldnt. Everything was on fire.

They picked their way among the mummied figures. The black skin stretched upon the bones and their faces split and shrunken on their skulls. Like victims of some ghastly envacuuming. Passing them in silence down that silent corridor through the drifting ash where they struggled forever in the road's cold coagulate.

They passed through the site of a roadside hamlet burned to nothing. Some metal storage tanks, a few standing flues of blackened brick. There were gray slagpools of melted glass in the ditches and the raw lightwires lay in rusting skeins for miles along the edge of the roadway. He was coughing every step of it. He saw the boy watching him. He was what the boy thought about. Well should he.

They sat in the road and ate leftover skilletbread hard as biscuit and their last can of tunafish. He opened a can of prunes and they passed it between them. The boy held the tin up and drained the last of the juice and then sat with the tin in his lap and passed his forefinger around the inside of it and put his finger in his mouth.

Dont cut your finger, the man said.

You always say that.

I know.

He watched him lick the lid of the tin. With great care. Like a cat licking its reflection in a glass. Stop watching me, he said.

Okay.

He folded down the lid of the can and set it in the road before him. What? he said. What is it?

Nothing.

Tell me.

I think there's someone following us.

That's what I thought.

That's what you thought?

Yes. That's what I thought you were going to say. What do you want to do?

I dont know.

What do you think?

Let's just go. We should hide our trash.

Because they'll think we have lots of food.

Yes.

And they'll try to kill us.

They wont kill us.

They might try to.

We're okay.

Okay.

I think we should lay in the weeds for them. See who they are.

And how many.

And how many. Yes.

Okay.

If we can get across the creek we could go up on the bluffs there and watch the road.

Okay.

We'll find a place.

They rose and piled their blankets in the cart. Get the tin, the man said.

.   .   .

It was late into the long twilight before the road crossed the creek. They trundled over the bridge and pushed the cart out through the woods looking for some place to leave it where it would not be seen. They stood looking back at the road in the dusk.

What if we put it under the bridge? the boy said.

What if they go down there for water?

How far back do you think they are?

I dont know.

It's getting dark.

I know.

What if they go by in the dark?

Let's just find a place where we can watch. It's not dark yet.

They hid the cart and went up the slope among the rocks carrying their blankets and they dug themselves in where they could see back down the road through the trees for perhaps half a mile. They were sheltered from the wind and they wrapped themselves in their blankets and took turns watching but after a while the boy was asleep. He was almost asleep himself when he saw a figure appear at the top of the road and stand there. Soon two more appeared. Then a fourth. They stood and grouped. Then they came on. He could just make them out in the deep dusk. He thought they might stop soon and he wished he'd found a place further from the road. If they stopped at the bridge it would be a long cold night. They came down the road and crossed the bridge. Three men and a woman. The woman walked with a waddling gait and as she approached he could see that she was pregnant. The men carried packs on their backs and the woman carried a small cloth suitcase. All of them wretchedlooking beyond description. Their breath steaming softly. They crossed the bridge and continued on down the road and vanished one by one into the waiting darkness.

It was a long night anyway. When it was light enough to see he pulled on his shoes and rose and wrapped one of the blankets around him and walked out and stood looking at the road below. The bare ironcolored wood and the fields beyond. The corrugate shapes of old harrowtroughs still faintly visible. Cotton perhaps. The boy was sleeping and he went down to the cart and got the map and the bottle of water and a can of fruit from their small stores and he came back and sat in the blankets and studied the map.

You always think we've gone further than we have.
He moved his finger. Here then.

More.

Here.

Okay.

He folded up the limp and rotting pages. Okay, he said.

They sat looking out through the trees at the road.

Do you think that your fathers are watching? That they weigh you in their ledgerbook? Against what? There is no book and your fathers are dead in the ground.

The country went from pine to liveoak and pine. Magnolias. Trees as dead as any. He picked up one of the heavy leaves and crushed it in his hand to powder and let the powder sift through his fingers.

On the road early the day following. They'd not gone far when the boy pulled at his sleeve and they stopped and stood. A thin stem of smoke was rising out of the woods ahead. They stood watching.

What should we do, Papa?

Maybe we should take a look.

Let's just keep going.

What if they're going the same way we are?

So? the boy said.

We're going to have them behind us. I'd like to know who it is.

What if it's an army?

It's just a small fire.

Why dont we just wait?

We cant wait. We're almost out of food. We have to keep going.

They left the cart in the woods and he checked the rotation of the rounds in the cylinder. The wooden and the true. They stood listening. The smoke stood vertically in the still air. No sound of any kind. The leaves were soft from the recent rains and quiet underfoot. He turned and looked at the boy. The small dirty face wide with fear. They circled the fire at a distance, the boy holding on to his hand. He crouched and put his arm around him and they listened for a long time. I think they've gone, he whispered.

What?

I think they're gone. They probably had a lookout.

It could be a trap, Papa.

Okay. Let's wait a while.

They waited. They could see the smoke through the trees. A wind had begun to trouble the top of the spire and the smoke shifted and they could smell it. They could smell something cooking. Let's circle around, the man said.

Can I hold your hand?

Yes. Of course you can.

The woods were just burned trunks. There was nothing to see. I think they saw us, the man said. I think they saw us and ran away. They saw we had a gun.

They left their food cooking.

Yes.

Let's take a look.

It's really scary, Papa.

There's no one here. It's okay.

They walked into the little clearing, the boy clutching his hand. They'd taken everything with them except whatever black thing was skewered over the coals. He was standing there checking the perimeter when the boy turned and buried his face against him. He looked quickly to see what had happened. What is it? he said. What is it? The boy shook his head. Oh Papa, he said. He turned and looked again. What the boy had seen was a charred human infant headless and gutted and blackening on the spit. He bent and picked the boy up and started for the road with him, holding him close. I'm sorry, he whispered. I'm sorry.

. . .

He didnt know if he'd ever speak again. They camped at a
river and he sat by the fire listening to the water running in
the dark. It wasnt a safe place because the sound of the
river masked any other but he thought it would cheer the
boy up. They ate the last of their provisions and he sat
studying the map. He measured the road with a piece of
string and looked at it and measured again. Still a long way
to the coast. He didnt know what they'd find when they
got there. He shuffled the sections together and put them
back in the plastic bag and sat staring into the coals.

The following day they crossed the river by a narrow iron
bridge and entered an old mill town. They went through
the wooden houses but they found nothing. A man sat on a
porch in his coveralls dead for years. He looked a straw
man set out to announce some holiday. They went down
the long dark wall of the mill, the windows bricked up.
The fine black soot raced along the street before them.

Odd things scattered by the side of the road. Electrical
appliances, furniture. Tools. Things abandoned long ago

by pilgrims enroute to their several and collective deaths. Even a year ago the boy might sometimes pick up something and carry it with him for a while but he didnt do that any more. They sat and rested and drank the last of their good water and left the plastic jerry jug standing in the road. The boy said: If we had that little baby it could go with us.

Yes. It could.

Where did they find it?

He didnt answer.

Could there be another one somewhere?

I dont know. It's possible.

I'm sorry about what I said about those people.

What people?

Those people that got burned up. That were struck in the road and got burned up.

I didnt know that you said anything bad.

It wasnt bad. Can we go now?

Okay. Do you want to ride in the cart?

It's okay.

Why dont you ride for while?

I dont want to. It's okay.

Slow water in the flat country. The sloughs by the roadside motionless and gray. The coastal plain rivers in leaden serpentine across the wasted farmland. They went on. Ahead in the road was a dip and a stand of cane. I think there's a bridge there, he said. Probably a creek.

Can we drink the water?

We dont have a choice.

It wont make us sick.

I dont think so. It could be dry.

Can I go ahead?

Yes. Of course you can.

The boy set off down the road. He'd not seen him run in a long time. Elbows out, flapping along in his outsized tennis shoes. He stopped and stood watching, biting his lip.

The water was little more than a seep. He could see it moving slightly where it drew down into a concrete tile under the roadway and he spat into the water and watched to see if it would move. He got a cloth from the cart and a plastic jar and came back and wrapped the cloth over the mouth of the jar and sank it in the water and watched it fill. He raised it up dripping and held it to the light. It didnt look too bad. He took the cloth away and handed the jar to the boy. Go ahead, he said.

The boy drank and handed it back.

Drink some more.

You drink some, Papa.

Okay.

They sat filtering the ash from the water and drinking until they could hold no more. The boy lay back in the grass.

We need to go.

I'm really tired.

I know.

He sat watching him. They'd not eaten in two days. In two more they would begin to get weak. He climbed the bank through the cane to check the road. Dark and black and trackless where it crossed the open country. The winds had swept the ash and dust from the surface. Rich lands at one time. No sign of life anywhere. It was no country that he knew. The names of the towns or the rivers. Come on, he said. We have to go.

They slept more and more. More than once they woke sprawled in the road like traffic victims. The sleep of death. He sat up reaching about for the pistol. In the leaden evening he stood leaning with his elbows on the cart handle and looking across the fields at a house perhaps a mile away. It was the boy who had seen it. Shifting in and out of the curtain of soot like a house in some uncertain dream. He leaned on the cart and looked at him. It would cost them some effort to get there. Take their blankets. Hide the cart someplace along the road. They could reach it before dark but they couldnt get back.

We have to take a look. We have no choice.

I dont want to.

We havent eaten in days.

I'm not hungry.

No, you're starving.

I dont want to go there Papa.

There's no one there. I promise.

How do you know?

I just know.

They could be there.

No they're not. It will be okay.

They set out across the fields wrapped in their blankets, carrying only the pistol and a bottle of water. The field had been turned a last time and there were stalks of stubble sticking out of the ground and the faint trace of the disc was still visible from east to west. It had rained recently and the earth was soft underfoot and he kept his eye on the ground and before long he stopped and picked up an arrowhead. He spat on it and wiped away the dirt on the seam of his trousers and gave it to the boy. It was white quartz, perfect as the day it was made. There are more, he said. Watch the ground, you'll see. He found two more.

Gray flint. Then he found a coin. Or a button. Deep crust of verdigris. He chipped at it with the nail of his thumb. It was a coin. He took out his knife and chiseled at it with care. The lettering was in spanish. He started to call to the boy where he trudged ahead and then he looked about at the gray country and the gray sky and he dropped the coin and hurried on to catch up.

They stood in front of the house looking at it. There was a gravel drive that curved away to the south. A brick loggia. Double stairs that swept up to the columned portico. At the rear of the house a brick dependency that may once have been a kitchen. Beyond that a log cabin. He started up the stairs but the boy pulled at his sleeve.

Can we wait a while?

Okay. But it's getting dark.

I know.

Okay.

They sat on the steps and looked out over the country.

There's no one here, the man said.

Okay.

Are you still scared?

Yes.

We're okay.

Okay.

.   .   .

They went up the stairs to the broad brickfloored porch.
The door was painted black and it was propped open with
a cinderblock. Dried leaves and weeds blown behind
it. The boy clutched his hand. Why is the door open,
Papa?

It just is. It's probably been open for years. Maybe the
last people propped it open to carry their things out.

Maybe we should wait till tomorrow.

Come on. We'll take a quick look. Before it gets too
dark. If we secure the area then maybe we can have a fire.

But we wont stay in the house will we?

We dont have to stay in the house.

Okay.

Let's have a drink of water.

Okay.

He took the bottle from the side pocket of his parka and
screwed off the top and watched the boy drink. Then he
took a drink himself and put the lid back on and took the
boy's hand and they entered the darkened hall. High ceiling. An imported chandelier. At the landing on the stairs
was a tall palladian window and the faintest shape of it
headlong on the stairwell wall in the day's last light.

We dont have to go upstairs, do we? the boy whispered.

No. Maybe tomorrow.

After we've secured the area.

Yes.

Okay.

They entered the drawingroom. The shape of a carpet beneath the silty ash. Furniture shrouded in sheeting. Pale squares on the walls where paintings once had hung. In the room on the other side of the foyer stood a grand piano. Their own shapes sectioned in the thin and watery glass of the window there. They entered and stood listening. They wandered through the rooms like skeptical housebuyers. They stood looking out through the tall windows at the darkening land.

In the kitchen there was cutlery and cooking pans and english china. A butler's pantry where the door closed softly behind them. Tile floor and rows of shelves and on the shelves several dozen quart jars. He crossed the room and picked one up and blew the dust from it. Green beans. Slices of red pepper standing among the ordered rows. Tomatoes. Corn. New potatoes. Okra. The boy watched him. The man wiped the dust from the caps of the jars and pushed on the lids with his thumb. It was getting dark fast. He carried a pair of the jars to the window and held them up and turned them. He looked at the boy. These may be poison, he said. We'll have to cook everything really well. Is that okay?

I dont know.

What do you want to do?

You have to say.

We both have to say.

Do you think they're okay?

I think if we cook them really good they'll be all right.

Okay. Why do you think nobody has eaten them?

I think nobody found them. You cant see the house from the road.

We saw it.

You saw it.

The boy studied the jars.

What do you think? the man said.

I think we've got no choice.

I think you're right. Let's get some wood before it gets any darker.

They carried armloads of dead limbs up the back stairs through the kitchen and into the diningroom and broke them to length and stuffed the fireplace full. He lit the fire and smoke curled up over the painted wooden lintel and rose to the ceiling and curled down again. He fanned the blaze with a magazine and soon the flue began to draw and the fire roared in the room lighting up the walls and the ceiling and the glass chandelier in its myraid facets. The flames lit the darkening glass of the window where the boy stood in hooded silhouette like a troll come in from the night. He seemed stunned by the heat. The man pulled the sheets off the long Empire table in the center of the room and shook them out and made a nest of them in front of the hearth. He sat the boy down and pulled off his shoes and pulled off the dirty rags with which his feet were wrapped. Everything's okay, he whispered. Everything's okay.

He found candles in a kitchen drawer and lit two of them and then melted wax onto the counter and stood them in the wax. He went outside and brought in more wood and piled it beside the hearth. The boy had not moved. There were pots and pans in the kitchen and he wiped one out and stood it on the counter and then he tried to open one of the jars but he could not. He carried a jar of green beans and one of potatoes to the front door and by the light of a candle standing in a glass he knelt and placed the first jar sideways in the space between the door and the jamb and pulled the door against it. Then he squatted in the foyer floor and hooked his foot over the outside edge of the door and pulled it against the lid and twisted the jar in his hands. The knurled lid turned in the wood grinding the paint. He took a fresh grip on the glass and pulled the door tighter and tried again. The lid slipped in the wood, then it held. He turned the jar slowly in his hands, then took it from the jamb and turned off the ring of the lid and set it in the floor. Then he opened the second jar and rose and carried them back into the kitchen, holding the glass in his other hand with the candle rolling about and sputtering. He tried to push the lids up off the jars with his thumbs but they were on too tight. He thought that was a good sign. He set the edge of the lid on the counter and punched the top of the jar with his fist and the lid snapped off and fell in the floor and he raised the jar and sniffed at it. It smelled delicious. He poured the potatoes and the beans into a pot and carried the pot into the diningroom and set it in the fire.

They ate slowly out of bone china bowls, sitting at opposite sides of the table with a single candle burning between them. The pistol lying to hand like another dining implement. The warming house creaked and groaned. Like a thing being called out of long hibernation. The boy nodded over his bowl and his spoon clattered to the floor. The man rose and came around and carried him to the hearth and put him down in the sheets and covered him with the blankets. He must have gone back to the table because he woke in the night lying there with his face in his crossed arms. It was cold in the room and outside the wind was blowing. The windows rattled softly in their frames. The candle had burned out and the fire was down to coals. He rose and built back the fire and sat beside the boy and pulled the blankets over him and brushed back his filthy hair. I think maybe they are watching, he said. They are watching for a thing that even death cannot undo and if they do not see it they will turn away from us and they will not come back.

The boy didnt want him to go upstairs. He tried to reason with him. There could be blankets up there, he said. We need to take a look.

I dont want you to go up there.

There's no one here.

There could be.

There's no one here. Dont you think they'd have come down by now?

Maybe they're scared.

I'll tell them we wont hurt them.

Maybe they're dead.

Then they wont mind if we take a few things. Look, whatever is up there it's better to know about it than to not know.

Why?

Why. Well, because we dont like surprises. Surprises are scary. And we dont like to be scared. And there could be things up there that we need. We have to take a look.

Okay.

Okay? Just like that?

Well. You're not going to listen to me.

I have been listening to you.

Not very hard.

There's no one here. There has been no one here for years. There are no tracks in the ash. Nothing disturbed. No furniture burned in the fireplace. There's food here.

Tracks dont stay in the ash. You said so yourself. The wind blows them away.

I'm going up.

They stayed at the house for four days eating and sleeping. He'd found more blankets upstairs and they dragged in great piles of wood and stacked the wood in the corner of the room to dry. He found an antique bucksaw of wood and wire that he used to saw the dead trees to length. The teeth were rusty and dull and he sat in front of the fire with a rattail file and tried to sharpen them but to little purpose. There was a creek some hundred yards from the house and he hauled endless pails of water across the stubble fields and the mud and they heated water and bathed in a tub off the back bedroom on the lower floor and he cut their hair and shaved his beard. They had clothes and blankets and pillows from the upstairs rooms and they fitted themselves out in new attire, the boy's trousers cut to length with his knife. He made a nesting place in front of the hearth, turning over a tallboy chest to use as a headboard for their bed and to hold the heat. All the while it continued to rain. He set pails under the downspouts at the housecorners to catch fresh water off the old standing-seam metal roof and at night he could hear the rain drumming in the upper rooms and dripping through the house.

They rummaged through the outbuildings for anything of use. He found a wheelbarrow and pulled it out and tipped it over and turned the wheel slowly, examining the tire. The rubber was glazed and cracked but he thought it might hold air and he looked through old boxes and jumbles of tools and found a bicycle pump and screwed the end of the hose to the valvestem of the tire and began to pump. The air leaked out around the rim but he turned the wheel and had the boy hold down the tire until it caught and he got it pumped up. He unscrewed the hose and turned the wheelbarrow over and trundled it across the floor and back. Then he pushed it outside for the rain to clean. When they left two days later the weather had cleared and they set out down the muddy road pushing the wheelbarrow with their new blankets and the jars of canned goods wrapped in their extra clothes. He'd found a pair of workshoes and the boy was wearing blue tennis shoes with rags stuffed into the toes and they had fresh sheeting for face masks. When they got to the blacktop they had to turn back along the road to fetch the cart but it was less than a mile. The boy walked alongside with one hand on the wheelbarrow. We did good, didnt we Papa? he said. Yes we did.

They ate well but they were still a long way from the coast. He knew that he was placing hopes where he'd no reason to. He hoped it would be brighter where for all he knew the world grew darker daily. He'd once found a lightmeter in a camera store that he thought he might use to average out readings for a few months and he carried it around with him for a long time thinking he might find some batteries for it but he never did. At night when he woke coughing he'd sit up with his hand pushed over his head against the blackness. Like a man waking in a grave. Like those disinterred dead from his childhood that had been relocated to accommodate a highway. Many had died in a cholera epidemic and they'd been buried in haste in wooden boxes and the boxes were rotting and falling open. The dead came to light lying on their sides with their legs drawn up and some lay on their stomachs. The dull green antique coppers spilled from out the tills of their eyesockets onto the stained and rotted coffin floors.

They stood in a grocery store in a small town where a mounted deerhead hung from the wall. The boy stood looking at it a long time. There was broken glass in the floor and the man made him wait at the door while he kicked through the trash in his workshoes but he found nothing. There were two gas pumps outside and they sat on the concrete apron and lowered a small tin can on a string into the underground tank and hauled it up and poured the cupful of gasoline it held into a plastic jug and lowered it again. They'd tied a small length of pipe to the can to sink it and they crouched over the tank like apes fishing with sticks in an anthill for the better part of an hour until the jug was full. Then they screwed on the cap and set the jug in the bottom rack of the cart and went on.

Long days. Open country with the ash blowing over the road. The boy sat by the fire at night with the pieces of the map across his knees. He had the names of towns and rivers by heart and he measured their progress daily.

They ate more sparingly. They'd almost nothing left. The boy stood in the road holding the map. They listened but they could hear nothing. Still he could see open country to the east and the air was different. Then they came upon it from a turn in the road and they stopped and stood with the salt wind blowing in their hair where they'd lowered the hoods of their coats to listen. Out there was the gray beach with the slow combers rolling dull and leaden and the distant sound of it. Like the desolation of some alien sea breaking on the shores of a world unheard of. Out on the tidal flats lay a tanker half careened. Beyond that the ocean vast and cold and shifting heavily like a slowly heaving vat of slag and then the gray squall line of ash. He looked at the boy. He could see the disappointment in his face. I'm sorry it's not blue, he said. That's okay, said the boy.

An hour later they were sitting on the beach and staring out at the wall of smog across the horizon. They sat with their heels dug into the sand and watched the bleak sea wash up at their feet. Cold. Desolate. Birdless. He'd left the cart in the bracken beyond the dunes and they'd taken blankets with them and sat wrapped in them in the windshade of a great driftwood log. They sat there for a long time. Along the shore of the cove below them windrows of small bones in the wrack. Further down the saltbleached ribcages of what may have been cattle. Gray salt rime on the rocks. The wind blew and dry seedpods scampered down the sands and stopped and then went on again.

Do you think there could be ships out there?

I dont think so.

They wouldnt be able to see very far.

No. They wouldnt.

What's on the other side?

Nothing.

There must be something.

Maybe there's a father and his little boy and they're sitting on the beach.

That would be okay.

Yes. That would be okay.

And they could be carrying the fire too?

They could be. Yes.

But we dont know.

We dont know.

So we have to be vigilant.

We have to be vigilant. Yes.

How long can we stay here?

I dont know. We dont have much to eat.

I know.

You like it.

Yeah.

Me too.

Can I go swimming?

Swimming?

Yes.

You'll freeze your tokus off.

I know.

It will be really cold. Worse than you think.

That's okay.

I dont want to have to come in after you.

You dont think I should go.

You can go.

But you dont think I should.

No. I think you should.

Really?

Yes. Really.

Okay.

He rose and let the blanket fall to the sand and then stripped out of his coat and out of his shoes and clothes.

He stood naked, clutching himself and dancing. Then he went running down the beach. So white. Knobby spine-bones. The razorous shoulder blades sawing under the pale skin. Running naked and leaping and screaming into the slow roll of the surf.

By the time he came out he was blue with cold and his teeth were chattering. He walked down to meet him and wrapped him shuddering in the blanket and held him until he stopped gasping. But when he looked the boy was crying. What is it? he said. Nothing. No, tell me. Nothing. It's nothing.

With dark they built a fire against the log and ate plates of okra and beans and the last of the canned potatoes. The fruit was long gone. They drank tea and sat by the fire and they slept in the sand and listened to the roll of the surf in the bay. The long shudder and fall of it. He got up in the night and walked out and stood on the beach wrapped in his blankets. Too black to see. Taste of salt on his lips. Waiting. Waiting. Then the slow boom falling downshore. The seething hiss of it washing over the beach and drawing away again. He thought there could be deathships out there yet, drifting with their lolling rags of sail. Or life in the deep. Great squid propelling themselves over the floor of the sea in the cold darkness. Shuttling past like trains, eyes the size of saucers. And perhaps beyond those shrouded swells another man did walk with another child on the dead gray sands. Slept but a sea apart on another beach among the bitter ashes of the world or stood in their rags lost to the same indifferent sun.

He remembered waking once on such a night to the clatter of crabs in the pan where he'd left steakbones from the night before. Faint deep coals of the driftwood fire pulsing in the onshore wind. Lying under such a myriad of stars. The sea's black horizon. He rose and walked out and stood barefoot in the sand and watched the pale surf appear all down the shore and roll and crash and darken again. When he went back to the fire he knelt and smoothed her hair as she slept and he said if he were God he would have made the world just so and no different.

When he got back the boy was awake and he was scared. He'd been calling out but not loud enough that he could hear him. The man put his arms around him. I couldnt hear you, he said. I couldnt hear you for the surf. He put wood on the fire and fanned it to life and they lay in their blankets watching the flames twist in the wind and then they slept.

In the morning he rekindled the fire and they ate and watched the shore. The cold and rainy look of it not so different from seascapes in the northern world. No gulls or shorebirds. Charred and senseless artifacts strewn down the shoreline or rolling in the surf. They gathered driftwood and stacked it and covered it with the tarp and then set off down the beach. We're beachcombers, he said.

What is that?

It's people who walk along the beach looking for things of value that might have washed up.

What kind of things?

Any kind of things. Anything that you might be able to use.

Do you think we'll find anything?

I dont know. We'll take a look.

Take a look, the boy said.

They stood on the rock jetty and looked out to the south. A gray salt spittle lagging and curling in the rock pool.

Long curve of beach beyond. Gray as lava sand. The wind coming off the water smelled faintly of iodine. That was all. There was no sea smell to it. On the rocks the remnants of some dark seamoss. They crossed and went on. At the end of the strand their way was blocked by a headland and they left the beach and took an old path up through the dunes and through the dead seaoats until they came out upon a low promontory. Below them a hook of land shrouded in the dark scud blowing down the shore and beyond that lying half over and awash the shape of a sailboat's hull. They crouched in the dry tufts of grass and watched. What should we do? the boy said.

Let's just watch for a while.

I'm cold.

I know. Let's move down a little ways. Out of the wind.

He sat holding the boy in front of him. The dead grass thrashed softly. Out there a gray desolation. The endless seacrawl. How long do we have to sit here? the boy said.

Not long.

Do you think there are people on the boat, Papa?

I dont think so.

They'd be all tilted over.

Yes they would. Can you see any tracks out there?

No.

Let's just wait a while.

I'm cold.

· · ·

They trekked out along the crescent sweep of beach, keeping to the firmer sand below the tidewrack. They stood, their clothes flapping softly. Glass floats covered with a gray crust. The bones of seabirds. At the tide line a woven mat of weeds and the ribs of fishes in their millions stretching along the shore as far as eye could see like an isocline of death. One vast salt sepulchre. Senseless. Senseless.

From the end of the spit to the boat there was perhaps a hundred feet of open water. They stood looking at the boat. Some sixty feet long, stripped to the deck, keeled over in ten or twelve feet of water. It had been a twin-masted rig of some sort but the masts were broken off close to the deck and the only thing remaining topside were some brass cleats and a few of the rail stanchions along the edge of the deck. That and the steel hoop of the wheel sticking up out of the cockpit aft. He turned and studied the beach and the dunes beyond. Then he handed the boy the pistol and sat in the sand and began to unlace the cords of his shoes.

What are you going to do, Papa?

Take a look.

Can I go with you?

No. I want you to stay here.

I want to go with you.

You have to stand guard. And besides the water's deep.

Will I be able to see you?

Yes. I'll keep checking on you. To make sure everything's okay.

I want to go with you.

He stopped. You cant, he said. Our clothes would blow away. Somebody has to take care of things.

He folded everything into a pile. God it was cold. He bent and kissed the boy on his forehead. Stop worrying, he said. Just keep a lookout. He waded naked into the water and stood and laved himself wet. Then he trudged out splashing and dove headlong.

He swam the length of the steel hull and turned, treading water, gasping with the cold. Amidships the sheer-rail was just awash. He pulled himself along to the transom. The steel was gray and saltscoured but he could make out the worn gilt lettering. Pájaro de Esperanza. Tenerife. An empty pair of lifeboat davits. He got hold of the rail and pulled himself aboard and turned and crouched on the slant of the wood deck shivering. A few lengths of braided cable snapped off at the turnbuckles. Shredded holes in the wood where hardware had been ripped out. Some terrible force to sweep the decks of everything. He waved at the boy but he didnt wave back.

The cabin was low with a vaulted roof and portholes along the side. He crouched and wiped away the gray salt and looked in but he could see nothing. He tried the low teak door but it was locked. He gave it a shove with his bony shoulder. He looked around for something to pry with. He was shivering uncontrollably and his teeth were chattering. He thought about kicking the door with the flat of his foot but then he thought that was not a good idea. He held his elbow in his hand and banged into the door again. He felt it give. Very slightly. He kept at it. The jamb was splitting on the inside and it finally gave way and he pushed it open and stepped down the companionway into the cabin.

A stagnant bilge along the lower bulkhead filled with wet papers and trash. A sour smell over everything. Damp and clammy. He thought the boat had been ransacked but it was the sea that had done it. There was a mahogany table in the middle of the saloon with hinged fiddles. The locker doors hanging open into the room and all the brasswork a dull green. He went through to the forward cabins. Past the galley. Flour and coffee in the floor and canned goods half crushed and rusting. A head with a stainless steel toilet and sink. The weak sea light fell through the clerestory portholes. Gear scattered everywhere. A mae west floating in the seepage.

He was half expecting some horror but there was none. The mattress pads in the cabins had been slung into the floor and bedding and clothing were piled against the wall. Everything wet. A door stood open to the locker in the bow but it was too dark to see inside. He ducked his head and stepped in and felt about. Deep bins with hinged wooden covers. Sea gear piled in the floor. He began to drag everything out and pile it on the tilted bed. Blankets, foulweather gear. He came up with a damp sweater and pulled it over his head. He found a pair of yellow rubber seaboots and he found a nylon jacket and he zipped himself into that and pulled on the stiff yellow breeches from the souwester gear and thumbed the suspenders up over his shoulders and pulled on the boots. Then he went back up on the deck. The boy was sitting as he'd left him, watching the ship. He stood up in alarm and the man realized that in his new clothes he made an uncertain figure. It's me, he called, but the boy only stood there and he waved to him and went below again.

· · ·

In the second stateroom there were drawers under the berth that were still in place and he lifted them free and slid them out. Manuals and papers in spanish. Bars of soap. A black leather valise covered in mold with papers inside. He put the soap in the pocket of his coat and stood. There were books in spanish strewn across the berth, swollen and shapeless. A single volume wedged in the rack against the forward bulkhead.

He found a rubberized canvas seabag and he prowled the rest of the ship in his boots, pushing himself off the bulkheads against the tilt, the yellow slicker pants rattling in the cold. He filled the bag with odds and ends of clothing. A pair of women's sneakers he thought would fit the boy. A foldingknife with a wooden handle. A pair of sunglasses. Still there was something perverse in his searching. Like exhausting the least likely places first when looking for something lost. Finally he went into the galley. He turned on the stove and turned it off again.

He unlatched and raised the hatch to the engine compartment. Half flooded and pitch dark. No smell of gas or oil.

He closed it again. There were lockers built into the benches in the cockpit that held cushions, sailcanvas, fishing gear. In a locker behind the wheel pedestal he found coils of nylon rope and steel bottles of gas and a toolbox made of fiberglass. He sat in the floor of the cockpit and sorted through the tools. Rusty but serviceable. Pliers, screwdrivers, wrenches. He latched the toolbox shut and stood and looked for the boy. He was huddled in the sand asleep with his head on the pile of clothes.

He carried the toolbox and one of the bottles of gas into the galley and went forward and made a last tour of the staterooms. Then he set about going through the lockers in the saloon, looking through folders and papers in plastic boxes, trying to find the ship's log. He found a set of china packed away unused in a wooden crate filled with excelsior. Most of it broken. Service for eight, carrying the name of the ship. A gift, he thought. He lifted out a teacup and turned it in his palm and put it back. The last thing he found was a square oak box with dovetailed corners and a brass plate let into the lid. He thought it might be a humidor but it was the wrong shape and when he picked it up and felt the weight of it he knew what it was. He unsnapped the corroding latches and opened it. Inside was a brass sextant, possibly a hundred years old. He lifted it from the fitted case and held it in his hand. Struck by the beauty of it. The brass was dull and there were patches of green on it that took the form of another hand that once had held it but otherwise it was perfect. He wiped the verdigris from the plate at the base. Hezzaninth, London. He held it to his eye and turned the wheel. It was the first thing he'd seen in a long time that stirred him. He held it in his hand and then he fitted it back into the blue baize lining of the case and closed the lid and snapped the latches shut and set it back in the locker and closed the door.

When he went back up on deck again to look for the boy the boy was not there. A moment of panic before he saw him walking along the bench downshore with the pistol hanging in his hand, his head down. Standing there he felt the hull of the ship lift and slide. Just slightly. Tide coming in. Slapping along the rocks of the jetty down there. He turned and went back down into the cabin.

He'd brought the two coils of rope from the locker and he measured the diameter of them with the span of his hand and that by three and then counted the number of coils. Fifty foot ropes. He hung them over a cleat on the gray teakwood deck and went back down into the cabin. He collected everything and stacked it against the table. There were some plastic jugs of water in the locker off the galley but all were empty save one. He picked up one of the empties and saw that the plastic had cracked and the water leaked out and he guessed they had frozen somewhere on the ship's aimless voyagings. Probably several times. He took the half full jug and set it on the table and unscrewed the cap and sniffed the water and then raised the jug in both hands and drank. Then he drank again.

The cans in the galley floor did not look in any way salvable and even in the locker there were some that were badly rusted and some that wore an ominous bulbed look. They'd all been stripped of their labels and the contents written on the metal in black marker pen in spanish. Not all of which he knew. He sorted through them, shaking them, squeezing them in his hand. He stacked them on the counter above the small galley refrigerator. He thought there must be crates of foodstuffs packed somewhere in the hold but he didnt think any of it would be edible. In any case there was a limit to what they could take in the cart. It occurred to him that he took this windfall in a fashion dangerously close to matter of fact but still he said what he had said before. That good luck might be no such thing. There were few nights lying in the dark that he did not envy the dead.

He found a can of olive oil and some cans of milk. Tea in a rusted metal caddy. A plastic container of some sort of meal that he did not recognize. A half empty can of coffee. He went methodically through the shelves in the locker, sorting what to take from what to leave. When he had carried everything into the saloon and stacked it against the companionway he went back into the galley and opened the toolbox and set about removing one of the burners from the little gimballed stove. He disconnected the braided flexline and removed the aluminum spiders from the burners and put one of them in the pocket of his coat. He unfastened the brass fittings with a wrench and took the burners loose. Then he uncoupled them and fastened the hose to the coupling pipe and fitted the other end of the hose to the gasbottle and carried it out to the saloon. Lastly he made a bindle in a plastic tarp of some cans of juice and cans of fruit and of vegetables and tied it with a cord and then he stripped out of his clothes and piled them among the goods he'd collected and went up onto the deck naked and slid down to the railing with the tarp and

swung over the side and dropped into the gray and freezing sea.

He waded ashore in the last of the light and swung the tarp
down and palmed the water off his arms and chest and
went to get his clothes. The boy followed him. He kept
asking him about his shoulder, blue and discolored from
where he'd slammed it against the hatch door. It's all right,
the man said. It doesnt hurt. We got lots of stuff. Wait till
you see.

They hurried down the beach against the light. What if the
boat washes away? the boy said.

It wont wash away.

It could.

No it wont. Come on. Are you hungry?

Yes.

We're going to eat well tonight. But we need to get a
move on.

I'm hurrying, Papa.

And it may rain.

How can you tell?

I can smell it.

What does it smell like?

Wet ashes. Come on.

Then he stopped. Where's the pistol? he said.

The boy froze. He looked terrified.

Christ, the man said. He looked back up the beach. They were already out of sight of the boat. He looked at the boy. The boy had put his hands on top of this head and he was about to cry. I'm sorry, he said. I'm really sorry.

He set down the tarp with the canned goods. We have to go back.

I'm sorry, Papa.

It's okay. It will still be there.

The boy stood with his shoulders slumped. He was beginning to sob. The man knelt and put his arms around him. It's all right, he said. I'm the one who's supposed to make sure we have the pistol and I didnt do it. I forgot.

I'm sorry, Papa.

Come on. We're okay. Everything's okay.

The pistol was where he'd left it in the sand. The man picked it up and shook it and he sat and pulled the cylinder pin and handed it to the boy. Hold this, he said.

Is it okay, Papa?

Of course it's okay.

He rolled the cylinder out into his hand and blew

the sand from it and handed it to the boy and he blew through the barrel and he blew the sand out of the frame and then took the parts from the boy and refitted everything and cocked the pistol and lowered the hammer and cocked it again. He aligned the cylinder for the true cartridge to come up and he let the hammer down and put the pistol in his parka and stood up. We're okay, he said. Come on.

Is the dark going to catch us?

I dont know.

It is, isnt it?

Come on. We'll hurry.

The dark did catch them. By the time they reached the headland path it was too dark to see anything. They stood in the wind from off the sea with the grass hissing all about them, the boy holding on to his hand. We just have to keep going, the man said. Come on.

I cant see.

I know. We'll just take it one step at a time.

Okay.

Dont let go.

Okay.

No matter what.

No matter what.

. . .

They went on in the perfect blackness, sightless as the blind. He held out one hand before him although there was nothing on that salt heath to collide with. The surf sounded more distant but he took his bearings by the wind as well and after tottering on for the better part of an hour they emerged from the grass and seaoats and stood again on the dry sand of the upper beach. The wind was colder. He'd brought the boy around on the lee side of him when suddenly the beach before them appeared shuddering out of the blackness and vanished again.

What was that, Papa?

It's okay. It's lightning. Come on.

He slung the tarp of goods up over his shoulder and took the boy's hand and they went on, tramping in the sand like parade horses against tripping over some piece of driftwood or seawrack. The weird gray light broke over the beach again. Far away a faint rumble of thunder muffled in the murk. I think I saw our tracks, he said.

So we're going the right way.

Yes. The right way.

I'm really cold, Papa.

I know. Pray for lightning.

. . .

They went on. When the light broke over the beach again he saw that the boy was bent over and was whispering to himself. He looked for their tracks going up the beach but he could not see them. The wind had picked up even more and he was waiting for the first spits of rain. If they got caught out on the beach in a rainstorm in the night they would be in trouble. They turned their faces away from the wind, holding on to the hoods of their parkas. The sand rattling against their legs and racing away in the dark and the thunder cracking just offshore. The rain came in off the sea hard and slant and stung their faces and he pulled the boy against him.

They stood in the downpour. How far had they come? He waited for the lightning but it was tailing off and when the next one came and then the next he knew that the storm had taken out their tracks. They trudged on through the sand at the upper edge of the beach, hoping to see the shape of the log where they'd camped. Soon the lightning was all but gone. Then in a shift in the wind he heard a distant faint patter. He stopped. Listen, he said.

What is it?

Listen.

I dont hear anything.

Come on.

What is it, Papa?

It's the tarp. It's the rain falling on the tarp.

They went on, stumbling through the sand and the trash along the tideline. They came upon the tarp almost at once and he knelt and dropped the bindle and groped about for the rocks he'd weighed the plastic with and pushed them beneath it. He raised up the tarp and pulled it over them and then used the rocks to hold down the edges inside. He got the boy out of his wet coat and pulled the blankets over them, the rain pelting them through the plastic. He shucked off his own coat and held the boy close and soon they were asleep.

In the night the rain ceased and he woke and lay listening. The heavy wash and thud of the surf after the wind had died. In the first dull light he rose and walked down the beach. The storm had littered the shore and he walked the tideline looking for anything of use. In the shallows beyond the breakwater an ancient corpse rising and falling among the driftwood. He wished he could hide it from the boy but the boy was right. What was there to hide? When he got back he was awake sitting in the sand watching him. He was wrapped in the blankets and he'd spread their wet coats over the dead weeds to dry. He walked up and eased himself down beside him and they sat watching the leaden sea lift and fall beyond the breakers.

They were most of the morning offloading the ship. He kept a fire going and he'd wade ashore naked and shivering and drop the towrope and stand in the warmth of the blaze while the boy towed in the seabag through the slack swells and dragged it onto the beach. They emptied out the bag and spread blankets and clothing out on the warm sand to dry before the fire. There was more on the boat than they could carry and he thought they might stay a few days on the beach and eat as much as they could but it was danger-ous. They slept that night in the sand with the fire stand-ing off the cold and their goods scattered all about them. He woke coughing and rose and took a drink of water and dragged more wood onto the fire, whole logs of it that sent up a great cascade of sparks. The salt wood burned orange and blue in the fire's heart and he sat watching it a long time. Later he walked up the beach, his long shadow reach-ing over the sands before him, sawing about with the wind in the fire. Coughing. Coughing. He bent over, holding his knees. Taste of blood. The slow surf crawled and seethed in the dark and he thought about his life but there was no life to think about and after a while he walked back. He got a can of peaches from the bag and opened it and sat before the fire and ate the peaches slowly with his spoon while the boy slept. The fire flared in the wind and sparks raced away down the sand. He set the empty tin between his feet. Every day is a lie, he said. But you are dying. That is not a lie.

They carried their new stores bundled in tarps or blankets down the beach and packed everything into the cart. The boy tried to carry too much and when they stopped to rest he'd take part of his load and put it with his own. The boat had shifted slightly in the storm. He stood looking at it. The boy watched him. Are you going back out there? he said.

I think so. One last look around.

I'm kind of scared.

We're okay. Just keep watch.

We've got more than we can carry now.

I know. I just want to take a look.

Okay.

He went over the ship from bow to stern again. Stop. Think. He sat in the floor of the saloon with his feet in the rubber boots propped against the pedestal of the table. It was already getting dark. He tried to remember what he knew about boats. He got up and went out on deck again. The boy was sitting by the fire. He stepped down into the cockpit and sat on the bench with his back against the bulkhead, his feet on the deck almost at eye level. He had on nothing but the sweater and the souwester outfit over that but there was little warmth to it and he could not stop shivering. He was about to get up again when he realized that he'd been looking at the fasteners in the bulkhead on the far side of the cockpit. There were four of them. Stainless steel. At one time the benches had been covered with cushions and he could see the ties at the corner where they'd ripped away. At the bottom center of the bulkhead just above the seat there was a nylon strap sticking out, the end of it doubled and cross-stitched. He looked at the fasteners again. They were rotary latches with wings for your thumb. He got up and knelt at the bench and turned each one all the way to the left. They were springloaded and when he had them undone he took hold of the strap at the bottom of the board and pulled it and the board slid down and came free. Inside under the deck was a space that held some rolled sails and what looked to be a two man rubber raft rolled and tied with bungee cords. A pair of small plastic oars. A box of flares. And behind that was a composite toolbox, the opening of the lid sealed with black electrical tape. He pulled it free and found the end of the tape and peeled it off all the way around and unlatched the chrome snaps and opened the box. Inside was a yellow plastic flashlight, an electric strobebeacon powered by a drycell, a first-aid kit. A yellow plastic EPIRB. And a black plastic case about the size of a book. He lifted it out and unsnapped the latches and opened it. Inside was fitted an old 37 millimeter bronze flarepistol. He lifted it from the case in both hands and turned it and looked at it. He depressed the lever and broke it open. The chamber was empty but there were eight rounds of flares fitted in a plastic container, short and squat and newlooking. He fitted the pistol back in the case and closed and latched the lid.

He waded ashore shivering and coughing and wrapped himself in a blanket and sat in the warm sand in front of the fire with the boxes beside him. The boy crouched and tried to put his arms around him which at least brought a smile. What did you find, Papa? he said.

I found a first-aid kit. And I found a flarepistol.

What's that?

I'll show you. It's to signal with.

Is that what you went to look for?

Yes.

How did you know it was there?

Well, I was hoping it was there. It was mostly luck.

He opened the case and turned it for the boy to see.

It's a gun.

A flaregun. It shoots a thing up in the air and it makes a big light.

Can I look at it?

Sure you can.

The boy lifted the gun from the case and held it. Can you shoot somebody with it? he said.

You could.

Would it kill them?

No. But it might set them on fire.

Is that why you got it?

Yes.

Because there's nobody to signal to. Is there?

No.

I'd like to see it.

You mean shoot it?

Yes.

We can shoot it.

For real?

Sure.

In the dark?

Yes. In the dark.

It could be like a celebration.

Like a celebration. Yes.

Can we shoot it tonight?

Why not?

Is it loaded?

No. But we can load it.

The boy stood holding the gun. He pointed it toward the sea. Wow, he said.

He got dressed and they set out down the beach carrying the last of their plunder. Where do you think the people went, Papa?

That were on the ship?

Yes.

I dont know.

Do you think they died?

I dont know.

But the odds are not in their favor.

The man smiled. The odds are not in their favor?

No. Are they?

No. Probably not.

I think they died.

Maybe they did.

I think that's what happened to them.

They could be alive somewhere, the man said. It's possible. The boy didnt answer. They went on. They'd wrapped their feet in sailcloth and bound them up in blue plastic pampooties cut from a tarp and they left strange tracks in their comings and going. He thought about the boy and his concerns and after a while he said: You're probably right. I think they're probably dead.

Because if they were alive we'd be taking their stuff.

And we're not taking their stuff.

I know.

Okay.

So how many people do you think are alive?

In the world?

In the world. Yes.

I dont know. Let's stop and rest.

Okay.

You're wearing me out.

Okay.

They sat among their bundles.

How long can we stay here, Papa?

You asked me that.

I know.

We'll see.

That means not very long.

Probably.

The boy poked holes in the sand with his fingers until he had a circle of them. The man watched him. I dont know how many people there are, he said. I dont think there are very many.

I know. He pulled his blanket about his shoulders and looked out down the gray and barren beach.

What is it? the man said.

Nothing.

No. Tell me.

There could be people alive someplace else.

Whereplace else?

I dont know. Anywhere.

You mean besides on earth?

Yes.

I dont think so. They couldnt live anyplace else.

Not even if they could get there?

No.

The boy looked away.

What? the man said.

He shook his head. I dont know what we're doing, he said.

The man started to answer. But he didnt. After a while he said: There are people. There are people and we'll find them. You'll see.

He fixed dinner while the boy played in the sand. He had a spatula made from a flattened foodtin and with it he built a small village. He dredged a grid of streets. The man walked down and squatted and looked at it. The boy looked up. The ocean's going to get it, isnt it? he said.

Yes.

That's okay.

Can you write the alphabet?

I can write it.

We dont work on your lessons any more.

I know.

Can you write something in the sand?

Maybe we could write a letter to the good guys. So if they came along they'd know we were here. We could write it up there where it wouldnt get washed away.

What if the bad guys saw it?

Yeah.

I shouldnt have said that. We could write them a letter.

The boy shook his head. That's okay, he said.

He loaded the flarepistol and as soon as it was dark they walked out down the beach away from the fire and he asked the boy if he wanted to shoot it.

You shoot it, Papa. You know how to do it.

Okay.

He cocked the gun and aimed it out over the bay and pulled the trigger. The flare arced up into the murk with a long whoosh and broke somewhere out over the water in a clouded light and hung there. The hot tendrils of magnesium drifted slowly down the dark and the pale foreshore tide started in the glare and slowly faded. He looked down at the boy's upturned face.

They couldnt see it very far, could they, Papa?

Who?

Anybody.

No. Not far.

If you wanted to show where you were.

You mean like to the good guys?

Yes. Or anybody that you wanted them to know where you were.

Like who?

I dont know.

Like God?

Yeah. Maybe somebody like that.

In the morning he built a fire and walked out on the beach while the boy slept. He was not gone long but he felt a strange unease and when he got back the boy was standing on the beach wrapped in his blankets waiting for him. He hurried his steps. By the time he got to him he was sitting down.

What is it? he said. What is it?

I dont feel good, Papa.

He cupped the boy's forehead in his hand. He was burning. He picked him up and carried him to the fire. It's okay, he said. You're going to be okay.

I think I'm going to be sick.

It's okay.

He sat with him in the sand and held his forehead while he bent and vomited. He wiped the boy's mouth with his hand. I'm sorry, the boy said. Shh. You didnt do anything wrong.

He carried him up to the camp and covered him with blankets. He tried to get him to drink some water. He put more wood on the fire and knelt with his hand on his forehead. You'll be all right he said. He was terrified.

Dont go away, the boy said.

Of course I wont go away.

Even for just a little while.

No. I'm right here.

Okay. Okay, Papa.

He held him all night, dozing off and waking in terror, feeling for the boy's heart. In the morning he was no better. He tried to get him to drink some juice but he would not. He pressed his hand to his forehead, conjuring up a coolness that would not come. He wiped his white mouth while he slept. I will do what I promised, he whispered. No matter what. I will not send you into the darkness alone.

He went through the first-aid kit from the boat but there was nothing much there of use. Aspirin. Bandages and disinfectant. Some antibiotics but they had a short shelflife. Still that was all he had and he helped the boy drink and put one of the capsules on his tongue. He was soaked in sweat. He'd already stripped him out of the blankets and now he unzipped him out of his coat and then out of his clothes and moved him away from the fire. The boy looked up at him. I'm so cold, he said.

I know. But you have a really high temperature and we have to get you cooled off.

Can I have another blanket?

Yes. Of course.

You wont go away.

No. I wont go away.

He carried the boy's filthy clothes into the surf and washed them, standing shivering in the cold salt water naked from the waist down and sloshing them up and down and wringing them out. He spread them by the fire on sticks angled into the sand and piled on more wood and went and sat by the boy again, smoothing his matted hair. In the evening he opened a can of soup and set it in the coals and he ate and watched the darkness come up. When he woke he was lying shivering in the sand and the fire had died almost to ash and it was black night. He sat up wildly and reached for the boy. Yes, he whispered. Yes.

He rekindled the fire and he got a cloth and wet it and put it over the boy's forehead. The wintry dawn was coming and when it was light enough to see he went into the woods beyond the dunes and came back dragging a great travois of dead limbs and branches and set about breaking them up and stacking them near the fire. He crushed aspirins in a cup and dissolved them in water and put in some sugar and sat and lifted the boy's head and held the cup while he drank.

He walked the beach, slumped and coughing. He stood looking out at the dark swells. He was staggering with fatigue. He went back and sat by the boy and refolded the cloth and wiped his face and then spread the cloth over his forehead. You have to stay near, he said. You have to be quick. So you can be with him. Hold him close. Last day of the earth.

The boy slept all day. He kept waking him up to drink the sugarwater, the boy's dry throat jerking and chugging. You have to drink he said. Okay, wheezed the boy. He twisted the cup into the sand beside him and cushioned the folded blanket under his sweaty head and covered him. Are you cold? he said. But the boy was already asleep.

He tried to stay awake all night but he could not. He woke endlessly and sat and slapped himself or rose to put wood on the fire. He held the boy and bent to hear the labored suck of air. His hand on the thin and laddered ribs. He walked out on the beach to the edge of the light and stood with his clenched fists on top of his skull and fell to his knees sobbing in rage.

It rained briefly in the night, a light patter on the tarp. He pulled it over them and turned and lay holding the child, watching the blue flames through the plastic. He fell into a dreamless sleep.

· · ·

When he woke again he hardly knew where he was. The fire had died, the rain had ceased. He threw back the tarp and pushed himself up on his elbows. Gray daylight. The boy was watching him. Papa, he said.

Yes. I'm right here.

Can I have a drink of water?

Yes. Yes, of course you can. How are you feeling?

I feel kind of weird.

Are you hungry?

I'm just really thirsty.

Let me get the water.

He pushed back the blankets and rose and walked out past the dead fire and got the boy's cup and filled it out of the plastic water jug and came back and knelt and held the cup for him. You're going to be okay, he said. The boy drank. He nodded and looked at his father. Then he drank the rest of the water. More, he said.

He built a fire and propped the boy's wet clothes up and brought him a can of apple juice. Do you remember anything? he said.

About what?

About being sick.

I remember shooting the flaregun.

Do you remember getting the stuff from the boat?

He sat sipping the juice. He looked up. I'm not a retard, he said.

I know.

I had some weird dreams.

What about?

I dont want to tell you.

That's okay. I want you to brush your teeth.

With real toothpaste.

Yes.

Okay.

He checked all the foodtins but he could find nothing suspect. He threw out a few that looked pretty rusty. They sat that evening by the fire and the boy drank hot soup and the man turned his steaming clothes on the sticks and sat watching him until the boy became embarrassed. Stop watching me, Papa, he said.

Okay.

But he didnt.

In two day's time they were walking the beach as far as the headland and back, trudging along in their plastic bootees.

They ate huge meals and he put up a sailcloth leanto with ropes and poles against the wind. They pruned down their stores to a manageable load for the cart and he thought they might leave in two more days. Then coming back to the camp late in the day he saw bootprints in the sand. He stopped and stood looking down the beach. Oh Christ, he said. Oh Christ.

What is it, Papa?

He pulled the pistol from his belt. Come on he said. Hurry.

The tarp was gone. Their blankets. The waterbottle and their campsite store of food. The sailcloth was blown up into the dunes. Their shoes were gone. He ran up through the swale of seaoats where he'd left the cart but the cart was gone. Everything. You stupid ass, he said. You stupid ass.

The boy was standing there wide-eyed. What happened, Papa?

They took everything. Come on.

The boy looked up. He was beginning to cry.

Stay with me, the man said. Stay right with me.

He could see the tracks of the cart where they sloughed up through the loose sand. Bootprints. How many? He lost the track on the better ground beyond the bracken and then picked it up again. When they got to the road he stopped the boy with his hand. The road was exposed to the wind from the sea and it was blown free of ash save for patches here and there. Dont step in the road, he said. And stop crying. We need to get all the sand off of our feet. Here. Sit down.

He untied the wrappings and shook them out and tied them back again. I want you to help, he said. We're looking for sand. Sand in the road. Even just a little bit. To see which way they went. Okay?

Okay.

They set off down the blacktop in opposite directions. He'd not gone far before the boy called out. Here it is, Papa. They went this way. When he got there the boy was crouched in the road. Right here, he said. It was a half teaspoon of beachsand tilted from somewhere in the understructure of the grocery cart. The man stood and looked out down the road. Good work, he said. Let's go.

They set off at a jogtrot. A pace he thought he'd be able to keep up but he couldnt. He had to stop, leaning over and coughing. He looked up at the boy, wheezing. We'll have to walk, he said. If they hear us they'll hide by the side of the road. Come on.

How many are there, Papa?

I dont know. Maybe just one.

Are we going to kill them?

I dont know.

They went on. It was already late in the day and it was another hour and deep into the long dusk before they overtook the thief, bent over the loaded cart, trundling down the road before them. When he looked back and saw them he tried to run with the cart but it was useless and finally he stopped and stood behind the cart holding a butcher knife. When he saw the pistol he stepped back but he didnt drop the knife.

Get away from the cart, the man said.

He looked at them. He looked at the boy. He was an outcast from one of the communes and the fingers of his right hand had been cut away. He tried to hide it behind him. A sort of fleshy spatula. The cart was piled high. He'd taken everything.

Get away from the cart and put down the knife.

He looked around. As if there might be help somewhere. Scrawny, sullen, bearded, filthy. His old plastic coat held together with tape. The pistol was a double action but the man cocked it anyway. Two loud clicks. Otherwise only their breathing in the silence of the salt moorland. They could smell him in his stinking rags. If you dont put down the knife and get away from the cart, the man said, I'm going to blow your brains out. The thief looked at the child and what he saw was very sobering to him. He laid the knife on top of the blankets and backed away and stood.

Back. More.

He stepped back again.

Papa? the boy said.

Be quiet.

He kept his eyes on the thief. Goddamn you, he said.

Papa please dont kill the man.

The thief's eyes swung wildly. The boy was crying.

Come on, man. I done what you said. Listen to the boy.

Take your clothes off.

What?

Take them off. Every goddamned stitch.

Come on. Dont do this.

I'll kill you where you stand.

Dont do this, man.

I wont tell you again.

All right. All right. Just take it easy.

He stripped slowly and piled his vile rags in the road.

The shoes.

Come on, man.

The shoes.

The thief looked at the boy. The boy had turned away and put his hands over his ears. Okay, he said. Okay. He sat naked in the road and began to unlace the rotting pieces of leather laced to his feet. Then he stood up, holding them in one hand.

Put them in the cart.

He stepped forward and placed the shoes on top of the blankets and stepped back. Standing there raw and naked, filthy, starving. Covering himself with his hand. He was already shivering.

Put the clothes in.

He bent and scooped up the rags in his arms and piled them on top of the shoes. He stood there holding himself. Dont do this, man.

You didnt mind doing it to us.

I'm begging you.

Papa, the boy said.

Come on. Listen to the kid.

You tried to kill us.

I'm starving, man. You'd have done the same.

You took everything.

Come on, man. I'll die.

I'm going to leave you the way you left us.

Come on. I'm begging you.

He pulled the cart back and swung it around and put the pistol on top and looked at the boy. Let's go, he said. And they set out along the road south with the boy crying and looking back at the nude and slatlike creature standing there in the road shivering and hugging himself. Oh Papa, he sobbed.

Stop it.

I cant stop it.

What do you think would have happened to us if we hadnt caught him? Just stop it.

I'm trying.

When they got to the curve in the road the man was still standing there. There was no place for him to go. The boy kept looking back and when he could no longer see him he stopped and then he just sat down in the road sobbing. The man pulled up and stood looking at him. He dug their shoes out of the cart and sat down and began to take the wrappings off the boy's feet. You have to stop crying, he said.

I cant.

He put on their shoes and then stood and walked back up the road but he couldnt see the thief. He came back and stood over the boy. He's gone, he said. Come on.

He's not gone, the boy said. He looked up. His face streaked with soot. He's not.

What do you want to do?

Just help him, Papa. Just help him.

The man looked back up the road.

He was just hungry, Papa. He's going to die.

He's going to die anyway.

He's so scared, Papa.

The man squatted and looked at him. I'm scared, he said. Do you understand? I'm scared.

The boy didnt answer. He just sat there with his head bowed, sobbing.

You're not the one who has to worry about everything.

The boy said something but he couldnt understand him. What? he said.

He looked up, his wet and grimy face. Yes I am, he said. I am the one.

They wheeled the tottering cart back up the road and stood there in the cold and the gathering dark and called but no one came.

He's afraid to answer, Papa.

Is this where we stopped?

I dont know. I think so.

They went up the road calling out in the empty dusk, their voices lost over the darkening shorelands. They stopped and stood with their hands cupped to their mouths, hallooing mindlessly into the waste. Finally he piled the man's shoes and clothes in the road. He put a rock on top of them. We have to go, he said. We have to go.

They made a dry camp with no fire. He sorted out cans for their supper and warmed them over the gas burner and they ate and the boy said nothing. The man tried to see his face in the blue light from the burner. I wasnt going to kill him, he said. But the boy didnt answer. They rolled themselves in the blankets and lay there in the dark. He thought he could hear the sea but perhaps it was just the wind. He could tell by his breathing that the boy was awake and after a while the boy said: But we did kill him.

In the morning they ate and set out. The cart was so loaded it was hard to push and one of the wheels was giving out. The road bent its way along the coast, dead sheaves of saltgrass overhanging the pavement. The leadcolored sea shifting in the distance. The silence. He woke that night with the dull carbon light of the crossing moon beyond the murk making the shapes of the trees almost visible and he turned away coughing. Smell of rain out there. The boy was awake. You have to talk to me, he said.

I'm trying.

I'm sorry I woke you.

It's okay.

He got up and walked out to the road. The black shape of it running from dark to dark. Then a distant low rumble. Not thunder. You could feel it under your feet. A sound without cognate and so without description. Something imponderable shifting out there in the dark. The earth itself contracting with the cold. It did not come again. What time of year? What age the child? He walked out into the road and stood. The silence. The salitter drying from the earth. The mudstained shapes of flooded cities burned to the waterline. At a crossroads a ground set with dolmen stones where the spoken bones of oracles lay moldering. No sound but the wind. What will you say? A living man spoke these lines? He sharpened a quill with his small pen knife to scribe these things in sloe or lampblack? At some reckonable and entabled moment? He is coming to steal my eyes. To seal my mouth with dirt.

He went through the cans again one by one, holding them in his hand and squeezing them like a man checking for ripeness at a fruitstand. He sorted out two he thought questionable and packed away the rest and packed the cart and they set out upon the road again. In three days they came to a small port town and they hid the cart in a garage behind a house and piled old boxes over it and then sat in the house to see if anyone would come. No one did. He looked through the cabinets but there was nothing there. He needed vitamin D for the boy or he was going to get rickets. He stood at the sink and looked out down the driveway. Light the color of washwater congealing in the dirty panes of glass. The boy sat slumped at the table with his head in his arms.

They walked through the town and down to the docks. They saw no one. He had the pistol in the pocket of his coat and he carried the flaregun in his hand. They walked out on the pier, the rough boards dark with tar and fastened down with spikes to the timbers underneath. Wooden bollards. Faint smell of salt and creosote coming in off the bay. On the far shore a row of warehouses and the shape of a tanker red with rust. A tall gantry crane against the sullen sky. There's no one here, he said. The boy didnt answer.

. . .

They wheeled the cart through the back streets and across the railroad tracks and came into the main road again at the far edge of the town. As they passed the last of the sad wooden buildings something whistled past his head and clattered off the street and broke up against the wall of the block building on the other side. He grabbed the boy and fell on top of him and grabbed the cart to pull it to them. It tipped and fell over spilling the tarp and blankets into the street. In an upper window of the house he could see a man drawing a bow on them and he pushed the boy's head down and tried to cover him with his body. He heard the dull thwang of the bowstring and felt a sharp hot pain in his leg. Oh you bastard, he said. You bastard. He clawed the blankets to one side and lunged and grabbed the flare-gun and raised up and cocked it and rested his arm on the side of the cart. The boy was clinging to him. When the man stepped back into the frame of the window to draw the bow again he fired. The flare went rocketing up toward the window in a long white arc and then they could hear the man screaming. He grabbed the boy and pushed him down and dragged the blankets over the top of him. Dont move, he said. Dont move and dont look. He pulled the blankets out into the street looking for the case for the flarepistol. It finally slid out of the cart and he snatched it up and opened it and took out the shells and reloaded the pistol and breeched it shut and put the rest of the loads in his pocket. Stay just like you are, he whispered. He patted the boy through the blankets and rose and ran limping across the street.

He entered the house through the back door with the flare-gun leveled at his waist. The house was stripped out to the wall studs. He stepped through into the livingroom and stood at the stair landing. He listened for movement in the upper rooms. He looked out the front window to where the cart lay in the street and then he went up the stairs.

A woman was sitting in the corner holding the man. She'd taken off her coat to cover him. As soon as she saw him she began to curse him. The flare had burned out in the floor leaving a patch of white ash and there was a faint smell of burnt wood in the room. He crossed the room and looked out the window. The woman's eyes followed him. Scrawny, lank gray hair.

Who else is up here?

She didnt answer. He stepped past her and went through the rooms. His leg was bleeding badly. He could feel his trousers sticking to the skin. He went back into the front room. Where's the bow? he said.

I dont have it.

Where is it?

I dont know.

They left you here, didnt they?

I left myself here.

He turned and went limping down the stairs and opened the front door and went out into the street backward watching the house. When he got to the cart he pulled it upright and piled their things back in. Stay close, he whispered. Stay close.

They put up in a store building at the end of the town. He wheeled the cart through and into a room at the rear and shut the door and pushed the cart against it sideways. He dug out the burner and the tank of gas and lit the burner and set it in the floor and then he unbuckled his belt and took off the bloodstained trousers. The boy watched. The arrow had cut a gash just above his knee about three inches long. It was still bleeding and his whole upper leg was discolored and he could see that the cut was deep. Some homemade broadhead beaten out of strapiron, an old spoon, God knows what. He looked at the boy. See if you can find the first-aid kit, he said.

The boy didnt move.

Get the first-aid kit, damn it. Dont just sit there.

He jumped up and went to the door and began digging under the tarp and the blankets piled in the cart. He came back with the kit and gave it to the man and the man took it without comment and set it in the concrete floor in front of him and unsnapped the catches and opened it. He reached and turned up the burner for the light. Bring me the water bottle, he said. The boy brought the bottle and the man unscrewed the lid and poured water over the wound and held it shut between his fingers while he wiped away the blood. He swabbed the wound with disinfectant and opened a plastic envelope with his teeth and took out a small hooked suture needle and a coil of silk thread and sat holding the silk to the light while he threaded it through the needle's eye. He took a clamp from the kit and caught the needle in the jaws and locked them and set about suturing the wound. He worked quickly and he took no great pains about it. The boy was crouching in the floor. He looked at him and he bent to the sutures again. You dont have to watch, he said.

Is it okay?

Yeah. It's okay.

Does it hurt?

Yes. It hurts.

He ran the knot down the thread and pulled it taut and cut off the silk with the scissors from the kit and looked at the boy. The boy was looking at what he'd done.

I'm sorry I yelled at you.

He looked up. That's okay, Papa.

Let's start over.

Okay.

In the morning it was raining and a hard wind was rattling the glass at the rear of the building. He stood looking out. A steel dock half collapsed and submerged in the bay. The wheelhouses of sunken fishingboats standing out of the gray chop. Nothing moving out there. Anything that could move had long been blown away. His leg was throbbing and he pulled away the dressing and disinfected the wound and looked at it. The flesh swollen and discolored in the truss of the black stitching. He dressed it and pulled his bloodstiffened trousers on.

They spent the day there, sitting among the boxes and crates. You have to talk to me, he said.

I'm talking.

Are you sure?

I'm talking now.

Do you want me to tell you a story?

No.

Why not?

The boy looked at him and looked away.

Why not?

Those stories are not true.

They dont have to be true. They're stories.

Yes. But in the stories we're always helping people and we dont help people.

Why dont you tell me a story?

I dont want to.

Okay.

I dont have any stories to tell.

You could tell me a story about yourself.

You already know all the stories about me. You were there.

You have stories inside that I dont know about.

You mean like dreams?

Like dreams. Or just things that you think about.

Yeah, but stories are supposed to be happy.

They dont have to be.

You always tell happy stories.

You dont have any happy ones?

They're more like real life.

But my stories are not.

Your stories are not. No.

The man watched him. Real life is pretty bad?

What do you think?

Well, I think we're still here. A lot of bad things have happened but we're still here.

Yeah.

You dont think that's so great.

It's okay.

They'd pulled a worktable up to the windows and spread out their blankets and the boy was lying there on his stomach looking out across the bay. The man sat with his leg stretched out. On the blanket between them were the two pistols and the box of flares. After a while the man said: I think it's pretty good. It's a pretty good story. It counts for something.

It's okay, Papa. I just want to have a little quiet time.

What about dreams? You used to tell me dreams sometimes.

I dont want to talk about anything.

Okay.

I dont have good dreams anyway. They're always about something bad happening. You said that was okay because good dreams are not a good sign.

Maybe. I dont know.

When you wake up coughing you walk out along the road or somewhere but I can still hear you coughing.

I'm sorry.

One time I heard you crying.

I know.

So if I shouldnt cry you shouldnt cry either.

Okay.

Is your leg going to get better?

Yes.

You're not just saying that.

No.

Because it looks really hurt.

It's not that bad.

The man was trying to kill us. Wasnt he.

Yes. He was.

Did you kill him?

No.

Is that the truth?

Yes.

Okay.

Is that all right?

Yes.

I thought you didnt want to talk?

I dont.

They left two days later, the man limping along behind the cart and the boy keeping close to his side until they cleared the outskirts of the town. The road ran along the flat gray coast and there were drifts of sand in the road that the winds had left there. It made for heavy going and they had to shovel their way in places with a plank they carried in the lower rack of the cart. They walked out down the beach and sat in the lee of the dunes and studied the map. They'd brought the burner with them and they heated water and made tea and sat wrapped in their blankets against the wind. Downshore the weathered timbers of an ancient ship. Gray and sandscrubbed beams, old hand-turned scarpbolts. The pitted iron hardware deep lilac in color, smeltered in some bloomery in Cadiz or Bristol and beaten out on a blackened anvil, good to last three hundred years against the sea. The following day they passed through the boarded ruins of a seaside resort and took the road inland through a pine wood, the long straight blacktop drifted in pineneedles, the wind in the dark trees.

He sat in the road at noon in the best light there would be and snipped the sutures with the scissors and put the scissors back in the kit and took out the clamp. Then he set about pulling the small black threads from his skin, pressing down with the flat of his thumb. The boy sat in the road watching. The man fastened the clamp over the ends of the threads and pulled them out one by one. Small pinlets of blood. When he was done he put away the clamp and taped gauze over the wound and then stood and pulled his trousers up and handed the kit to the boy to put away.

That hurt, didnt it? the boy said.

Yes. It did.

Are you real brave?

Just medium.

What's the bravest thing you ever did?

He spat into the road a bloody phlegm. Getting up this morning, he said.

Really?

No. Dont listen to me. Come on, let's go.

In the evening the murky shape of another coastal city, the cluster of tall buildings vaguely askew. He thought the iron armatures had softened in the heat and then reset again to leave the buildings standing out of true. The melted window glass hung frozen down the walls like icing on a cake. They went on. In the nights sometimes now he'd wake in the black and freezing waste out of softly colored worlds of human love, the songs of birds, the sun.

.   .   .

He leaned his forehead on his arms crossed upon the bar handle of the cart and coughed. He spat a bloody drool. More and more he had to stop and rest. The boy watched him. In some other world the child would already have begun to vacate him from his life. But he had no life other. He knew the boy lay awake in the night and listened to hear if he were breathing.

The days sloughed past uncounted and uncalendared. Along the interstate in the distance long lines of charred and rusting cars. The raw rims of the wheels sitting in a stiff gray sludge of melted rubber, in blackened rings of wire. The incinerate corpses shrunk to the size of a child and propped on the bare springs of the seats. Ten thousand dreams ensepulchred within their crozzled hearts. They went on. Treading the dead world under like rats on a wheel. The nights dead still and deader black. So cold. They talked hardly at all. He coughed all the time and the boy watched him spitting blood. Slumping along. Filthy, ragged, hopeless. He'd stop and lean on the cart and the boy would go on and then stop and look back and he would raise his weeping eyes and see him standing there in the road looking back at him from some unimaginable future, glowing in that waste like a tabernacle.

. . .

The road crossed a dried slough where pipes of ice stood out of the frozen mud like formations in a cave. The remains of an old fire by the side of the road. Beyond that a long concrete causeway. A dead swamp. Dead trees standing out of the gray water trailing gray and relic hagmoss. The silky spills of ash against the curbing. He stood leaning on the gritty concrete rail. Perhaps in the world's destruction it would be possible at last to see how it was made. Oceans, mountains. The ponderous counterspectacle of things ceasing to be. The sweeping waste, hydroptic and coldly secular. The silence.

They'd begun to come upon dead windfalls of pinetrees, great swaths of ruin cut through the countryside. The wreckage of buildings strewn over the landscape and skeins of wire from the roadside poles garbled like knitting. The road was littered with debris and it was work to get the cart through. Finally they just sat by the side of the road and stared at what was before them. Roofs of houses, the trunks of trees. A boat. The open sky beyond where in the distance the sullen sea lagged and shifted.

. . .

They sorted through the wreckage strewn along the road and in the end he came up with a canvas bag that he could tote over his shoulder and a small suitcase for the boy. They packed their blankets and the tarp and what was left of the canned goods and set out again with their knapsacks and their bags leaving the cart behind. Clambering through the ruins. Slow going. He had to stop and rest. He sat in a roadside sofa, the cushions bloated in the damp. Bent over, coughing. He pulled the bloodstained mask from his face and got up and rinsed it in the ditch and wrung it out and then just stood there in the road. His breath pluming white. Winter was already upon them. He turned and looked at the boy. Standing with his suitcase like an orphan waiting for a bus.

In two day's time they came to a broad tidal river where the bridge lay collapsed in the slow moving water. They sat on the broken abutment of the road and watched the river backing upon itself and coiling over the iron trelliswork. He looked across the water to the country beyond.

What are we going to do Papa? he said.

Well what are we, said the boy.

. . .

They walked out the long spit of tidal mud where a small boat lay half buried and stood there looking at it. It was altogether derelict. There was rain in the wind. They trudged up the beach with their baggage looking for shelter but they found none. He scuffled together a pile of the bonecolored wood that lay along the shore and got a fire going and they sat in the dunes with the tarp over them and watched the cold rain coming in from the north. It fell harder, dimpling the sand. The fire steamed and the smoke swung in slow coils and the boy curled up under the pattering tarp and soon he was asleep. The man pulled the plastic over himself in a hood and watched the gray sea shrouded away out there in the rain and watched the surf break along the shore and draw away again over the dark and stippled sand.

The next day they headed inland. A vast low swale where ferns and hydrangeas and wild orchids lived on in ashen effigies which the wind had not yet reached. Their progress was a torture. In two days when they came out upon a road he set the bag down and sat bent over with his arms crossed at his chest and coughed till he could cough no more. Two more days and they may have traveled ten miles. They crossed the river and a short ways on they came to a crossroads. Downcountry a storm had passed over the isthmus and leveled the dead black trees from east to west like weeds in the floor of a stream. Here they camped and when he lay down he knew that he could go no further and that this was the place where he would die. The boy sat watching him, his eyes welling. Oh Papa, he said.

He watched him come through the grass and kneel with the cup of water he'd fetched. There was light all about him. He took the cup and drank and lay back. They had for food a single tin of peaches but he made the boy eat it and he would not take any. I cant, he said. It's all right.

I'll save your half.

Okay. You save it until tomorrow.

He took the cup and moved away and when he moved the light moved with him. He'd wanted to try and make a tent out of the tarp but the man would not let him. He said that he didnt want anything covering him. He lay watching the boy at the fire. He wanted to be able to see. Look around you, he said. There is no prophet in the earth's long chronicle who's not honored here today. Whatever form you spoke of you were right.

.   .   .

The boy thought he smelled wet ash on the wind. He went up the road and come dragging back a piece of plywood from the roadside trash and he drove sticks into the ground with a rock and made of the plywood a rickety leanto but in the end it didnt rain. He left the flarepistol and took the revolver with him and he scoured the countryside for anything to eat but he came back emptyhanded. The man took his hand, wheezing. You need to go on, he said. I cant go with you. You need to keep going. You dont know what might be down the road. We were always lucky. You'll be lucky again. You'll see. Just go. It's all right.

I cant.

It's all right. This has been a long time coming. Now it's here. Keep going south. Do everything the way we did it.

You're going to be okay, Papa. You have to.

No I'm not. Keep the gun with you at all times. You need to find the good guys but you cant take any chances. No chances. Do you hear?

I want to be with you.

You cant.

Please.

You cant. You have to carry the fire.

I dont know how to.

Yes you do.

Is it real? The fire?

Yes it is.

Where is it? I dont know where it is.

Yes you do. It's inside you. It was always there. I can see it.

Just take me with you. Please.

I cant.

Please, Papa.

I cant. I cant hold my son dead in my arms. I thought I could but I cant.

You said you wouldnt ever leave me.

I know. I'm sorry. You have my whole heart. You always did. You're the best guy. You always were. If I'm not here you can still talk to me. You can talk to me and I'll talk to you. You'll see.

Will I hear you?

Yes. You will. You have to make it like talk that you imagine. And you'll hear me. You have to practice. Just dont give up. Okay?

Okay.

Okay.

I'm really scared Papa.

I know. But you'll be okay. You're going to be lucky. I know you are. I've got to stop talking. I'm going to start coughing again.

It's okay, Papa. You dont have to talk. It's okay.

. . .

He went down the road as far as he dared and then he came back. His father was asleep. He sat with him under the plywood and watched him. He closed his eyes and talked to him and he kept his eyes closed and listened. Then he tried again.

He woke in the darkness, coughing softly. He lay listening. The boy sat by the fire wrapped in a blanket watching him. Drip of water. A fading light. Old dreams encroached upon the waking world. The dripping was in the cave. The light was a candle which the boy bore in a ringstick of beaten copper. The wax spattered on the stones. Tracks of unknown creatures in the mortified loess. In that cold corridor they had reached the point of no return which was measured from the first solely by the light they carried with them.

Do you remember that little boy, Papa?
Yes. I remember him.
Do you think that he's all right that little boy?
Oh yes. I think he's all right.
Do you think he was lost?
No. I dont think he was lost.
I'm scared that he was lost.

I think he's all right.

But who will find him if he's lost? Who will find the little boy?

Goodness will find the little boy. It always has. It will again.

He slept close to his father that night and held him but when he woke in the morning his father was cold and stiff. He sat there a long time weeping and then he got up and walked out through the woods to the road. When he came back he knelt beside his father and held his cold hand and said his name over and over again.

He stayed three days and then he walked out to the road and he looked down the road and he looked back the way they had come. Someone was coming. He started to turn and go back into the woods but he didnt. He just stood in the road and waited, the pistol in his hand. He'd piled all the blankets on his father and he was cold and he was hungry. The man that hove into view and stood there looking at him was dressed in a gray and yellow ski parka. He carried a shotgun upside down over his shoulder on a braided leather lanyard and he wore a nylon bandolier filled with shells for the gun. A veteran of old skirmishes, bearded, scarred across his cheek and the bone stoven and the one eye wandering. When he spoke his mouth worked imperfectly, and when he smiled.

Where's the man you were with?

He died.

Was that your father?

Yes. He was my papa.

I'm sorry.

I dont know what to do.

I think you should come with me.

Are you one of the good guys?

The man pulled back the hood from his face. His hair was long and matted. He looked at the sky. As if there were anything there to be seen. He looked at the boy. Yeah, he said. I'm one of the good guys. Why dont you put the pistol away?

I'm not supposed to let anyone take the pistol. No matter what.

I dont want your pistol. I just dont want you pointing it at me.

Okay.

Where's your stuff?

We dont have much stuff.

Have you got a sleeping bag?

No.

What have you got? Some blankets?

My papa's wrapped in them.

Show me.

The boy didnt move. The man watched him. He squatted on one knee and swung the shotgun up from under his arm and stood it in the road and leaned on the forestock. The shotgun shells in the loops of the bandolier were handloaded and the ends sealed with candlewax. He smelled of woodsmoke. Look, he said. You got two choices here. There was some discussion about whether to even come after you at all. You can stay here with your papa and die or you can go with me. If you stay you need to keep out of the road. I dont know how you made it this far. But you should go with me. You'll be all right.

How do I know you're one of the good guys?

You dont. You'll have to take a shot.

Are you carrying the fire?

Am I what?

Carrying the fire.

You're kind of weirded out, arent you?

No.

Just a little.

Yeah.

That's okay.

So are you?

What, carrying the fire?

Yes.

Yeah. We are.

Do you have any kids?

We do.

Do you have a little boy?

We have a little boy and we have a little girl.

How old is he?

He's about your age. Maybe a little older.

And you didnt eat them.

No.

You dont eat people.

No. We dont eat people.

And I can go with you?

Yes. You can.

Okay then.

Okay.

They went into the woods and the man squatted and looked at the gray and wasted figure under the tilted sheet of plywood. Are these all the blankets you have?

Yes.

Is that your suitcase?

Yes.

He stood. He looked at the boy. Why dont you go back out to the road and wait for me. I'll bring the blankets and everything.

What about my papa?

What about him.

We cant just leave him here.

Yes we can.

I dont want people to see him.

There's no one to see him.

Can I cover him with leaves?

The wind will blow them away.

Could we cover him with one of the blankets?

I'll do it. Go on now.

Okay.

He waited in the road and when the man came out of the woods he was carrying the suitcase and he had the blankets over his shoulder. He sorted through them and handed one to the boy. Here, he said. Wrap this around you. You're cold. The boy tried to hand him the pistol but he wouldnt take it. You hold onto that, he said.

Okay.

Do you know how to shoot it?

Yes.

Okay.

What about my papa?

There's nothing else to be done.

I think I want to say goodbye to him.

Will you be all right?

Yes.

Go ahead. I'll wait for you.

He walked back into the woods and knelt beside his father. He was wrapped in a blanket as the man had promised and the boy didnt uncover him but he sat beside him and he was crying and he couldnt stop. He cried for a long time. I'll talk to you every day, he whispered. And I wont forget. No matter what. Then he rose and turned and walked back out to the road.

The woman when she saw him put her arms around him and held him. Oh, she said, I am so glad to see you. She would talk to him sometimes about God. He tried to talk to God but the best thing was to talk to his father and he did talk to him and he didnt forget. The woman said that was all right. She said that the breath of God was his breath yet though it pass from man to man through all of time.

Once there were brook trout in the streams in the mountains. You could see them standing in the amber current where the white edges of their fins wimpled softly in the flow. They smelled of moss in your hand. Polished and muscular and torsional. On their backs were vermiculate patterns that were maps of the world in its becoming. Maps and mazes. Of a thing which could not be put back. Not be made right again. In the deep glens where they lived all things were older than man and they hummed of mystery.

ALSO BY CORMAC MCCARTHY

ALL THE PRETTY HORSES

All the Pretty Horses—the first volume of the Border Trilogy and winner of the National Book Award—tells of young John Grady Cole, the last of a long line of Texas ranchers. Across the border Mexico beckons—beautiful and desolate, rugged and cruelly civilized. With two companions, he sets off on an idyllic, sometimes comic adventure, to a place where dreams are paid for in blood.

Fiction/Literature/978-0-679-74439-9

THE CROSSING

In the late 1930s, sixteen-year-old Billy Parham captures a she-wolf that has been marauding his family's ranch. But instead of killing it, he decides to take it back to the mountains of Mexico. With that crossing, he begins an arduous and often dreamlike journey into a country where men meet like ghosts and violence strikes as suddenly as heat-lightning. The second volume of the Border Trilogy, *The Crossing* is an essential novel by any measure, one that touches, stops, and starts the heart and mind at once.

Fiction/Literature/978-0-679-76084-9

CITIES OF THE PLAIN

It is 1952 and John Grady Cole and Billy Parham are working as ranch hands in New Mexico, not far from the proving grounds of Alamogordo and the cities of El Paso and Juarez. Their life is made up of trail drives and horse auctions and stories told by campfire light. They value that life all the more because they know it is about to change forever. The change comes when John Grady falls in love with a beautiful, ill-starred Mexican prostitute and sets in motion a chain of events as violent as they are unstoppable. Haunting in its beauty, filled with sorrow, humor, and awe, *Cities of the Plain* is a genuine American epic.

Fiction/Literature/978-0-679-74719-2

BLOOD MERIDIAN
Or the evening redness in the west

Based on historical events that took place on the Texas-Mexico border in the 1850s, *Blood Meridian* traces the fortunes of the Kid, a fourteen-year-old Tennesseean who stumbles into a nightmarish world where Indians are being murdered and the market for their scalps is thriving. An epic novel of the violence and depravity that attended America's westward expansion, *Blood Meridian* brilliantly subverts the conventions of the Western novel and the mythology of the "Wild West."

Fiction/Literature/978-0-679-72875-7

NO COUNTRY FOR OLD MEN

A good old boy named Llewellyn Moss finds a pickup truck surrounded by dead men. A load of heroin and two million dollars in cash are still in the back. When Moss takes the money, he sets off a chain reaction of catastrophic violence that not even the law can contain. Encompassing themes as ancient as the Bible and as bloodily contemporary as this morning's headlines, *No Country for Old Men* is a triumph.

Fiction/Literature/978-0-375-70667-7

ALSO AVAILABLE:

Child of God, 978-0-679-72874-0
The Orchard Keeper, 978-0-679-72872-6
Outer Dark, 978-0-679-72873-3
The Stonemason, 978-0-679-76280-5
The Sunset Limited, 978-0-307-27836-4
Suttree, 978-0-679-73632-5

VINTAGE INTERNATIONAL
Available at your local bookstore, or visit
www.randomhouse.com

MORTAL ENGINES

"Philip Reeve's debut novel, *Mortal Engines*, seems
to have leapt fully formed from a startling
imagination ... a gripping yarn"
Daily Telegraph

"truly memorable characters... This big, brave,
brilliant book combines a thrilling adventure story with
endless moral conundrums ... the reader is constantly
forced to reassess his or her attitudes"
Guardian

"No 11–16-year-old should miss the superbly imagined
debut novel from Philip Reeve, *Mortal Engines*"
The Times

Point

MORTAL ENGINES

PHILIP REEVE

■SCHOLASTIC

Scholastic Children's Books,
Commonwealth House, 1-19 New Oxford Street,
London, WC1A 1NU, UK
a division of Scholastic Ltd
London ~ New York ~ Toronto ~ Sydney ~ Auckland
Mexico City ~ New Delhi ~ Hong Kong

First published by Scholastic Ltd, 2001
This edition published by Scholastic Ltd, 2002

Copyright © Philip Reeve, 2001
Cover illustration copyright © David Frankland, 2001

ISBN 0 439 97943 9

Typeset by M Rules
Printed and bound by Nørhaven Paperback A/S, Denmark

10 9 8 7

CONTENTS

PART TWO

For Sarah

PART ONE

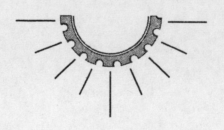

1
THE HUNTING GROUND

It was a dark, blustery afternoon in spring, and the city of London was chasing a small mining town across the dried-out bed of the old North Sea.

In happier times, London would never have bothered with such feeble prey. The great Traction City had once spent its days hunting far bigger towns than this, ranging north as far as the edges of the Ice Waste and south to the shores of the Mediterranean. But lately prey of any kind had started to grow scarce, and some of the larger cities had begun to look hungrily at London. For ten years now it had been hiding from them, skulking in a damp, mountainous, western district which the Guild of Historians said had once been the island of Britain. For ten years it had eaten nothing but tiny farming towns and static settlements in those wet hills. Now, at last, the Lord Mayor had decided that the time was right to take his city back over the land-bridge into the Great Hunting Ground.

It was barely halfway across when the look-outs on the high watch-towers spied the mining town, gnawing at the salt-flats twenty miles ahead. To the people of London it seemed like a sign from the gods, and even the Lord Mayor (who didn't believe in gods or signs) thought it was a good beginning to the journey east, and issued the order to give chase.

The mining town saw the danger and turned tail, but already the huge caterpillar tracks under London were starting to roll faster and faster. Soon the city was lumbering in hot pursuit, a moving mountain of metal which rose in seven tiers like the layers of a wedding cake, the lower levels wreathed in engine-smoke, the villas of the rich gleaming white on the higher decks, and above it all the cross on top of St Paul's Cathedral glinting gold, two thousand feet above the ruined earth.

                          ○ ○ ○ ○ ○

Tom was cleaning the exhibits in the London Museum's Natural History section when it started. He felt the tell-tale tremor in the metal floor, and looked up to find the model whales and dolphins that hung from the gallery roof swinging on their cables with soft creaking sounds.

He wasn't alarmed. He had lived in London for all of his fifteen years, and he was used to its movements. He knew that the city was changing course and putting on speed. A prickle of excitement ran through him, the ancient thrill of the hunt that all Londoners shared. There must be prey in sight! Dropping his brushes and dusters he pressed his hand to the wall, sensing the vibrations that came rippling up from the huge engine-rooms down in the Gut. Yes, there it was – the deep throb of the auxiliary motors cutting in, *boom, boom, boom*, like a big drum beating inside his bones.

The door at the far end of the gallery slammed open and Chudleigh Pomeroy came storming in, his toupee askew and his round face red with indignation. "What in the name of Quirke. . .?" he blustered, gawping at the gyrating whales, and the stuffed birds jigging and twitching in their cases as if they were shaking off their long captivity and getting ready to take wing again. "Apprentice Natsworthy! What's going on here?"

"It's a chase, sir," said Tom, wondering how the Deputy Head of the Guild of Historians had managed to live aboard London for so long and still not recognize its heartbeat. "It must be something good," he explained. "They've brought all the auxiliaries on line. That hasn't happened for ages. Maybe London's luck has turned!"

"Pah!" snorted Pomeroy, wincing as the glass in the display cases started to whine and shiver in sympathy with the beat of the engines. Above his head the biggest of the models – a thing called a blue whale that had become extinct thousands of years ago – was jerking back and forth on its hawsers like a plank-swing. "That's as may be, Natsworthy," he said. "I just wish the Guild of Engineers would fit some decent shock-absorbers in this building. Some of these specimens are very delicate. It won't do. It won't do at all." He tugged a spotted handkerchief out of the folds of his long black robes and dabbed his face with it.

"Please, sir," asked Tom, "could I run down to the observation platforms and watch the chase, just for half an hour? It's been years since there was a really good one. . ."

Pomeroy looked shocked. "Certainly not, Apprentice! Look at all the dust that this wretched chase is shaking down! All the exhibits will have to be cleaned again and checked for damage."

"Oh, but that's not fair!" cried Tom. "I've just dusted this whole gallery!"

He knew at once that he had made a mistake. Old Chudleigh Pomeroy wasn't bad as Guildsmen went, but he didn't like being answered back by a mere Third Class Apprentice. He drew himself up to his full height (which was only slightly more than his full width) and frowned so sternly that his Guild-mark almost vanished between his bushy eyebrows. "*Life* isn't fair, Natsworthy," he boomed. "Any more cheek from you and you'll be on Gut-duty as soon as this chase is over!"

Of all the horrible chores a Third Class Apprentice had to perform, Gut-duty was the one Tom hated most. He quickly shut up, staring meekly down at the beautifully buffed toes of the Chief Curator's boots.

"You were told to work in this department until seven o'clock, and you *will* work until seven o'clock," Pomeroy went on. "Meanwhile, I shall consult the other curators about this dreadful, dreadful shaking. . ."

He hurried off, still muttering. Tom watched him go, then picked up his gear and went miserably back to work. Usually he didn't mind cleaning, especially not in this gallery, with its amiable, moth-eaten animals and the blue whale smiling its big blue smile. If he grew bored, he simply took refuge in a daydream, in which he was a hero who rescued beautiful girls from air-pirates, saved London from the Anti-Traction League and lived happily ever after. But how could he daydream, with the rest of the city enjoying the first proper chase for ages?

He waited for twenty minutes, but Chudleigh Pomeroy did not return. There was nobody else about. It was a Wednesday, which meant the Museum was closed to the public, and most of the senior Guildsmen and First and Second Class Apprentices would be having the day off. What harm could it do if he slipped outside for ten minutes, just to see what was happening? He hid his bag of cleaning stuff behind a handy yak and hurried through the shadows of dancing dolphins to the door.

Out in the corridor all the argon lamps were dancing too, spilling their light up the metal walls. Two black-robed Guildsmen hurried past, and Tom heard the reedy voice of old Dr Arkengarth whine, "Vibrations!

Vibrations! It's playing merry hell with my 35th Century ceramics. . ." He waited until they had vanished around a bend in the corridor, then slipped quickly out and down the nearest stairway. He cut through the 21st Century gallery, past the big plastic statues of Pluto and Mickey, animal-headed gods of lost America. He ran across the main hall and down galleries full of things that had somehow survived through all the millennia since the Ancients destroyed themselves in that terrible flurry of orbit-to-earth atomics and tailored-virus bombs called the Sixty Minute War. Two minutes later he slipped out through a side entrance into the noise and bustle of the Tottenham Court Road.

The London Museum stood at the very hub of Tier Two, in a busy district called Bloomsbury, and the underbelly of Tier One hung like a rusty sky a few feet above the rooftops. Tom didn't worry about being spotted as he pushed his way along the dark, crowded street towards the public Goggle-screen outside the Tottenham Court Road elevator station. Joining the crowd in front of it he had his first glimpse of the distant prey; a watery, blue-grey blur captured by cameras down on Tier Six. *"The town is called Salthook,"* boomed the voice of the announcer. *"A mining platform of nine hundred inhabitants. She is currently moving at eighty miles per hour, heading due east, but the Guild of Navigators predicts London will catch her before sundown. There are sure to be many more towns awaiting us beyond the land-bridge; clear proof of just how wise our beloved Lord Mayor was when he decided to bring London east again. . ."*

Eighty miles per hour! thought Tom in awe. It was an astonishing speed, and he longed to be down at the observation deck, feeling the wind on his face. He was probably already in trouble with Mr Pomeroy. What difference could it make if he stole a few more minutes?

He set off at a run, and soon reached Bloomsbury Park, out in the open air on the tier's brim. It had been a proper park once, with trees and duck-ponds, but because of the recent shortage of prey it had been given over to food production and its lawns grubbed up to make way for cabbage-plots and algae-pans. The observation platforms were still there though, raised balconies jutting out from the edge of the tier where Londoners could go to watch the passing view. Tom hurried towards the nearest. An even bigger crowd had gathered there, including quite a few people in the black of the Historian's Guild, and Tom tried to look inconspicuous as he pushed his way through to the front and peered over the railings. Salthook was only five miles ahead, travelling flat out with black smoke spewing from its exhaust-stacks.

"Natsworthy!" called a braying voice, and his heart sank. He looked round and found that he was standing next to Melliphant, a burly First Class Apprentice, who grinned at him and said, "Isn't it wonderful? A fat little salt-mining platform, with C20 land-engines! Just what London needs!"

Herbert Melliphant was the worst sort of bully; the sort who didn't just hit you and stick your head down the lavatory, but made it his business to find out all your secrets and the things that upset you most and taunt you with them. He enjoyed picking on Tom, who was small and shy and had no friends to stick up for him – and Tom could not get back at him, because Melliphant's family had paid to make him a First Class Apprentice, while Tom, who had no family, was a mere Third. He knew Melliphant was only bothering to talk to him because he was hoping to impress a pretty young Historian named Clytie Potts, who was standing just behind. Tom nodded and turned his back, concentrating on the chase.

"Look!" shouted Clytie Potts.

The gap between London and its prey was narrowing fast, and a dark shape had lifted clear of Salthook. Soon there was another and another. Airships! The crowds on London's observation platforms cheered, and Melliphant said, "Ah, air-merchants. They know the town is doomed, you see, so they are making sure they get away before we eat it. If they don't, we can claim their cargoes along with everything else aboard!"

Tom was glad to see that Clytie Potts looked thoroughly bored by Melliphant: she was a year above him and must already know this stuff, because she had passed her Guild exams and had the Historian's mark tattooed on her forehead. "Look!" she said again, catching Tom's glance and grinning. "Oh, look at them go! Aren't they beautiful!"

Tom pushed his untidy hair out of his eyes and watched as the airships rose up and up and vanished into the slate-grey clouds. For a moment he found himself longing to go with them, up into the sunlight. If only his poor parents had not left him to the care of the Guild, to be trained as a Historian! He wished he could be cabin-boy aboard a sky-clipper and see all the cities of the world: Puerto Angeles adrift on the blue Pacific and Arkangel skating on iron runners across the frozen northern seas, the great ziggurat-towns of the Nuevo-Mayans and the unmoving strongholds of the Anti-Traction League. . .

But that was just a daydream, better saved for some dull Museum afternoon. A fresh outbreak of cheering warned him that the chase was nearing its end, and he forgot the airships and turned his attention back to Salthook.

The little town was so close that he could see the ant-like shapes of people running about on its upper tiers. How frightened they must be, with London bearing down on them and nowhere to hide! But he knew he mustn't feel sorry for them: it was natural that cities ate towns, just as the towns ate smaller towns, and smaller towns snapped up the miserable static settlements. That was Municipal Darwinism, and it was the way the world had worked for a thousand years, ever since the great engineer Nikolas Quirke had turned London into the first Traction City. "London! London!" he shouted, adding his voice to the cheers and shouts of everybody else on the platform, and a moment later they were rewarded by the sight of one of Salthook's wheels breaking loose. The town slewed to a halt, smokestacks snapping off and crashing down into the panicked streets, and then London's lower tiers blocked it from view and Tom felt the deck-plates shiver as the city's huge hydraulic Jaws came slamming shut.

There was frantic cheering from observation platforms all over the city. Loudspeakers on the tier-support pillars started to play "London Pride", and somebody Tom had never even seen before hugged him tight and shouted in his ear, "A catch! A catch!" He didn't mind; at that moment he loved everybody on the platform, even Melliphant. "A catch!" he yelled back, struggling free, and felt the deck-plates trembling again. Somewhere below him the city's great steel teeth were gripping Salthook, lifting it and dragging it backwards into the Gut.

". . .and perhaps Apprentice Natsworthy would like to come as well," Clytie Potts was saying. Tom had no idea what she was talking about, but as he turned she touched his arm and smiled. "There'll be celebrations in Kensington Gardens tonight," she explained. "Dancing and fireworks! Do you want to come?"

People didn't usually invite Third Class Apprentices to parties – especially not people as pretty and popular as Clytie – and Tom wondered at first if she were making fun of him. But Melliphant obviously didn't think so, for he tugged her away and said, "We don't want Natsworthy's sort there."

"Why not?" asked the girl.

"Well, you know," huffed Melliphant, his square face turning almost as red as Mr Pomeroy's. "He's just a Third. A skivvy. He'll never get his Guild-mark. He'll just end up as a curator's assistant. Won't you, Natsworthy?" he asked, leering at Tom. "It's a pity your dad didn't leave you enough money for a *proper* apprenticeship. . ."

"That's none of your business!" shouted Tom angrily. His elation at the catch had evaporated and he was on edge again, wondering what punishments would be in store when Pomeroy found out that he had sneaked away. He was in no mood for Melliphant's taunts.

"Still, that's what comes of living in a slum on the lower tiers, I suppose," smirked Melliphant, turning back to Clytie Potts. "Natsworthy's mum and dad lived down on Four, see, and when the Big Tilt happened they both got squashed flat as a couple of raspberry pancakes: *splat!*"

Tom didn't mean to hit him; it just happened. Before

he knew what he was doing his hand had curled into a tight fist and he lashed out. "Ow!" wailed Melliphant, so startled that he fell over backwards. Someone cheered, and Clytie stifled a giggle. Tom just stood staring at his trembling fist and wondering how he had done it.

But Melliphant was much bigger and tougher than Tom, and he was already back on his feet. Clytie tried to restrain him, but some other Historians were cheering him on and a group of boys in the green tunics of Apprentice Navigators clustered close behind and chanted, "Fight! Fight! Fight!"

Tom knew he stood no more chance against Melliphant than Salthook had stood against London. He took a step backwards, but the crowd was hemming him in. Then Melliphant's fist hit him on the side of the face and Melliphant's knee crashed up hard between his legs and he was bent double and stumbling away with his eyes full of tears. Something as big and softly yielding as a sofa stood in his way, and as he rammed his head against it, it said, "Ooof!"

He looked up into a round, red, bushy-eyebrowed face under an unconvincing wig; a face that grew even redder when it recognized him.

"Natsworthy!" boomed Chudleigh Pomeroy. "What in Quirke's name do you think you're playing at?"

2
VALENTINE

And so Tom found himself being sent off to do Gut-duty while all the other apprentices were busy celebrating the capture of Salthook. After a long, embarrassing lecture in Pomeroy's office ("Disobedience, Natsworthy... Striking a senior Apprentice... What would your poor parents have thought?") he trudged over to Tottenham Court Road station and waited for a down elevator.

When it came, it was crowded. The seats in the upper compartment were packed with arrogant-looking men and women from the Guild of Engineers, the most powerful of the four Great Guilds which ran London. They gave Tom the creeps, with their bald heads and those long white rubber coats they wore, so he stayed standing in the lower section, where the stern face of the Lord Mayor stared down at him from posters saying, *Movement is Life – Help the Guild of Engineers keep London moving!* Down and down went the elevator, stopping at all the familiar stations – Bakerloo, High Holborn, Low Holborn, Bethnal Green – and at every stop another crowd of people surged into the car, squashing him against the back wall until it was almost a relief to reach the bottom and step out into the noise and bustle of the Gut.

The Gut was where London dismantled the towns it caught: a stinking sprawl of yards and factories between the Jaws and the central engine-rooms. Tom loathed it. It was always noisy, and it was staffed by workers from the lower tiers, who were dirty and frightening, and convicts from the Deep Gut Prisons, who were worse. The heat down there always gave him a headache and the sulphurous air made him sneeze and the flicker of the argon globes which lit the walkways hurt his eyes. But the Guild of Historians always made sure some of its staff were on hand when a town was being digested, and tonight he would have to join them and go about reminding the tough old foremen of the Gut that any books and antiques aboard the new catch were the rightful property of his Guild and that history was just as important as bricks and iron and coal.

He fought his way out of the elevator terminus and hurried towards the Guild of Historians' warehouse, through tubular corridors lined with green ceramic tiles and across metal catwalks high above the fiery gulfs of the Digestion Yards. Far below him he could see Salthook being torn to pieces. It looked tiny now, dwarfed by the vastness of London. Big yellow dismantling machines were crawling around it on tracks and swinging above it on cranes and clambering over it on hydraulic spider-legs. Its wheels and axles had already been taken off, and work was starting on the chassis. Circular saws as big as Ferris wheels bit into the deckplates, throwing up plumes of sparks. Great blasts of heat came billowing from furnaces and smelters, and before he had gone twenty paces Tom could feel the sweat starting to soak through the armpits of his black uniform tunic.

But when he finally reached the warehouse, things started to look a bit brighter. Salthook had not had a museum or a library, and the small heaps that had been salvaged from the town's junk-shops were already being packed into crates for their journey up to Tier Two. If he was lucky he might be allowed to finish early and catch the end of the celebrations! He wondered which Guildsman was in charge tonight. If it was old Arkengarth or Dr Weymouth he was doomed – they always made you work your whole shift whether there was anything to do or not. If it was Potty Pewtertide or Miss Plym he might be all right. . .

But as he hurried towards the supervisor's office he began to realize that someone much more important than any of them was on Gut-duty tonight. There was a bug parked outside the office, a sleek black bug with the Guild's emblem painted on its engine cowling, much too flash for any of the usual staff. Two men in the livery of high-ranking Guild staff stood waiting beside it. They were rough-looking types, in spite of their plush clothes, and Tom knew at once who they were – Pewsey and Gench, the reformed air-pirates who had been the Head Historian's faithful servants for twenty years and who piloted the *13th Floor Elevator* whenever he flew off on an expedition. *Valentine is here!* Tom thought, and tried not to stare as he hurried past them up the steps.

Thaddeus Valentine was Tom's hero: a former scavenger who had risen to become London's most famous archaeologist – and also its Head Historian, much to the envy and disgust of people like Pomeroy. Tom kept a picture of him tacked to the dormitory wall above his bunk, and he had read his books, *Adventures of a Practical Historian* and *America Deserta – Across the Dead Continent with Gun, Camera and Airship*, until he knew them by heart. The proudest moment of his life had been when he was twelve and Valentine had come down to present the apprentices' end-of-year prizes, including the one Tom had won for an essay on identifying fake antiquities. He still remembered every word of the speech the great man had made. *"Never forget, Apprentices, that we Historians are the most important Guild in our city. We don't make as much money as the Merchants, but we create knowledge, which is worth a great deal more. We may not be responsible for steering London, like the Navigators, but where would the Navigators be if we hadn't preserved the ancient maps and charts? And as for the Guild of Engineers, just remember that every machine they have ever developed is based on some fragment of Old-Tech – ancient high technology that our museum-keepers have preserved or our archaeologists have dug up."*

All Tom had been able to manage by way of reply was a mumbled, "Thank you, sir," before he scurried back to his seat, so it never occurred to him that Valentine would remember him. But when he opened the door of the supervisor's office the great man looked up from his desk and grinned.

"It's Natsworthy, isn't it? The apprentice who's so good at spotting fakes? I'll have to watch my step tonight, or you'll find me out!"

It wasn't much of a joke, but it broke through the awkwardness that usually existed between an apprentice and a senior Guildsman, and Tom relaxed enough to stop hovering on the threshold and step right inside, holding out his note from Pomeroy. Valentine jumped to his feet and came striding over to take it. He was a tall, handsome man of nearly forty with a mane of silver-flecked black hair and a trim black beard. His grey, mariner's eyes twinkled with humour, and on his forehead a third eye – the Guild-mark of the Historian, the blue eye that looks backwards into time – seemed to wink as he raised a quizzical eyebrow.

"Fighting, eh? And what did Apprentice Melliphant do to deserve a black eye?"

"He was saying stuff about my mum and dad, sir," mumbled Tom.

"I see." The explorer nodded, watching the boy's face. Instead of telling him off he asked, "Are you the son of David and Rebecca Natsworthy?"

"Yes sir," admitted Tom. "But I was only six when the Big Tilt happened. . . I mean, I don't really remember them."

Valentine nodded again, and his eyes were sad and kind. "They were good Historians, Thomas. I hope you'll follow in their footsteps."

"Oh, yes, sir!" said Tom. "I mean – I hope so too!" He thought of his poor mum and dad, killed when part of Cheapside collapsed on to the tier below. Nobody had ever spoken like that about them before, and he felt his eyes filling with tears. He felt as if he could tell Valentine anything, anything at all, and he was just on the point of saying how much he missed his parents and how lonely and boring it was being a Third Class Apprentice, when a wolf walked into the office.

It was a very large wolf, and white, and it appeared through the door that led out into the stock-room. As soon as it saw Tom it came running towards him, baring its yellow fangs. "Aaaah!" he shrieked, leaping on to a chair. "A wolf!"

"Oh, do behave!" a girl's voice said, and a moment later the girl herself was there, bending over the beast and tickling the soft white ruff of fur under its chin. The fierce amber eyes closed happily, and Tom heard its tail whisking against her clothes. "Don't worry," she laughed, smiling up at him. "He's a lamb. I mean, he's a wolf really, but he's as *gentle* as a lamb."

"Tom," said Valentine, his eyes twinkling with amusement, "meet my daughter Katherine, and Dog."

"Dog?" Tom came down off his chair, feeling foolish and still a little scared. He had thought the brute must have escaped from the zoo in Circle Park.

"It's a long story," said Valentine. "Katherine lived on the raft-city of Puerto Angeles until she was five. Then her mother died, and she was sent to live with me. I brought Dog back for her as a present from my expedition to the Ice Wastes, but Katherine couldn't speak very much Anglish in those days and she'd never heard of wolves, so when she first saw him she said, 'Dog!', and it sort of stuck."

"He's perfectly tame," the girl promised, still smiling up at Tom. "Father found him when he was just a cub. He had to shoot the mother, but he hadn't the heart to finish poor Dog off. He likes it best if you tickle his tummy. Dog, I mean, not Father." She laughed. She had a lot of long, dark hair, and her father's grey eyes and the same quick, dazzling smile, and she was dressed in the narrow silk trousers and flowing tunic that were all the rage in High London that summer. Tom gazed at her in wonder. He had seen pictures of Valentine's daughter, but he had never realized how beautiful she was.

"Look," she said, "he likes you!"

Dog had ambled over to sniff at the hem of Tom's tunic. His tail swished from side to side and a wet, pink tongue rasped over Tom's fingers.

"If Dog likes people," said Katherine, "I usually find I

like them too. So come along Father; introduce us properly!"

Valentine laughed. "Well, Kate, this is Tom Natsworthy, who has been sent down here to help, and if your wolf has finished with him, I think we will have to let him get to work." He put a kindly hand on Tom's shoulder. "There's not much to be done; we'll just take a last look around the Yards and then. . ." He glanced at the note from Pomeroy, then tore it up into little pieces and dropped them into the red recycling bin beside his desk. "Then you can go."

Tom was not sure what surprised him more – that Valentine was letting him off, or that he was coming down to the yards in person. Senior Guildsmen usually preferred to sit in the comfort of the office and let the apprentices do the hard work down in the heat and fumes, but here was Valentine pulling off his black robes, clipping a pen into the pocket of his waistcoat, pausing to grin at Tom from the doorway.

"Come along then," he said. "The sooner we start, the sooner you can be off to join the fun in Kensington Gardens. . ."

Down they went and down, with Dog and Katherine following, down past the warehouse and on down twisting spirals of metal stairs to the Digestion Yards, where Salthook was growing smaller by the minute. All that remained of it now was a steel skeleton, and the machines were ripping even that apart, dragging deckplates and girders away to the furnaces to be melted down. Meanwhile, mountains of brick and slate and timber and salt and coal were trundling off on conveyor belts towards the heart of the Gut, and skips of furniture and provisions were being wheeled clear by the salvage gangs.

The salvagemen were the true rulers of this part of London, and they knew it. They swaggered along the narrow walkways with the agility of tomcats, their bare chests shiny with sweat and their eyes hidden by tinted goggles. Tom had always been frightened of them, but Valentine hailed them with an easy charm and asked them if they had seen anything amongst the spoils that might be of interest to the Museum. Sometimes he stopped to joke with them, or ask them how their families were doing – and he was always careful to introduce them to, "My colleague, Mr Natsworthy." Tom felt himself swell with pride. Valentine was treating him like a grown-up, and so the salvagemen treated him the same way, touching the peaks of their greasy caps and grinning as they introduced themselves. They all seemed to be called Len, or Smudger.

"Take no notice of what they say about these chaps up at the Museum," warned Valentine, as one of the Lens led them to a skip where some antiques had been stowed. "Just because they live down in the nether boroughs and don't pronounce their 'H's doesn't mean they're fools. That's why I like to come down in person when the Yards are working. I've often seen salvagemen and scavengers turn up artefacts that Historians might have missed. . ."

"Yes sir. . ." agreed Tom, glancing at Katherine. He longed to do something that would impress the Head Historian and his beautiful daughter. If only he could find some wonderful fragment of Old-Tech amongst all this junk, something that would make them remember him after they had gone back to the luxury of High London. Otherwise, after this wander around the yards, he might never see them again!

Hoping to amaze them, he hurried to the skip and looked inside. After all, Old-Tech *did* turn up from time to time in small-town antique shops, or on old ladies' mantelpieces. Imagine being the one to rediscover some legendary secret, like heavier-than-air flying machines, or pot noodles! Even if it wasn't something that the Guild of Engineers could use it might still end up in the Museum, labelled and preserved in a display case with a notice saying, *"Discovered by Mr T. Natsworthy"*. He peered hopefully at the heap of salvage in the skip: shards of plastic, lamp stands, a flattened toy ground-car... A small metal box caught his eye. When he pulled it out and opened it his own face blinked back at him, reflected in a silvery plastic disc. "Mr Valentine! Look! A seedy!"

Valentine reached into the box and lifted out the disc, tilting it so that rainbow light darted across its surface. "Quite right," he said. "The Ancients used these in their computers, as a way of storing information."

"Could it be important?" asked Tom.

Valentine shook his head. "I'm sorry, Thomas. The people of the old days may only have lived in static settlements, but their electronic machines were far beyond anything London's Engineers have been able to build. Even if there is still something stored on this disc we have no way of reading it. But it's a good find. Keep hold of it, just in case."

He turned away as Tom put the seedy back in its box and slid it into his pocket. But Katherine must have sensed Tom's disappointment, because she touched his hand and said, "It's lovely, Tom. Anything that has survived all those thousands of years is lovely, whether it's any use to the horrible old Guild of Engineers or not. I've got a necklace made of old computer discs. . ." She smiled at him. She was as lovely as one of the girls in his daydreams, but kinder and funnier, and he knew that from now on the heroines he rescued in his imagination would all be Katherine Valentine.

There was nothing else of interest in the skip; Salthook had been a practical sort of town, too busy gnawing at the old sea-bed to bother about digging up the past. But instead of going straight back to the warehouse Valentine led his companions up another staircase and along a narrow catwalk to the Incomers' Station, where the former inhabitants were queuing to give their names to the Clerk of Admissions and be taken up to new homes in the hostels and workhouses of London. "Even when I'm not on duty," he explained, "I always make a point of going down to see the scavengers when we make a catch, before they have a chance to sell their finds at the Tier Five antique markets and melt back into the Out-Country."

There were always some scavengers aboard a catch – townless wanderers who roamed the Hunting Ground on foot, scratching up pieces of Old-Tech. Salthook was no exception; at the end of a long queue of dejected townsfolk stood a group more ragged than the rest, with long, tattered coats that hung down to their ankles and goggles and dust-masks slung about their grubby necks.

Like most Londoners, Tom was horrified by the idea that people still actually *lived* on the bare earth. He hung back with Katherine and Dog, but Valentine went over to speak with the scavengers. They came clustering

22

round him, all except one, a tall, thin one in a black coat – a girl, Tom thought, although he could not be sure because she wore a black scarf wrapped across her face like the turban of a desert nomad. He stood near her and watched while Valentine introduced himself to the other scavengers and asked, "So – have any of you found anything the Historians' Guild might wish to purchase?"

Some of the men nodded, some shook their heads, some rummaged in their bulging packs. The girl in the black head-scarf slid one hand inside her coat and said, "I have something for you, Valentine."

She spoke so softly that only Tom and Katherine heard her, and as they turned to look she suddenly sprang forward, whipping out a long, thin-bladed knife.

3
THE WASTE CHUTE

There was no time to think: Katherine screamed, Dog growled, the girl hesitated for a moment and Tom saw his chance and threw himself forward, grabbing her arm as she drove the knife at Valentine's heart. She hissed, writhing, and the knife dropped to the deck as she twisted free and darted away along the catwalk. "Stop her!" bellowed Valentine, starting forward, but the other refugees had seen the knife and were milling about in fright, barring his way. Several of the scavengers had pulled out firearms and an armoured policeman came lumbering through the crowd like a huge blue beetle, shouting, "No guns allowed in London!"

Glancing over the scavengers' heads, Tom glimpsed a dark silhouette against the distant glare of furnaces. The girl was at the far end of the catwalk, climbing nimbly up a ladder to a higher level. He ran after her and snatched at her ankle as she reached the top. He missed by a few inches, and at the same moment a dart hissed past him, striking sparks from the rungs. He looked back. Two more policemen were thrusting through the crowd with crossbows raised. Beyond them he could see Katherine and her father watching him. "Don't shoot!" he shouted. "I can catch her!"

He flung himself at the ladder and scrambled eagerly upwards, determined to be the one to capture the would-be assassin. He could feel his heart pounding with excitement. After all those dull years spent dreaming of adventures, suddenly he was having one! He had saved Mr Valentine's life! He was a hero!

The girl was already heading along the maze of high-level catwalks which led towards the furnace district. Hoping that Katherine could still see him, Tom set off in pursuit. The catwalk forked and narrowed, the handrails only a yard apart. Below him the work of the Digestion Yards went on regardless; no one down there had noticed the drama being played out above their heads. He plunged through deep shadows and warm, blinding clouds of steam with the girl always a few feet ahead. A low duct caught her head-scarf and ripped it off. Her long hair was coppery in the dim glow of the furnaces, but Tom still couldn't see her face. He wondered if she was pretty; a beautiful assassin from the Anti-Traction League.

He ducked past the dangling head-scarf and ran on, gasping for breath, fumbling his collar open. Down a giddy spiral of iron stairs and out on to the floor of the Digestion Yards, flashing through the shadows of conveyor belts and huge spherical gas-tanks. A gang of convict labourers looked up in amazement as the girl raced by. "Stop her!" yelled Tom. They just stood gawping as he passed, but when he looked back he saw that one of the Apprentice Engineers who had been supervising them had broken off his work to join the chase. Tom immediately regretted shouting out. He wasn't going to give up his victory to some stupid Engineer! He put on an extra spurt of speed, so that he should be the one who caught her.

Ahead, the way was barred by a circular hole in the deckplate, ringed by rusty handrails – a waste chute, scorched and blackened where clinker from the furnaces had been tipped down. The girl broke her pace for a moment, wondering which way to turn. When she went on, Tom had narrowed her lead. His outstretched fingers grabbed her pack; the strap broke and she stopped and spun to face him, lit by the red glare of the smelters.

She was no older than Tom, and she was hideous. A terrible scar ran down her face from forehead to jaw, making it look like a portrait that had been furiously crossed out. Her mouth was wrenched sideways in a permanent sneer, her nose was a smashed stump and her single eye stared at him out of the wreckage, as grey and chill as a winter sea.

"Why didn't you let me kill him?" she hissed.

He was so shocked that he couldn't move or speak, could only stand there as the girl reached down for her fallen pack and turned to run on. But behind him police whistles were blowing, and crossbow darts came sparking against the metal deck-plates and the overhead ducts. The girl dropped the pack and fell sideways, gasping a filthy curse. Tom hadn't even imagined that girls *knew* such words. "Don't shoot!" he yelled, waving towards the policemen. They were lumbering down the spiral stair beyond the gas-tanks, shooting as they came, as if they didn't much care that Tom was in the way. "Don't shoot!"

The girl scrambled up, and he saw that a crossbow-dart had gone through her leg just above the knee. She clutched at it, blood welling out between her fingers. Her breath came in sobs as she backed up against the handrail, lifting herself awkwardly over it. Behind her, the waste-chute gaped like an open mouth.

"NO!" shouted Tom, seeing what she meant to do. He didn't feel like a hero any more – he just felt sorry for this poor, hideous girl, and guilty at being the one who had trapped her here. He held out his hand to her, willing her not to jump. "I couldn't let you hurt Mr Valentine!" he said, shouting to make her hear him above the din of the Gut. "He's a good man, a kind, brave, wonderful. . ."

The girl lunged forward, shoving her awful noseless face towards him. "Look at me!" she said, her voice all twisted by her twisted mouth. "Look what your brave, kind Valentine did to me!"

"What do you mean?"

"Ask him!" she screamed. "Ask him what he did to Hester Shaw!"

The police were closer now; Tom could feel their footsteps drumming on the deck. The girl glanced past him, then heaved her wounded leg over the handrail, crying out at the pain. "No!" pleaded Tom again, but too late. Her ragged greatcoat snapped and fluttered and she was gone. He flung himself forward and peered down the shadowed chute. A cool blast of air came up at him, mingled with the smell of mud and crushed vegetation; the smell of the speeding earth beneath the city.

"No!"

She had jumped! She had jumped right out of the city to her death! *Hester Shaw.* He would have to remember that name, and say a prayer for her to one of London's many gods.

Shapes loomed out of the drifting smoke. The policemen were advancing cautiously, like watchful crabs, and Valentine was with them, running ahead. In the shadows under a gas-tank Tom saw the young Engineer looking on, shocked. Tom tried to smile at him, but his face felt frozen, and the next moment another thick swag of smoke had folded over him, blotting out everything.

"Tom! Are you all right?" Valentine ran up, barely

winded by the long chase. "Where is she? Where is the girl?"

"Dead," Tom said lamely.

Valentine stood beside him at the handrail and peered over. The shadows of the drifting smoke moved over his face like cobwebs. There was a strange light in his eyes, and his face was tight and white and frightened. "Did you see her, Tom? Did she have a scar?"

"Yes," said Tom, wondering how Valentine could know that. "It was horrible! Her eye was gone, and her nose. . ." Then he remembered the terrible thing the girl had told him. "And she said. . ." But he wasn't sure if he should tell Mr Valentine what she had said – it was a lie, insane. "She said her name was Hester Shaw."

"Great Quirke!" hissed Valentine, and Tom flinched backwards, wishing he had never mentioned it. But when he looked up again Valentine was smiling kindly at him, his eyes full of sorrow. "Don't worry, Tom," he said. "I'm sorry. . ."

Tom felt a big, gentle hand on his shoulder and then – he was never sure quite how it happened – a twist, a shove, and he was pitching over the handrail and falling, just as Hester Shaw had fallen, flailing wildly for a hold on the smooth metal at the brim of the waste chute. *He pushed me!* he thought, and it was more amazement that he felt than fear as the black throat swallowed him down into the dark.

4
THE OUT-COUNTRY

Silence. Silence. He couldn't understand it. Even when London wasn't moving there was usually some sort of noise in the dormitory; the whirr of ventilators, the hum and rattle of distant elevator shafts, the snores of other apprentices in the neighbouring bunks. But now – silence. His head ached. In fact, *all* of him ached. His bunk felt strange, too, and when he moved his hands there was something cold and slimy that oozed between his fingers like. . .

MUD! He sat up, gasping. He wasn't in the Third Class dormitory at all. He was lying on a great humpbacked mound of mud, on the edge of a deep trench, and in the thin, pearl-grey light of dawn he could see the girl with the ruined face sitting nearby. His horrible dream of sliding down that fire-blackened chute had been true: he had fallen out of London, and he was alone with Hester Shaw on the bare earth!

He moaned in terror, and the girl glanced quickly round at him and then away. "You're alive, then," she said. "I thought you'd died." She sounded as if she didn't much care either way.

Tom scrambled up on to all fours, so that only his knees and his toes and the palms of his hands were touching the mud. His arms were bare, and when he looked down he saw that his bruised body was naked to the waist. His tunic lay on the mud nearby, but he couldn't find his shirt at all, until he crawled closer to the scarred girl and realized that she was busily tearing it into strips which she was using to bandage her wounded leg.

"Hey!" he said. "That's one of my best shirts!"

"So?" she replied without looking up. "It's one of my best legs."

He pulled his tunic on. It was tattered and filthy from his fall down the waste-chute, full of rents that let the chill Out-Country air through. He hugged himself, shivering. *Valentine pushed me! He pushed me and I fell down the shaft into the Out-Country! He pushed me. . . No, he can't have done. It must have been a mistake. I slipped, and he tried to grab me, that's what must have happened.*

Hester Shaw finished her bandaging and stood up, grunting at the pain as she pulled her filthy, blood-stiffened breeches on over the wound. Then she threw what was left of Tom's shirt back at him, a useless rag. "You should have let me kill him," she said, and turned away, setting off with a kind of furious limp up the long curve of the mud.

Tom watched her go, too shocked and bewildered to move. It was only when she vanished over the top of the slope that he realized he didn't want to be left alone here; he would prefer any company, even hers, to the silence.

He flung the torn shirt away and ran after her, slithering in the thick, clagging mud, stubbing his toes on fragments of rock and torn-up roots. The deep, sheer-walled trench yawned on his left, and as he reached the crest of the rise he realized that it was just one of a hundred identical trenches; the huge track-marks of London stretching ruler-straight into the distance. Far, far ahead he saw his city, dark against the brightening eastern sky, wrapped in the smoke of its own engines. He felt the cold tug of homesickness. Everyone he had ever known was aboard that dwindling mountain, everyone except

Hester, who was stomping angrily after it, dragging her injured leg behind her.

"Stop!" he shouted, half-running, half-wading to catch her up. "Hester! Miss Shaw!"

"Leave me alone!" she snapped.

"But where are you going?"

"I've got to get back into London, haven't I?' she said. "Two years it took me to find it, trudging across the Out-Country on foot, jumping aboard little townlets in the hope it would be London that scoffed them. And when I finally get there and find Valentine, come down to strut round the yards just like the scavengers told me he would, what happens? Some idiot stops me from cutting his heart out like he deserves." She stopped walking and turned to face Tom. "If you hadn't shoved your oar in he'd be dead, and I'd have fallen down and died beside him and I'd be at peace by now!"

Tom stared at her, and before he could stop himself his eyes filled with stinging tears. He hated himself for looking like a fool in front of Hester Shaw, but he couldn't help it; the shock of what had happened to him and the thought of being abandoned out here over-whelmed him, and the hot tears flooded down his face and cut white runnels through the mud on his cheeks.

Hester, who had been on the point of turning away, stopped and watched, as if she wasn't sure what was happening to him. "You're crying!" she said at last, quite gently, sounding surprised.

"Sorry," he sniffed.

"I never cry. I can't. I didn't even cry when Valentine murdered my mum and dad."

"What?" Tom's voice was all wobbly from weeping. "Mr Valentine would never do something like that!

Katherine said he couldn't even bring himself to shoot a wolf cub. You're lying!"

"How come you're here, then?" she asked, mocking him. "He shoved you out after me, didn't he? Just because you'd seen me."

"You're lying!" said Tom again. But he remembered those big hands thrusting him forward; remembered falling, and the strange light that had shone in the archaeologist's eyes.

"Well?" asked Hester.

"He pushed me!" murmured Tom, amazed.

Hester Shaw just shrugged, as if to say, *See? See what he's really like?* Then she turned away and started walking again.

Tom hurried along at her side. "I'll come with you! I've got to get back to London, too! I'll help you!"

"You?" She gave a hissing laugh and spat on the mud at his feet. "I thought you were Valentine's man. Now you want to help me kill him?"

Tom shook his head. He didn't know what he wanted. Part of him still clung to the hope that it was all a misunderstanding and Valentine was good and kind and brave. He certainly didn't want to see him murdered and poor Katherine left without a father. . . But he *had* to catch up with London somehow, and he couldn't do it alone. And anyway, he felt responsible for Hester Shaw. It was his fault that she had been wounded, after all. "I'll help you walk," he said. "You're injured. You need me."

"I don't need anybody," she said fiercely.

"We'll go after London together," Tom promised. "I'm a member of the Guild of Historians. They'll listen to me. I'll tell Mr Pomeroy. If Valentine really did the things you said then the law will deal with him!"

"The *law*?" she scoffed. "Valentine is the law in London. Isn't he the Lord Mayor's favourite? Isn't he the Head Historian? No, he'll kill me unless I kill him first. Kill you too, probably. *Ssshinnng!*" She mimed drawing a sword and driving it through Tom's chest.

The sun was rising, lifting wreaths of steam from the wet mud. London was still moving, visibly smaller since the last time he looked. The city usually stopped for a few days when it had eaten, and some part of Tom's brain that was not quite numb wondered idly, *Where on earth is it going?*

But just then the girl stumbled and fell, her bad leg crumpling under her. Tom scrambled to help her up. She didn't thank him, but she didn't push him away either. He pulled her arm around his shoulders and hauled her up, and they set off together along the mud ridge, following London's tracks into the east.

5
THE LORD MAYOR

A hundred miles ahead the sunrise shone on Circle Park, the elegant loop of lawns and flower-beds that encircled Tier One. It gleamed in ornamental lakes and on pathways glistening with dew, and it glittered on the white metal spires of Clio House, Valentine's villa, which stood among dark cedars at the park's edge like some gigantic conch shell abandoned by a freak high tide.

In her bedroom on the top floor Katherine awoke and lay watching the sunbeams filter through the tortoise-shell shutters on her window. She knew she was unhappy, but at first she did not know why.

Then she remembered the previous evening; the attack in the Gut and how that poor, sweet, young apprentice had chased after the assassin and got himself killed. She had gone running after Father, but by the time she reached the waste-chute it was all over; a young Apprentice Engineer was stumbling away, his shocked face as white as his rubber coat, and beyond him she found Father, looking pale and angry, surrounded by policemen. She had never seen him look like that before, nor heard the harsh, unnatural voice in which he snapped at her to go straight home.

Part of her just wanted to curl up and go back to sleep, but she had to see him and make sure he was all right. She flung back the quilt and got up, pulling on the clothes from last night that lay all crumpled on the floor, still smelling of furnaces.

Outside her bedroom door a hallway sloped gently downward, round-roofed, curling about on itself like the inside of an ammonite. She hurried down it, pausing to pay her respects before the statue of Clio, goddess of History, who stood in a niche outside the door to the dining room. In other niches lay treasures that her father had brought back from his expeditions; potsherds, fragments of computer keyboards and the rusting metal skulls of Stalkers, those strange, half-mechanical soldiers from a forgotten war. Their cracked glass eyes stared balefully at Katherine as she hurried by.

Father was drinking coffee in the atrium, the big open space at the centre of the house. He was still in his dressing-gown, his long face serious as he paced up and down between the potted ferns. A glance at his eyes was enough to tell Katherine that he had not slept at all. "Father?" she asked. "What's happened?"

"Oh, Kate!" He came and hugged her tight. "What a night!"

"That poor boy," Katherine whispered. "Poor Tom! I suppose they didn't . . . *find* anything?"

Valentine shook his head. "The assassin dragged him with her when she jumped. They were both drowned in the mud of the Out-Country, or crushed beneath the tracks."

"Oh," whispered Katherine, and sat down on the edge of a table, not even noticing Dog when he came padding in to rest his great head on her knee. *Poor Tom!* she thought. He had been so sweet, so eager to please. She had really liked him. She had even thought of asking Father about bringing him up to work at Clio House so she and Dog could get to know him better. And now he was dead, his soul fled down to the Sunless Country and his body lying cold in the cold mud, somewhere in the city's wake.

"The Lord Mayor isn't happy," said Valentine, glancing at the clock. "An assassin loose in the Gut on London's first day back in the Hunting Ground. He is coming down here in person to discuss it. Will you sit with me while I wait for him? You can have some of my breakfast if you like. There is coffee on the table – rolls – butter. I have no appetite at all."

Katherine had no appetite either, but she glanced at the food, and noticed a battered leather pack lying on the far side of the table. It was the pack the girl assassin had dropped in the Gut last night, and its contents were spread out around it like exhibits in a strange museum: a metal water-bottle, a first-aid kit, some string, a few strips of dried meat that looked tougher than the tongues of old boots and a stained and crumpled sheet of paper with a photograph stapled to it. Katherine picked it up. It was an identity form, issued in a town called "Strole", filthy and faded and coming apart along the creases. Before she could study the writing her eye was drawn to the photograph. She gasped. "Father! Her face!"

Valentine turned, saw her holding the paper and snatched it from her hand with an angry cry. "No, Kate! That is not for your eyes! It is not for anybody's eyes. . ."

He pulled out his lighter and carefully lit a corner of the form, folding it into the ashtray on his desk as it burned. Then he went back to his pacing, and Katherine sat and watched him. In the ten years since she arrived in London Katherine had come to think of him as her best friend as well as her father. They liked the same things, and laughed at the same jokes, and never kept secrets from each other – but she could see that he was keeping something from her about this girl. She had never seen him so worried by anything. "Who is she, Father?" she asked. "Do you know her from one of your expeditions? She is so young, and so. . . Whatever happened to her *face*?"

There were footsteps, a knock at the door, and Pewsey burst into the room. "Lord Mayor's on his way, Chief."

"Already?" gasped Valentine.

"'Fraid so. Gench just saw him coming across the park in his bug. Said he didn't look pleased."

Valentine didn't look pleased either. He grabbed his robes from the chair-back where they had been flung and started trying to make himself presentable. Katherine stepped forward to help, but he waved her away, so she kissed him quickly on the cheek and hurried out with Dog trotting behind her. Through the big oval windows of the drawing room she could see a white official bug pulling in through the gates of Clio House. A squad of soldiers ran ahead of it, dressed in the bright red armour of the Beefeaters, the Lord Mayor's personal bodyguard. They took up positions around the garden like ugly lawn ornaments as Gench and one of the other servants hurried forward to open the bug's glastic lid. The Lord Mayor stepped out and came striding towards the house.

Magnus Crome had been ruler of London for nearly twenty years, but he still didn't *look* like a Lord Mayor. The Lord Mayors in Katherine's history books were chubby, merry, red-faced men, but Crome was as thin as an old crow, and twice as gloomy. He didn't even wear the scarlet robes that had been the pride and joy of other mayors, but still dressed in his long white rubber coat and wore the red wheel of the Guild of Engineers upon his brow. Those earlier Lord Mayors had had their Guild-marks removed to show that they were serving the whole of London, but things had changed when Crome seized power – and even if some people said it was unfair for one man to be master of the Engineers *and* Lord Mayor, they still admitted that Crome made a good job of running the city.

Katherine didn't like him. She had never liked him, even though he had been so good to her father, and she was not in any mood to meet him this morning. As soon as she heard the front door iris open she hurried back into the corridor and started up it, calling softly for Dog to follow her. She stopped as soon as she was around the first bend, hidden in a shallow alcove, resting the tips of her fingers on the wolf's head to keep him still. She could tell that some terrible trouble had overtaken her father, and she was not going to let him keep the truth from her as if she was still a little girl.

A few seconds later she saw Gench arrive at the door to the atrium, clutching his hat in his hands. "This way, yer worshipful honour," he mumbled, bowing. "Mind yer step, yer Mayorness."

Close behind came Crome. He paused for a moment, his head flicking from side to side in an oddly reptilian way, and Katherine felt his gaze sweep the corridor like a wind from the Ice Wastes. She squeezed herself tighter into the alcove and prayed to Quirke and Clio that he would not see her. For a moment she could hear his breathing and the faint squeaks and creakings of his rubber coat. Then Gench led him into the atrium, and the danger was past.

With one hand firmly on Dog's collar she crept back to the door and listened. She could hear Father's voice and imagined him standing beside the ornamental fountain while his men showed Crome to a seat. He started to make some polite comment about the weather, but the cold, thin voice of the Lord Mayor interrupted him. "I have been reading your report of last night's escapade, Valentine. You assured me that the whole family had been dealt with."

Katherine flinched away from the door as though it had burned her. How dare the old man talk to Father like that! She did not want to hear any more, but curiosity got the better of her and she set her ear against the wood again.

". . .a ghost from my past," Father was saying. "I can't imagine how she escaped. And Quirke alone knows where she learned to be so agile and cunning. But she is dead now. So is the boy who caught her, poor Natsworthy. . ."

"You are sure of that?"

"They fell out of the city, Crome."

"That means nothing. We are travelling over soft ground; they may have survived. You should have sent men down to check. Remember, we don't know how much the girl knew of her mother's work. If she were to tell another city that we have MEDUSA, before we are ready to use it. . ."

"I know, I know," said Valentine irritably, and Katherine heard a chair creak as he flung himself down in it. "I'll take the *13th Floor Elevator* back and see if I can find the bodies. . ."

"No," ordered Crome. "I have other plans for you and your airship. I want you to fly ahead and see what lies between London and its goal."

"Crome, that is a job for a Planning Committee scout-ship, not the *Elevator*. . ."

"No," snapped Crome again. "I don't want too many

people to know where we are taking the city. They will find out when the time is ripe. Besides, I have a task in mind that only you can be trusted with."

"And the girl?" asked Valentine.

"Don't worry about her," said the Lord Mayor. "I have an agent who can be relied on to track her down and finish the job you failed to do. Concentrate on preparing your airship, Valentine."

The meeting was at an end. Katherine heard the Lord Mayor getting ready to leave, and hurried away up the corridor before the door opened, her mind whirling faster than one of the tumble-dryers in the London Museum's Hall of Ancient Technology.

Back in her room she sat down to wonder about the things she had heard. She had hoped to solve a mystery, but instead it had grown deeper. All she was sure of was that Father had a secret. He had never kept anything from her before. He always told her everything, and asked her opinion, and wanted her advice, but now he was whispering with the Lord Mayor about the girl being *a ghost from his past* and some agent being sent back to look for her and do . . . what? Could Tom and the assassin really still be alive? And why was the Lord Mayor packing Father off on a reconnaissance flight amid such secrecy? And why didn't he want to say where London was going? And what, what on earth was *MEDUSA*?

6
SPEEDWELL

All that day they struggled onwards, trudging along in the scar that London had clawed through the soft earth of the Hunting Ground. The city was never out of their sight, but it grew smaller and smaller, more and more distant, pulling away from them towards the east, and Tom realized that it might soon be lost for ever beyond the horizon. Loneliness wrenched at him. He had never much enjoyed his life as an Apprentice Historian (Third Class), but now his years in the Museum felt like a beautiful, golden dream. He found himself missing fussy old Dr Arkengarth and pompous Chudleigh Pomeroy. He missed his bunk in the draughty dormitory and the long hours of work, and he missed Katherine Valentine, although he had known her for only a few minutes. Sometimes, if he closed his eyes, he could see her face quite clearly, her kind grey eyes and her lovely smile. He was sure that she didn't know what sort of man her father was. . .

"Watch where you're going!" snapped Hester Shaw, and he opened his eyes and realized that he had almost led her over the brink of one of the gaping track-marks.

On they went, and on, and Tom started to think that what he missed most about his city was the food. It had never been up to much, the stuff they served in the Guild canteen, but it was better than nothing, and nothing was what he had now. When he asked Hester Shaw what they were supposed to live on out here she just said, "I bet you wish you hadn't lost my pack for me now, London boy. I had some good dried dog meat in my pack."

In the early afternoon they came across a few dull, greyish bushes that London's tracks had not quite buried, and Hester tore some leaves off and mashed them to a pulp between two stones. "They'd be better cooked," she said, as they ate the horrid vegetable goo. "I had the makings of a fire in my pack."

Later, she caught a frog in one of the deep pools that were already forming in the chevroned track-prints. She didn't offer Tom any, and he tried not to watch while she ate it.

He still did not know what to make of her. She was silent mostly, and glared so fiercely at him when he tried to talk to her that he quickly learned to walk in silence too. But sometimes, quite suddenly, she would start talking. "The land's rising," she might say. "That means London'll go slower. It would waste fuel, going full speed on an uphill stretch." Then, an hour or two later, "My mum used to say Traction Cities are stupid. She said there was a reason for them a thousand years ago when there were all those earthquakes and volcanoes and the glaciers pushing south. Now they just keep rolling around and eating each other 'cos people are too stupid to stop them."

Tom liked it when she talked, even though he did think that her mum sounded like a dangerous Anti-Tractionist. But when he tried to keep the conversation going she would go quiet again, and her hand would go up to hide her face. It was as if there were two Hesters sharing the same thin body; one a grim avenger who thought only of killing Valentine, the other a quick, clever, likeable girl whom he sometimes sensed peeking out at him from behind that scarred mask. He wondered if she was slightly mad. It would be enough to send anyone mad, seeing your parents murdered.

"How did it happen?" he asked her gently. "I mean, your mum and dad, are you sure it was Valentine who—?"

"Shut up and walk," she said.

But long after dark, as they huddled in a hollow of the mud to escape the chill night wind, she suddenly started telling him her story.

"I was born on the bare earth," she said, "but it wasn't like this. I lived on Oak Island, in the far west. It used to be a part of the Hunting Ground once, but the earthquakes drowned all the land around and made an island of it, too far off-shore for any hungry city to attack, and too rocky for the amphibious towns to get at. It was lovely; green hills and great outcrops of stone and the streams running through tangly oak woods, all grey with lichen – the trees shaggy with it, like old dogs."

Tom shuddered. Every Londoner knew that only savages lived on the bare earth. "I prefer a nice firm deckplate under me," he said, but Hester didn't seem to hear him; the words kept spilling out of her twisted mouth as if she had no choice in the matter.

"There was a town there called Dunroamin'. It was mobile once, but the people got sick of running all the time from bigger towns, so they floated it across to Oak Island and took its wheels and engines off and dug it into a hillside. It's been sitting there a hundred years or more, and you'd never know it used to move at all."

"But that's awful!" Tom gasped. "It's downright Anti-Tractionist!"

"My mum and dad lived down the road a way," she went on, talking straight over him. "They had a house on the edge of the moor, where the sea comes in. Dad was a farmer, and Mum was a historian like you – only a lot cleverer than you, of course. She flew off each summer in her airship, digging for Old-Tech, but in the autumn she'd come home. I used to go up to her study in the attic on winter's nights and eat cheese on toast and she'd tell me about her adventures.

"And then one night, seven years ago, I woke up late and there were voices up in the attic arguing. So I went up the ladder and looked, and Valentine was there. I knew him, because he was Mum's friend and used to drop in on us when he was passing. Only he wasn't being very friendly that night. 'Give me the machine, Pandora,' he kept saying. 'Give me MEDUSA.' He didn't see me watching him. I was at the top of the ladder, looking into the attic, too scared to go up and too scared to go back. Valentine had his back to me and Mum was stood facing him, holding this machine, and she said, 'Damn you, Thaddeus, I found it, it's *mine*!'

"And then Valentine drew his sword and he . . . and he. . ."

She paused for breath. She wanted to stop, but she was riding a wave of memory and it was carrying her backwards to that night, that room, and the blood that had spattered her mother's star-charts like the map of a new constellation.

"And then he turned round and saw me watching, and he came at me and I dived back so his sword only cut my face, and I fell back down the ladder. He must have thought he'd killed me. I heard him go to Mum's desk and start rustling through the papers there, and I got up and ran. Dad was lying on the kitchen floor; he was dead too. Even the dogs were dead.

"I ran out of the house and saw Valentine's great black

ship moored at the end of the garden with his men waiting. They came after me, but I escaped. I ran down to the boathouse and shoved off in Dad's skiff. I think I meant to go round to Dunroamin' and get help – I was only little, and I thought a doctor could help Mum and Dad. But I was so weak with the pain and all the blood. . . I untied the boat somehow, and the current swept it out, and the next thing I knew I was waking up on the shores of the Hunting Ground.

"I lived in the Out-Country after that. At first I didn't remember much. It was as if when he cut my head open some of my memories spilled out, and the rest got muddled about. But slowly I started remembering, and one day I remembered Valentine and what he'd done. That's when I decided to come and find him. Kill him the same way he killed my mum and dad."

"What was this machine?" asked Tom, in the long silence. "This MEDUSA thing?"

Hester shrugged. (It was too dark to see her by this time, but he *heard* her shrug, the hunch of her shoulders inside her filthy coat.) "Something my mum found. Old-Tech. It didn't look important. Like a metal football, all bashed and dented. But that's what he killed her for."

"Seven years ago," whispered Tom. "That's when Mr Valentine got made head of the Guild. They said he'd found something in the Out-Country and Crome was so pleased that he promoted him, straight over the heads of Chudleigh Pomeroy and all the rest. But I never heard what it was he'd found. And I never heard of a MEDUSA before."

Hester said nothing at all. After a few minutes she began to snore.

Tom sat awake for a long time, turning her story over

and over in his mind. He thought of the daydreams that had kept him going through long, tedious days in the Museum. He had dreamed of being trapped in the Out-Country with a beautiful girl, on the trail of some murderous criminal, but he had never imagined it would be so wet and cold, or that his legs would ache so, or that the murderer would be London's greatest hero. And as for the beautiful girl. . .

He looked at the blunt wreck of Hester Shaw's face in the faint moonlight, scowling even in her sleep. He understood her better now. She hated Valentine, but she hated herself even more, for being so ugly, and for being still alive when her parents were dead. He remembered how he had felt when the Big Tilt happened, and he came home and found his house flattened and Mum and Dad gone. He had thought that it was all his fault somehow. He had felt full of guilt, because he had not been there to die with them.

"I must help her," he thought. "I won't let her kill Mr Valentine, but I'll find a way to get the truth out. If it *is* the truth. Maybe tomorrow London will have slowed down a bit and Hester's leg will be better. We'll be back in the city by sundown, and *somebody* will listen to us. . ."

But next morning they woke to find that the city was even further ahead, and Hester's leg was worse. She moaned with pain at almost every step now; her face was the colour of old snow and fresh blood was soaking through her bandages and running down into her boot. Tom cursed himself for throwing those rags of shirt away, and for making Hester lose her pack, and her first-aid kit. . .

In the middle of the morning, through shifting veils of rain, they saw something ahead of them. A pile of slag and clinker lay spilled across the track-marks, where London had vented it the day before. Drawn up beside it was a strange little town, and as they got closer Hester and Tom could see that people were scrambling up and down the spoil-heap, sifting out collops of melted metal and fragments of unburnt fuel.

The sight gave them hope and they pressed forward faster. By early afternoon they were walking under the shadow of the townlet's huge wheels, and Tom was staring up in amazement at its single tier. It was smaller than a lot of the houses in London, and it appeared to have been built out of wood by somebody whose idea of good carpentry was to bang a couple of nails in and hope for the best. Behind the shed-like town hall rose the huge, crooked chimneys of an experimental engine array.

"Welcome!" shouted a tall, white-bearded man, picking his way down the clinker-heap, grubby brown robes flapping. "Welcome to Speedwell. I am Orme Wreyland, Mayor. Do you speak Anglish?"

Hester hung back suspiciously, but Tom thought the old man looked friendly enough. He stepped forward and said, "Please, sir, we need some food, and a doctor to look at my friend's leg. . ."

"I'm not your friend," hissed Hester Shaw. "And there's nothing wrong with my leg." But she was white and trembling and her face shone with sweat.

"No doctor in Speedwell anyway," laughed Wreyland. "Not one. And as for food. . . Well, times are hard. Do you have anything you can trade?"

Tom patted the pockets of his tunic. He had a little money, but he didn't see what use London money would be to Orme Wreyland. Then he touched something hard. It was the seedy he had found in the Gut. He pulled it out and looked wistfully at it for a moment before he handed it to the old man. He had been planning to make a present of it to Katherine Valentine one day, but now food was more important.

"Pretty! Very pretty!" admitted Orme Wreyland, tilting the disc and admiring the rippling rainbows. "Not a lot of use, but worth a few nights' shelter and a bit of food. It's not very good food, mind, but it's better than nothing. . ."

○ ○ ○ ○ ○

He was right: it *wasn't* very good, but Tom and Hester ate greedily anyway and then held out their bowls for more.

"It's made from algae, mostly," explained Orme Wreyland, as his wife slopped out second helpings of the bluish muck. "We grow it in vats down under the main engine room. Nasty stuff, but it keeps body and soul together when pickings is thin, and between you and me, pickings has never been thinner. That's why we were so glad to come across this mound of trash we're scraping through."

Tom nodded, leaning back in his chair and looking around the Wreylands' quarters. It was a tiny, cheese-shaped room, and not at all what he would have expected of a mayoral residence – but then Orme Wreyland was not exactly what he would have expected of a mayor. The shabby old man seemed to rule over a town composed mainly of his own family; sons and daughters, grandchildren, nieces, nephews, and the husbands and wives that they had met on passing towns.

But Wreyland was not a happy man. "It's no fun, running a traction town," he kept saying. "No, no fun at all, not any more. There was a time when a little place like Speedwell could go about its business quite safely, being too small for any other town to bother eating. But not now. Not with prey so scarce. Everyone we see wants to eat us. We even found ourselves running from a city the other day. One of those big Frankish-speaking *Villes Mobiles* it was. I ask you, what good would a place like Speedwell be to a monster like that? We'd barely take the edge off its appetite. But they chased us anyway."

"Your town must be very fast," said Tom.

"Oh, yes," agreed Wreyland, beaming, and his wife put in, "Hundred miles an hour, top speed. That's Wreyland's doing. He's a wizard with those big engines of his."

"Could you help us?" asked Tom, leaning forward in his seat. "We need to get to London, as quickly as possible. I'm sure you could catch it up, and there might be more spoil-heaps along the way. . ."

"Bless you, lad," said Wreyland, shaking his head. "What London drops isn't worth going far for, not these days. Everything's recycled now that prey's so short. Why, I remember the days when cities' waste-heaps used to dot the Hunting Ground like mountains. Oh, there was good pickings then! But not any more. Besides," he added with a shudder, "I wouldn't take my town too close to London, or any other city. You can't trust them these days. They'd turn round and snaffle us, like as not. Chomp! No, no."

Tom nodded, trying not to show his disappointment. He glanced across at Hester, but her head was hanging down and she seemed to be asleep, or unconscious. He hoped it was just the effects of her long walk and her full stomach, but as he started up to check that she was all right Wreyland said, "I tell you what, though, lad; we'll take you to the cluster!"

"To the what?"

"To the trading-cluster! It's a gathering of small towns, a couple of days run south-east of here. We were going anyway."

"There'll be lots of towns at the cluster," Mrs Wreyland agreed. "And even if none of them is prepared to take you and your friend to London, you'll soon find an air-trader who will. Bound to be air-traders at a cluster."

"I. . ." said Tom, and stopped. He wasn't feeling very well. The room seemed to waver, then started to roll like the picture on a badly-tuned Goggle-screen. He looked at Hester and saw that she had slipped off her seat on to the floor. The Wreylands' household gods grinned at him from their shrine on the wall, and one of them seemed to be saying in Orme Wreyland's voice, "Sure to be airships there, Tom, always airships at a trading-cluster. . ."

"Would you like some more algae, dear?" enquired Mrs Wreyland, as he fell to his knees. From a long, long way away he heard her saying, "It took an awfully long time to take effect, didn't it, Ormey?", and Wreyland replying, "We'll have to put more in next time, my sweet." Then the swirling patterns on the carpet reached up and twined around him and pulled him down into a sleep that was as soft as cotton wool, and filled with dreams of Katherine.

7

HIGH LONDON

Above Tier One, above the busy shops of Mayfair and Piccadilly, above Quirke Circus, where the statue of London's saviour stands proudly on its fluted steel column, Top Tier hangs over the city like an iron crown, supported by vast pillars. It is the smallest, highest and most important of the seven Tiers, and, though only three buildings stand there, they are the three greatest buildings in London. To sternward rise the towers of the Guildhall, where the greater and lesser Guilds all have their offices and meet in council once a month. Opposite it is the building where the *real* decisions are taken: the black glass claw of the Engineerium. Between them stands St Paul's, the ancient Christian temple that Quirke re-erected up here when he turned London into a Traction City. It is a sad sight now, covered in scaffolding and shored up with props, for it was never meant to move, and London's journeys have shaken the old stonework terribly. But soon it will be open to the public again: the Guild of Engineers has promised to restore it, and if you listen closely you can hear the drills and hammers of their men at work inside.

Magnus Crome hears them as his bug goes purring through the old cathedral's shadow to the Engineerium. They make him smile a faint, secret smile.

Inside the Engineerium the sunlight is kept at bay behind black windows. A cold neon glow washes the metal walls, and the air smells of antiseptic, which Crome thinks is a welcome relief from the stench of flowers and new-mown grass that hangs over High London on this warm spring day. A young apprentice leaps to attention as he stalks into the lobby and bows her bald head when he barks, "Take me to Doctor Twix."

A monorail car is waiting. The apprentice helps the Lord Mayor into it and it takes him sweeping up in a slow spiral through the heart of the Engineerium. He passes floor after floor of offices and conference rooms and laboratories, and glimpses the shapes of strange machines through walls of frosted glass. Everywhere he looks he sees his Engineers at work, tinkering with fragments of Old-Tech, performing experiments on rats and dogs, or guiding groups of shaven-headed children who are up on a day-trip from the Guild's nurseries in the Deep Gut. He feels safe and satisfied, here in the clean, bright, inner sanctum of his Guild. It makes him remember why he loves London so much, and why he has devoted his whole career to finding ways to keep it moving.

When Crome was a young apprentice, many years ago, he read gloomy forecasts which said that prey was running out and Traction Cities were doomed. He has made it his life's work to prove them wrong. Clawing his way to the top of his Guild and then on to the Lord Mayor's throne was just the start. His fierce recycling and anti-waste laws were merely a stop-gap. Now he is almost ready to unveil his real plan.

But first he must be certain that the Shaw girl can make no more trouble.

The car comes sighing to a halt outside one of the upper laboratories. A squat, white-coated barrel of a woman stands waiting at the entrance, hopping nervously from foot to foot. Evadne Twix is one of the best Engineers in London. She may look like someone's dotty auntie and decorate her laboratory with pictures of flowers and puppies (a clear breach of Guild rules), but when it comes to her work she is utterly ruthless. "Hello, Lord Mayor," she simpers, bowing. "How lovely to see you! Have you come to visit my babies?"

"I want to see Shrike," he snaps, brushing past, and she dances along in his wake like a leaf in the slipstream of a passing city.

Through her laboratory they go, past startled, bowing Engineers, past glittering racks of glassware – and past tables where rusting metal skeletons are being painstakingly repaired. Dr Twix's team has spent years studying the Stalkers, the Resurrected Men whose remains turn up sometimes in the Out-Country – and lately they have had more than just remains to work on.

"You have completed your researches on Shrike?" asks Crome as he strides along. "You are certain he is of no further use to us?"

"Oh, I've learned everything we can, Lord Mayor," twitters the doctor. "He's a fascinating piece of work, but really far more complicated than is good for him; he has almost developed his own personality. And as for his strange fixation with this girl. . . I shall make sure my new models are much simpler. Do you wish me to have him dismantled?"

"No." Crome stops at a small, round door and touches a stud that sends it whirling open. "I intend to keep my promise to Shrike. And I have a job for him."

Beyond the door hang shadows and a smell of oil. A tall shape stands motionless against a far wall. As the Lord Mayor steps into the room two round, green eyes snap on like headlights.

"Mr Shrike!" says Crome, sounding almost cheery. "How are we today? I hope you were not asleep?"

"I DO NOT SLEEP," replies a voice from the darkness. It is a horrible voice, sharp as the squeal of rusty cogs. Even Dr Twix, who knows it well, shudders inside her rubber coat. "DO YOU WISH TO EXAMINE ME AGAIN?"

"No, Shrike," Crome says. "Do you remember what you warned me of when you first came to me, a year and a half ago? About the Shaw girl?"

"I TOLD YOU THAT SHE IS ALIVE, AND ON HER WAY TO LONDON."

"Well, it seems you were right. She turned up just as you said she would."

"WHERE IS SHE? BRING HER TO ME!"

"Impossible, I'm afraid. She jumped down a waste-chute, back into the Out-Country."

There is a slow hiss, like steam escaping. "I MUST GO AFTER HER."

Crome smiles. "I was hoping you'd say that. One of my Guild's Goshawk 90 reconnaissance airships has been made ready for you. The pilots will retrace the city's tracks until you find where the girl fell. If she and her companion are dead, all well and good. If they are alive, kill them. Bring their bodies to me."

"AND THEN?" asks the voice.

"And then, Shrike," Crome replies, "I will give you your heart's desire."

○ ○ ○ ○ ○

It was a strange time for London. The city was still travelling at quite high speed, as if there was a catch in sight, but there was no other town to be seen on the grey, muddy plains of the north western Hunting Ground, and everybody was wondering what the Lord Mayor could be planning. "We can't just go driving on like this," Katherine heard one of her servants mutter. "There are big cities further east, and they'll scoff us up and spit out the bones!" But Mrs Mallow the housekeeper whispered back, "Don't you know nothing, Sukey Blinder? Ain't Mr Valentine himself being sent off on a hexpedition to spy out the land ahead? Him and Magnus Crome have got their eye on some vast great prize, you can be sure of it!"

Some vast great prize perhaps, but nobody knew what, and when Valentine came home at lunchtime from another meeting with the Guild of Engineers Katherine asked him, "Why do they have to send *you* off on a reconnaissance flight? That's a job for a Navigator, not the best archaeologist in the world. It's not fair!"

Valentine sighed patiently. "The Lord Mayor trusts me, Kate. And I will soon be back. Three weeks. A month. No more. Now, come down to the hangar with me, and we'll see what Pewsey and Gench have been doing to that airship of mine."

In the long millennia since the Sixty Minute War, airship technology had reached levels that even the Ancients had never dreamed of. Valentine had had the *13th Floor Elevator* specially constructed, using some of the money that Crome had paid him for the Old-Tech he found on his trip to America, twenty years before. He said she was the finest airship ever built, and Katherine saw no reason to doubt him. Of course he didn't keep her down at the Tier Five air-harbour with the common merchantmen, but at a private air-quay a few hundred yards from Clio House.

Katherine and her father walked towards it through the sunlit park. The hangar and the metal apron in front of it were busy with people and bugs as Pewsey and Gench set about loading the *Elevator* with provisions for the coming flight. Dog went hurrying ahead to sniff at the stacks of crates and drums: tinned meat, lifting gas, medicines, airship-puncture repair kits, sun lotion, gas-masks, flame-proof suits, guns, rain-capes, cold-weather coats, map-making equipment, portable stoves, spare socks, plastic cups, three inflatable dinghies and a carton labelled "Pink's Patent Out-Country Mud-Shoes – *Nobody Sinks with Pink's!*"

In the shadows of the hangar the great airship waited, her sleek, black, armoured envelope screened by tarpaulins. As usual, Katherine felt a rising thrill at the thought of that huge vessel lifting Father up into the sky – and a sadness too, that he was leaving her; and a fear that he might not return. "Oh, I wish I could go with you!" she said.

"Not this time, Kate," her father told her. "One day, perhaps."

"Is it because I'm a girl?" she asked. "But that doesn't matter. I mean, in Ancient times women were allowed to do all the same things men did, and anyway, the air-trade is full of women pilots. You had one yourself, on the American trip, I remember seeing pictures of her. . ."

"It's not that, Kate," he said, hugging her. "It's just that it may be dangerous. Anyway, I don't want you to start turning into an old ragamuffin adventurer like me; I want you to stay here and finish school and become a fine, beautiful High London lady. And most of all I want you to stop Dog from peeing over all my crates of soup. . ."

When Dog had been dragged away and scolded they sat down together in the shadow of the hangar and Katherine said, "So will you tell me where you are going, that is so important and dangerous?"

"I am not supposed to say," said Valentine, glancing down at her out of the corner of his eye.

"Oh, come on!" she laughed. "We're best friends, aren't we? You know I'd never tell anybody else. And I'm desperate to know where London is going to! Everyone at school keeps asking. We've been travelling east at top speed for days and days. We didn't even stop when we ate Salthook. . ."

"Well, Kate," he admitted, "the fact is, Crome has asked me to take a look into Shan Guo."

Shan Guo was the leading nation of the Anti-Traction League, the barbarian alliance which controlled the old Indian sub-continent and what was left of China, protected from hungry cities by a great chain of mountains and swamps that marked the eastern limits of the Hunting Ground. Katherine had studied it in Geography. There was only one pass through those mountains, and it was protected by the dreadful fortress-city of Batmunkh Gompa, the Shield-Wall, beneath whose guns a hundred cities had come to grief in the first few centuries of Traction. "But why there?" she asked. "London can't be going there!"

"I didn't say it was," replied Valentine. "But one day we may *have* to go to Shan Guo and breach the League's defences. You know how short prey has become. Cities are starting to starve, and turn on one another."

Katherine shivered. "But there must be some other solution," she protested. "Can't we talk to the Lord Mayors of other cities and work something out?"

He laughed gently. "I'm afraid Municipal Darwinism doesn't work like that, Kate. It's a town eat town world. But you mustn't worry. Crome is a great man, and he will find a way."

She nodded unhappily. Her father's eyes had that haunted, hunted look again. He had still not confided in her about the girl assassin, and now she could tell that he was keeping something else from her, something about this expedition and the Lord Mayor's plans for London. Was it all connected somehow? She could not ask him directly about the things she had overheard in the atrium without admitting that she had spied on him, but just to see what he would say she asked, "Does this have something to do with that awful girl? Was *she* from Shan Guo?"

"No," said Valentine quickly, and she saw the colour drain from his face. "She is dead, Kate, and there is no reason to worry about her any more. Come on." He stood up quickly. "We have a few days more together before I set off; so let's make the most of them. We'll sit by the fire and eat buttered toast and talk about old times, and not think about . . . about that poor disfigured girl."

As they walked back hand in hand across the park a shadow slid over them; a Goshawk 90 departing from the Engineerium. "You see?" said Katherine. "The Guild of Engineers has airships of its own. I think it's horrid of Magnus Crome, sending you away from me."

But her father just shaded his eyes to watch as the white airship circled Top Tier and flew quickly towards the west.

8

THE TRADING CLUSTER

Tom was dreaming of Katherine. She was walking arm in arm with him through the familiar rooms of the Museum, only there were no curators or Guildsmen about, nobody to say, "Polish the floor, Natsworthy," or "Dust the 43rd Century glassware." He was showing her around the place as if he owned it, and she was smiling at him as he explained the details of the replica airships and the great cut-away model of London. Through it all a strange, moaning music sounded, and it wasn't until they reached the Natural History gallery that they realized it was the blue whale, singing to them.

The dream faded, but the weird notes of the whale's song lingered. He was lying on a quivering wooden deck. Wooden walls rose on either side, with morning sunlight glinting through the gaps between the planks, and overhead a mad confusion of pipes and ducts and tubes crawled over the ceiling. It was Speedwell's plumbing, and its burblings and grumbles were what he had mistaken for the song of the whale.

He rolled over and looked around the tiny room. Hester was sitting against the far wall. She nodded when she saw that he was awake.

"Where am I?" he groaned.

"I didn't know anybody really said that," she said. "I thought that was just in books. 'Where am I?' How interesting."

"No, really," Tom protested, looking around at the rough walls and the narrow metal door. "Is this still Speedwell? What happened?"

"The food, of course," she replied.

"You mean Wreyland drugged us? But why?" He got up and made his way to the door across the pitching deck. "Don't bother," Hester warned him, "it's locked." He tried it anyway. She was right. Next he stumbled over to peer through a crack in the wall. Beyond it he could see a narrow wooden walkway that flickered like a Goggle-screen picture as the shadow of one of Speedwell's wheels flashed across it. The Out-Country was rushing past, looking much rockier and steeper than when last he saw it.

"We've been heading south by south east since first light," explained Hester wearily, before he could ask. "Probably longer, but I was asleep too."

"Where are they taking us?"

"How should I know?"

Tom sat down in a heap with his back to the shuddering wall. "That's it then!" he said. "London must be hundreds of miles away! I'll never get home now!"

Hester said nothing. Her face was white, making the scars stand out even more than usual, and blood had soaked into the planking around her injured leg.

An hour crawled by, and then another. Sometimes people went hurrying along the walkway outside, their shadows blocking out the skinny shafts of sunlight. The plumbing burbled to itself. At last Tom heard the sound of a padlock being undone. A hatch low down on the door popped open and a face peered in. "Everybody all right?" it asked.

"All right?" shouted Tom. "Of course we're not all right!" He scrambled towards the door. Wreyland was on hands and knees outside, crouching down so he could see through the hatch (which Tom suspected was really a cat-flap). Behind him were the booted feet of some of his men, standing guard. "What have you done this for?" Tom asked. "We haven't done you any harm!"

The old mayor looked embarrassed. "That's true, dear boy, but times are hard, you see, cruel hard these days. No fun, running a traction town. We have to take what we can get. So we took you. We're going to sell you as slaves, you see. That's how it is. There'll be some slaving towns at the cluster, and we're going to sell you. It has to be done. We need spare parts for our engines, if we're to keep a step ahead of the bigger towns. . ."

"Sell us?" Tom had heard of cities that used slaves to work their engine rooms, but it had always seemed like something distant and exotic that would never affect him. "I've got to catch London! You can't sell me!"

"Oh, I'm sure you'll fetch a good price," Wreyland said, as if it were something Tom should be pleased about. "A handsome, healthy lad like you. We'll make sure you go to a good owner. I don't know about your friend, of course: she looks half dead, and she was no oil-painting to start with. But maybe we can sell you off together, 'buy one, get one free' sort of thing." He pushed two bowls through the flap, round metal bowls such as a dog would eat from. One contained water, the other more of the blue-ish algae. "Eat up!" he said cheerfully. "We want you looking nice and well-fed for the auction. We'll be at the cluster by sundown, and sell you in the morning."

"But. . ." Tom protested.

"Yes, I know, and I'm terribly sorry about it, but what can I do?" said Wreyland sadly. "Times are hard, you know."

The hatch slammed shut. "What about my seedy?" shouted Tom. There was no answer. He heard

Wreyland's voice in the passage outside, talking to the guard, then nothing. He cupped his hands and drank some water, then took the bowl across to Hester. "We've got to get away!" he told her.

"How?"

Tom looked around their cell. The door was no use, locked and guarded as it was. He peered up at the plumbing until he had a crick in his neck, but although some of the pipes looked big enough for a person to crawl through he could see no way to get into them, or even to reach them. Anyway, he wouldn't have fancied crawling through whatever that thick fluid was which he could hear gurgling inside them. He turned his attention to the wall, feeling his way along the planks. At last he found one that felt slightly loose, and gradually, as he worked at it, it started to get looser still.

It was slow, hard, painful work. Tom's fingers filled with splinters and the sweat ran down his face and he had to stop each time someone passed along the walkway outside. Hester watched silently, until he started to feel cross with her for not helping. But by evening, as the sky outside turned red and the racing townlet started to slow, he had made a gap just wide enough to get his head through.

He waited until he was sure there was no one about, then leaned out. Speedwell was passing through the shadows of some tall spines of rock, the town-gnawed cores of old mountains. Ahead lay a natural amphitheatre, a shallow bowl between more rock-spires, and it was full of towns. Tom had never seen so many trading suburbs and traction villages gathered in one place before. "We're here!" he told Hester. "It's the trading cluster!"

Speedwell slowed and slowed, manoeuvring into a space between a ragged little sail-powered village and a larger market town. Tom could hear the people on the new towns hailing Speedwell, asking where it had come from and what it had to trade. "Scrap metal," he heard Mrs Wreyland bellow back, "and some wood, and a pretty seedy and two fine, fresh, healthy, young slaves!"

"Oh, Quirke!" muttered Tom, working away at enlarging the hole he had made.

"It'll never be big enough," said Hester, who always expected the worst and was usually right.

"You could try helping, instead of just sitting there!" Tom snapped back, but he regretted it at once, for he could see that she was very ill. He wondered what would happen if she was too weak to escape. He couldn't run off into the Out-Country alone and leave her here. But if he stayed, he would end up as a slave on one of these filthy little towns!

He tried not to think about it and concentrated on making the hole bigger, while the sky outside grew dark and the moon rose. He could hear music and laughter drifting across the trading cluster and the sounds of gangways being run out as some of Wreyland's people went off to enjoy themselves aboard the other towns. He scrabbled and scratched at the hole, prising at the planks, scraping at them with a rusty nail, but it was no use. At last, desperate, he turned to Hester and hissed, "Please! Help!"

The girl stood up unsteadily and walked over to where he crouched. She looked sick, but not quite as bad as he'd feared. Perhaps she had been saving herself, harbouring her last reserves of strength until it was dark enough to escape. She felt around the edges of the hole he had made and nodded. Then, leaning all her weight on Tom's shoulder, she swung her good foot up hard against the wall. Once, twice she kicked it, the wood around the hole splintering and yielding, and at the third kick a whole section of planking fell out, spilling across the walkway outside.

"*I* could have done that!" said Tom, staring at the ragged hole and wondering why he hadn't thought of it.

"But you didn't, did you?" said Hester, and tried to smile. It was the first time he had seen her smile; an ugly, crooked thing, but very welcome; it made him feel that she was starting to like him and didn't just regard him as an annoyance.

"Come on then," she said, "if you're coming."

۞ ۞ ۞ ۞ ۞

Hundreds of miles away across the moonlit mud, Shrike spots something. He signals to the Engineer pilots, who nod and grumble as they steer the Goshawk 90 down to land. "What now? How much longer are we going to keep flying back and forth along these track-marks before he'll admit the kids are dead?" But they grumble quietly: they are terrified of Shrike.

The hatch opens and Shrike stalks out. His green eyes sweep from side to side until he finds what he is looking for. A rag of white fabric from a torn shirt, soggy with rain, half-buried in the mud. "HESTER SHAW WAS HERE," he tells the Out-Country at large, and begins sniffing for her scent.

9

THE *JENNY HANIVER*

A t first it looked as if their luck might hold. They scrambled quickly across the dimly-lit walkway and down into the shadows under one of Speedwell's wheel-arches. They could see the dark bulks of the other towns, with lights burning in their windows and a big bonfire on the top deck of one of them, a mining townlet on the far side of the cluster where a noisy party·was in progress.

They crept along the outside edge of Speedwell to a place where a gangplank stretched across to the market town which was parked next door. It was unguarded, but brightly lit, and as they reached the far end and stepped on to the deck of the market town a voice somewhere behind them shouted, "Hey!" and then, louder, "Hey! Hey! Uncle Wreyland! Them slaves is 'scaping!"

They ran, or rather, Tom ran, and dragged Hester along beside him, hearing her whimper in pain at every step. Up a stairway, along a catwalk, past a shrine to Peripatetia, goddess of wandering towns, and they were in a market square lined with big iron cages, in some of which thin, miserable slaves were waiting to be sold off. Tom forced himself to slow down and tried to look inconspicuous, listening all the time for sounds of pursuit. There were none. Maybe the Wreylands had given up the chase, or maybe they weren't allowed to chase people on to other towns – Tom didn't know what the rules were in a trading cluster.

"Head for the bows," said Hester, letting go his arm and pulling the collar of her coat up to hide her face. "If we're lucky there'll be an air-harbour at the bows."

They were lucky. At the front of the town's top deck was a raised section where half a dozen small airships were tethered, their dark, gas-filled envelopes like sleeping whales. "Are we going to steal one?" Tom whispered.

"Not unless you know how to fly an airship," said Hester weakly. "There's an airman's café over there; we'll have to try and book passage like normal people."

The café was just an ancient, rusting airship gondola that had been bolted to the deck. A few metal tables stood in front beneath a stripy awning. Hurricane lamps were burning there and an old aviator slumped snoring in a chair. The only other customer was a sinister-looking Oriental woman in a long, red leather coat who sat in the shadows near the bar. In spite of the dark she wore sunglasses, the tiny lenses black as the wing-cases of beetles. She turned to stare at Tom as he walked up to the counter.

A small man with a huge, drooping moustache was polishing glasses. He glanced up without much interest when Tom said, "I'm looking for a ship."

"Where to?"

"London," said Tom. "Me and my friend have to get back to London, and we have to leave tonight."

"London, is it?" The man's moustachios twitched like the tails of two squirrels which had been shoved up his nose and were starting to get a bit restless. "Only ships with a licence from the London Merchant's Guild can dock there. We've got nuffink like that here. Stayns ain't that sort of town."

"Perhaps I may be of help?" suggested a soft, foreign-sounding voice at Tom's shoulder. The woman in the red coat had come silently to his side; a lean, handsome woman with badgery slashes of white in her short black hair. Reflections of the hurricane lamps danced in her sunglasses, and when she smiled Tom noticed that her teeth were stained red. "I haven't a licence for London, but I am going to Airhaven. You could find a ship there that will take you the rest of the way. Have you some money?"

Tom hadn't thought about that part. He rummaged in his tunic and fished out two tatty banknotes with the face of Quirke on the front and Magnus Crome gazing sternly from the back. He had put them in his pocket the night he fell out of London, hoping to spend them at the catch-party in Kensington Gardens. Here, under the fizzing hurricane lamps of the air-harbour, they looked out of place, like toy money.

The woman seemed to think so too. "Ah," she said. "Twenty Quirkes. But notes like that can only be spent in London. Not much use to a poor wandering skyfarer like me. Don't you have any gold? Or Old-Tech?"

Tom shrugged and mumbled something. Out of the corner of his eye he saw some newcomers pushing their way between the tables. "Look, Uncle Wreyland!" he heard one of them shout. "Here they are! We've got 'em!"

Tom looked round and saw Wreyland and a couple of his boys closing in, carrying heavy clubs. He grabbed Hester, who was leaning against the counter, barely conscious. One of the Speedwell men moved to cut off their escape, but the woman in the red coat barred his way and Tom heard her say, "These are my passengers. I was just arranging a fee."

"They're our slaves!" shouted Wreyland, pushing past her. "Tom Nitsworthy and his friend. Found 'em in the Out-Country, fair and square. Finders keepers. . ."

Tom hurried Hester across the metal deck, past stairways leading up to the quays where the airships moored. He could hear Wreyland's men splitting up, shouting to each other as they searched, then a grunt and a crash as if one of them had fallen over. *Good*, he thought, but he knew that the others would soon find him.

He dragged Hester up a short iron stairway to the quays. There were lights in some of the ships that hung at anchor there, and he had a vague idea about forcing his way aboard one of them and making them take him to London. But he had nothing that would serve as a weapon, and before he could look for one there were feet ringing on the ladder behind him and Wreyland's voice saying, "Please try and be reasonable, Mr Nitsworthy! I don't want to have to hurt you. Fred!" he added. "I've got the rotters cornered. Fred?"

Tom felt the hope drain out of him. There was no escape now. He stood there meekly as Wreyland stepped forward into the light from the portholes of a nearby airship, hefting his club. Hester slumped against a dockside winch and moaned.

"It's only fair," said Wreyland, as if he thought she was complaining. "I don't like this slaving lark any more than you do, but times are hard, and we *did* catch you, there's no denying it. . ."

Suddenly, faster than Tom would have thought possible, Hester moved. She dragged a metal lever out of the winch and swung it at Wreyland. His club went whirling out of his hand and hit the deck with a glockenspiel sound, and the metal bar struck him a glancing blow on the side of his head. "Ow!" he wailed, crumpling to the floor. Hester lurched forward and raised the bar again, but before she could bring it down on the old man's skull Tom grabbed her arm. "Stop! You'll kill him!"

"So?" She swung towards him, snaggle teeth bared, looking like a demented monkey. "So?"

"He's right, my dear," said a gentle voice. "There is no need to finish him."

Out of the shadows stepped the woman from the bar, her red coat swirling around her ankles as she walked towards them. "I think we should get aboard my ship before the rest of his people come looking for you."

"You said we didn't have enough money," Tom reminded her.

"You don't, Mr Nitsworthy," said the aviatrix. "But I can hardly stand by and watch you taken away to be sold as slaves, can I? I was a slave myself once, and I wouldn't recommend it." She had taken off her glasses. Her eyes were dark and almond-shaped, and fine webs of laughter lines crinkled at their corners when she smiled. "Besides," she added, "you intrigue me. Why is a Londoner wandering about in the Hunting Ground, getting into trouble?" She held out her hand to Tom, a long, brown hand with the thin machinery of bones and tendons clearly visible, sliding under papery skin.

"How do we know you won't betray us like Wreyland did?" he demanded.

"You don't, of course!" she laughed. "You will just have to trust me."

After Valentine and the Wreylands, Tom didn't think he would ever be able to trust anybody again, but this strange foreigner was the only hope he had. "All right," he said. "But Wreyland got my name wrong, it's *Natsworthy*."

"And mine is Fang," said the woman. "Miss Anna

Fang." She still had her hand outstretched as if he was a scared animal she wanted to tame, and she was still smiling her alarming red smile. "My ship is on air-quay six."

So they went with her, and somewhere in the oily shadows under the quays they stepped over Wreyland's companions, who lay slumped against a stanchion with their heads lolling drunkenly. "Are they. . .?" whispered Tom.

"Out cold," said Miss Fang. "I'm afraid I just don't know my own strength."

Tom wanted to stop and check that the men were all right, but she led him quickly past and up a ladder to Quay Six. The ship that hung at anchor there was not the elegant sky-clipper Tom had been expecting. In fact, it was little more than a shabby scarlet gasbag and a cluster of rusty engine pods bolted to a wooden gondola.

"It's made of junk!" he gasped.

"Junk?" laughed Miss Fang. "Why, the *Jenny Haniver* is built from bits of the finest airships that ever flew! An envelope of silicon-silk from a Shan Guo clipper, twin Jeunet-Carot aëro-engines off a Paris gunship, the reinforced gas-cells of a Spitzbergen war-balloon. . . It's amazing what you can find in the scrapyards. . ."

She led them up the gangplank into the cramped, spice-smelling gondola. It was just a narrow wooden tube with a flight-deck at the front and Miss Fang's quarters at the stern, a jumble of other little cabins in between. Tom had to keep ducking to avoid braining himself on overhead lockers and dangerous-looking bundles of cables that hung from instrument panels on the roof, but the aviatrix flitted around with practised ease, mumbling in some strange foreign tongue as she set switches, pulled levers and lit dim green electrics which filled the cabin with an aquarium glow. She laughed when she saw Tom's worried look. "That is Airsperanto, the common language of the sky. It's a lonely life on the bird-roads, and I have a habit of talking to myself. . ."

She pulled on a final lever and the creak and sigh of gas-valves echoed through the gondola. There was a clang as the magnetic docking clamps released, and the radio crackled into life and snapped, "*Jenny Haniver*, this is the Stayns Harbour Board. You are not cleared for departure!"

But the *Jenny Haniver* was departing anyway. Tom felt his stomach turn over as she lifted into the midnight sky. He scrambled to a porthole, and saw the market town falling away below. Then Speedwell came into view, and soon the whole cluster was spread out below him like a display of model towns in the Museum.

"*Jenny Haniver*," insisted the loud speaker, "return to your berth at once! We have a request from the Speedwell town council that you give up your passengers, or they will be forced to—"

"Boring!" trilled Miss Fang, flicking the radio off. A home-made rocket battery on the roof of Speedwell town hall spat a fizzing flock of missiles after them. Three hissed harmlessly past, a fourth exploded off the starboard quarter, making the gondola swing like a pendulum, and the fifth came even closer. (Anna Fang raised an eyebrow at that one, while Tom and Hester ducked for cover like frightened rabbits.) Then they were out of range; the *Jenny Haniver* was climbing into the cold clear spaces of the night, and the trading cluster was just a distant smear of light beneath the clouds.

10

THE *13TH FLOOR ELEVATOR*

I t rained that night on London, but by first light the sky was as clear and pale as still water, and the smoke from the city's engines rose straight up into the windless air. Wet decks shone silver in the sunrise and all the banners of Tier One hung limp and still against their flagpoles. It was a fine spring morning, the morning that Valentine had been hoping for, and Katherine had been dreading. It was perfect flying weather.

Although it was so early, crowds had gathered all along the edge of Tier One to watch the *13th Floor Elevator* lift off. As Gench drove Katherine and her father over to the air-quay she saw that Circle Park was crowded too; it looked as if the whole of High London had come to cheer Valentine on his way. None of them knew where he was going, of course, but as London sped eastward the city's rumour-mills had been grinding night and day: everyone was sure that Valentine's expedition was connected with some huge prize that the Lord Mayor hoped to catch out in the central Hunting Ground.

Temporary stands had been erected for the Council and Guilds and, when she and Dog had wished Father goodbye in the bustling shadows of the hangar, Katherine went to take her place with the Historians, squeezed between Chudleigh Pomeroy and Dr Arkengarth. All around her stood the great and good of London: the sober black robes of Father's Guild and the purple of the Guild of Merchants, sombre Navigators in their neat green tunics and a row of Engineers robed and hooded in white rubber, looking like novelty erasers.

Even Magnus Crome had risen to the occasion, and the Lord Mayor's ancient chain of office hung gleaming around his thin neck.

Katherine wished they had all just stayed at home. It was difficult saying goodbye to someone when you were part of a great cheering mob all waving flags and blowing kisses. She stroked Dog's knobbly head and told him, "Look, there's Father, going up the gangplank now. They'll start the engines in a moment."

"I just hope nothing goes wrong," muttered Dr Arkengarth. "One hears stories about these air-ships suddenly going off bang for no reason."

"Perhaps we should stand a little further back?" suggested Miss Plym, the Museum's twittery curator of furniture.

"Nonsense," Katherine told them crossly. "Nothing is going to go wrong."

"Yes, do shut up, Arkengarth, you silly old coot," agreed Chudleigh Pomeroy, surprising her. "Never fear, Miss Valentine. Your father has the finest airship and the best pilots in the world: nothing can go wrong."

Katherine smiled gratefully at him, but she kept her fingers crossed just the same, and Dog caught something of her mood and started to whimper softly.

From inside the hangar came the sound of hatches slamming shut and the rattle of boarding-ladders being dragged clear. An expectant hush fell over the stands. Along the tier's edge High London held its breath. Then, as the band struck up "Rule Londinium", Valentine's ground-crew began dragging the *13th Floor Elevator* out into the sunlight, a sleek, black dart whose armoured envelope shone like silk. On the open platform at the stern of the control gondola Valentine stood waving. He saluted the ground-crew and the flag-decked stands and then smiled straight at Katherine, picking her face out of all the others without a moment's hesitation.

She waved back frantically, and the crowd cheered themselves hoarse as the *13th Floor Elevator*'s engine-pods swivelled into take-off position. The ground crew cast off the mooring-hawsers, the propellers began to turn and blizzards of confetti eddied in the down-drafts as the huge machine lifted into the air. Some Apprentice Historians spread out a banner reading *Happy Valentine's Day!* and the cheers went on and on, as if the crowds thought it was their love alone which was keeping the explorer airborne. *"Val-en-tine! Val-en-tine!"*

But Valentine took no notice of the noise or the flags. He stood watching Katherine, one hand raised in farewell, until the airship was so high and far away that she could not make him out any more.

At last, when the *Elevator* was just a speck in the eastern sky and the stands were emptying, she wiped away her tears, took Dog's lead and turned to go home. She was already missing her father, but she had a plan now. While he was away she would make her own enquiries and find out who that mysterious girl had been, and why she scared him so.

11
AIRHAVEN

Once he had washed and slept and had something to eat, Tom began to decide that adventuring might not be so bad after all. By sunrise he was already starting to forget the misery of his trek across the mud and imprisonment in Speedwell. The view from the *Jenny Haniver*'s big forward windows as the airship flew between golden mountains of dawn-lit cloud was enough to make even the pain of Valentine's betrayal fade a little. At breakfast-time, drinking hot chocolate with Miss Fang on the flight deck, he found that he was enjoying himself.

As soon as the *Jenny Haniver* was safely out of the range of Speedwell's rockets the aviatrix had become all smiles and kindness. She locked her airship on course and set about finding Tom a warm fleece-lined coat and making up a bed for him in the hold, a space high up inside the airship's envelope, heaped with a cargo of sealskins from Spitzbergen. Then she led Hester into the medical bay and went to work on her injured leg. When Tom looked in on her after breakfast that morning the girl was sleeping soundly under a white blanket. "I gave her something for the pain," explained Miss Fang. "She will sleep for hours, but you need have no fear for her."

Tom stared at Hester's sleeping face. Somehow he had expected her to look better now that she had been washed and fed and had her leg fixed, but of course she was as hideous as ever.

"He has made a mess of her, your wicked Mr Valentine," the aviatrix said, leading him back to the flight deck, where she took the controls off their automatic setting.

"How do you know about Valentine?" asked Tom.

"Oh, everyone has heard about Thaddeus Valentine," she laughed. "I know that he is London's greatest historian, and I also know that that is just a cover for his *real* work: as Crome's secret agent."

"That's not true!" Tom started to say, still instinctively defending his ex-hero. But there had always been rumours that Valentine's expeditions involved something darker than mere archaeology, and now that he had seen the great man's ruthless handiwork, he believed them. He blushed, ashamed for Valentine, and ashamed of himself for having loved him.

Miss Fang watched him with a faint, sympathetic smile. "Hester told me a great deal more last night, while I was tending to her wound," she said gently. "You are both very lucky to be alive."

"I know," agreed Tom, but he could not help feeling uneasy that Hester had shared their story with this stranger.

He sat down in the co-pilot's seat and studied the controls; a baffling array of knobs and switches and levers labelled in mixtures of Airsperanto, Anglish and Chinese. Above them a little lacquered shrine had been fixed to the bulkhead, decorated with red ribbons and pictures of Miss Fang's ancestors. That smiling Manchu air-merchant must be her father, he supposed. And had that red-haired lady from the Ice Wastes been her mum?

"So tell me, Tom," asked Miss Fang, setting the ship on a new course, "where *is* London going?"

The question was unexpected. "I don't know!" Tom said.

"Oh, surely you must know *something*!" she laughed.

"Your city has left its hidey-hole in the west, come back across the land-bridge, and now it is whizzing off into the central Hunting Ground 'like a bat out of Hull', as the saying goes. You must have heard at least a rumour. No?"

Her long eyes slid towards Tom, who licked his lips nervously, wondering what to say. He had never paid any attention to the stupid tales the other apprentices swapped about where London was heading; he really had no idea. And even if he had, he knew it would be wrong to go revealing his city's plans to mysterious Oriental aviatrices. What if Miss Fang flew off and told some larger city where to lie in wait for London, in exchange for a finder's fee? And yet, if he didn't tell her *something*, she might kick him off her airship – perhaps without even bothering to land it first!

"Prey!" he blurted out. "The Guild of Navigators say there is lots and lots of prey in the central Hunting Ground."

The red smile grew even broader. "Really?"

"I heard it from the Head Navigator himself," said Tom, growing bolder.

Miss Fang nodded, beaming. Then she hauled on a long brass lever. Gas-valves grumbled up inside the envelope and Tom's ears popped as the *Jenny Haniver* started to descend, plunging into a thick, white layer of cloud. "Let me show you the central Hunting Ground," she chuckled, checking the charts that were fastened to the bulkhead beside her shrine.

Down, and down, and then the cloud thinned and parted and Tom saw the vast Out-Country spread below him like a crumpled sheet of grey-brown paper, slashed with long, blue shapes that were the flooded track-marks of countless towns. For the first time since the airship lifted away from Stayns he felt afraid, but Miss Fang murmured, "Nothing to fear, Tom."

He calmed himself and gazed out at the amazing view. Far to the north he could see the cold glitter of the Ice Wastes and the dark cones of the Tannhäuser fire-mountains. He looked for London, and eventually thought he saw it, a tiny, grey speck that raised a cloud of dust behind it as it trundled along, much further off than he had hoped. There were other towns and cities too, dotted here and there across the plain, or lurking in the shadows of half-eaten mountain ranges, but not nearly as many as he had expected. To the south-east there were none at all, just a dingy layer of mist above a tract of marshland, and beyond that the silvery shimmer of water.

"That is the great inland Sea of Khazak," said the aviatrix, when he pointed to it. "I'm sure you've heard the old land-shanty," and in a lilting, high-pitched voice she sang, *"Beware, beware of the Sea of Khazak, for the town that goes near it will never come back. . ."*

But Tom wasn't listening. He had noticed something much more terrible than any inland sea.

Directly below, with the tiny shadow of the *Jenny Haniver* flickering across its skeletal girders, lay a dead city. It stood on ground scarred by the tracks of hundreds of smaller towns, tilting over at a strange angle, and as the *Jenny Haniver* swept down for a closer look Tom realized that its tracks and gut were gone, and that its deckplates were being stripped out by a swarm of small towns which seethed in the shadows of its lower levels, tearing off huge rusting sections in their jaws and landing salvage parties whose blow-torches glittered and sparked in the shadows between the tiers like fairy lights on a Quirkemas tree.

There was a puff of smoke from one of the towns and a rocket came winding up towards the airship and exploded a few hundred feet below. Miss Fang's hands moved swiftly over the controls and Tom felt the ship lift again. "Half the scavengers of the Hunting Ground are working on the wreck of Motoropolis," she said, "and they are a jealous lot. Shoot at anybody who comes near, and when nobody does, they shoot at each other."

"But how did it get like that?" asked Tom, staring back at the huge skeleton as the *Jenny Haniver* carried him up and away.

"It starved," said the aviatrix. "It ran out of fuel, and as it stood motionless there a pack of smaller towns came and started tearing it apart. The feeding frenzy has been going on for months, and I expect another city will come along soon and finish off the job. You see, Tom, there isn't enough prey to go round in the central Hunting Ground – so it can't be that which has brought London out of hiding."

Tom twisted round to watch as the dead city fell behind. A pack of tiny predator-suburbs were harrying the scavenger towns on the north-western side, singling out the weakest and slowest and charging after it, but before they caught it the *Jenny Haniver* rose up again into the pure, clean world above the clouds, and the carcass of Motoropolis was hidden from view.

When Miss Fang looked at him again she was still smiling, but there was an odd gleam in her eyes. "So if it isn't prey that Magnus Crome is after," she said, "what can it be?"

Tom shook his head. "I'm only an Apprentice

Historian," he confessed. "Third Class. I don't *really* know the Head Navigator."

"Hester mentioned something," the aviatrix went on. "The thing Mr Valentine took from her poor parents. MEDUSA. A strange name. Have you heard of it? Do you know what it means?"

Tom shook his head and she watched him closely, watched his eyes until he felt as if she were looking right into his soul. Then she laughed. "Well, no matter. I must get you to Airhaven, and we'll find a ship to take you home."

❉ ❉ ❉ ❉ ❉

Airhaven! It was one of the most famous towns of the whole Traction Era, and when the warble of its homing-beacon came over the radio that evening Tom went racing forward to the flight deck. He met Hester in the companion-way outside the sick-bay, tousled and sleepy and limping. Anna Fang had done her best with the wounded leg, but she hadn't improved the girl's manners; she hid her face when she saw Tom and only glared and grunted when he asked her how she felt.

On the flight deck the aviatrix turned to greet them with a radiant smile. "Look, my dears!" she said, pointing ahead through the big windows. "Airhaven!"

They went and stood behind her seat and looked, and far away across the sea of clouds they saw the westering sun glint on a single tier of light-weight alloy and a nimbus of brightly coloured gas-bags.

Long ago, the town of Airhaven had decided to escape the hungry cities by taking to the sky. It was a trading post and meeting place for aviators now, drifting above the Hunting Ground all summer, then flying south to winter in warmer skies. Tom remembered how it had once anchored over London for a whole week; how the sight-seeing balloons had gone up and down from Kensington Gardens and Circle Park, and how jealous he had been of people like Melliphant who were rich enough to take a trip in one and come back full of stories about the floating town. Now he was going there himself, and not just as a sightseer, either! What a story he would be able to tell the other apprentices when he got home!

Slowly the airship rose towards the town, and as the sun dipped behind the cloud-banks in the west Miss Fang cut her engines and let her drift in towards a docking strut, while harbour officers in sky-blue livery waved multi-coloured flags to guide her safely to her berth. Behind them the dock was crowded with sightseers and aviators, and even a little gaggle of airship-spotters who dutifully jotted down the *Jenny Haniver*'s number in their notebooks as the mooring clamps engaged.

A few moments later Tom was stepping out into the twilight and the chill, thin air, gazing at the airships coming and going; elegant high-liners and rusty scows, trim little air-cutters with see-through envelopes and tiger-striped spice-freighters from the Hundred Islands. "Look!" he said, pointing up at the rooftops. "There's the Floating Exchange, and that church is St Michael's-in-the-Sky, there's a picture of it in the London Museum!" But Miss Fang had seen it many, many times before, and Hester just scowled at the crowds on the quayside and hid her face.

The aviatrix locked the *Jenny*'s hatches with a key that hung on a thong around her neck, but when a little barefoot boy ran up and tugged at her coat saying, "Watch yer airship for yer, Missus?" she laughed and dropped three square bronze coins into his palm. "I won't let nobody sneak aboard!" he promised, taking up his post beside the gangplank. Uniformed dockhands appeared, grinning at Miss Fang but staring suspiciously at her new groundling friends. They checked that the new-comers had no metal toecaps on their boots or lighted cigarettes about their persons, then led them back to the harbour-office where huge, crudely-lettered notices insisted NO SMOKING, TURN OFF ALL ELECTRICS and MAKE NO SPARKS. Sparks were the terror of the air-trade, because of the danger that they might ignite the gas in the airships' envelopes. In Airhaven even over-vigorous hair-brushing was a serious crime, and all new arrivals had to sign strict safety agreements and con-vince the harbourmaster that they were not likely to burst into flames.

At last they were allowed up a metal stairway to the High Street. Airhaven's single thoroughfare was a hoop of lightweight alloy deckplates lined with shops and stalls, chandleries, cafés and airshipmen's hotels. Tom turned around and around, trying to take everything in and make sure he would remember it for ever. He saw turbines whirling on every rooftop, milling the wind to feed the central power plant, and mechanics crawling like spiders over the huge engine pods. The air was thick with the exotic smells of foreign food, and everywhere he looked there were aviators, striding along with the care-less confidence of people who had lived their whole life in the sky, their long coats fluttering behind them like leathery wings.

Miss Fang pointed along the curve of the High Street

to a building with a sign in the shape of an airship. "That's the Gasbag and Gondola," she told her companions. "I'll buy you dinner, and then we'll find a friendly captain to take you back to London."

They strode towards it, the aviatrix in the lead, Hester hiding from the world behind her upraised hand, Tom still looking about in wonder and thinking it a pity that his adventures would soon be over. He didn't notice a Goshawk 90 circling among a shoal of larger vessels, waiting for a berth. Even if he had, he would not have been able to read its registration numbers at this distance, or see that the insignia on its envelope was the red wheel of the Guild of Engineers.

12
THE GASBAG AND GONDOLA

The inn was big and dark and busy. The walls were decorated with airships in bottles and the propellers of famous old sky-clippers with their names carefully painted on the blades, *Nadhezna* and *Aerymouse* and *Invisible Worm*. Aviators clustered round the metal tables, talking of cargoes and the price of gas. There were Jains and Tibetans and Xhosa, Inuit and Air-Tuareg and fur-clad giants from the Ice Wastes. An Uighur girl played "Slipstream Serenade" on her forty-string guitar, and now and then a loudspeaker would announce, "Arrival on strut three; the *Idiot Wind* fresh from the Nuevo-Mayan Palatinates with a cargo of chocolate and vanilla," or, "Now boarding at strut seven; *My Shirona* outbound for Arkangel. . ."

Anna Fang stopped at a little shrine just inside the door and said her thanks to the gods of the sky for a safe journey. The God of Aviators was a friendly-looking fellow – the fat red statue on the shrine reminded Tom of Chudleigh Pomeroy – but his wife, the Lady of the High Heavens, was cruel and tricky; if offended she might brew up hurricanes or burst a gas-cell. Anna made her an offering of rice-cakes and lucky money, and Tom and Hester nodded their thank-yous just in case.

When they looked up the aviatrix was already hurrying away from them towards a group of aviators at a corner table. "Khora!" she shouted, and by the time they caught up with her she was being whirled round and round in the arms of a handsome young African and talking quickly in Airsperanto. Tom was almost sure he heard her mention "MEDUSA" as she glanced back at him and Hester, but by the time they drew near the talk had switched into Anglish and the African was saying, "We rode high-level winds all the way from Zagwa!" and shaking red Sahara sand out of his flying helmet to prove it.

He was Captain Khora of the gunship *Mokele Mbembe* and he came from a static enclave in the Mountains of the Moon, an ally of the Anti-Traction League. Now he was bound for Shan Guo, to begin a tour of duty in the League's great fortress at Batmunkh Gompa. Tom was shocked at first to be sharing a table with a soldier of the League, but Khora seemed a good man, as kind and welcoming as Miss Fang herself. While she ordered food he introduced his friends: the tall gloomy one was Nils Lindstrom of the *Garden Aëroplane Trap*, and the beautiful Arab lady with the laugh was Yasmina Rashid of the Palmyrene privateer *Zainab*. Soon the aviators were all laughing together, reminding each other of battles above the Hundred Islands and drunken parties in the airmen's quarter on Panzerstadt-Linz, and between stories Anna Fang pushed dishes across the table to her guests. "More battered dormouse, Tom? Hester, try some of this delicious devilled bat!"

While Tom poked the strange foreign food around his plate with the pair of wooden sticks he had been given instead of a knife and fork, Khora leaned close and said softly, "So are you and your girlfriend crewing aboard the *Jenny* now?"

"No, no!" Tom assured him quickly. "I mean, no, she's not my girlfriend, and no, we are just passengers. . ." He fumbled with some mashed locust and asked, "Do you know Miss Fang well?"

"Oh yes!" laughed Khora. "The whole air-trade knows Anna. And the whole of the League too, of course. In Shan Guo they call her 'Feng Hua', the Wind-Flower."

Tom wondered why Miss Fang would have a special name in Shan Guo, but before he could ask, Khora went on, "Do you know, she built the *Jenny Haniver* herself? When she was just a girl she and her parents had the bad luck to be aboard a town that was eaten by Arkangel. They were put to work as slaves in the airship-yards there, and over the years she managed to sneak an engine here, a steering vane there, until she built herself the *Jenny* and escaped."

Tom was impressed. "She didn't *say*," he murmured, looking at the aviatrix in a new light.

"She doesn't talk about it," said Khora. "You see, her parents did not live to escape with her; she watched them die in the slave-pits."

Tom felt a rush of sympathy for poor Miss Fang, his fellow orphan. Was that why she smiled all the time, to hide her sorrow? And was that why she had rescued Hester and himself, to save them from her parents' fate? He smiled at her as kindly as he could, and she caught his eye and smiled back and passed him a plate of crooked black legs. "Here, Tom, try a sautéed tarantula. . ."

"Arrival on strut fourteen!" blared the loudspeaker overhead. "London airship GE47 carrying passengers only."

Tom jumped up and his chair fell backwards with a crash. He could remember the little fast-moving scout ships that the Engineers used to survey London's tracks and superstructure, and he remembered how they didn't have names, just registration codes, and how all the codes started with GE. "They've sent someone after us!" he gasped.

Miss Fang was rising to her feet as well. "It might just be coincidence," she said. "There must be lots of airships from London... And even if Valentine has sent someone after you, you are among friends. We are more than a match for your horrible Beefburgers."

"Beef*eaters*," Tom corrected her automatically, although he knew that she had made the mistake deliberately, just to break the tension. He saw Hester smile and felt glad that she was there, and fiercely determined to protect her.

Then all the lights went out.

There were shouts, boos, a crash of falling crockery from the kitchens. The windows were dim twilight-coloured shapes cut out of the dark. "The electrics are off all over Airhaven!" said Lindstrom's gloomy voice. "The power-plant must have failed!"

"No," said Hester quickly. "I know this trick. It's meant to create chaos and stop us leaving. Someone's here, coming for us..." There was an edge of panic in her voice that Tom hadn't heard before, not even in the chase at Stayns. Suddenly he felt very frightened.

From the far end of the room, where crowds of people were spilling out on to the moonlit High Street, a sudden scream arose. Then came another, and a long crash of breaking glass, shrieks, curses, the clatter of chairs and tables falling. Two green lamps bobbed above the crowd like corpse-lanterns.

"That's no Beefeater!" said Hester.

Tom couldn't tell if she was frightened, or relieved.

"HESTER SHAW!" screeched a voice like a saw cutting

metal. Over by the doorway a sudden cloud of vapour bloomed, and out of it stepped a Stalker.

It was seven feet tall, and beneath its coat shone metal armour. The flesh of its long face was pale, glistening with a slug-like film of mucus, and here and there a blue-white jag of bone showed through the skin. Its mouth was a slot full of metal teeth. Its nose and the top of its head were covered by a long metal skull-piece with tubes and flexes trailing down like dreadlocks, their ends plugged into ports on its chest. Its round glass eyes gave it a startled look, as if it had never got over the horrible surprise of what had happened to it.

Because that was the worst thing about the Stalkers: they had been human once, and somewhere beneath that iron cowl a human brain was trapped.

"It's impossible!" Tom whimpered. "There *aren't* any Stalkers! They were all destroyed centuries ago!" But the Stalker stood there still, horribly real. Tom tried to back away, but he couldn't move. Something was trickling down his legs, as hot as spilled tea, and he realized that he had wet himself.

The Stalker came forward slowly, shoving aside the empty chairs and tables. Fallen glasses burst under its feet. From the shadows behind an aviator swung at it with a sword, but the blade rebounded from its armour and it smashed the man aside with a sweeping blow of one huge fist, not even bothering to glance back.

"HESTER SHAW," it said. "THOMAS NATSWORTHY."

It knows my name! he thought.

"I. . ." began Miss Fang, but even she seemed lost for words. She pulled Tom backwards while Khora and the others drew their swords and stepped between the creature and its prey. But Hester pushed past them. "It's all right," she said in a strange, thin voice. "I know him. Let me talk to him."

The Stalker swung its dead-white face from Tom to Hester, lenses whirring inside mechanical eyes. "HESTER SHAW," it said, caressing her name with its gas-leak hiss of a voice.

"Hello, Shrike," said Hester.

The great head tilted to stare down at her. A metal hand rose, hesitated, then touched her face, leaving streaks of oil.

"I'm sorry I never got the chance to say goodbye. . ."

"I WORK FOR THE LORD MAYOR OF LONDON NOW," said Shrike. "HE HAS SENT ME TO KILL YOU."

Tom whimpered again. Hester gave a brittle little laugh. "But . . . you won't do it, will you, Shrike? You wouldn't kill *me*?"

"YES," said Shrike flatly, still staring down at her.

"No, Shrike!" whispered Hester, and Miss Fang seized her chance. She drew a little fan-shaped sliver of metal from a pocket in the sleeve of her coat and sent it whirling towards the Stalker's throat. It made an eerie moaning sound as it flew, unfolding into a shimmering, razor-edged disc. "A Nuevo-Mayan Battle Frisbee!" gasped Tom, who had seen such weapons safe in glass cases in the Weapons & Warfare section at the Museum. He knew that they could sever a man's neck at sixty paces, and he tensed, waiting for the Stalker's skull to drop from its shoulders – but the frisbee just hit Shrike's armoured throat with a clang and lodged there, quivering.

The slit of a mouth lengthened into a long smile and the Stalker darted forward, quick as a lizard. Miss Fang sidestepped, jumped past it and swung a high kick, but it was far too fast for her. "Run!" she shouted at Hester and Tom. "Get back to the *Jenny*! I'll follow!"

What else could they do? They ran. The thing snatched at them as they ducked past, but Khora was there to grab its arm and Nils Lindstrom swung his sword at its face. The Stalker flung Khora off and raised its hand; there were sparks and a shriek of metal on metal, and Lindstrom dropped the broken sword and howled and clutched his arm. It threw him aside and lifted Anna off her feet as she came at it again, swinging her hard against Khora and Yasmina when they rushed to her aid.

"Miss Fang!" shouted Tom. For a moment he thought of going back, but he knew enough about Stalkers to know that there was nothing he could do. He ran after Hester, over a heap of bodies in the doorway and out into shadows and twilight and the frightened, milling crowds. A siren was keening mournfully. There was acrid smoke on the breeze and over by the power-plant he thought he saw the flicker of the thing all aviators feared the most: fire!

"I don't understand," gasped Hester, talking to herself, not Tom. "He wouldn't kill *me*, he *wouldn't*!" But she kept running, and together they dashed out on to Strut Seven where the *Jenny Haniver* was waiting for them.

But Shrike had already made certain that the little airship would not be going anywhere that night. The envelope had been slashed, the cowling of the starboard engine pod had been wrenched open like an old tin can and a spaghetti of torn wiring spilled out on to the quay. Among it lay the broken body of the boy Miss Fang had paid to guard her ship.

Tom stood staring at the wreckage. Behind him,

faintly, growing closer, footsteps trod the metal deck: *pung, pung, pung, pung.*

He looked round for Hester, and found her gone; limping away along the docking ring – running *downhill*, he realized, for the damaged air-town was developing a worrying tilt. He shouted her name and sprinted after her, following her out on to a neighbouring strut. A tatty-looking balloon had just arrived there, spilling out a family of startled sightseers who weren't sure if the darkness and the shouting meant an emergency or some sort of carnival. Hester shouldered her way through them and grabbed the balloonist by his goggles, heaving him out of his basket. It sagged away from the quay as she leaped in. "Stop! Thieves! Hijackers! Help!" the balloonist was shouting, but all Tom could hear was that faint, appalling *pung-pung-pung* approaching fast along the High Street.

"Tom! Come on!"

He summoned all his courage and leaped after Hester. She was fumbling at the mooring ropes as he landed in the bottom of the basket. "Throw everything overboard," she shouted at him.

He did as he was told and the balloon lurched upwards, level with the first-floor windows, with the rooftops, with the spire of St Michael's. Soon Airhaven was a doughnut of darkness falling away behind them and below, and Shrike was just a speck, his green eyes glowing as he stalked out along the strut to watch them go.

13

THE RESURRECTED MAN

In the dark ages before the dawn of the Traction Era, nomad empires had battled each other across the volcano-maze of Europe. It was they who had built the Stalkers, dragging dead warriors off the battlefields and bringing them back to a sort of life by wiring weird Old-Tech machines into their nervous systems.

The empires were long forgotten, but the terrible Resurrected Men were not. Tom could remember playing at being one when he was a child in the Guild Orphanage, stomping about with his arms held out straight in front of him, shouting, "I-AM-A-STAL-KER! EX-TER-MIN-ATE!" until Miss Plym came and told him to keep the noise down.

But he had never expected to *meet* one.

As the stolen balloon scudded eastward, on the night-wind he sat shuddering in the swaying basket, twisted sideways so that Hester wouldn't see the wet stain on his breeches, and said, "I thought they all died hundreds of years ago! I thought they were all destroyed in battles, or went mad and tore themselves apart. . ."

"Not Shrike," said Hester.

"And he *knew* you!"

"Of course he did," she said. "We're old friends, Shrike and me."

✿ ✿ ✿ ✿ ✿

She had met him the morning after her parents died, the morning when she woke up on the shores of the Hunting Ground in the whispering rain. She had no idea how she came to be there, and the pain in her head was so bad that she could barely move or think.

Drawn up nearby was the smallest, filthiest town that she had ever seen. People with big wicker baskets on their backs were coming down out of it on ladders and gangplanks and sifting through the flotsam on the tide-line before returning with their baskets full of scrap and driftwood. A few were carrying her father's rowing boat away, and it wasn't long before some of them discovered Hester. Two men came and looked down at her. One was a typical scavenger, small and filthy, with bits of an old bug piled in his basket. After he had peered at her for a while he stepped back and said to his companion, "Sorry, Mr Shrike – I thought she might be one for your collection, but she's flesh and blood all right. . ."

He turned and stumped away across the steaming garbage, losing all interest in Hester. He only wanted stuff he could sell, and there was no value in a half-dead child. Old bug tyres, now – *those* were worth something. . .

The other man stayed where he was, looking down at Hester. It was only when he reached down and touched her face and she felt the cold, hard iron beneath his gloves that she realized he was not really a man at all. When he spoke, his voice sounded like a wire brush being scraped across a blackboard. "YOU CAN'T STAY HERE, CHILD," he said, and picked her up and slung her over his shoulder and took her aboard the town.

It was called Strole, and it was home to fifty tough, dust-hardened scavengers who robbed Old-Tech sites when they could find them and scrounged salvage from the leavings of larger towns when they could not. Shrike lived with them, but he was no scavenger. When criminals from one of the great Traction Cities escaped into the Out-Country, Shrike would track them and cut off their heads, which he carefully preserved. When he crossed that city's path again he would take the head to the authorities, and collect his reward.

Why he bothered to rescue her Hester never did discover. It could not have been out of pity, for he had none. The only sign of tenderness she ever saw in him was when he busied himself with his collection. He was fascinated by old automata and mechanical toys, and he would buy any that passing scavengers brought to him. His ramshackle quarters in Strole were full of them: animals, knights in armour, clockwork soldiers with keys in their backs, even a life-size Angel of Death pulled from some elaborate clock. But his favourites were all women or children: beautiful ladies in moth-eaten gowns and pretty girls and boys with porcelain faces. All night long Shrike would patiently dismantle and repair them, exploring the intricate escapements of their hearts as if searching for some clue to the workings of his own.

Sometimes it seemed to Hester that she too was part of his collection. Did she remind him of the wounds that he had suffered on the battlefields of forgotten wars, when he had still been human?

She shared his home for five long years, while her face healed badly into a permanent ruined scowl and her memories came slowly back to her. Some were startlingly clear, the waves on the shores of Oak Island, her mum's voice, the moor-wind with its smells of wet grass and the dung of animals. Others were murky and hard to understand; they flashed into her mind just as she was falling asleep, or caught her unawares while she wandered amongst the silent mechanical figures in Shrike's house. *Blood on the star-charts. A metallic noise. A man's long, handsome face with sea-grey eyes.* They were broken shards of memory, and they had to be carefully collected and pieced together, just like the bits of machinery the scavengers dug up.

It was not until she overheard some men telling stories about the great Thaddeus Valentine that she started to make sense of it all. She found that she recognized that name: it was the name of the man who had killed her mum and dad and turned her into a monster. She knew what she had to do without even having to think about it. She went to Shrike and told him she wanted to go after Valentine.

"YOU MUST NOT," was all the Stalker said. "YOU'LL BE KILLED."

"Then come with me!" she had pleaded, but he would not. He had heard about London and about Magnus Crome's love of technology. He thought that if he went there the Guild of Engineers would overpower him and cut him into pieces to study in their secret laboratories. "YOU MUST NOT GO," was all that he would say.

So she went anyway, waiting till he was busy with his automata, then slipping out of a window and out of Strole, and setting off across the wintry Out-Country with a stolen knife in her belt, in search of London and revenge.

❁ ❁ ❁ ❁

"I've never seen him since that," she told Tom, shivering in the basket of the stolen balloon. "Strole was down on the shores of the Anglish Sea when I left, but here Shrike is, working for Magnus Crome, and wanting to kill me. It doesn't make sense!"

"Maybe you hurt his feelings when you ran away?" suggested Tom.

"Shrike doesn't have feelings," said Hester. "They cleaned all *his* memories and feelings away when they made a Stalker of him."

She sounds as if she envies him, thought Tom. But at least the sound of her voice had helped to calm him, and he had stopped shaking. He sat and listened to the wind sigh through the balloon's rigging. There was a black stain on the western clouds which he thought must be the smoke from Airhaven. Had the aviators managed to get the fires under control, or had their town been destroyed? And what about Anna Fang? He realized that Shrike had probably murdered her, along with all her friends. That kind, laughing aviatrix was dead, as dead as his own parents. It was as if there was a curse on him that destroyed everybody who was kind to him. If only he had never met Valentine! If only he had stayed safely in the Museum where he belonged!

"She might be all right," said Hester suddenly, as if she had guessed what he was thinking about. "I think Shrike was just playing with her; he didn't have his claws out or anything."

"He's got *claws*?!"

"As long as she didn't annoy him too much he probably wouldn't waste time killing her."

"What about Airhaven?"

"I suppose if it's really badly damaged it'll put down somewhere for repairs."

Tom nodded. Then a happy thought occurred to him. "Do you think Miss Fang'll come after us?"

"I don't know," said Hester. "But Shrike will."

Tom looked over his shoulder again, horrified.

"Still," she said, "at least we're heading in the right direction for London."

He peered gingerly over the edge of the basket. The clouds lay below them like a white eiderdown drawn across the land, hiding anything that might give a clue as to where they were, or where they were going. "How can you tell?" he asked.

"From the stars, of course," said Hester. "Mum showed me. She was an aviator, too, remember? She'd been all over the place. She even went to America once. You have to use the stars to find your way in places like that where they don't have charts or landmarks. Look, that's the Pole Star, and that constellation is what the Ancients used to call the Great Bear, but most people nowadays call it the City. And if we keep *that* one to starboard we'll know we're heading north-east. . ."

"There are so many!" he said, trying to follow her pointing finger. Here above the clouds, without veils of city-smoke and Out-Country dust to hide it, the night sky sparkled with a million cold points of light. "I never knew there were so many stars before!"

"They're all suns, burning away far out in space, thousands and thousands of miles away," said Hester, and Tom had the feeling that she felt proud to show him how much she knew. "Except for the ones that aren't really stars at all. Some of the really bright ones are mechanical moons that the Ancients put up into orbit thousands of years ago, still circling and circling the poor old Earth."

Tom stared up at the glittering dark. "And what's that one?" he asked, pointing to a bright star low in the west.

Hester looked at it, and her smile faded away. He saw her hands clench into fists. "That one?" she said. "That's an airship, and it's coming after us."

"Perhaps Miss Fang has come to rescue us?" said Tom hopefully.

But the distant airship was gaining quickly, and in another few minutes they could see that it was a small, London-built scoutship, a Spudbury Sunbeam or a Goshawk 90. They could almost feel Shrike's green eyes watching them across the deserts of the sky.

Hester started fumbling with the rusty wheels and levers that controlled the gas-pressure in the balloon. After a few seconds she found the one she wanted and a fierce hiss came from somewhere overhead.

"What are you doing?" squeaked Tom. "You'll let the gas out! We'll crash!"

"I'm hiding us from Shrike," said the girl, and opened the valve still further. Looking up, Tom saw the gasbag start to sag. He glanced back at the pursuing airship. It was gaining, but it was still a few miles away. Hopefully from that distance it would look as if some accident had struck the balloon. Hopefully Shrike would not guess Hester's plan. Hopefully his little ship was not armed with rocket-projectors. . .

And then they sank down into the clouds and could see nothing but swirling dark billows and sometimes a quick glimpse of the moon scudding dimly above them. The basket creaked and the envelope flapped and the gas-valve hissed like a tetchy snake.

"When we touch down, get out of the basket as quick as you can," said Hester.

"Yes," he said, and then, "but . . . you mean we're going to leave the balloon?"

"We don't stand a chance against Shrike in the air," she explained. "Hopefully on the ground I can outwit him."

"On the ground?" cried Tom. "Oh, not the Out-Country again!"

The balloon was sinking fast. They saw the black landscape looming up below, dark blots of vegetation and a few thin glimmers of moonlight. Overhead, thick clouds were racing into the east. There was no sign of Shrike's airship. Tom braced himself. The ground was a hundred feet below, then fifty, then ten. Branches came rattling and scraping along the keel and the basket bucked and plunged, crashing against muddy earth and leaping up into the sky and down again and up.

"Jump!" screamed Hester, the next time it touched down. He jumped, falling through scratchy branches into a soft mattress of mud. The balloon shot upwards again and for a moment he was afraid that Hester had abandoned him to perish on the bare earth. "Hester!" he shouted, so loud it hurt his throat. "Hester!" And then there was a rustling in the scrub away to his left and she was limping towards him. "Oh, thank Quirke!" he whispered.

He expected her to stop and sit down with him to rest a while and thank the gods for dropping them on to soft, wet earth instead of hard stone. Instead, she walked straight past him, limping away towards the north-east.

"Stop!" shouted Tom, still too winded and shivery to even stand. "Wait! Where are you going?"

She looked back at him as if he were mad. "London," she said.

Tom rolled on to his back and groaned, gathering his strength for another weary trek.

Above him, freed of their weight, the balloon was returning to the sky, a dark tear-drop that was quickly swallowed into the belly of the clouds. A few moments later he heard the purr of engines as Shrike's airship went hurrying after it. Then there was only the night and the cold wind, and rags of moonlight prowling the broken hills.

14

THE GUILDHALL

Katherine decided to start at the top. The day after her father left London she sent a message up the pneumatic tube system to the Lord Mayor's office from the terminal in her father's room, and half an hour later a reply came back from Crome's secretary: the Lord Mayor would see Miss Valentine at noon.

Katherine went to her dressing room and put on her most businesslike clothes – her narrow black trousers and her grey coat with the shoulder-fins. She tied back her hair with a clip made from the tail-lights of an ancient car and fetched out a stylish hat with trailing ear-flaps which she had bought six weeks before but hadn't got round to wearing yet. She put colour on her lips and soft oblongs of rouge high on her cheekbones and painted a little blue triangle between her eyebrows, a mock Guild-mark like the fashionable ladies wore. She found a notebook and a pencil and slipped them both into one of Father's important-looking black briefcases along with the pass he had given her on her fifteenth birthday, the gold pass which allowed her access to almost every part of London. Then she studied her appearance in the mirror, imagining herself a few weeks from now going to meet the returning expedition. She would be able to tell Father, *"It's all right now, I under-stand everything; you needn't be afraid any more. . ."*

At a quarter to twelve she walked with Dog to the elevator station in Quirke Circus, enjoying the looks that people gave her as she passed. *"There goes Miss Katherine Valentine,"* she imagined them saying. *"Off to see the Lord Mayor. . ."* The elevator staff all knew her face, and they smiled and said, "Good morning, Miss Katherine," and patted Dog and didn't bother looking at her pass as she boarded the 11.52 for Top Tier.

The elevator hummed upwards. She walked briskly across Paternoster Square, where Dog stared thoughtfully at the wheeling pigeons and pricked up his ears at the sounds of the repair-work going on inside St Paul's. Soon she was climbing the steps of the Guildhall and being ushered into a tiny internal elevator, and at one minute to twelve she was shown through the circular bronze door of the Lord Mayor's private office.

"Ah, Miss Valentine. You are one minute early." Crome glanced up at her from the far side of his huge desk and went back to the report that he had been reading. Behind his head was a round window with a view of St Paul's, looking wavery and unreal through the thick glass, like a sunken temple seen through clear water. Sunlight shone dimly on the tarnished bronze panels of the office walls. There were no pictures, no hangings or decorations of any sort, and the floor was bare metal. Katherine shivered, feeling the cold rise up through the soles of her shoes.

The Lord Mayor kept her waiting for fifty-nine silent seconds which seemed to stretch on for ever. She was feeling thoroughly uncomfortable by the time he set down the report. He smiled faintly, like somebody who had never seen a smile, but had read a book on how to do it.

"You will be glad to hear that I have just received a coded radio signal sent from your father's expedition shortly before he flew out of range," he said. "All is well aboard the *13th Floor Elevator*."

"Good!" said Katherine, knowing that it would be the last she would hear of Father until he was on his way home; even the Engineers had never been able to send radio signals more than a few hundred miles.

"Was there anything else?" asked Crome.

"Yes. . ." said Katherine, and hesitated, afraid that she was going to sound foolish. Faced with Crome's cold office and still colder smile she found herself wishing she had not put on so much make-up or worn these stiff, formal clothes. But this was what she had come here for, after all. She blurted out, "I want to know about that girl, and why she tried to kill my father."

The Lord Mayor's smile vanished. "Your father has never seen fit to tell me who she is. I have no idea why she is so keen to murder him."

"Do you think it is something to do with MEDUSA?"

Crome's gaze grew a few degrees colder. "That matter does not concern you!" he snapped. "What has Valentine told you?"

"Nothing!" said Katherine, getting flustered. "But I can see he's scared, and I need to know why, because. . ."

"Listen to me, child," said Crome, standing up and coming around the desk at her. Thin hands gripped her shoulders. "If Valentine has secrets from you it is for good reason. There are aspects of his work that you could not begin to understand. Remember, he started out with nothing; he was a mere Out-Country scavenger before I took an interest in him. Do you want to see him reduced to that again? Or worse?"

Katherine felt as if he had slapped her. Her face burnt red with anger, but she controlled herself.

"Go home and wait for his return," ordered Crome. "And leave grown-up matters to those who understand them. Don't speak to anyone about the girl, or MEDUSA."

"Grown-up matters?" thought Katherine angrily. *"How old does he think I am?"* But she bowed her head and said meekly, "Yes, Lord Mayor," and "Come along, Dog."

"And do not bring that animal to Top Tier again," called Crome, his voice following her into the outer office, where the secretaries turned to stare at her furious, tearful face.

Riding the elevator back to Quirke Circus, she whispered in her wolf's ear, "We'll show him, Dog!"

⚙ ⚙ ⚙ ⚙ ⚙

Instead of going straight home she called in at the Temple of Clio on the edge of Circle Park. There in the scented darkness she calmed herself and tried to work out what to do next.

Ever since Nikolas Quirke had been declared a god, most Londoners had stopped giving much thought to the older gods and goddesses, and so Katherine had the temple to herself. She liked Clio, who had been her mother's goddess back in Puerto Angeles, and whose statue looked a bit like Mama too, with its kind dark eyes and patient smile. She remembered what Mama had taught her, about how the poor goddess was being blown constantly backwards into the future by the storm of progress, but how she could reach back sometimes and inspire people to change the whole course of history. Looking up now at the statue's gentle face she said, "What must I do, Clio? How can I help Father if the Lord Mayor won't tell me anything?"

She hadn't really expected an answer, and none came, so she said a quick prayer for Father and another for poor Tom Natsworthy, and made her offerings and left.

It wasn't until she was halfway back to Clio House that the idea struck her, a thought so unexpected that it could have been sent to her by the goddess herself. She remembered how, as she ran towards the waste chutes on the night Tom fell, she had passed someone heading in the other direction; a young Apprentice Engineer, looking so white and shocked that she was *sure* he must have witnessed what happened.

She hurried homeward through the sunlit park. That young Engineer would have the answer! She would go back to the Gut and find him! She would find out what was going on without any help from wicked old Magnus Crome!

15

THE RUSTWATER MARSHES

Tom and Hester had walked all night, and when the pale, flat sun rose behind drifts of morning fog they kept walking, stopping only now and then to catch their breath. This landscape was quite different from the mud-plains they had crossed a few days ago. Here they had to keep making detours around bogs and pools of brackish water, and although they sometimes stumbled into the deep, weed-choked scars of old town-tracks it was clear that no town had been this way for many years. "See how the scrub has grown up," said Hester, pointing out ruts filled with brambles and hillsides green with young trees. "Even a little semi-static would have felled those saplings for fuel."

"Perhaps the earth here is just too soft," suggested Tom, sinking to his waist for the twentieth time in the thick mud. He was recalling the huge map of the Hunting Ground that hung in the lobby of the London Museum, and the great sweep of marsh-country that stretched all the way from the central mountains to the shores of the Sea of Khazak, mile after mile of reed-beds and thin blue creeks and all of it marked, *Unsuitable for Town or City*. He said, "I think this must be the edge of the Rustwater Marshes. They call it that because the water is supposed to be stained red with the rust of towns that have strayed into it and sunk. Only the most foolhardy mayor would bring his town here."

"Then Wreyland and Anna Fang brought us much further south than I thought," whispered Hester to herself. "London must be almost a thousand miles away by now.

It'll take months to catch it up again, and Shrike will be on my tail the whole way."

"But you fooled him!" Tom reminded her. "We escaped!"

"He won't stay fooled for long," she said. "He'll soon pick up our tracks again. Why do you think he's called a Stalker?"

✿ ✿ ✿ ✿ ✿

On and on she led him, dragging him over hills and through mires and down valleys where the air was speckly with swarms of whining, stinging flies. They both grew weary and peevish. Once Tom suggested they sit down and rest a while, and Hester snapped back, "Do what you like. What do I care?" After that he trudged on in silence, angry at her. What a horrible, ugly, vicious, self-pitying girl she was! After all they had come through, and the way he had helped her in the Out-Country, she was still ready to abandon him. He wished Shrike had got her and it was Miss Fang or Khora who he had escaped with. *They* would have let him rest his aching feet. . .

But he was glad enough of Hester when the darkness fell, when thick clots of fog rose out of the marshes like the ghosts of mammoths and every rustle in the under-growth sounded like a Stalker's footfall. She found a place for them to spend the night, in the shelter of some stunted trees, and later, when the sudden shriek of a hunting owl brought him leaping out of his uneasy sleep he found her sitting guard beside him like a friendly gar-goyle. "It's all right," she told him. And after a moment, in one of those sudden flashes of softness that he had noticed before, she said, "I miss them, Tom. My mum and dad."

"I know," he said. "I miss mine too."

"You've got no family at all in London?"

"No."

"No friends?"

He thought about it. "Not really."

"Who was that girl?' she asked, after a little while.

"What? Where?"

"In the Gut that night, with you and Valentine."

"That was Katherine," he said. "She's. . . Well, she's Valentine's daughter."

Hester nodded. "She's pretty," she said.

After that he slept easier, dreaming that Katherine was coming down to rescue them in an airship, carrying them back into the crystal light above the clouds. When he next opened his eyes it was dawn and Hester was shaking him.

"Listen!"

He listened, and heard a sound that was not the sound of woods or water.

"Is it a town?" he asked hopefully.

"No. . ." Hester tilted her head to one side, tasting the sound. "It's a Rotwang aëro-engine. . ."

It grew louder, throbbing down out of the sky. Above the swirling mist a London scoutship flickered by.

They froze, hoping that the wet black cage of branches overhead would hide them. The growl of the airship faded and then rose again, circling. "Shrike can see us," whispered Hester, staring up at the blind, white fog. "I can feel him watching us. . ."

"No, no," Tom insisted. "If we can't see the airship, how can he see us? It stands to reason. . ."

⚙ ⚙ ⚙ ⚙ ⚙

But high overhead the Resurrected Man tunes his eyes to ultra-red and switches on his heat-sensors and sees two glowing human shapes amid the soft grey static of the trees. "TAKE ME CLOSER," he orders.

"If you can see them so clearly now," the airship's pilot grumbles, "it's a pity you couldn't tell that bloomin' balloon was empty before we went chasing it across half the Hunting Ground."

Shrike says nothing. Why should he explain himself to this whining Once-born? He had seen that the balloon was empty as soon as it popped back up above the clouds, but he had decided to keep it to himself. He was pleased at Hester Shaw's quick thinking, and he decided to let her live a few more hours as a reward, while this slow-witted Engineer-aviator pursued her empty balloon.

He flicks his eyes back to their normal setting. He will hunt Hester the hard way, with scent and sound and ordinary vision. He calls up a memory of her face and sets it turning in his mind as the airship sweeps down through the fog.

⚙ ⚙ ⚙ ⚙ ⚙

"Run!" said Hester. The airship loomed out of the whiteness a few yards away, settling towards the ground with its rotors beating the fog like egg-whisks. She hauled Tom out of their useless hiding place and away across sodden ground, knuckled with tree-roots. White scuts of water spurted at every step, and black slime gurgled into their boots. They ran blindly, until Hester came to such an abrupt stop that Tom crashed into her from behind and they both went sprawling.

They had come in a circle. The airship hung just ahead of them, and a giant shape barred their path. Two beams of pale green light stabbed towards them, filled with dancing water droplets. "HESTER," grated a metal voice.

Hester groped for something she could use as a weapon and came up with a gnarled old length of wood. "Don't come any closer, Shrike!" she warned. "I'll smash those pretty green eyes of yours! I'll bash your brains out!"

"Come on!" squeaked Tom, plucking at her coat and trying to drag her away.

"Where to?" asked Hester, risking a quick glance back at him. She shifted her grip on the makeshift club and stood her ground as Shrike stalked closer.

"YOU HAVE DONE WELL, HESTER, BUT THE HUNT IS ENDED." The Stalker was moving carefully over the wet ground. Each time he set down his metal foot a wreath of steam hissed up. He raised his hands and claw-like blades slid out.

"What made you change your mind about London, Shrike?" shouted Hester angrily. "How do you come to be Crome's odd-job man?"

"YOU LED ME TO LONDON, HESTER." Shrike paused, and his dead face widened in a steely smile. "I KNEW YOU WOULD GO THERE. I SOLD MY COLLECTION AND CHARTERED AN AIRSHIP SO THAT I COULD GET THERE BEFORE YOU."

"You sold your clockwork people?" Hester sounded astonished. "Shrike, if you wanted me back that badly, why didn't you just track me down?"

"I DECIDED TO LET YOU CROSS THE HUNTING GROUND ALONE," said Shrike. "IT WAS A TEST."

"Did I pass?"

Shrike ignored her. "WHEN I REACHED LONDON I WAS TAKEN STRAIGHT TO THE ENGINEERIUM, AS I EXPECTED. I SPENT EIGHTEEN MONTHS THERE WAITING FOR YOU TO ARRIVE. THE ENGINEERS TOOK ME APART AND PUT ME TOGETHER AGAIN A DOZEN TIMES. BUT IT WAS WORTH IT. I MADE A DEAL WITH MAGNUS CROME. HE HAS PROMISED ME MY HEART'S DESIRE."

"Oh, good," said Hester weakly, wondering what on earth he was talking about.

"BUT FIRST YOU MUST DIE."

"But Shrike, why?"

The reply was drowned out by a thick, warbling hum that made Tom wonder if the Stalker's airship was about to lift off without him. He glanced up at it. It was still holding the same position as before, but the steady chirrup of the propellers had been masked by the new noise, a rumbling, slithering roar that grew louder every second. Even Shrike seemed disturbed: his eyes flickered and he tilted his head to one side, listening. Underfoot, the ground began to tremble.

Out of the fog behind the Stalker burst a wall of mud and water, curling over at the top, capped with white foam. Behind it came a town, a very small, old-fashioned town, racing along on eight fat wheels. Hester scrambled backwards, and Shrike saw the look on her face and turned to see what caused it. Tom dived sideways, grabbing the girl by the scruff of her neck and hurling her to safety. The airship tried to veer away but the wheels of the speeding town caught it and blew it apart and ploughed the blazing debris down into the mud. An instant later they heard the Stalker bellow "HESTER!" as the huge front wheel came crashing down on him.

They clung together, rolling over and over as the town howled past, a flicker of spokes and pistons, firelight on metal, tiny figures staring down from observation decks, the long-drawn-out moan of a klaxon echoing through the fog. Then, just as suddenly as it had appeared, it was gone. The air stank of smoke and hot metal.

They sat up. Bits of airship were drifting down, blazing merrily. Where the Stalker had been standing a deep wheel-mark was quickly filling with black, glistening mud. Something which might have been an iron hand jutted from the ooze and a pale cloud of steam rose into the air above it and slowly faded.

"Is it . . . *dead*?" asked Tom, his voice all quivery with fright.

"A town just ran over him," said Hester. "I shouldn't think he's very well. . ."

Tom wondered dimly what Shrike had meant about his "heart's desire". Why would he have sold his precious collection to come after Hester if all he wanted to do was kill her? There was no way of knowing now. "And the poor men on that airship. . ." he whispered.

"They were sent to help him kill us, Natsworthy," said the girl. "Don't waste your pity on them."

They were quiet for a moment, staring at the mist. Then Tom said, "I wonder what it was running from?"

"What do you mean?"

"That town," said Tom. "It was moving so fast. . . Something must be chasing it. . ."

Hester looked at him and slowly realized what he meant.

"Oh, *knackers*!" she said.

The second town was upon them almost at once. It was bigger than the first, with vast, barrel-shaped wheels. On its gaping jaws some wag had drawn a toothy grin and the words, *"HAPPY EETER"*.

There was no time to run out of its way. Hester grabbed Tom this time and he saw her shouting something, but the shrieking thunder of the engines meant that it took him a moment to work out what it was.

"We can jump it! Do as I do!"

The town rolled over them, its wheels passing on either side so that they were lifted up like two ants in the path of a plough, lifted on a wave of mud that almost smashed them against the lumbering metal belly overhead. Hester crouched on the crest of the wave like a surfer and Tom wobbled beside her, expecting at any moment to be swatted out of his life by a passing derrick or hurled under the wheels. Hester was shouting at him again, and pointing. An exhaust duct was rushing past them like a monstrous snake, and by the flare of furnace-light from vents on the town's underside he made out the handrail of a maintenance platform. Hester grabbed at it and swung herself up, and Tom flung himself after her. For a moment his hands clutched wildly at nothing, then there was rusty iron under his fingers, almost jerking his arms from their sockets, and Hester reached down and took a firm grip on his belt and hauled him to safety.

It was a long time before they stopped shaking and clambered to their feet. They both looked as if they had been modelled crudely from the Out-Country mud; it covered their clothes and clagged in their hair and plastered their faces. Tom was laughing helplessly at the closeness of their escape and at the sheer surprise of finding himself still alive, and Hester laughed with him. He had never heard her laugh before, and he had never felt as close to anyone as he felt to her at that moment.

"We'll be all right!" she said. "We'll be all right now! Let's go up and find out who we've hitched a lift with!"

✿ ✿ ✿ ✿ ✿

Whatever the town was, it was small, only a suburb really. Tom amused himself by trying to work out what it might be while Hester picked the lock on a hatchway and led him up a long stairwell with rusty walls that steamed in the heat from the engines. He thought it looked a bit like Crawley, or Purley Spokes, the suburbs that London had built back in the great old days when there was so much prey that cities could afford to build little satellite towns. If so, it might have its own merchant airships, licensed to trade with London.

But something still nagged at the back of his mind. *Only the most foolhardy mayor would bring his town here...*

Why on earth would Crawley or Purley Spokes be chasing a townlet into the dreaded Rustwater Marshes?

They climbed on up the stairwell until they reached a second hatch. It wasn't locked, and swung open to let them out on to the upper deck. A cold wind blew fog between the metal buildings and the deckplates shook and lurched as the suburb raced onwards. The streets seemed deserted, but Tom knew that small towns often had only a few hundred inhabitants. Perhaps they were all busy in the engine-rooms, or waiting safe indoors until the chase was over.

But there was something about this place he didn't like; it certainly wasn't the trim little suburb he had been hoping for. The deckplates were rusty and pitted and the shabby houses were dwarfed by huge auxiliary engines that had been ripped out of other towns and bolted haphazardly to this one, linked to the main engines on the deck below by a cat's-cradle of gigantic ducts that wrapped around the buildings and burrowed down through holes cut in the deckplate. Beyond them, where Tom would have expected parks and observation platforms, a mess of gun-emplacements and wooden palisades ringed the edge of the suburb.

Hester motioned for him to keep quiet and led him towards the foggy stern, where he could see a tall building that must be the Town Hall. As they drew nearer they made out a sign above the entrance which read:

Welcome to
TUNBRIDGE WHEELS
Population: ~~500~~ ~~467~~ 212
and still rising!

Above it flapped a black and white flag; a grinning skull and two crossed bones.

"Great Quirke!" gasped Tom. "This is a pirate suburb!"

And suddenly, from foggy side-streets all around them, came men and women as shabby as the town, lean and hard and fierce-eyed, and carrying the biggest guns that he had ever seen.

◎ ◎ ◎ ◎ ◎

As the pirate suburb speeds on its way, silence returns to the Rustwater, broken only by the sounds of small creatures moving in the reed-beds. Then the ooze in one of the deep wheel-ruts burbles and heaves and vomits up the jerking wreck of Shrike.

He has been driven far down into the mud like a screaming tent-peg, ground and crushed and twisted. His left arm hangs by a few frayed wires; his right leg will not move. One of his eyes is dark and blind and the view from the other is cloudy, so that he has to keep twitching his head to clear it. Bits of his memory have vanished, but others come up unbidden. As he wades out of the suburb's wheel-marks he remembers the ancient wars that he was built for. At Hill 20 the Tesla Guns crackled like iced lightning, wrapping him in fire until his flesh began to fry on his iron bones. But he survived. He is the last of the Lazarus Brigade, and he always survives. It will take a lot more than being run over by a couple of towns to finish Shrike.

Slowly, slowly, he claws his way to firmer ground, and sniffs and scouts and scans until he is sure that Hester escaped alive. He feels very proud of her. His heart's desire! Soon he will find her again, and the loneliness of his everlasting life will be over.

The suburb has left deep grooves across the landscape. It will be easy to track, even with his leg dragging uselessly, even with an eye gone and his mind misfiring. The Stalker throws back his head and bellows his hunting cry at the empty marshes.

16

THE TURD TANKS

London kept on moving, day after day, grinding its way across the continent formerly known as Europe as if there were some fantastic prize ahead – but all that the look-outs had sighted since the city ate Salthook were a few tiny scavenger towns, and Magnus Crome would not even alter course to catch them. People started to grow restless, asking each other in whispers what the Lord Mayor thought he was playing at. London had never been meant to go so far, so fast. There was talk of food shortages, and the heat from the engines spread up through the deckplates until it was said you could fry an egg on the pavements of Tier Six.

Down in the Gut the heat was appalling, and when Katherine stepped off the elevator at Tartarus Row she felt as if she had just walked into an oven. She had never been so deep into the Gut before, and for a while she stood blinking on the steps of the elevator terminus, dazed by the noise and darkness. Up on Tier One she had left the sun shining down on Circle Park and a cool wind stirring the rose-bushes: down here gangs of men were were running about, klaxons were honking and huge hoppers of fuel were grinding past her on their way to the furnaces.

For a moment she felt like going home, but she knew that she had do what she had come here for, for Father's sake. She took a deep breath and went out into the street.

It was nothing like High London. Nobody knew her face down here; passers-by were surly when she asked them for directions, and off-duty labourers lounging on the pavements whistled as she went by and shouted, "Hello, darling!" and "Where'd you get that hat?" A burly foreman shoved her aside to lead a gang of shackled convicts past. From shrines under the fuel-ducts leered statues of Sooty Pete, the hunch-backed god of engine rooms and smoke-stacks. Katherine lifted her chin and kept a tight grip on Dog's leash, glad that he was there to protect her.

But she knew that this was the only place where she could hope to find the truth. With Father away and Tom lost or dead, and Magnus Crome unwilling to talk, there was only one person left in London who might know the secret of the scarred girl.

It had been hard work finding him, but luckily the staff in the records office at the Guild of Salvagemen, Stokers, Wheel-Tappers and Associated Gut Operatives were happy enough to oblige Thaddeus Valentine's daughter. If there was an Apprentice Engineer near the waste-chutes that night, they said, he must have been supervising convict labourers, and if he was supervising convict labourers he must have come from the Engineers' experimental prison in the Deep Gut. A few more questions and a bribe to a Gut foreman and she had a name: Apprentice Engineer Pod.

Now, nearly a week after her meeting with the Lord Mayor, she was on her way to talk to him.

✿ ✿ ✿ ✿ ✿

The Deep Gut Prison was a complex of buildings the size of a small town which clustered around the base of a giant support pillar. Katherine followed signposts to the administration block, a spherical metal building jacked up on rust-streaked gantries and slowly revolving so that the supervisors could look down from its windows and watch their cell-blocks and exercise yards and algae-mat farms spin endlessly around them. In the entrance hall, neon light glimmered on acres of white metal. An Engineer came gliding up to Katherine as she stepped inside. "No dogs allowed," he said.

"He's not a dog, he's a wolf," replied Katherine, with her sweetest smile, and the man jumped back as Dog sniffed at his rubber coat. He was prim-looking, with a thin, pursed mouth and patches of eczema on his bald head. The badge on his coat said, *Gut Supervisor Nimmo.* Katherine smiled at him, and before he could raise any more objections she showed her gold pass and said, "I'm here on an errand for my father, the Head Historian. I have to see one of your apprentices, a boy called Pod."

Supervisor Nimmo blinked at her and said, "But. . . But. . ."

"I've come straight from Magnus Crome's office," Katherine lied. "Call his secretary if you want to check. . ."

"No, I'm sure it's all right. . ." mumbled Nimmo. Nobody from outside the Guild had ever wanted to interview an apprentice before, and he didn't like it. There was probably a rule against it. But he didn't want to argue with someone who knew the Lord Mayor. He asked Katherine to wait and scurried away, vanishing into a glass-walled office on the far side of the hall.

Katherine waited, stroking Dog's head and smiling politely at bald, white-coated passers-by. Soon Nimmo was back. "I have located Apprentice Pod," he announced. "He has been transferred to Section 60."

"Oh, well done, Mr Nimmo!" beamed Katherine. "Can you send him up?"

"Certainly not," retorted the Engineer, who wasn't sure he liked being ordered about by a mere Historian's daughter. But if she wanted to see Section 60, he would take her there. "Follow me," he said, leading the way to a small elevator. "Section 60 is on the underdecks."

The underdecks were where London kept its plumbing. Katherine had read about them in her school books so she was prepared for the long descent, but nothing could have prepared her for the smell. It hit her as soon as the elevator reached the bottom and the door slid open. It was like walking into a wall of wet sewage.

"This is Section 60, one of our most interesting experimental labour units," said Nimmo, who didn't seem to notice the smell. "The convicts assigned to this sector are helping to develop some very exciting new ways of recycling the city's waste products."

Katherine stepped out, clamping her handkerchief over her nose. She found herself standing in a huge, dimly-lit space. Ahead of her were three tanks, each larger than Clio House and all its gardens. Stinking yellow-brown filth was dribbling into the tanks from a maze of pipes that clung to the low ceiling, and people in drab grey prison coveralls were wading chest-deep in it, skimming the surface with long-handled rakes.

"What are they doing?" asked Katherine. "What *is* that stuff?"

"Detritus, Miss Valentine," said Nimmo, sounding proud. "Effluent. Ejecta. Human nutritional by-products."

"You mean . . . poo?" said Katherine, appalled.

"Thank you, Miss Valentine; perhaps that is the word for which I was groping." Nimmo glared at her. "There is nothing disgusting about it, I assure you. We all . . . ah . . . use the toilet from time to time. Well, now you know where your . . . um . . . *poo* ends up. 'Waste not, want not' is the Engineers' motto, Miss. Properly processed human ordure makes very useful fuel for our city's engines. And we are experimenting with ways of turning it into a tasty and nutritious snack. We feed our prisoners on nothing else. Unfortunately they keep dying. But that is just a temporary set-back, I'm sure."

Katherine walked to the edge of the nearest tank. *I have come down to the Sunless Country!* she thought. *Oh, Clio! This is the land of the dead!*

But even the Sunless Country could not be as terrible as this place. The slurry swilled and shifted, slapping at the edges of the tanks as London trundled over a range of rugged hills. Flies buzzed in thick clouds beneath the vaulted roof and settled on the faces and bodies of the labourers. Their shaven heads gleamed in the dim half-light, faces set in blank stares as they skimmed the thick crust from the surface and transferred it into hoppers which other convicts wheeled on rails along the sides of the tank. Grim-faced Apprentice Engineers looked on, swinging long, black truncheons. Only Dog seemed happy; he was straining at his leash, his tail wagging, and every now and then he would look up eagerly at Katherine as if to thank her for bringing him somewhere with such interesting smells.

She fought down her rising lunch and turned to Nimmo. "These poor people! Who are they?"

"Oh, don't worry about *them*," said the supervisor. "They're convicts. Criminals. They deserve it."

"What did they do?'

"Oh, this and that. Petty theft. Tax-dodging. Criticizing our Lord Mayor. They're very well-treated, considering. Now, let's see if we can find Apprentice Pod. . ."

While he spoke, Katherine had been watching the nearest tank. One of the men working it had stopped moving and let go of his rake, holding his head as if overcome by dizziness. Now a girl apprentice had also noticed him, and stepping up to the edge of the tank she jabbed at the man with her truncheon. Blue sparks flickered where it touched him, and he thrashed and howled and floundered, finally vanishing under the heaving surface. Other prisoners stared towards the place where he had sunk, too scared to go and help.

"Do something!" gasped Katherine, turning to Nimmo, who seemed not to have noticed.

Another apprentice came running along the edge of the tank, shouting at the prisoners below him to help their comrade. Two or three of them dredged him up, and the new apprentice leaned down into the tank and hauled him out, splattering himself with slurry in the process. He was wearing a little gauze mask, like many of the warders, but Katherine was sure she recognized him, and at her side she heard Nimmo growl, *"Pod!"*

They hurried towards him. Apprentice Pod had dragged the half-drowned convict on to the metal walkway between the tanks and was trying to wash the slurry from his face with water from a stand-pipe nearby. The other apprentice, the one who had jabbed the poor man in the first place, looked on with an expression of disgust. "You're wasting water again, Pod!" she said, as Katherine and Nimmo ran up.

"What is going on here, Apprentices?" asked Nimmo crossly.

"This man was slacking," the girl said. "I was just trying to get him to work a bit faster."

"He's feverish!" said Apprentice Pod, looking up plaintively, covered in stinking muck. "It's no wonder he couldn't work."

Katherine knelt beside him and he noticed her for the first time, his eyes widening in surprise. He had succeeded in washing most of the slurry from the man's face, and she reached out and laid her hand on the damp brow. Even by the standards of the Deep Gut it felt hot. "He's really sick," she said, looking up at Nimmo. "He's burning up. He should be in hospital. . ."

"Hospital?" replied Nimmo. "We have no hospital down here. These are prisoners, Miss Valentine. Criminals. They don't require medical care."

"He'll be another case for K Division soon," observed the girl apprentice.

"Be quiet!" hissed Nimmo.

"What does she mean, K Division?" asked Katherine. Nimmo wouldn't answer. Apprentice Pod was staring at her, and she thought she saw tears trickling down his face, although it might have been perspiration. She looked down at the convict, who seemed to have slid into a sort of half-sleep. The metal decking looked terribly hard, and on a sudden impulse she pulled off her hat and folded it and slipped it under his head as a pillow. "He shouldn't be here!" she said angrily. "He's far too weak to work in your horrible tanks!"

"It's appalling," agreed Nimmo. "The sort of prisoners

we are being sent these days are just too feeble. If the Guild of Merchants made more of an effort to solve the food shortage they might be a bit healthier, or if the Navigators pulled their fingers out and tracked down some decent prey for once. . . But I think you have seen enough, Miss Valentine. Kindly ask Apprentice Pod whatever it is your father wishes to know, and I shall take you back to the elevators."

Katherine looked round at Pod. He had pulled down his mask, and he was unexpectedly handsome, with big dark eyes and a small, perfect mouth. She stared at him for a moment, feeling stupid. Here he was, being brave, trying to help this poor man, and she was bothering him with something that suddenly seemed quite trivial.

"It's Miss Valentine, Miss, isn't it?" he said nervously, as Dog pushed past him to sniff at the sick man's fingers.

Katherine nodded. "I saw you in the Gut that night when we ate Salthook," she said. "Down by the waste-chutes. I think you saw the girl who tried to kill my father. Could you tell me everything you remember?"

The boy stared at her, fascinated by the long dark strands of hair that were falling down across her face now that her hat was off. Then his eyes flicked away to look at Nimmo. "I didn't see anything, Miss," he said. "I mean, I heard shouting and I ran to help, but with all the smoke and stuff. . . I didn't see anybody."

"Are you sure?" pleaded Katherine. "It could be terribly important."

Apprentice Pod shook his head, and wouldn't meet her eye. "I'm sorry. . ."

The man on the deck suddenly stirred and gave a great sigh, and they all looked down at him. It took Katherine a moment to understand that he was dead.

"See?" said the girl apprentice smugly. "Told you he was for K Division."

Nimmo was prodding the body with the toe of his boot. "Take him away, Apprentice."

Katherine was shaking. She wanted to cry, but she couldn't. If only she could do something to help these poor people! "I'm going to tell my father all about this when he gets home," she promised. "And when he finds out what's going on in this dreadful place. . ." She wished she had never come here. Beside her she heard Pod say again, "Sorry, Miss Valentine," and wasn't sure if he was sorry because he couldn't help her or sorry for her because she had learned the truth of what life was like under London.

Nimmo was growing edgy. "Miss Valentine, I insist that you leave now. You shouldn't be here. Your father should have sent an official member of his Guild if he had business with this apprentice. What did he hope to learn from the boy anyway?"

"I'm coming," said Katherine, and did the only thing she could for the dead convict: she reached out and gently shut his eyes.

"I'm sorry," whispered Apprentice Pod, as they led her away.

17

THE PIRATE SUBURB

ate that night, and deep in the Rustwater Marshes, Tunbridge Wheels finally caught up with its prey. The exhausted townlet had blundered into a sink-hole and the suburb hit it side-on without bothering to slow its thunderous speed. The impact tore the townlet to pieces and splinters came raining down into the suburb's streets as it turned and sped back to swallow the wreckage. "Meals on wheels!" the pirates howled.

From their cage in the suburb's gut, Tom and Hester watched in horror as the dismantling-engines went to work, ripping the townlet into heaps of scrap without even bothering to let the survivors off. The few who did come stumbling out were grabbed by the waiting pirates. If they were young and fit they were dragged off to other tiny cages like the one in which Hester and Tom had been imprisoned. If not, they were killed, and their bodies were added to the rubbish heap at the edge of the digestion yard.

"Oh, great Quirke!" Tom whispered. "This is horrible! They're breaking every rule of Municipal Darwinism. . ."

"It's a pirate suburb, Natsworthy," said Hester. "What did you expect? They strip their prey as quickly as they can and make the captives slaves in their engine-rooms. They don't waste food and space on people who are too weak to work. It's not really so different from what your precious London gets up to. At least this lot have the honesty to call themselves pirates."

The flash of a crimson robe out in the digestion yards caught Tom's eye. The mayor of the pirate suburb had come down to take a look at his latest catch, and he was strutting along the walkway outside the cells, surrounded by his bodyguards. He was a tiny little man, stooping and hunch-shouldered, a bald head and scrawny neck jutting from the cat-fur collar of his gown. He didn't look friendly. "He looks more like a moth-eaten vulture than a mayor!" whispered Tom, tugging at Hester's sleeve and pointing. "What do you think he'll do with us?"

She shrugged, glancing up at the approaching party. "We'll be slung into the engine-rooms, I suppose. . ." Then she stopped short, staring at the mayor as if he was the most amazing thing she had ever seen. Shouldering Tom aside she thrust her face against the bars of the cage and started to shout. "Peavey!" she hollered, straining to make herself heard over the thunder of the gut. "Peavey! Over here!"

"Do you know him?" asked Tom, confused. "Is he a friend? Is he all right?"

"I don't have friends," snapped Hester, "and he's not all right; he's a ruthless, murdering animal and I've seen him kill people for just looking at him in a funny way. So let's hope the catch has put him in a good mood. Peavey! Over here! It's me! It's Hester Shaw!"

The ruthless, murdering animal turned towards their cage and scowled.

"His name's Chrysler Peavey," Hester explained hoarsely. "He stopped to trade in Strole a couple of times when I lived there with Shrike. He was mayor of another little scavenger town. The gods alone know how he got himself a flash suburb like this. . . Now hush; and let me do the talking!"

Tom studied Chrysler Peavey as he came stalking over to peer at the captives, henchmen clustering behind. He wasn't much to look at. His lumpy scalp reflected the glare of furnaces and the sweat draining off it made pale stripes in the grime on his face. As if to make up for his bald head he had hair almost everywhere else; grubby white bristles pushing out of his chin, thick grey tufts sprouting from his ears and nostrils, and a pair of enormous, bushy, wriggling eyebrows. A tarnished chain of office hung round his neck, and on one shoulder perched a scrawny monkey.

"Who're they?" he said.

"Couple of hitchhikers, boss – I mean, Your Worship. . ." said one of his guards, a woman whose hair had been plaited and lacquered into two long, curving horns.

"Come aboard in the middle of the chase, Your Worship," added another, the man who had overseen the newcomers' capture. He showed Peavey the coat he was wearing; the fleece-lined aviator's coat he had taken from Tom. "I got this off one of 'em. . ."

Peavey grunted. He seemed about to turn away, but Hester kept grinning her crooked grin at him and saying, "Peavey! It's me!" until she lit a spark of recognition in his greedy black eyes.

"Bloody Hull!" he growled. "It's the tin man's kid!"

"You're looking good, Peavey," said Hester, and Tom noticed that she didn't try to hide her face from the pirates, as if she knew that she mustn't let them see any sign of weakness.

"Blimey!" said Peavey, looking her up and down. "Blimey! It really is you! The Stalker's little helper, all growed up and uglier than ever! Where's old Shrikey then?"

"Dead," said Hester.

"Dead? What was it, metal fatigue?" He gave a great guffaw and the bodyguards all joined in obediently, until even the monkey on his shoulder started shrieking and rattling its chain. "Metal fatigue! Get it?"

"So how come you're running Tunbridge Wheels?" asked Hester, while he was still wiping the tears from his eyes and chuckling. "The last I heard of this place it was a respectable suburb. It used to hunt up north, on the edges of the ice."

Peavey chuckled, leaning against the bars. "Flashy, innit?" he said. "This place ate my old town a couple of years back. Come racing up one day and scoffed it straight down. They was soft, though: they hadn't reckoned with me and my boys. We busted out of the gut and took over the whole place; set the mayor and the council to work stoking their own boilers, settled ourselves down in their comfy houses and their posh Town Hall. No more scavenging for me! I'm a proper mayor now. His Worship Chrysler Peavey at your service!"

Tom shuddered, imagining the dreadful things that must have happened here when Peavey's roughs took over – but Hester just nodded as if she was impressed. "Congratulations," she said. "It's a good town. Fast, I mean. Well-built. You're taking a risk, though. If your prey hadn't stopped when it did, you'd've plunged straight into the heart of the Rustwater and sunk like a stone."

Peavey waved the warning away. "Not Tunbridge Wheels, sweetheart. This suburb's specialized. Mires and marshes don't bother us. There're fat towns hiding in these swamps, and fatter prey still where I'm planning to go next."

Hester nodded. "So how about letting us out then?"

she asked casually. "With all this prey to catch you could probably use a couple of good tough helpers up top."

"Ha ha!" chortled Peavey. "Nice try, Hettie, but you're out of luck. Prey's been short these last couple of years. I need all the loot and grub I can find just to keep the lads happy, and they won't be happy if I start bringing new faces aboard. 'Specially not faces as 'orrible as yours." He bellowed with laughter again, looking round at his bodyguards to make sure they were joining in. The monkey ran up on to the top of his head and squatted there, chattering.

"But you need me, Peavey!" Hester told him, forgetting all about Tom in her desperation. "I'm not soft. I'm probably tougher than half of your best lads. I'll fight for a place up top, if that's what it takes. . ."

"Oh, I can use you, all right," agreed Peavey. "But not up top. It's in the engine rooms where I need help. Sorry, Hettie!" He turned away, and beckoned to the woman with the horns. "Chain 'em up, Maggs, and take 'em to the slave pits."

Hester slumped down on the floor of the cage, despairing. Tom touched her shoulder, but she shrugged him irritably away. He looked past her, at Peavey stalking away across his blood-stained yards and the pirates advancing on the cage with guns and manacles. To his surprise, he felt more angry than afraid. After all that they had been through, they were going to become slaves after all! It wasn't *fair*! Before he knew what he was doing he was on his feet and pounding at the greasy bars, and, in a strange, thin-sounding voice, he heard himself shouting, "NO!"

Peavey turned round. His eyebrows climbed his craggy forehead like mountaineering caterpillars.

"NO!" shouted Tom again. "You know her, and she asked you for help, and you ought to help her! You're just a coward, eating up little towns that can't escape, and murdering people, and sticking people in the slave pit because you're too scared of your own men to help them!"

Maggs and the other guards all raised their guns and looked at Peavey expectantly, waiting for him to give the order to blow the impertinent prisoner to pieces. But he just stood and stared, and then came walking slowly back towards the cage.

"What did you say?" he asked.

Tom took a step backwards. When he tried to speak again, no words came out.

"You're from London, ain't yer?" asked Peavey. "I'd recognize that accent anywhere! And you're not from the Nether Boroughs, neither. What Tier d'you come from?"

"T-two," stammered Tom.

"Tier Two?" Peavey looked round at his companions. "You 'ear that? That's almost High London, that is! This bloke's a High London gentleman. What did you want to go slinging a gentleman like this in the lock-ups for, Maggs?"

"But you said. . ." Maggs protested.

"Never mind what I *SAID*," screamed Peavey. "Get him OUT!"

The horned woman fumbled at the lock until the door slid open, and the other pirates grabbed Tom and dragged him out of the cage. Peavey pushed them aside and started dusting him down with a sort of rough gentleness, muttering, "That's no way to treat a gentleman! Spanner, give him back his coat!"

"What?" cried the pirate wearing Tom's coat. "No way!"

Peavey pulled out a gun and shot him dead. "I said, give the gentleman back his COAT!" he shouted at the startled-looking corpse, and the others hurried to pull the coat off and put it back on Tom. Peavey patted at the smouldering bullet hole on the breast. "Sorry about the blood," he said earnestly. "These blokes, they've got no manners. Please allow me to apologize most 'umbly for the misunderstanding, and welcome you aboard my 'umble town. It's an honour to 'ave a real gentleman aboard at last, sir. I do hope you'll join me for afternoon tea in the Town Hall. . ."

Tom gaped at him. He had only just realized that he wasn't going to be killed. Afternoon tea was the last thing he was expecting. But as the pirate mayor started to lead him away he remembered Hester, still cowering in the cage. "I can't leave her down here!" he said.

"What, *Hettie*?" Peavey looked bewildered.

"We're travelling together," explained Tom. "She's my friend. . ."

"There's plenty of other girls in Tunbridge Wheels," said Peavey. "Much better ones, with noses and everyfink. Why, my own lovely daughter would be very pleased to make your acquainternce. . ."

"I can't leave Hester behind," said Tom, as firmly as he dared, and the mayor simply bowed and gestured to his men to open the cage again.

✿ ✿ ✿ ✿ ✿

At first Tom thought that Peavey was interested in the same thing as Miss Fang – information about where

London was headed, and what had brought it out into the central Hunting Ground. But although the pirate mayor was full of questions about Tom's life in the city, he didn't seem to have much interest in its movements; he was just pleased to have what he called "a High London gent" aboard his town.

He gave Tom and Hester a guided tour of the Town Hall, and introduced them to his "councillors", a rough-looking gang with names to match; Janny Maggs and Thick Mungo and Stadtsfesser Zeb, Pogo Nadgers and Zip Risky and the Traktiongrad Kid. Then it was time for afternoon tea in his private quarters, a room full of looted treasures high in the Town Hall where his rabble of whining, snot-nosed children kept getting under everybody's feet. His eldest daughter Cortina brought tea in delicate porcelain cups, and cucumber sandwiches on a blast-glass tray. She was a dim, terrified girl with watery blue eyes, and when her father saw that she hadn't cut the crusts off the sandwiches he knocked her backwards over the pouffe. "Thomas 'ere is from LONDON!" he shouted, hurling the sandwiches at her. "He expects fings POSH! And you should have done 'em in little TRIANGLES!"

"What can you do?" he said plaintively, turning to Tom. "I've tried to brung her up lady-like, but she won't learn. She's a good girl though. I look at her sometimes and almost wish I hadn't shot her mum. . ." He sniffed and dabbed at his eyes with a huge skull-and-crossbones hanky, and Cortina came trembling back with fresh sandwiches.

"The fing is," Peavey explained, through a mouthful of bread and cucumber, "the fing is, Tom, I don't want to be a pirate all me life."

"Um, no?" said Tom.

"No," said Peavey. "You see, Tommy boy, I didn't have the advantages what you've got when I was a kid. I didn't get no education or nuffink, and I've always been ugly as sin. . ."

"Oh, I wouldn't say that," Tom mumbled politely.

"I had to look out for meself, in the dust-heaps and the ditches. But I always knew one day I'd make it big. I saw London once, see. From a distance, like. Off on its travels somewhere. I fought it was the most beautiful place I'd ever seen, all them tiers, and the white villas up top all shining in the sun. And then I 'eard about them rich people what live up there, and I decided that's how I want to live; all them posh outfits and garden parties and trips to the theatre and that. So I become a scavenger, and then I got a little town of me own, and now I got a bigger one. But what I really want . . ." (he leaned close to Tom) "what I really want is to be *respectable*."

"Yes, yes, of course," agreed Tom, glancing at Hester.

"You see, what I'm finking is this," Peavey went on. "If this hunting trip works out like I hope, Tunbridge Wheels is goin' ter be rich soon. Really rich. I love this suburb, Tom. I wanna see it grow. I wanna 'ave a proper upper level wiv parks and posh mansions and no oiks allowed, and elevators goin' up and down. I want Tunbridge Wheels to turn into a city, a proper big city wiv me as Lord Mayor, sumfink I can 'and down to me sprogs. And you Tommy, I want you to tell me how a city ought to be, and teach me manners. Ettyket, like. So I can hob nob wiv' other Lord Mayors and not 'ave them laugh at me behind my back. And all my lads as well; they live like pigs at the moment. So what do you say? Will you turn us into gentlemen?"

Tom blinked at him, remembering the hard faces of Peavey's gang and wondering what they would do if he started telling them to open doors for each other and not to chew with their mouths open. He didn't know what to say, but in the end Hester said it for him.

"It was a lucky day for you when Tom came aboard," she told the mayor. "He's an expert on etiquette. He's the politest person I know. He'll tell you anything you want, Peavey."

"But. . ." said Tom, and winced as she kicked his ankle.

"Lovely-jubbley!" cackled Peavey, spraying them both with half-eaten sandwich. "You stick with old Chrysler, Tommy boy, and you won't go far wrong. As soon as we've scoffed our big catch you can start work. It's waiting for us on the far side of these marshes. We should reach it by the end of the week. . ."

Tom sipped at his tea. In his mind's eye he saw again the great map of the Hunting Ground; the broad sweep of the Rustwater, and beyond it. . . "Beyond the marshes?" he said. "But beyond the marshes there's nothing but the Sea of Khazak!"

"Relax, Tommy boy!" chuckled Chrysler Peavey. "Didn't I tell you? Tunbridge Wheels is *specialized*!" Just you wait and see. Wait and *sea*, get it? Wait and *sea*, ha ha ha ha!" And he slapped Tom on the back and swigged his tea, his little finger delicately raised.

18
BEVIS

A few days later London sighted prey again; a scattering of small Slavic-speaking tractionvilles which had been trying to hide among the crags of some old limestone hills. To and fro the city went, snapping them up, while half of London crowded on to the forward observation platforms to watch and cheer. The dismal plains of the western Hunting Ground were behind them now, and the discontent of yesterday was forgotten. Who cared if people were dying of heat stroke down in the Nether Boroughs? Good old London! Good old Crome! This was the best run of catches for years!

The city chased down and ate the faster towns and then turned back for the slower ones. It was nearly a week before the last of them was caught, a big, once proud place that was limping along with its tracks ripped off after an attack by predator suburbs. On the night it was finally eaten there were catch-parties in all the London parks, and the celebrations grew still more frantic when a cluster of lights was sighted far away to the north. A rumour started to circulate: that the lights belonged to a huge but crippled city; that it was what Valentine had been sent to find, and radio signals from the *13th Floor Elevator* would lead London north to its greatest meal ever. Fireworks banged and racketed until two in the morning, and Chudleigh Pomeroy, the acting Head Historian, reduced Herbert Melliphant to Apprentice Third Class after he let off a fire-cracker in the Museum's Main Hall.

But at dawn the happiness and the rumours died away. The lights in the north belonged to a huge city all right, but it was not crippled; it was heading south at top speed, and it had a hungry look. The Guild of Navigators soon identified it as Panzerstadt-Bayreuth, a conurbation formed by the coupling together of four huge *Traktionstadts,* but nobody else cared very much *what* it was called; they just wanted to get away from it.

London fired up its engines and raced on into the east until the conurbation sank below the horizon. But next morning, there it was again, upperworks glinting in the sunrise, even closer than before.

○ ○ ○ ○ ○

Katherine Valentine had not joined in with the parties and the merrymaking, nor did she join in the panic that now gripped her city.

Since her return from the Deep Gut she had kept to her room, washing and washing herself to get rid of the awful slurry-pit stink of Section 60. She hardly ate anything, and she made the servants fling all the clothes she had been wearing that day into the recycling bins. She stopped going to school. How could she face her friends, with all their silly talk of clothes and boys, knowing what she knew? Outside, sunlight dappled the lawns and the flowers were blooming and the trees were all unfurling fresh green leaves, but how could she enjoy the beauty of High London ever again? All she could think of were the thousands of Londoners who were toiling and dying in misery so that a few lucky, wealthy people like herself could live in comfort.

She wrote a letter to the Goggle-screen people about it, and another to the police, but she tore them both up. What was the point of sending them, when everyone knew that Magnus Crome controlled the police and the Goggle-screens? Even the High Priest of Clio had been appointed by Crome. She would have to wait for her father's return before anything could be done about the Deep Gut – providing that London hadn't got itself eaten by the time he came home.

As for her search for the truth about the scarred girl, it had ground to a halt. Apprentice Pod had known nothing – or pretended as much – and she could think of nowhere else to turn.

Then, at breakfast time on the third day of London's flight from Panzerstadt-Bayreuth, a letter came for her. She had no idea who would have written to her, and she turned the envelope over in her hands a couple of times, staring at the Tier Six postmark and feeling oddly afraid.

When she finally tore it open a sliver of paper dropped into her algae-flakes; ordinary London notepaper, recycled so many times that it was as soft and hairy as felt, with a watermark that said "Waste not – want not".

Dear Miss Vallentine,
Please help me there is something I must tell you. I will be at Pete's Eats in Belsize Park, Tier Five today at 11am.
Singed yours truly,
A Friend.

A few weeks earlier Katherine would have been excited, but she was in no mood for mysteries any more. It was probably somebody's idea of a joke, she thought. She was in no mood for jokes, either. How could she be, with London fleeing for its life and the lower tiers full of suffering and misery? She flung the note into the recycling bin and pushed her breakfast away uneaten, then went off to wash again.

But she was curious, in spite of herself. When nine o'clock came she said, "I will not go."

At nine-thirty she told Dog, "It would be pointless, there won't be anybody there."

At ten she muttered, "Pete's Eats – what sort of name is that? They probably made it up."

Half an hour later she was waiting at the Central Shaft terminus for a down elevator.

She got off at Low Holborn and walked to the tier's edge through streets of shabby metal flats. She had put on her oldest clothes and walked fast with her head down and Dog close against her. She didn't feel proud any more when people stared. She imagined them saying, *"That's Katherine Valentine, a stuck-up little miss from Tier One. They don't know they're born, those High Londoners."*

Belsize Park was almost deserted, the air thick with grainy smog from London's engines. The lawns and flowerbeds had all been given over to agriculture years and years before and the only people she could see were some labourers from Parks & Gardens who were moving along the rows of cabbages, spraying them with something to kill greenfly. Nearby stood a tatty conical building with a sign on its roof that read "Pete's Eats" and, in smaller letters underneath, "Café". There were metal tables under awnings on the pavement outside the door, and more tables inside. People sat talking and smoking in the thin flicker of a half-power argon globe. A boy sitting alone at a table near the door stood up and waved. Dog wagged his tail. It took Katherine a moment to recognize Apprentice Pod.

"I'm Bevis," he said, smiling nervously as Katherine sat down opposite him. "Bevis Pod."

"I remember."

"I'm glad you came, Miss. I've been wanting to talk to you ever since you come down to Section 60, but I didn't want the Guild to know I'd been in touch with you. They don't like us talking to outsiders. But I've got the day off 'cos they're preparing for a big meeting, so I came up here. You don't see many Engineers eating in here."

"I'm not surprised," said Katherine to herself, looking at the menu. There was a big colour picture of something called a "Happy Meal", a wedge of impossibly pink meat sandwiched between two rounds of algae-bread. She ordered mint tea. It came in a glastic tumbler and tasted of chemicals. "Are all Tier Five restaurants like this?"

"Oh no," said Bevis Pod. "This one's much nicer than the rest." He could not stop staring at her hair. He had spent his whole life in the Engineer warrens of the Gut and he had never seen anyone before with hair like hers, so long and shining and full of life. The Engineers said hair was unnecessary; a vestige of the ground-dwelling past, but when he saw Katherine's, it made him wonder. . .

"You said you needed my help. . ." Katherine prompted.

"Yes," said Bevis. He glanced over his shoulder as if to check that nobody was watching them. "It's about what you asked. I couldn't tell you down at the Turd Tanks. Not with Nimmo watching. I was in enough trouble already, for trying to help that poor man. . ."

His dark eyes were full of tears again, and Katherine thought it strange that an Engineer could cry so easily.

"Bevis, it's not your fault," she said. "Now what about the girl? Did you see her?"

Bevis nodded, thinking back to the night London ate Salthook. "I saw her run past, with that Apprentice Historian chasing after her. He shouted for help, so I ran after him. I saw the girl turn when she got to the waste-chutes. There was something wrong with her face. . ."

Katherine nodded. "Go on."

"I heard her shouting at him. I couldn't catch it all, over the engines and the noise of the Dismantling Yards. But she said something about your father, Miss. And then she pointed at herself and said, 'something something something Hester Shaw'. And then she jumped."

"And dragged poor Tom with her."

"No, Miss. He was left there, looking a bit stupid. Then the smoke came down and I couldn't see nothing, and next thing I knew there were policemen everywhere, so I made myself scarce. I wasn't supposed to leave my post, you see, so I couldn't tell anyone what I'd seen."

"But you're telling me," said Katherine.

"Yes, Miss." The apprentice blushed.

"Hester Shaw?" Katherine turned the name over in her mind, but it meant nothing to her. Nor did she understand his description of events, which didn't seem to tally with Father's. Bevis must have made a mistake, she decided.

He glanced around nervously again, then lowered his voice to a whisper. "Did you mean what you said, Miss, about your dad? Could he really do something to help the prisoners?"

"He will when I tell him what's happening," vowed Katherine. "I'm sure he doesn't know. But there's no need to call me Miss; I'm Katherine. Kate."

"Right," said Bevis solemnly. "Kate." He smiled again, but he still looked troubled. "I'm loyal to the Guild," he explained. "I never wanted to be anything but an Engineer. But I never expected to get assigned to the experimental prison. Keeping people in cages and making them work in the Gut, and wade about in those turd-tanks – that's not Engineering. That's just wicked. I do what I can to help them, but I can't do much, and the supervisors just want to work them to death and then send them up to K Division in plastic bags, so even when they're dead they won't get no rest."

"What is this K Division?" asked Katherine, remembering how Nimmo had hushed the other apprentice when she mentioned it. "Is it part of the prison?"

"Oh no. It's up top. In the Engineerium. It's some sort of experimental department, run by Dr Twix."

"What does she use dead bodies for?" asked Katherine nervously, not at all sure that she wanted to know.

Bevis Pod went a little paler. "It's just a rumour, Miss, but some people in the Guild say she's building Stalkers. Resurrected Men."

"Great Clio!" Katherine thought of what she had been taught about the Stalkers. She knew that her father had dug up some rusty skeletons for the Engineers to study, but he had told her they were only interested in the electrical brains. Could they really be trying to make new ones?

"Why?" she asked. "I mean, they were soldiers, weren't they? Sort of human tanks, built for some old war. . ."

"Perfect workers, Miss," said Bevis, wide-eyed. "They don't need feeding or clothing or housing, and when there's no work to be done you can just switch 'em off and stack 'em in a warehouse, so they're much easier to store. The Guild says that in the future everybody who dies on the lower tiers will be resurrected, and we won't need living people at all, except as supervisors."

"But that's horrible!" protested Katherine. "London would be a city of the dead!"

Bevis Pod shrugged. "Down in the Deep Gut it feels like that already. I'm just telling you what I've heard. Crome wants Stalkers built, and that's what Dr Twix does with the bodies from our section."

"I'm sure if people knew about this awful plan. . ." Katherine started to say. Then an idea occurred to her. "Does it have a code-name? Do they call it MEDUSA?"

"Blimey! How do you know about MEDUSA?" Bevis's face had turned paler than ever. "Nobody's supposed to know about that!"

"Why?" asked Katherine. "What is it? If it's not to do with these new Stalkers. . ."

"It's a big Guild secret," whispered Bevis. "Apprentices aren't supposed to even know the name. But you hear the Supervisors talking about it. Whenever something goes wrong, or the city is in trouble, they talk about how everything will be all right once we awaken MEDUSA. Like this week, with this conurbation chasing us. Everybody's running around in a panic thinking it's the end of London, but the top Guildsmen just tell each other, 'MEDUSA will sort things out.' That's why they're having this big meeting at the Engineerium tonight. Magnus Crome is making an announcement about it."

Katherine shivered, thinking about the Engineerium and the mysterious things that went on behind its black windows. That was where she would find the clue to her father's troubles. MEDUSA. It all had something to do with MEDUSA.

She leaned closer to the boy and whispered, "Bevis, listen; are you going to this meeting? Can you tell me what Crome says?"

"Oh no, Miss ... I mean Kate. No! It's strictly Guildsmen only. No apprentices..."

"Couldn't you pose as a Guildsman or something?" Katherine urged him. "I have a feeling that there is something bad going on, and I think this MEDUSA thing is at the bottom of it."

"I'm sorry, Miss," said Bevis, shaking his head. "I wouldn't dare. I don't want to get killed and carted off to Top Tier and turned into a Stalker."

"Then help *me* go!" said Katherine eagerly. She reached across the table to take his hand, and he flinched at her touch and pulled back, staring at his fingers in amazement, as if it had never occurred to him that anybody would want to touch them. Katherine persisted, gently taking both his trembling hands in hers and looking deep into his eyes.

"I have to find out what Crome is really up to," she explained, "for Father's sake. Please, Bevis. I have to get inside the Engineerium!"

19
THE SEA OF KHAZAK

A few hours later, as the evening mists came curling from the Rustwater Marshes, Tunbridge Wheels rolled down to the edge of the sea. It paused there a while, gazing out towards a cluster of islands that rose dark and rugged from the silver water. Birds were streaming in off the sea in long skeins and as the suburb cut its engines the beat of their wings came echoing over the mudflats. Small waves beat steadily against the shore and a wind from the east blew hissing through the thin, grey marram grass. There was no other sound, no other movement, no light or smoke-trail of a wandering town anywhere on the marshes or the sea.

"Natswurvy!" shouted Chrysler Peavey, standing with a telescope to his eye at the window of his observation bridge, high in the Town Hall. "Where is the lad? Pass the word for Natswurvy!" When a couple of his pirates ushered Tom and Hester in he turned with a broad grin and held out the telescope, saying, "Take a look, Tommy boy! I told you I'd get you here, didn't I? I told you I'd get you through these marshes safe? Now, have a look at where we're going!"

Tom took the telescope and put it to his eye, blinking at the trembling, blurred circle of view until it came clear. There were dozens of little islands speckling the sea ahead, and a larger one which loomed in the east like the back of an enormous prehistoric monster breaking the water.

He lowered the telescope and shuddered. "But there's nothing there. . ." he said.

It had taken more than a week for Tunbridge Wheels to pick its slow way through the quagmire, and although Chrysler Peavey had taken quite a shine to Tom he had still not explained what he hoped to find on the far side. His men had not been told either, but they were happy enough snapping up the tiny townships which had taken shelter in the mazes of the Rustwater, semi-static places with moss-covered wheels and delicate, beautiful carvings on their wooden upperworks. They were so small that they were barely worth eating, but Tunbridge Wheels ate them anyway, and murdered or enslaved their people and fed the lovely carvings to its furnaces.

It was a horrible, confusing time for Tom. He had been brought up to believe that Municipal Darwinism was a noble, beautiful system, but he could see nothing noble or beautiful about Tunbridge Wheels.

He was still an honoured guest in the Town Hall, and so was Hester, although Peavey clearly didn't understand his attachment to the scarred, sullen, silent girl. "Why don'cha ask my Cortina out?" he wheedled one night, sitting next to Tom in the old council chamber that was now his dining hall. "Or why not one of them girls we took off the last catch? Lovely lookers they was, an' not a word of Anglish, so they can't give you any lip. . ."

"Hester isn't my girlfriend!" Tom started to say, but he didn't want to have to go out with the mayor's daughter and he knew Peavey would never understand the truth; that he was in love with the image of Katherine Valentine, whose face had hung in his mind like a lantern through all the miles of his adventures. So he said, "Hester and I have been through a lot together, Mr Peavey. I promised I'd help her catch up with London."

"But that was before," the mayor reasoned. "You're a Tunbridge-Wheelsian now. You're going to stay here with me, like the son I never had, and I'm just thinking that maybe the lads would accept you a bit more easily if you had a better-looking girl; you know, more lady-like."

Tom looked across the clutter of tables and saw the other pirates glaring at him, fingering their knives. He knew that they would never accept him. They hated him for being a soft city-dweller, and for being Peavey's favourite, and he couldn't really blame them.

Later, in the little room he shared with Hester, he said, "We have to get off this town. The pirates don't like us, and they're starting to get tired of Peavey going on at them about manners and stuff. I don't even like to think about what will happen to us if they mutiny."

"Let's wait and see," muttered the girl, curled up in a far corner. "Peavey's tough, and he'll be able to keep his lads in line as long as he finds them this big catch he's been promising. But Quirke alone knows what it is."

"We'll find out tomorrow," said Tom, drifting into an uneasy sleep. "This time tomorrow these horrible bogs will be behind us. . . ."

◌ ◌ ◌ ◌ ◌

This time tomorrow, and the horrible bogs *were* behind them. As Peavey's navigator spread out his maps in the observation bridge a strange hissing sound echoed up the stairwells of the Town Hall. Tom glanced up at the faces of Peavey's henchmen as they clustered around the chart-table, but apart from Hester no one seemed to have heard it. She looked nervously at him and shrugged.

The navigator was a thin, bespectacled man named Mr Ames. He had been the suburb's schoolteacher until Peavey took over. Now he was settling happily into his new life as a pirate: it was a lot more fun, and the hours were better, and Peavey's ruffians were better behaved than most of his old pupils. Smoothing his maps with his long, thin hands he said, "It used to be the hunting ground for hundreds of little aquatic towns, but they all ate each other, and now Anti-Tractionist squatters have started coming down out of the mountains and setting up home on islands like this one. . ."

Tom craned closer. The great inland Sea of Khazak was speckled with dozens of islands, but the one Ames was pointing to was the biggest, a tattered diamond shape some twenty miles long. He couldn't imagine what was so interesting about it, and most of the other pirates looked baffled too, but Peavey was chuckling and rubbing his hands together in glee.

"The Black Island," he said. "Not much to look at, is it? But it's goin' ter make us rich, boys, rich. After tonight, ol' Tunbridge Wheels'll be able to set up as a proper city."

"How?" demanded Mungo, the pirate who trusted Chrysler Peavey least, and most resented Tom. "There's nothing there, Peavey. Just a few old trees and some worthless Mossies."

"What are 'Mossies'?" Tom whispered to Hester.

"He means people who live in static settlements," she hissed back. "You know, like in that old saying, 'A rolling town gathers no moss. . .'"

"The fact is, ladies and gentlemen," announced

Peavey, "that there *is* something on the Black Island. A few days ago – just before you come aboard, Tom – we shot down an airship that was footling about over the marshes. Its crew told me something very interesting before we killed 'em. It seems there's been a big battle up in Airhaven; fires, engine-damage, gas-spills, the whole place knocked about so bad they couldn't stay up in the sky but had to come down for repairs. And where d'you fink they've landed?"

"The Black Island?" suggested Tom, guessing as much from Peavey's greedy grin.

"That's my boy, Tommy! There's an air-caravanserai there, where sky-convoys refuel on their way up from the League's lands south of the mountains. That's where Airhaven's put down. They think they're safe, with sea all round them and their Mossie friends to help 'em. But they ain't safe from Tunbridge Wheels!"

A ripple of excitement ran through the assembled pirates. Tom turned to Hester, but she was staring out across the sea towards the distant island. Half of him was appalled by the thought that the lovely flying town was lying crippled there, waiting to be eaten – the other half was busy wondering how on earth Peavey planned to reach it.

"To yer stations, me hearties!" the pirate mayor yelled. "Fire up the engines! Prime the guns! By dawn tomorrow, we'll all be rich!"

The pirates scrambled to obey his orders, and Tom ran to the window. It was almost dark outside now, with a last ominous glow of sunset bruising the sky above the marshes. But the streets of Tunbridge Wheels were full of light, and all around the edge of the suburb huge orange shapes were unfolding, growing like fungus in a speeded-up film. Now the hissing from the lower deck made sense; while Peavey talked his town had been busily pumping air into flotation chambers and these inflatable rubber skirts.

"Let's go swimmin'!" shouted the pirate mayor, sitting back in his swivel chair and signalling the engine rooms. The huge motors rumbled into life, a plume of exhaust gases drifted aft, and Tunbridge Wheels surged forward across the beach and into the sea.

o o o o o

At first all went well; nothing stirred on the darkening waters as Tunbridge Wheels went chugging eastward, and up ahead the Black Island grew steadily larger. Tom opened a small side window on the bridge and stood there feeling the salt night air spill over him, feeling strangely excited. He could see pirates gathering in the old market square at the suburb's forward end, readying grappling hooks and boarding ladders, because Airhaven would be far too large to fit into the jaws – they would have to take it by force and tear it apart at their leisure. He didn't like the idea, especially when he remembered that his aviator friends might still be on Airhaven, but it was a town eat town world, after all – and there *was* something exciting about the cut-throat recklessness of Peavey's plan.

And then suddenly something fell out of the sky and exploded in the market square, and there was a black gash in the deck and the men he had been watching weren't there any more. Others came running with buckets and fire extinguishers. "Airship! Airship! Airship!" someone was shouting, and then there were more rushing things and buildings were exploding all over the suburb, with people flung tumbling high up into the air like mad acrobats.

"For Sooty Pete's sake!" shouted Peavey, running to the shattered observation window and staring down into the smoke-filled streets. His monkey jumped up and down on his shoulders, jabbering. "These Mossies are better organized than we gave 'em credit for," he said. "Searchlights, quick!"

Two wavering fingers of light rose above the town, feeling their way across the smoke-dappled sky. Where they met, Tom saw a fat rising shape shine briefly red. The suburb's guns swung upward and fired a rippling broadside, and pulses of flame stalked the drifting clouds.

"Missed!" hissed Peavey, squinting through his telescope. "Curse it, I should have known Airhaven would send up spotter ships. And if I'm not mistaken it was that witch Fang's old rustbucket!"

"The *Jenny Haniver*!" gasped Tom.

"No need to sound so pleased about it," snarled Peavey. "She's a menace. Ain't you heard of the Wind-Flower?"

Tom hadn't told the pirate mayor of his adventures aboard Airhaven. He tried to hide his happiness at the thought that Miss Fang was still alive and said, "I've *heard* of her. She's an air-trader. . ."

"Oh, yeah?" Peavey spat on the deck. "You think a trader carries that sort of fire-power? She's one of the Anti-Traction League's top agents. She'll stop at nothing to hurt us poor traction towns. It was her who planted the bomb that sank Marseilles, and her what strangled the poor Sultana of Palau Pinang. She's got the blood of a thousand murdered townsfolk on her hands! Still, we'll show her, won't we, Tommy boy? I'll have her guts for goulash! I'll hang her carcass out for the buzzards! Mungo! Pogo! Maggs! An extra cut of the spoils to whoever shoots down that red airship!"

No one did shoot down that red airship; it was long out of range, buzzing back towards the Black Island to warn Airhaven of the approaching danger. But Tom could not have been more filled with grief and anger if he had seen it falling in flames. So that was why Miss Fang had rescued him, and been so kind! All she had wanted was information for the League – and her friend Captain Khora had been in on it, spinning that tale about her just to win Tom's sympathy. Thank Quirke he had not been able to tell her anything!

Tunbridge Wheels was battered and burning, but the *Jenny Haniver's* rockets had been too small to do any serious damage, and now that the element of surprise was lost Miss Fang did not risk another attack. The suburb chugged on into the east, pushing a thick bore of flame-lit water ahead of it. Tom could see lights on the Black Island now, lanterns flickering along the shore. Closer, between the island and the suburb, shone another cluster of lights. "Boats!" shouted Mungo, peering through the sights of his gun.

Peavey went and stood at the window, robes flapping on the rising breeze. "Fishing fleet!" he grunted, sounding satisfied. "First meal of the night; we'll eat 'em up by way of an *aperitif.* That's 'starters' to you lot."

The fishing-boats started scattering as Tunbridge Wheels bore down, running goose-winged for the shelter of the shore, but one, bigger and slower than the rest, sagged away to windward. "We'll have him," growled

Peavey, and Maggs relayed his order into the intercom. The suburb changed course slightly, engines grumbling. The steep crags of the Black Island filled the sky ahead, blotting out the eastern stars. *What if there are guns on the heights?* thought Tom – but if there were any, they stayed silent. He could see the white wake of the boat ahead, and beyond it a faint pale line of breakers on the shore. . .

And then there were other, closer breakers, dead ahead, and Hester was shouting, "Peavey! It's a trap!"

They all saw it then, but it was much too late. The fishing boat with its shallow keel ran clear through the reef, but the great lumbering bulk of Tunbridge Wheels struck at full speed and the sharp rocks clawed its belly open. The suburb lurched and settled, throwing Tom off his feet and rolling him hard against the legs of the chart table. The engines failed, and in the terrible silence that followed a klaxon began lowing like a frightened bull.

Tom crawled back to the window. Down below he saw the streets going dark as a great rush of water came bursting through the palisades. White geysers of foam sprayed up through gratings from the flooded under-deck, and mingled with the whiteness he saw black flecks of debris and tiny, struggling figures. The boat was far away, tacking to admire her handiwork. A hundred yards of sea separated the doomed suburb from the steep shores of the island.

A hand grabbed his shoulder, heaving him towards the exits. "You're coming wiv me, Tommy boy," snarled Chrysler Peavey, snatching a huge gun from a rack on the wall and swinging it on to his shoulder. "You too, Amesy, Mungo, Maggs, you're wiv me. . ."

They were with him, the pirates forming a tight

protective knot around their mayor as he hurried Tom down the stairs. Hester came limping behind. There were screams below, and frightened faces staring up at them from a third-floor landing already knee-deep in water. "Abandon town!" hollered Peavey. "Women and mayors first!"

They crashed into his private quarters, where his daughter stood clutching her frightened brothers and sisters. Peavey ignored her and waded to a chest in the corner, scowling with concentration as he twirled the combination lock this way and that. The chest sprang open, he dragged out a little orange bundle and then they were on the move again, out on to the balcony where the sea was already spilling through the railings. Tom turned back into the room, meaning to help Cortina and the children, but Peavey had forgotten all about them. He flung the bundle down into the waves and it unfolded with a complicated hiss, flowering into a small, circular life-raft. "Get aboard," he snapped, taking hold of Tom and thrusting him towards it.

"But. . ."

"Get aboard!" A boot in the seat of his breeches sent him tumbling over the balcony rail and down on to the yielding rubber floor of the raft. Mungo was next, then the others piled in so fast that the raft wallowed deep and water spilled over the gunwales. "Oh! Oh! Oh!" wailed Cortina Peavey somewhere away to the left, but by the time Tom had scrambled out from under Mr Ames the suburb was already far away, its stern submerged and its bows tilted high into the night sky. He looked for Hester and found her crouching beside him. Peavey's monkey jabbered with fear, bouncing up and down on his head. "Oh! Oh! Oh!" came the distant cries, and there were white splashes, dozens of splashes as people leaped from palisades and the useless tatters of the air-bags. Hands clutched at the sides of the raft and Mungo and Peavey beat them away. Frantic figures came splashing through the swell towards them, and Janny Maggs stood up and fired her machine-gun, churning up red water all around the raft. The suburb was tilting steeper, steeper; there was a rush of steam as the sea poured into its boilers and then with sudden, shocking speed it slid under. The water boiled and heaved. For a while there were screams, faint cries for help, a brief rattle of gunfire as a drifting fragment of debris changed hands, a longer one as a few lucky pirates battled their way on to a beach.

Then there was silence, and the raft turning slow circles as the current drew it in towards the shore.

20
THE BLACK ISLAND

*A*t dawn Shrike comes to the edge of the sea. The tide is turning and the deep wheel marks that lead down into the surf are already starting to blur. Eastward, smoke rises from settlements on the shores of the Black Island. The Stalker wrenches his dead face into a smile, feeling very pleased with Hester Shaw and the trail of destruction that she has left behind her.

The thought of Hester is all that dragged him through the marshes. On and on it has drawn him, through mud that sucked at his damaged leg and sloughs whose bitter waters sometimes closed over his head. But at least the tracks the suburb left were easy to follow. He follows them again now, stalking down the beach and into the waves like a swimmer bent on a morning dip. Salt water slaps at the lenses of his eyes and seeps stinging through the gashes in his armour. The sounds of the gulls and the wind fade, replaced by the dim hiss of the underneath of the sea. Air or water, it makes no difference to the Resurrected Men. Fish goggle at him and dart away into forests of kelp. Crabs sidle out of his path, rearing up and waving their pincers at him, as if they are worshipping a crab-god, armoured, invincible. He ploughs on, following the water-scent of oil and axle-grease that will lead him to Tunbridge Wheels.

❖ ❖ ❖ ❖ ❖

A few miles from the inlet where they had come ashore, Chrysler Peavey paused at the top of a steep rise and waited for the others to catch up. They came slowly, first

Tom and Hester, then Ames with his map, finally Maggs and Mungo, bent under the weight of their guns. Looking back they could see the steep rocky flanks of the island falling to the sea, and a cluster of boats gathered above the wreck of Tunbridge Wheels, where a raft with a crane on it had already been anchored. The islanders were wasting no time in looting the drowned suburb.

"Mossie scum," growled Peavey.

Tom had barely spoken to the mayor since they first came struggling ashore. Now he was surprised to see tears gleaming in the little man's eyes. He said, "I'm so sorry about your family, Mr Peavey. I tried to reach them, but. . ."

"Little twerps!" snorted Peavey. "I wasn't sniffling over *them*. It's my lovely suburb! Look at it! Damn Mossies. . ."

Just then, from somewhere to the south, they heard the faint clatter of gunfire.

Peavey's face brightened. He turned to the others. "Hear that! Some of the lads must have got ashore! They'll be more'n a match for them Mossies! We'll link up with 'em! We'll capture Airhaven yet, keep a few of its people alive to repair it, kill the rest and fly back to the mainland rich. Drop out of the sky on a few fat towns before word gets round that Airhaven's gone pirate! Catch ourselves a city, maybe!"

He set off again, hauling himself up from boulder to boulder with the monkey riding on his hunched shoulders. The others followed behind. Maggs and Mungo seemed dazed by the loss of Tunbridge Wheels and not convinced by Peavey's latest plan. They kept exchanging glances and muttering together when their mayor was out of earshot – but they were in strange country, and

Tom didn't think they had the nerve to move against Peavey, not yet. As for Mr Ames, he had never set foot on the bare earth before. "It's horrible!" he grumbled. "So difficult to walk on. . . All this grass! There may be wild animals, or snakes. . . I can quite see why our ancestors decided to stop living on the ground!"

Tom knew exactly how he felt. To north and south of them the steep side of the Black Island stretched away, and above them the slope climbed almost vertically to dark crags which moaned with ghostly voices as the wind blew around them. Some of the higher pinnacles of rock had been sculpted into such wild shapes that from the beach they had looked like fortresses, and Peavey had led his party on a long detour to avoid them before he realized they were only stones.

"It's lovely," sighed Hester, limping along at Tom's side. She was smiling to herself, which he had never seen her do, and whistling a little tune through her teeth.

"What are you so happy about?" he asked.

"We're going to Airhaven, aren't we?" she replied in a whisper. "It's laired up ahead somewhere, and Peavey's little gang will never take it, not with Mossies and the Airhaven people ranged against them. They'll be killed, and we'll find a ship to take us north to London. Anna Fang's there, remember. She might help us again."

"Oh, her!" said Tom angrily. "Didn't you hear what Peavey said? She's a League spy."

"I thought so," admitted Hester. "I mean, all those questions she kept asking us about London, and Valentine."

"You should have told me!" he protested. "I might have revealed an important secret!"

"Why would I care?" asked Hester. "And since when

have Apprentice Historians known any important secrets? Anyway, I thought you realized she was a spy."

"She didn't look like one."

"Well, spies don't, generally. You can't expect them to wear a big sandwich board with 'SPY' on it, or a special spying hat." She was in a strange, jokey mood, and Tom wondered if it was because these dismal steeps reminded her of her girlhood on that other island. Suddenly she touched his arm and said, "Poor Tom. You're learning what Valentine taught me all those years ago; you can't trust anybody."

"Huh," said Tom.

"Oh, I don't mean *you*," she added hurriedly. "I think I trust you, almost. And what you did for me back in Tunbridge Wheels – making Peavey let me out of the lock-ups like that. . . A lot of people wouldn't have bothered. Not for somebody like me."

Tom looked round at her, and saw more clearly than ever before the kind, shy Hester peeping from behind the grim mask. He smiled at her with such warmth that she blushed (at least, her strange face turned red in patches and her scar went purple) and Peavey looked back at them and hollered, "Come on, you two lovebirds! Stop whispering sweet nothings and *march*!"

Afternoon, the cloud clearing eastwards and sunlight dazzling down through the wave-tops, flickering on the upperworks of Tunbridge Wheels. Shrike moves through the suburb's streets with his head swinging slowly from side to side. Bodies drift in the flooded rooms like cold teabags left too long in the pot. Small fish dart in and out

of a pirate's mouth. A girl's hair coils on the current. Dark keels of salvage boats move overhead. He waits hidden in the shadows while three naked boys come diving down, flying past him with urgent motions of their arms and legs and leaving trails of silver bubbles. They kick back to the surface carrying guns, bottles, a leather belt.

Hester is not here. Shrike turns away from the sunken suburb, following the shadows of drifting oil-slicks over the silt. Wreckage is strewn along the sea floor, and floating bodies beckon him towards the roots of the Black Island.

It is evening by the time he walks out of the surf, trailing flags of seaweed, water draining from inside his battered armour. He shakes his head to clear his vision and stares about him at a beach of black sand beneath dark cliffs. It takes him most of another hour to find the life-raft, hidden in a tumble of house-sized boulders. He unsheathes his metal claws and tears the bottom out of it, cutting off her escape. Hester is his again now. When she is dead he will carry her gently through the drowned sunlight and the forests of kelp, back through the marshes and the long leagues of the Hunting Ground to Crome. He will take her into London in his arms like a father carrying his sleeping child.

He drops on all fours in the sand and starts sniffing for her scent.

Towards sundown, they finally reached the top of the slope, and found themselves looking down into the centre of the Black Island.

Tom hadn't realized until now that it was an extinct volcano, but from here it was obvious; the steep, black crags ringed an almost circular bowl of land, green, and patched with fields. Almost directly below the place where the pirates crouched, a small static settlement stood beside a blue lake. There were airship hangars and mooring masts beside the stone buildings, and on the flat ground behind them, dwarfing the whole place, Airhaven perched on a hundred skinny landing legs, looking as helpless as a grounded bird.

"The air-caravanserai!" chuckled Peavey. He pulled out his telescope and put it to his eye. "Look at 'em work! They're pumping their gasbags back up, desperate to get back into the sky. . ." He swung the glass quickly across the surrounding hillsides. "No sign of any of our boys. Oh, if only we had a cannon left! But we'll manage, eh lads? A bunch of airy-fairies is no match for us! Come on, let's get closer. . ."

There was a strange edge to the mayor's voice. *He's frightened*, Tom realized. *But he can't admit it, in case Mungo and Maggs and Ames lose faith in him.* He had never thought he would feel sorry for the pirate mayor, but he did. Peavey had been kind to him, in his way, and it hurt to see him reduced to this, scrambling across the wet ground with his people muttering and cursing him behind his back.

They still followed him though, down between the screes into the crater of the old fire-mountain. Once they saw riders silhouetted on a distant crag; a patrol of islanders hunting for survivors from the sunken pirate town. Once an airship flew low overhead, and Peavey hissed at everybody to lie flat and stay still, wrapping his monkey under his robes to muffle its shrill complaints.

The airship circled, but by that time the sun had gone down, and the pilot did not see the figures who cowered in the twilight below him like mice hiding from an owl. He flew back down to land at the caravanserai as a fat moon heaved itself over the eastern crags.

Tom gave a sharp sob of relief and scrambled up. Around him the others were also starting to move, grunting, dislodging small stones which went clattering away down the hillside. He could see people hurrying about with lanterns and torches in the streets of the air-caravanserai, and lamp-lit windows that made him think how wonderful it would be to be warm and safe indoors. Airhaven was bright with electric lights, and the wind brought the distant sounds of shouted orders, music, cheering.

"For Pete's sake!" hissed Mungo. "We're too late! It's leaving!"

"Never," scoffed Peavey.

But they could all see that Airhaven's gasbags were almost full. A few minutes later the growl of its engines came rumbling up the slope, rising and falling as the wind gusted. The flying town was straining upwards, its crab-like legs folding back into place underneath it.

"No!" shouted Peavey.

Then he was running downhill, scrambling and tumbling down clattering spills of scree towards the flat, boggy land in the crater floor, and as he ran they heard him screaming "Come back! You're my *catch*! I sank my town for you!"

Mungo and Maggs and Ames set off after him, with Hester and Tom behind. At the foot of the slope the ground grew soft and squashy underfoot and pools of water reflected the moon and the lights of the rising town.

"Come back!" they could hear Peavey shouting, somewhere ahead of them. "Come back!" and then, "Ah! Oh! Help!"

They hurried towards the sound of his voice and the harsh screams of the monkey, and all came to a halt together at the edge of a deep patch of bog. Peavey was already up to his waist in it. The monkey perched on top of his head like a sailor on a foundering ship, grinning with fear. "Give me a hand, boys!" the mayor pleaded. "Help me! We can still get it! It's only testing its liftin' engines! It'll come down again!"

The pirates watched him silently. They knew they had no chance of taking the flying town, and that his shouts had probably warned the islanders of their presence.

"We've got to help him!" whispered Tom, starting forward, but Hester held him back.

"Too late," she said.

Peavey was sinking deeper, the weight of his chain of office pulling him down. He spluttered as the black mud swilled into his mouth. "Come on, lads! Maggs? Mungo? I'm your mayor! I done all this for you!" He searched for Tom with wild, terrified eyes. "Tell 'em, Tommy boy!" he whimpered. "Tell 'em I wanted to make Tunbridge Wheels great! I wanted to be respectable! Tell 'em—"

Mungo's first shot blew the monkey off the top of Peavey's head in a cloud of singed fur. The second and third went through his chest. He bowed his head, and the mud gulped him down with soft farting noises.

The pirates turned to look at Tom.

"We prob'ly wouldn't be 'ere if it weren't for you," muttered Mungo.

"If you hadn't of gone filling the Chief's head up with

all them ideas about manners and cities and stuff,"
agreed Maggs.

"Different forks for every course, and no talking with
your mouth full!" sneered Ames.

Tom started to back away. To his surprise, Hester
stepped quickly between him and the pirates. "It's not
Tom's fault!" she said.

"An' you're no use to us, neither," Mungo growled.
"Neither of you is. We're pirates. We don't need no lessons in etiquette an' we don't need no lame scarface girl
to hold us up." He raised his gun, and Maggs followed
suit. Even Mr Ames pulled out a little revolver.

And a voice out of the darkess said, "THEY'RE MINE."

21

IN THE ENGINEERIUM

London was climbing towards a high plateau where the town-torn earth was dusted with thin layers of snow. A hundred miles behind it rolled Panzerstadt-Bayreuth, not just a threatening blur on the horizon any more but a huge dark mass of tracks and tiers, the gold filigree-work of its ornate top deck clearly visible above the smoke of factories and engines. Londoners crowded on to the aft observation platforms and watched in silence as the gap between the two cities slowly narrowed. That afternoon the Lord Mayor announced that there was no need for panic and that the Guild of Engineers would bring the city safely through this crisis – but there had already been riots and looting on the lower tiers, and squads of Beefeaters had been sent down to keep order in the Gut.

"Old Crome doesn't know what he's talking about," muttered one of the men on duty at the Quirke Circus Elevator Station that evening. "I never thought I'd hear myself say it, but he's a fool. Bringing poor old London way out east like this, day after day of travelling, week after week, just to get scoffed by some big old conurbation. I wish Valentine was here. He'd know what to do. . ."

"Quiet, Bert," hissed his companion, "here comes some more of 'em."

Both men bowed politely as two Engineers strode up to the turnstiles, a young man and a girl, dressed identically in green glastic goggles and white rubber hoods and coats. The girl flashed a gold pass. When she and her companion had gone up into the waiting elevator

Bert turned to his friend and whispered, "It must be important, this do at the Engineerium. They've been swarming up out of their nests in the Deep Gut like a load of old white maggots. Imagine having a Guild meeting at a time like this!"

Inside the elevator Katherine sat down next to Bevis Pod, already feeling hot and self-conscious inside the coat that he had lent her. She glanced at him, and then checked her reflection in the window, making sure that the red wheels they had drawn so carefully on each other's foreheads had not got smudged. She thought they both looked ridiculous in these hoods and goggles, but Bevis had assured her that a lot of Engineers wore them these days, and the other occupant of the elevator, a fat Navigator, didn't so much as look at them while the car lurched towards Top Tier.

Katherine had spent the whole day restlessly waiting for Bevis to arrive with her disguise. To while away the time she had looked up the name HESTER SHAW in the indices of all her father's books, but couldn't find it. *A Complete Catalogue of the London Museum* contained one brief reference to a *Pandora* Shaw, but it just said she was an Out-Country scavenger who had supplied a few minor fossils and pieces of Old-Tech to the Historian's Guild, and gave the date of her death, seven years ago. After that she tried looking up MEDUSA, only to learn that it was some sort of monster in an old story. She didn't think Magnus Crome and his Engineers believed in monsters.

Nobody gave a second glance as she and Bevis

strode across Top Tier towards the main entrance of the Engineerium. Scores of Engineers were already hurrying up the steps. Katherine joined them, clutching her gold pass and keeping close to the apprentice, terrified that she might lose him in this crowd of identical white coats. *This will never work!* she kept thinking, but the Guildsman on duty at the door wasn't bothering to look at passes. She took a last look at the fading sunset behind the dome of St Paul's, then stepped inside.

It was bigger than she expected, and brighter, lit by hundreds of argon globes that hung in the great open shaft at the centre of the building like planets hanging in space. She looked around for the staircase, but Bevis tugged at her arm and said, "We go up by monorail. Look. . ."

The Engineers were clambering into little monorail cars. Katherine and Bevis joined the queue, listening to their muttered conversations and the squeaky rustle of their coats rubbing together. Bevis's eyes were wide and frightened behind his goggles. Katherine had hoped that they would be able to get a monorail car to themselves so that they could talk, but more Engineers were arriving all the time and she ended up sitting on the far side of a packed car from him, wedged tightly in with a group from the Mag-Lev Research Division.

"Where are you from, Guildsperson?" asked the man sitting beside her.

"Um. . ." Katherine looked frantically at Bevis, but he was too far away to whisper an answer. She blurted out the first thing that came to mind. "K Division."

"Old Twixie, eh?" said the man. "I hear she's having amazing results with her new models!"

"Oh, yes, very," she replied. Then the car moved off with a lurch and her neighbour turned to the window, fascinated by the passing view.

Katherine had expected the monorail to feel like an elevator, but the speed and the spiralling movement made it quite different and for a moment she had to concentrate hard on not being sick. The other Engineers seemed not to notice. "What do you think the Lord Mayor's speech will be about?" one of them asked.

"It must be MEDUSA," said another. "I heard they are preparing for a test."

"Let's hope it works," said a woman sitting just in front of Katherine. "It was Valentine who found the machine, after all, and he's only a Historian, you know. You can't trust them."

"Oh, Valentine is the Lord Mayor's man," said another. "Don't let that Historian's guild-mark fool you. He's as loyal as a dog, so long as we give him plenty of money and he gets to pretend that foreign daughter of his is a High London lady."

Round and round they went, and up past offices and workshops full of busy Engineers, like an enormous hive of insects. The car stopped on level five and Katherine climbed out, still flushed with anger at what the others had said. She linked up with Bevis again and they all trotted together along chilly, white corridors and through hanging curtains of transparent plastic. She could hear the babble of voices ahead, and after a few twists and turns they emerged into an immense auditorium. Bevis led the way to a seat near one of the exits. She looked about her to see if she could spot Supervisor Nimmo, but it was impossible to make him out. The auditorium was a sea of white coats and bald or hooded heads, and more were pouring through the entrances all the time.

"Look!" hissed Bevis, nudging her. "That's Dr Twix, the one I told you about!" He pointed to a squat little barrel-shaped woman who was taking a seat in the front row, chattering animatedly with her neighbours. "All the top Guildspersons are here! Twix, Chubb, Garstang . . . and there's Dr Vambrace, the head of security!"

Katherine began to feel frightened. If she had been unmasked at the door she might have been able to pass it off as a silly prank, but now she was deep in the Engineers' inner sanctum, and she could tell that something important was about to happen. She reminded herself that even if they discovered her, the Engineers would never dare harm Thaddeus Valentine's daughter. She tried not to think about what they might do to Bevis.

At last the doors were closed and the lights dimmed. An expectant hush filled the auditorium, broken only by the slithery whisper of five hundred Engineers rising to their feet.

Katherine and Bevis jumped up with them, peering at the stage over the shoulders of the people in front. Magnus Crome was standing at a metal lectern, his cold eyes sweeping the audience. For a moment he seemed to stare straight at Katherine, and she had to remind herself that he couldn't possibly recognize her, not with her hood and her goggles and the tall collar of her coat turned up.

"You may be seated," said Crome, and waited until they had settled themselves before going on. "This is a glorious day for our Guild, my friends."

A ripple of excitement ran through the auditorium, and through Katherine too. Crome motioned for quiet.

Up in the ceiling of the auditorium a slide-projector whirred into life, and a picture appeared on a screen behind his head. It was a diagram of an enormous, complicated machine.

"MEDUSA," announced Crome, and there was a sort of echo as all the Engineers sighed, "*MEDUSA!*"

"As some of you already know," he went on, "MEDUSA is an experimental energy weapon from the Sixty Minutes War. We have known about it for some time – in fact, ever since Valentine found these documents on his trip to America, twenty years ago."

The projector-screen was flickering with faded diagrams and spidery writing. *Father never told me that!* Katherine thought.

"Of course, these fragmentary plans were not enough to let us reconstruct MEDUSA." Crome was saying. "But seven years ago, thanks again to Valentine, we acquired a remarkable piece of Old-Tech, taken from a long-lost military site in the American desert. It is perhaps the best preserved Ancient computer-core ever discovered, and it is more than that; it is the brain of MEDUSA, the artificial intelligence that once powered this remarkable machine. Thanks to the hard work of Dr Splay and his comrades in B Division, we have at last been able to restore it to working order. Guildspersons, the days when London had to run and hide from other hungry cities are at an end! With MEDUSA at our command we will be able to reduce any one of them to ashes in the blink of an eye!"

The Engineers applauded wildly, and Bevis Pod nudged at Katherine to join in, but her hands seemed to have become frozen to the metal arm-rests of her seat. She felt giddy with shock. She remembered everything she had heard about the Sixty Minute War and how the Ancients' terrible thunder-weapons had blasted their static cities and poisoned the earth and sky. Father would never have helped the Engineers to recreate such a terrible thing!

"Nor will we have to go chasing after scraps like Salthook," Crome continued. "In another week London will be within range of Batmunkh Gompa, the Shield-Wall. For a thousand years the Anti-Traction League has cowered behind it, holding out against the tide of history. MEDUSA will destroy it at a single stroke. The lands beyond it, with all their huge static cities, their crops and forests, their untapped mineral wealth, will become London's new hunting ground!"

You could hardly hear him now; the cheers of the Engineers rolled like breakers against the wall behind him, and it slid slowly open, revealing a long window that looked out towards St Paul's Cathedral and the turrets of the Guildhall.

"But first," he shouted, "we have more pressing business to attend to. Although I had hoped we might keep MEDUSA hidden until we reached the Shield-Wall, it has become necessary to give a demonstration of its power. Even as I speak, Dr Splay's team is preparing a test-firing of the new weapon."

Even if Katherine had wanted to hear more it would soon have become impossible, for Crome's audience were all talking excitedly among themselves. A few Engineers, presumably those connected with the MEDUSA project, were hurrying to the exits. Standing up, Katherine started pushing her way to the door. A moment later she was out in the antiseptic corridor, wondering what to do next.

"Kate?" Bevis Pod appeared behind her. "Where are you going? People noticed you leave! I saw some Guild security people watching us. . ."

"We've got to get out of here," whispered Katherine. "Where's the way out?"

"I don't know," admitted the boy. "I've never been to this level before. I suppose we'll have to find our way back to the monorail. . ." He shook Katherine away as she tried to take his hand. "No! Somebody will see. Engineers aren't supposed to touch each other. . ."

They hurried along the tubular corridors, and Katherine said, "Crome was lying! My father didn't go to America seven years ago. He just went on a little trip to the islands of the Western Ocean. And he never told me he'd found anything important. He'd have told me, if he'd really found MEDUSA. He wouldn't want anything to do with old-world weapons, anyway. . ."

"But why would the Lord Mayor lie?" asked Bevis, who was secretly rather pleased that his Guild had stumbled upon the keys to yet another Ancient secret. "Anyway, he didn't say your dad went to America for this thing, he just said he acquired it. Maybe he bought it from a scavenger or something. I wonder what Crome meant about a demonstration. . ."

He stopped. They had come to the end of the corridor, and there were no monorails in sight. Three doorways faced them. Two were locked, the third led only on to a narrow balcony that jutted out from the Engineerium's flank, high above Paternoster Square.

"What now?" asked Katherine, hearing her own voice high and thin with fright, and Bevis, just as nervously, replied, "I don't know."

She stepped out on to the balcony to catch her breath.

The moon was up, but veiled by thin cloud, and a cool drizzle was falling. She pulled off her goggles and let the rain spill down her face, glad to be free of the heat and the chemical stench. She thought about Father. Had he really found MEDUSA? Bevis was right; Crome had no reason to lie. Poor Father! He would be in the air now, somewhere above the snow-peaks of Shan Guo. If only she had some way to warn him what they were planning to do with his discovery!

A low, mechanical rumble came drifting across the moonlit square. She looked down at the wet deckplates, but could not see what was making the noise. Then something made her glance up at St Paul's. She gasped. "Bevis! Look!"

Slowly, like a huge bud blooming, the dome of the ancient cathedral was splitting open.

Had the Stalker only just arrived, or had he been standing watching them squabble, dark and still on the stone-strewn hillside like a stone himself? He took a step forward, and the damp grass smouldered where he set his foot. "THEY ARE MINE."

The pirates swung round, Maggs's machine gun spraying streams of tracer at the iron man while Mungo's hand-cannon punched black holes in his armour and Ames blazed away with his revolver. Caught in the web of gunfire, Shrike stood swaying for a moment. Then, slowly, like a man walking into a strong wind, he started forward. Bullets sparked off his armour and his coat tore away in rags and tatters. The holes the cannon made spewed something that might have been blood, might have been oil. He stretched out his arms, and an iron claw was ripped away, and another. Then he reached Maggs and she made a choking sound and went backwards into the bracken and down. Ames flung down his gun and turned to run, but Shrike was suddenly behind him and he stopped short, gawping at a handful of red spikes that sprouted from his chest.

Mungo's gun was empty. He threw it aside and pulled his sword out, but before he could swing it Shrike had grabbed him by the hair and wrenched his head back and severed his neck with one scything blow.

"Tom," said Hester. "*Run!*"

Shrike flung the head aside and stalked forward, and Tom ran. He didn't want to; he knew there was no point, and he knew he should stand by Hester, but his legs had other ideas; his whole body wanted only to be away from the terrible, dead thing that was coming towards him down the hill. Then the ground gave way under him; he plunged into cold mud and fell, rolled over, and came to a rest against an outcrop of stone on the edge of the same mire that had swallowed Chrysler Peavey.

He looked back. The Stalker stood among the sprawling bodies. Airhaven was overhead, testing its engines one by one, and its lights kindled cold reflections on his moon-silvered skull.

Hester stood facing him, bravely holding her ground. Tom thought, *She's trying to save me! She's buying time so that I can get away! But I can't just let him kill her, I can't!*

Ignoring the countless voices of his body that were still screaming at him to run, he started to crawl back up the hill.

"HESTER SHAW," he heard Shrike say, and the voice slurred and caught like a faulty recording. Steam hissed from holes in the Stalker's chest and black ichor dripped from him and bubbled at the corners of his mouth.

"Are you going to kill me?" the girl asked.

Shrike nodded his great head, just once. "FOR A LITTLE WHILE."

"What do you mean?"

The long mouth dragged sideways, smiling. "WE ARE TWO OF A KIND, YOU AND I. I KNEW IT AS SOON AS I FOUND YOU THAT DAY ON THE SHORE. AFTER YOU LEFT ME, THE LONELI-NESS. . ."

"I had to go, Shrike," she whispered. "I wasn't part of your collection."

"YOU WERE VERY DEAR TO ME."

Something's wrong with him, thought Tom, inching up the hill. Stalkers weren't meant to have *feelings.* He remembered what he had been taught about the Resurrected Men all going mad. Was that seaweed hanging from the ducts on Shrike's head? Had his brains gone rusty? Sparks were flickering inside his chest, behind the bullet-holes. . .

"HESTER," Shrike grated, falling heavily to his knees so that his face was at the same level as hers. "CROME HAS MADE ME A PROMISE. HIS SERVANTS HAVE LEARNED THE SECRET OF MY CONSTRUCTION."

Fear prickled the back of Tom's neck.

"I WILL TAKE YOUR BODY TO LONDON," Shrike told the girl. "CROME WILL RESURRECT YOU AS AN IRON WOMAN. YOUR FLESH WILL BE REPLACED WITH STEEL, YOUR NERVES WITH WIRE, YOUR THOUGHTS WITH ELECTRICITY. YOU WILL BE BEAUTIFUL! YOU WILL BE MY COMPANION, FOR ALL TIME."

"Shrike," Hester snorted. "Crome won't want *me* Resurrected. . ."

"WHY NOT? NO ONE WILL RECOGNIZE YOU IN YOUR NEW BODY; YOU WILL HAVE NO MEMORIES, NO FEELINGS, YOU WILL BE NO THREAT TO HIM. BUT *I* WILL REMEMBER FOR YOU, MY DAUGHTER. WE WILL HUNT DOWN VALENTINE TOGETHER."

Hester laughed; a strange, mad, terrible sound that set Tom's teeth on edge as he reached the place where Mungo's body lay. The heavy sword was still clamped in the pirate's fist, and Tom reached out and started prising it free. Glancing up, he saw that Hester had taken a step closer to the Stalker. She tilted her head back, baring her throat, readying herself for his claws. "All right," she said. "But let Tom go."

"HE MUST DIE," insisted Shrike. "IT IS PART OF MY BARGAIN WITH CROME. YOU WILL NOT REMEMBER HIM WHEN YOU WAKE IN YOUR NEW BODY."

"Oh please, Shrike, no," begged Hester. "Tell Crome

he escaped or drowned or something, died somewhere in the Out-Country and you couldn't bring him back. Please."

Tom clung to the sword, its hilt still clammy with Mungo's sweat. Now that the moment had come he was so scared that he could barely breathe, let alone stand up and confront the Stalker. *I can't do this!* he thought. *I'm a Historian, not a warrior!* But he couldn't desert Hester, not while she was bargaining away her life for his. He was close enough to see the fear in her eye, and the sharp glitter of Shrike's claws as he reached for her.

"VERY WELL," the Stalker said. Gently, he stroked Hester's face with the tips of the blades. "THE BOY CAN LIVE." The hand drew back to strike. Hester shut her eye.

"Shrike!" howled Tom, hurling himself up and forward with the sword held out stiffly in front of him, feeling the green light spill across his face as Shrike spun hissing to meet him. An iron arm lashed out, hurling him backwards. He felt a searing pain in his chest and for a moment he was sure that he had been torn in two, but it was the Stalker's forearm that struck him, not the bladed hand, and he landed in one piece and rolled over, gasping at the pain, expecting to see Shrike lunge at him and then nothing, ever again.

But Shrike was on the ground, and Hester was bending over him, and as Tom watched the Stalker's eye flickered and something exploded inside him with a flash and a crack and a coil of smoke leaking upwards. The hilt of the sword jutted from one of the gashes in his chest, crackling with blue sparks.

"Oh, Shrike!" whispered Hester

Shrike carefully sheathed his claws so that she could take his hand. Unexpected memories fluttered through his disintegrating mind, and he suddenly knew who he had been before they dragged him on to the Resurrection Slab to make a Stalker of him. He wanted to tell Hester, and he lifted his great iron head towards her, but before he could force the words out his death was upon him, and it was no easier this time than the last.

The great iron carcass settled into stillness, and smoke blew away on the wind. Down in the valley, horns were blowing, and Tom could see a party of riders starting up the hill from the caravanserai, alerted by the sound of gunfire. They carried spears and flaming torches, and he didn't think they would be friendly. He tried to push himself upright, but the pain in his chest almost made him faint.

Hester heard him groan and swung towards him. "What did you do that for?" she shouted.

Tom could not have been more surprised if she had slapped him. "He was going to kill you!" he protested.

"He was going to make me like *him*!" screamed Hester, hugging Shrike. "Didn't you hear what he said? He was going to make me everything I ever wanted; no memories, no feelings. Imagine Valentine's face when I came for him! Oh, *why* do you keep *interfering*?"

"He would have turned you into a monster!" Tom heard his own voice rising to a shout as all his pain and fear flared into anger.

"I'm already a monster!" she shrieked.

"No, you're not!" Tom managed to heave himself to his knees. "You're my friend!" he shouted.

"I hate you! I hate you!" Hester was yelling

"Well, I care about you, whether you like it or not!" Tom screamed. "Do you think you're the only person who's lost their mum and dad? I feel just as angry and lonely as you, but you don't see me going around wanting to kill people and trying to get myself turned into a Stalker! You're just a rude, self-pitying –"

But the rest of what he had been planning to tell her died away in an astonished sob, because suddenly he could see the town below him and Airhaven and the approaching riders as clearly as if it were the middle of the day. He saw the stars fade; he saw Hester's face freeze in mid-shout with spittle trailing from the corners of her mouth; he saw his own wavering shadow dancing on the blood-soaked grass.

Above the crags, the night sky was filling with an unearthly light, as if a new sun had risen from the Out-Country, somewhere far away towards the north.

23
MEDUSA

Katherine watched, transfixed, as the dome of St Paul's split along black seams and the sections folded outwards like petals. Inside, something was rising slowly up a central tower and opening as it rose, an orchid of cold, white metal. The grumble of vast hydraulics echoed across the square and shivered through the fabric of the Engineerium.

"MEDUSA!" whispered Bevis Pod, standing behind her in the open doorway. "They haven't really been repairing the cathedral at all! They've built MEDUSA inside St Paul's!"

"Guildspersons?"

They turned. An Engineer was standing behind them. "What are you doing?" he snapped. "This gantry is off-limits to everyone but L Division –"

He stopped, staring at Katherine, and she saw that Bevis was staring too, his dark eyes wide and horrified. For a moment she couldn't imagine what was wrong with him. Then she understood. The rain! She had forgotten about the Guild-mark he had painted so carefully between her eyebrows, and now it was trickling down her face in thin red rills.

"What in Quirke's name?" the Engineer gasped.

"Kate, run!" shouted Bevis, pushing the Engineer aside, and Katherine ran, and heard the man's angry shout behind her as he fell. Then Bevis was with her, grabbing her by the hand, darting left and right down empty corridors until a stairway opened ahead. Down one flight and then another, and behind them they heard more shouts and the sudden jarring peal of an alarm bell. Then they were at the bottom, in a small lobby, somewhere at the rear of the Engineerium. There were big glass doors opening on to Top Tier, and two Guildsmen standing guard.

"There's an intruder!" panted Bevis, pointing back the way they had come. "On the third floor! I think he's armed!"

The Guildsmen were already startled by the sudden ringing of the alarm bell. They exchanged shocked glances, then one started up the stairs, dragging a gas-pistol from his belt.

Bevis and Katherine seized their chance and hurried on. "My colleague's been hurt," explained Bevis, pointing at Katherine's red-streaked face. "I'm taking her round to the infirmary!" The door swung open and spilled them out into the welcome dark.

They ran as fast as they could into the shadow of St Paul's, then stopped and listened. Katherine could hear the heavy throbbing of machinery, and a closer, louder throb that was the beat of her own heart. A man's voice was shouting orders somewhere, and there was a crash of armoured feet, coming closer. "Beefeaters!" she whimpered. "They'll want to see our papers! They'll take off my hood! Oh, Bevis, I should never have asked you to get me in there! Run! Leave me!"

Bevis looked at her and shook his head. He had defied his Guild and risked everything to help her, and he wasn't about to abandon her now.

"*Oh, Clio help us!*" breathed Katherine, and something made her glance towards Paternoster Square. There was old Chudleigh Pomeroy standing on the Guildhall steps with his arms full of envelopes and folders, staring upward. She had never been so happy to see anyone in her whole life, and she ran to him, dragging Bevis Pod along with her and calling softly, "Mr Pomeroy!"

He looked blankly at them, then gasped in surprise as Katherine pulled the stupid hood off and he saw her face and her sweat-draggled hair. "Miss Valentine! What in Quirke's name is happening? Look what those damned interfering Engineers have done to St Paul's!"

She looked up. The metal orchid was open to its full extent now, casting a deep shadow on the square below. Only it was not an orchid. It was a cowled, flaring thing like the hood of some enormous cobra, and it was swinging round to point at Panzerstadt-Bayreuth.

"MEDUSA!" she said.

"Who?" asked Chudleigh Pomeroy.

A bug siren wailed. "Oh, please!" she cried, turning to the plump Historian, "They're after us! If they catch Bevis, I don't know what will happen to him. . ."

Bless him – he did not say "Why?" or "What have you done wrong?", just took Katherine by one arm and Bevis Pod by the other and hurried them towards the Guildhall garage where his bug was waiting. As the chauffeur helped them into it a squad of Beefeaters came clattering past, but they paid no attention to Pomeroy and his companions. He hid Katherine's coat and hood behind his seat, and made Bevis Pod crouch down on the floor of the bug. Then he squeezed himself in beside Katherine on the back seat and said, "Let me do the talking," as the bug went purring out into Paternoster Square.

There was a throng of people outside the elevator station, gazing up in amazement at the thing which had sprouted from St Paul's. Beefeaters stopped the bug while a young Engineer peered in. Pomeroy opened a vent in the glastic lid and asked, "Is there a problem, Guildsman?"

"A break-in at the Engineerium. Anti-Tractionist terrorists. . ."

"Well, don't look at us," laughed Pomeroy. "I've been working in my office at the Guildhall all evening, and Miss Valentine has been kindly helping me to sort out some papers. . ."

"All the same, sir, I'll have to search your bug."

"Oh, really!" cried Pomeroy. "Do we look like terrorists? Haven't you got better things to do, on the last night of London, with a dirty great conurbation bearing down on us? I shall complain to the Council in the strongest possible terms! It's outrageous!"

The man looked uncertain, then nodded and stepped aside to let Pomeroy's chauffeur steer the bug into a waiting freight elevator. As the doors closed behind it Pomeroy let out a sigh of relief. "Those damned Engineers. No offence, Apprentice Pod. . ."

"None taken," said Bevis's muffled voice from somewhere below.

"Thank you!" whispered Katherine. "Oh, thank you for helping us!"

"Don't mention it," chuckled Pomeroy. "I'm always happy to do anything that upsets Crome and his lackeys. Thousands of years old, that cathedral, and they go and turn it into a . . . into whatever they've turned it into, without so much as a by-your-leave. . ." He looked nervously at Katherine and saw that she wasn't really listening. Gently he asked, "But whatever have you done to stir them up, Miss Valentine? You don't have to tell me if you don't want to, but if you and your friend are in trouble, and if there's anything an old coot like me can do. . ."

Katherine felt helpless tears prickling her eyes. "Please," she whispered, "could you just take us home?"

"Of course."

They sat in awkward silence as the bug drove through the streets of Tier One into the park. The darkness was full of people running and shouting, pointing up towards the cathedral. But there were other runners too: Engineer security men leading squads of Beefeaters. When the bug stopped outside Clio House, Pomeroy climbed out to walk Katherine to the door. She whispered a heartfelt goodbye to Bevis and followed him. "Could you take Apprentice Pod to an elevator station?' she asked. "He needs to get back to the Gut."

Pomeroy looked worried. "I don't know, Miss Valentine," he sighed. "You've seen how het-up the Engineers are. If I know them they'll have all their factories and dormitory blocks locked down tight by now, and security checks in progress. They may already have worked out that he's missing, along with two coats and hoods. . ."

"You mean, he can't go back?" Katherine felt dizzy at the thought of what she had done to poor Pod. "Not ever?"

Pomeroy nodded.

"Then I'll keep him with me at Clio House!" Katherine decided.

"He's not a stray cat, my dear."

"But when Father gets home he'll be able to sort everything out, won't he? Explain to the Lord Mayor that it was nothing to do with Bevis. . ."

"It's possible," agreed Pomeroy. "Your father is very close to the Guild of Engineers. A damned sight *too* close, some people say. But I don't think Clio House is

185

the place to keep your friend. I'll take him down to the Museum. There's plenty of room for him there, and the Engineers won't be able to search for him without giving us warning first."

"Would you really do that?" asked Katherine, afraid that she was dragging yet another innocent person into the trouble she had created. But after all, it would only be for a few days, until Father came home. Then everything would be all right. "Oh, thank you!" she said happily, standing on tiptoe to kiss Pomeroy's cheek. "Thank you!"

Pomeroy blushed and beamed at her, and started to say something else – but although his mouth moved she could not hear the words. Her head was filled with a strange sound, a whining roar that grew louder and louder until she realized that it wasn't inside her at all, but pounding down from somewhere overhead.

"Look!" shouted the Historian, pointing upwards.

Her fear had made her forget St Paul's. Now, looking up at Top Tier, she saw the cobra-hood of MEDUSA start to crackle with violet lightning. The hair on her arms and the back of her neck prickled, and when she reached for Pomeroy's hand pale sparks jumped between the tips of her fingers and his robes. "Mr Pomeroy!" she shouted. "What's happening?"

"Great Quirke!" the Historian cried. "What have those fools awoken now?"

Ghostly spheres of light detached themselves from the glowing machine and drifted down over Circle Park like fire-balloons. Lightning danced around the spires of the Guildhall. The rushing, whining roar grew louder and louder, higher and higher, until even with her hands clapped over her ears Katherine felt she could not bear a moment more of it. Then, quite suddenly, a stream of incandescent energy burst from the cobra's hood and stretched northwards, a snarling, spitting cat-o'-nine-tails lashing out to lick at the upperworks of Panzerstadt-Bayreuth. The night split apart and went rushing away to hide in the corners of the sky. For a second Katherine saw the tiers of the distant conurbation limned in fire, and then it was gone. A pulse of brightness lifted from the earth, blinding white, then red, a pillar of fire rushing up in silence into the sky, and across the flame-lit snow the sound-wave came rolling, a low, long-drawn-out boom as if a great door had slammed shut somewhere in the depths of the earth.

The beam snapped off, plunging Circle Park into sudden darkness, and in the silence she heard Dog howling madly inside the house.

"Great Quirke!" Pomeroy whispered. "All those poor people. . .!"

"No!" Katherine heard herself say. "Oh, no, no, no!" She started to run across the garden, staring towards the lightning-flecked cloud which wreathed the wreckage of the conurbation. From Circle Park and all the observation platforms came the sound of wordless voices, and she thought at first that they were crying out in horror, the way she wanted to – but no; they were cheering, cheering, cheering.

PART TWO

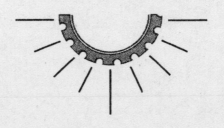

24

AN AGENT OF THE LEAGUE

The strange light in the north had died away and the long thunderclap had spent itself, echoing and re-echoing from the walls of the old volcano. Mastering their panicked horses, the men of the Black Island came on along the margins of the bog amid a drum-roll of galloping hooves and the torn-silk sound of windblown torches.

Tom raised his hands and shouted, "We're friends! Not pirates! Travellers! From London!" But the horsemen were in no mood to listen, even the few who understood. They had been hunting survivors from the sunken suburb all day, they had seen what Peavey's pirates had done in the fishing villages along the western shore, and now they shouted to each other in their own language and galloped closer, raising their bows. A grey-feathered arrow thudded into the ground at Tom's feet, making him stumble backwards. "We're friends!" he shouted again.

The leading man drew his sword, but another rider spurred in front of him, shouting something in the Island tongue, then in Anglish. "I want them alive!"

It was Anna Fang. She reined in her horse, swung herself down from the saddle and ran towards Tom and Hester, her coat flapping against the firelight like a red flag. She wore a sword in a long scabbard on her back, and on her breast Tom saw a bronze badge in the shape of a broken wheel – the symbol of the Anti-Traction League.

"Tom! Hester!" She hugged them one by one, smiling her sweetest smile. "I thought you were dead! I sent

Lindstrom and Yasmina to look for you, the morning after the fight at Airhaven. They found your balloon wrecked in those horrible marshes, and said you must be dead, dead. I wanted to search for your poor bodies, but the *Jenny* had been damaged, and I was so busy helping guide the town down to the repair-yard here... But we said prayers for you, and made funeral sacrifices to the gods of the sky. Do you think we could ask them for a refund?"

Tom kept quiet. His chest was hurting so that he could hardly breathe, let alone speak. Anyway, the badge on the aviatrix's coat told him that Peavey's stories had been true: she was an agent of the League. He wasn't charmed any more by her kindness and her tinkling laugh.

She shouted something over her shoulder to the waiting riders, and a couple jumped down from their ponies and led them forward, staring in wonder at Shrike's corpse. "I have to leave you for a while," she explained. "I'm taking the *Jenny* north to see what devilry has lit up the sky. The islanders will look after you. Can you ride?"

Tom had never even seen a horse before, let alone sat on one, but he was so dazed with pain and shock that he could not protest as they heaved him up into the saddle of a shaggy little pony and started to lead it downhill. He looked back for Hester and saw her scowling at him, hunched in the saddle of a second pony. Then the knot of riders closed about her, and he lost sight of her in the narrow, crowded streets of the caravanserai, where whole families were standing outside their homes to stare at the northern sky, and dust and litter whirled between the buildings as Airhaven dipped overhead, trying out its rotors one by one.

There was a small stone house where someone found a seat for him, and a man in black robes and a big white turban who examined his bruised chest. "Broken!" he said cheerfully. "I am Ibrahim Nazghul, physician. Four of your ribs are quite smashed up!"

Tom nodded, giddy with the pain and shock, but starting to feel lucky that he was still alive, and glad that these people weren't the Anti-Tractionist savages he had been expecting. Dr Nazghul wound bandages around his chest, and his wife brought a steaming bowl of mutton stew and helped Tom eat, spooning it into his mouth. Lantern-light lapped at the corners of the room, and in the doorway the doctor's children stood staring at Tom with huge dark eyes.

"You are a hero!" explained the doctor. "They say you fought with an iron djinn who would have killed us all."

Tom blinked sleepily at him. He had almost forgotten the squalid little battle at the edge of the bog: the details were fading quickly, like a dream. *I killed Shrike*, he thought. *All right, so he was dead already, technically, but he was still a person. He had hopes and plans and dreams, and I put a stop to them all.* He didn't feel like a hero, he felt like a murderer, and the feeling of guilt and shame stayed with him, staining his dreams as his head drooped over the bowl of stew and he slipped away into sleep.

Then he was in another room, in a soft bed, and there was a blustery blue-and-white sky beyond the window and a patch of sunlight coming and going on the lime-washed wall.

"How are you feeling, Stalker-killer?" a voice asked. Miss Fang stood over him, watching him with the gentle smile of an angel in an old picture.

Tom said, "Everything hurts."

"Well enough to travel? The *Jenny Haniver* is waiting, and I would like to be away before sundown. You can eat once we're airborne; I've made toad in the hole, with real toad."

"Where's Hester?" Tom asked groggily.

"Oh, she's coming too."

He sat up, wincing at the sharp pain in his chest and the memory of all that had happened. "I'm not going anywhere with *you*," he said.

The aviatrix laughed as if she thought he was joking, then realized he wasn't and sat down on the bed, looking concerned. "Tom? Have I done something to upset you?"

"You work for the League!" he said angrily. "You're a spy, no better than Valentine! You only helped us because you hoped we'd tell you things about London!"

Miss Fang's smile faded entirely. "Tom," she said gently, "I helped you because I like you. And if you had seen your family slave to death aboard a ruthless city, might you not have decided to help the League in its fight against Municipal Darwinism?"

She reached out to brush the tousled hair away from his forehead, and Tom remembered something he had forgotten, a time when he was little and very ill and his mother had sat with him like this. But the badge of the League was still on Miss Fang's breast, and the wound of Valentine's betrayal was still raw: he would not let himself be tricked by smiles and kindness again. "You kill people!" he said, pushing her hand away. "You sank Marseilles. . ."

"If I had not, it would have attacked the Hundred Islands, killing or enslaving hundreds more people than I drowned with my little bomb."

"And you strangled the . . . the Raisin of Somewhere-or-Other!"

"The Sultana of Palau Pinang?" The smile came flickering back. "I didn't strangle her! What a horrible suggestion! I simply broke her neck. She let amphibious raft-cities refuel at her island, so she had be disposed of."

Tom didn't see that it was anything to smile about. He remembered Wreyland's men slumped in the shadows of the air-quay at Stayns, and Miss Fang telling him they were just unconscious.

"I may be no better than Valentine," she went on, "but there is a difference between us. Valentine tried to kill you, and I want to keep you alive. So, will you come with me?"

"Where to?" asked Tom suspiciously.

"To Shan Guo," she replied. "I'm willing to bet that what lit up the sky last night had something to do with the thing Valentine took from Hester's mother. And I have learned that London is heading straight for the Shield-Wall."

Tom was amazed. Could the Lord Mayor really have found a way to breach the League's borders? If so, it was the best news for years! As for going to Shan Guo, that was the heart of the Anti-Traction League, the last place in the world a decent Londoner should go. "I won't do anything to help you harm London," he told her. "It's still my home."

"Of course," she replied. "But if the Wall is about to be attacked, don't you think the people who live behind it deserve a chance to get away? I am going to warn them of their danger, and I want Hester to come with me and tell her side of the story. And Hester will only go if you come too."

Tom laughed, and found that it hurt. "I don't think so!" he said. "Hester hates me!"

"Nonsense," giggled Miss Fang. "She likes you very much. Did she not spend half the night telling me how kind you have been, and how wonderfully brave you were, killing that machine-man?"

"Did she?" Tom blushed, feeling suddenly proud. He didn't think he would ever get used to Hester Shaw and her see-sawing moods. Nevertheless, she was the closest thing he had to a friend in this huge, confusing world, and he still remembered how she had pleaded with Shrike for his life. Wherever she was going, he had to go too: even into the savage heartland of the League; even to Shan Guo.

"All right," he said. "I'll come."

25
THE HISTORIANS

It is raining on London, steady rain out of the low, bruised sky, raining hard enough to wash away the snow and churn the mud beneath the city's tracks into thick yellow slurry, but not to quench the fires of Panzerstadt-Bayreuth, which are still blazing like a Titan's pyre away in the north-west.

Magnus Crome stands on the windswept roof of the Engineerium and watches the rising smoke. An apprentice holds an umbrella over him, and behind her wait six tall, motionless figures dressed in black versions of the Guild's rubber coats. The terrorists who breached the Engineerium last night have still not been caught, and security is being strengthened: from now on the Lord Mayor will go nowhere without his new bodyguard; the first batch of Dr Twix's Stalkers.

A Guild spotter-ship swings overhead and touches down. Dr Vambrace, the Engineers' security chief, steps out and comes hurrying to where the Lord Mayor waits, his rubber coat flapping thickly in the wind.

"Well, Doctor?" Crome asks eagerly. "What did you see? Were you able to land?"

Vambrace shakes his head. "Fires are still burning all over the wreck. But we circled as low as we dared and took photographs. The upper tiers have melted and collapsed on to the lower, and it looks as if all the boilers and fuel-stores exploded at the first touch of our energy beam."

Crome nods. "Were there any survivors?"

"A few signs of life, between the tiers, but otherwise. . ." The security man's eyes go wide behind his thick glasses, looking like a pair of jellyfish in an aquarium. His department is always keen to find new and inventive ways to kill people, and he is still excited at the thought of the dry, charred shapes he saw littering the streets and squares of Panzerstadt-Bayreuth, many of them still standing upright, flashed into clinker statues by the gaze of MEDUSA.

"Do you intend to turn back and devour the wreck, Lord Mayor?" he asks after a moment. "The fires will burn themselves out in a day or two."

"Absolutely not," snaps Crome. "We must press on towards the Shield-Wall."

"The people will not like that," Vambrace warns. "They have had their victory, now they want the spoils. The scrap metal and spare parts from that conurbation—"

"I have not brought London all this way for scrap metal and spare parts," Crome interrupts. He stands at the handrail on the roof's rim and stares east. He can already see the white summits of high mountains on the horizon, like a row of pearly teeth. "We must press on. A few more days will bring us within range of the Shield-Wall. I have announced a public holiday, and a reception at the Guildhall to mark the great event. Think of it, Vambrace! A whole new hunting ground!"

"But the League know we are coming now," warns Vambrace. "They will try to stop us."

Crome's eyes are bright and cold, gazing at the future. He says, "Valentine has his orders. He will deal with the League."

And so London kept moving, dragging itself eastward as the smoke of the dead conurbation towered up into the sky behind, and Katherine walked to the elevator stations through the wet wreckage of last-night's celebrations. Broken Chinese lanterns blew across the shuddering deckplates, and men in the red livery of the Recycling Department wheeled bins around, gathering up abandoned party-hats and soggy banners whose messages were still dimly to be read: *We ♡ Magnus Crome* and *Long Live London.* Dog played chase with a billowing paperchain, but Katherine called him sharply to heel. This was no time for games.

At least in the Museum there were no banners and no paperchains. The Historians' Guild had never been as quick as the rest of London to welcome new inventions from the Engineers, and they made no exception for MEDUSA. In the dusty shadows of the exhibition galleries there was a decent silence, as befitted the morning after the death of a whole city. The sounds of the streets outside seemed muffled, as if thick, soft curtains of time hung in the dim air between the display cabinets. The quietness helped Katherine to gather her thoughts, and by the time she reached Chudleigh Pomeroy's office she was quite clear about what she had to say.

She had not yet told Mr Pomeroy what she had learned in the Engineerium, but he had seen how shaken she was when he left her at Clio House the night before. He did not seem surprised to find her and Dog at his door.

"Mr Pomeroy," she whispered, "I have to talk to you. Is Bevis here? Is he all right?"

"Of course," he said at once. "Come in!"

Bevis Pod was waiting for her in the little

teak-panelled office, dressed in borrowed Historian's robes, his pale skull looking as fragile as an eggshell in the dim yellow glow of the Museum lamps. She wanted to run to him and hold him and apologize for what she had led him into, but crammed in around him were about a dozen Historians, some perching on the arms of chairs and the corners of Pomeroy's desk. They all looked up guiltily at Katherine, and she looked back at them with a sudden, horrible fear that Pomeroy had betrayed her.

"Don't worry," said Pomeroy kindly. "If Pod's to be a guest of the Museum I thought my fellow Historians should be introduced to him. None of us are friends of the Lord Mayor. We have agreed that Apprentice Pod can stay as long as necessary."

The Historians made a space for her next to Bevis. "Are you all right?" she asked him, and was relieved when he managed a nervous smile. "Not bad," he whispered. "It's strange here. All this wood everywhere, and old stuff. But the Historians are very kind. . ."

Katherine looked around the room at them. She knew many of them by sight; Dr Arkengarth, Dr Karuna, Professor Pewtertide, young Miss Potts, Norman Nancarrow from Prints and Paintings and Miss Plym, who was sniffling into her hankie.

"We've been talking about the destruction of Panzerstadt-Bayreuth," said Pomeroy, pressing a hot mug of cocoa into her hands. "This horrible MEDUSA device."

"Everybody else seems to think it's wonderful," said Katherine bitterly. "I could hear them laughing and shouting 'Good old Crome' half the night. I know they're relieved that we didn't get eaten, but. . . Well, I don't think blowing up another city is anything to be happy about."

"It's a disaster!" agreed old Dr Arkengarth, wringing his bony hands. "The vibrations from that vile machine played havoc with my ceramics!"

"Oh, bother your ceramics, Arkengarth," snapped Pomeroy, who could see how upset Katherine was. "What about Panzerstadt-Bayreuth? Burned to a cinder!"

"That's what comes of the Engineers' obsession with Old-Tech!" said Professor Pewtertide. "Countless centuries of history to learn from, and all they are interested in is a few ancient machines!"

"And what did the Ancients ever achieve with their devices anyway?" whined Arkengarth. "They just made a horrible mess of their world and then blew themselves up!"

The others nodded dolefully.

"There was a great museum in Panzerstadt-Bayreuth," said Dr Karuna.

"I believe they had some wonderful paintings," agreed Nancarrow.

"Unique examples of 30th Century c-c-cabinet-making!" wailed Miss Plym, and collapsed in tears on Arkengarth's knobbly shoulder.

"You must excuse poor Moira, Katherine," whispered Pomeroy. "She had terrible news this morning. Crome has ordered that our furniture collection be broken up to feed the furnaces. It's the fuel shortage, you see, a result of this mad journey east."

Katherine couldn't have cared less about furniture or ceramics at that moment, but she felt glad that she was not the only one in London appalled by what the Lord

Mayor had unleashed. She took a deep breath, then quickly explained what she and Bevis had heard in the Engineerium; about MEDUSA and the next step in Crome's great plan; the attack on the Shield-Wall.

"But that's terrible!" they whispered when she had finished.

"Shan Guo is a great and ancient culture, Anti-Traction League or no Anti-Traction League. Batmunkh Gompa can't be blown up. . .!"

"Think of all those temples!"

"Ceramics!"

"Prayer-wheels. . ."

"Silk paintings. . ."

"F-f-furniture!"

"Think of the *people*!" said Katherine angrily. "We must do something!"

"Yes! Yes!" they agreed, and then all looked sheepishly at her. After twenty years of Crome's rule they had no idea how to stand up to the Guild of Engineers.

"But what *can* we do?" asked Pomeroy at last.

"Tell people what is happening!" urged Katherine. "You're Acting Head Historian. Call a meeting of the Council! Make them see how wrong it is!"

Pomeroy shook his head. "They won't listen, Miss Valentine. You heard the cheering last night."

"But that was only because Panzerstadt-Bayreuth had been going to eat us! When they learn that Crome plans to turn his weapon on yet another city. . ."

"They'll just cheer all the louder," sighed Pomeroy.

"He has packed the other Guilds with his allies anyway," observed Dr Karuna. "All the great old Guildsmen are gone; dead or retired or arrested on his orders. Even our own apprentices are as besotted with

Old-Tech as the Engineers, especially since Crome foisted his man Valentine on us as Head Historian. . . Oh, I mean no offence, Miss Katherine. . ."

"Father isn't Crome's man," said Katherine angrily. "I'm sure he's not! If he knew what Crome was planning he would never have helped him. That's probably why he was packed off on this reconnaissance mission, to get him out of the way. When he gets home and finds out he'll do something to stop it. You see, it was he who found MEDUSA in the first place. He would be horrified to think of it killing all those people. He will want to make amends, I'm sure he will!"

She spoke so passionately that some of the Historians believed her, even the ones like Dr Karuna who had been passed over for promotion when Crome put Valentine in charge of their Guild. As for Bevis Pod, he watched her with shining eyes, filled with a feeling that he couldn't even name; something that they had never taught him about in the Learning Labs. It made him shiver all over.

Pomeroy was the first to speak. "I hope you're right, Miss Valentine," he said. "Because he is the only man who can hope to challenge the Lord Mayor. We must wait for his return."

"But. . ."

"In the meantime, we have agreed to keep Mr Pod safe, here at the Museum. He can sleep up in the old Transport Gallery, and help Dr Nancarrow catalogue the art collection, and if the Engineers come hunting for him we'll find a hiding place. It isn't much of a blow against Crome, I know. But please understand, Katherine; we are old, and frightened, and there really is nothing more that we can do."

The world was changing. That was nothing new, of course; the first thing an Apprentice Historian learned was that the world was always changing, but now it was changing so fast that you could actually see it happening. Looking down from the flight-deck of the *Jenny Haniver*, Tom saw the wide plains of the eastern Hunting Ground speckled with speeding towns, spurred into flight by whatever it was that had bruised the northern sky, heading away from it as fast as their tracks or wheels could carry them, too preoccupied to try and catch each other.

"MEDUSA," he heard Miss Fang whisper to herself, staring towards the far off, flame-flecked smoke.

"What *is* a MEDUSA?" asked Hester. "You know something, don't you? About what my mum and dad were killed for?"

"I'm afraid not," the aviatrix replied. "I wish I did. But I heard the name once. Six years ago another League agent managed to get into London, posing as a crewman on a licensed airship. He had heard something that must have intrigued him, but we never learned what it was. The League had only one message from him, just two words: *Beware MEDUSA*. The Engineers caught him and killed him."

"How do you know?" asked Tom.

"Because they sent us back his head," said Miss Fang. "Cash on Delivery."

That evening she set the *Jenny Haniver* down on one of the fleeing towns, a respectable four-decker called Peripatetiapolis which was steering south to lair in the mountains beyond the Sea of Khazak. At the air-harbour there they heard more news of what had happened to Panzerstadt-Bayreuth.

"I saw it!" said an aviator. "I was a hundred miles away, but I still saw it. A tongue of fire, reaching out from London's Top Tier and bringing death to everything it touched!"

"London's dug up something from the Sixty Minute War," a freelance archaeologist told them. "The old American Empire was quite insane towards the end; I've heard stories about terrible weapons: quantum energy beams that drew their power from places outside the real universe. . ."

"Who'll dare defy them now, when Magnus Crome has the power to burn any city that disobeys him?" asked a panic-stricken Peripatetiapolitan merchant. "'Come here and let us eat you,' London will tell us, and we will have to go. It's the end of civilization as we know it! Again!"

But one good thing had come out of it; the people of Peripatetiapolis were suddenly quite glad to accept Tom's London money. On an impulse he bought a red silk shawl to replace the scarf that Hester had lost on that long-ago night when he chased her through the Gut.

"For *me*?" she said incredulously when he gave it to her. She couldn't remember anyone ever giving her a gift before. She had not spoken to him much since they left the Black Island, ashamed of her outburst the night before, but now she said, "Thank you. And I suppose I should thank you for saving my life, too. Though I don't know why you keep bothering."

"I knew you didn't really want to end up as a Stalker," Tom told her.

"Oh, I did," she said. "It would make things so much easier. But you did the right thing." She looked away from him, embarrassed, staring down at the shawl in her hands. "I try to be nice," she said. "Nobody's ever made me feel they *like* me before, the way you do. So I try to be kind and smiley, like you want me to be, but then I catch sight of my reflection or I think of *him* and it all goes wrong and I can only think horrible things and scream at you and try to hurt you. I'm sorry."

"It's all right," said Tom awkwardly. "I know. It's OK." He picked up the shawl and tied it carefully round her neck, but as he had expected she pulled it up at once to hide her mouth and nose. He felt strangely sad: he had grown used to that face, and he would miss her lop-sided smiles.

They flew on before dawn, crossing a range of steep hills like crumpled brown paper. All day the land rose up and up, and soon Tom realized that they were leaving the Hunting Ground altogether. By evening the *Jenny Haniver* was flying over landscapes too rugged for most towns to travel. He saw dense forests of pine and rhododendron, with now and then a little static village squatting in its cove of farmland, and once a white settlement perched on a mountain top with roads reaching out from it like the spokes of a wheel; real roads with carts moving up and down and a bright flutter of prayer-flags at the intersections. He watched until they were out of sight. He had heard about roads in his history lessons, but he had never thought he'd *see* one.

Next day, Anna Fang handed out balls of reddish paste to her passengers. "Powdered betel-nut," she explained, "mixed with some dried leaves from Nuevo Maya. They help at these high altitudes. But don't make a habit of

chewing them, or your teeth will turn as red as mine."
The gritty paste made Tom's mouth tingle, but it cured
the faint sense of nausea and light-headedness that
had been growing in him as the airship flew higher
and higher, and it also helped to numb the pain of his
broken ribs.

By now the *Jenny*'s tiny shadow was flickering over
high snow-clad summits, and ahead lay summits still
higher, white spires which hung like a mirage above the
clouds. Beyond them stretched an even higher range,
and then another, higher yet. Tom strained his eyes, peering towards the south in the hope that he might catch a
glimpse of old Chomolungma, Everest of the Ancients,
but storms were brewing in the high Himalayas and it
was wrapped in cloud.

They flew for three days through a black-and-white
world of snow and glaciers and the sheer dark rock of
young mountains, where Tom or Hester sometimes had
to mind the controls while Anna Fang took cat-naps in
the seat beside them, afraid to risk leaving her flight-
deck. And still they climbed, until at last they were
skimming over the lower buttresses of great Zhan Shan,
tallest of the earth's new mountains, whose snow-capped
caldera jutted into the endless cold above the sky. After
that the peaks were lower, white and lovely, with sometimes a green vale between, where huge herds of animals
scattered and wheeled at the sound of the airship's
engines. These were the Mountains of Heaven, and they
swept away towards the north and east and sank down
in the far distance to steppe and taiga and the glitter of
impassable swamps.

"This is Shan Guo of the many horses," Anna Fang
told Tom and Hester. "I had hoped to retire here, when

my work for the League was done. Now I suppose it may all be eaten by London; our fortresses blasted by MEDUSA and our settlements devoured, the green hills split open and made to give up their minerals, the horses extinct, just like the rest of the world."

Tom didn't think it was such a bad idea, because it was only natural that Traction Cities should eventually spread right across the globe. But he couldn't help liking Miss Fang, even if she was a spy and an Anti-Tractionist, and to comfort her he said, "However powerful MEDUSA is, it will take years for London to gnaw its way through these great big mountains."

"It won't have to," she replied. "Look."

He looked where she pointed, and saw a break in the mountain-chain ahead, a broad pass that a city could have crawled along – except that stretching across it, so vast that it seemed at first glance just another spur of the mountains, was the Shield-Wall.

It was like a wall of night, black, black, built from huge blocks of volcanic stone, armoured with the rusting deckplates of cities that had dared to challenge it and been destroyed by the hundreds of rocket batteries on its western face. On its snow-clad summit, four thousand feet above the valley floor, the banner of the broken wheel snapped and raced in the wind and the sunlight gleamed on armoured gun-emplacements and the steel helmets of the League's soldiers.

"If only it were as strong as it looks," sighed the aviatrix, bringing the *Jenny Haniver* down towards it it in a long sweeping curve. A small flying machine, little more than a motorized kite, came soaring to meet them, and she held a brief radio conversation with its pilot. It circled the *Jenny* once and then whirred ahead, guiding the newcomer over the top of the Shield-Wall. Tom looked down at broad battlements and the faces of soldiers gazing upwards, yellow, brown, black, white, faces from every part of the world where barbarian statics still held out against Municipal Darwinism. Then they were gone; the *Jenny* was sinking down the sheltered eastern side of the Wall, and he saw that it was a city, a vertical city with hundreds of terraces and balconies and windows all carved into the black rock, tier upon tier of shops and barracks and houses with balloons and brightly coloured kites drifting up and down between them like petals.

"Batmunkh Gompa," announced Miss Fang. "The City of Eternal Strength. Although the people who call it that have never heard of MEDUSA, of course."

It was beautiful. Tom, who had always been taught that static settlements were dingy, squalid, backward places, went to the window and stared, and Hester came and pressed her face to the glass beside him, safe behind her veil and almost girlish. "Oh! It's just like the cliffs on Oak Island where the sea-birds nest!" she cried. "Look! Look!" Down at the base of the Wall a lake shone azure blue, flecked with the sails of pleasure-boats. "Tom, we'll go swimming, I'll teach you how. . ."

The *Jenny Haniver* landed among some other merchant ships at a mooring-terrace halfway down the Wall, and Miss Fang led Tom and Hester to a waiting balloon that took them up again past parks and tea-shops to the governor's palace; the ancient monastery from which Batmunkh Gompa took its name, whitewashed and many-windowed, carved out of the steep side of the mountain at the Wall's end. Other balloons were converging on the landing deck below the palace gardens, their envelopes bright in the mountain sunlight, and in one of the dangling baskets Tom saw Captain Khora waving.

They met on the landing deck, the young airman touching down just ahead of them and running across to embrace Miss Fang and help her friends out of the skittish gondola. He had flown here from Airhaven the morning after Shrike's attack, and he seemed amazed and happy to see Tom and Hester alive. Turning to the aviatrix he said, "The Governor and his officers are eager for your report, Feng Hua. Terrible rumours have reached us about London. . ."

It was good to meet a friendly face in this strange new city, and Tom fell into step beside Khora as he led the newcomers up the long stair to the palace entrance. He remembered seeing a trim Achebe 2100 berthed at one of the lower platforms and asked, "Was that your machine we saw at the mooring-place, the one with oxhide outriggers?"

Khora laughed delightedly. "That old air-scow? No, thank the gods! My *Mokele Mbembe* is a warship, Tom. Every ally of the League supplies a ship to the Northern Air-Fleet, and they are stabled together, up there." He stopped and pointed, and Tom saw the gleam of bronze doors far up near the summit of the Wall. "The High Eyries."

"We'll take you up there one day, Tom," promised Miss Fang, leading them past the warrior-monks who guarded the door and on into a maze of cool stone corridors. "The League's great Air Destroyers are one of the wonders of the skies! But first, Governor Khan must hear Hester's story."

Governor Ermene Khan was a gentle old man with the long, mournful face of a kindly sheep. He welcomed them all into his private quarters and gave them tea and honey-cakes in a room whose round windows looked down towards the lake of Batmunkh Nor, gleaming among patchwork farmlands, far below. For a thousand years his family had helped to man the Shield-Wall, and he seemed dazed by the news that all his guns and rockets were suddenly useless. "No city can pass Batmunkh Gompa," he kept saying, as the room filled with officers eager to hear the aviatrix's advice. "My dear Feng Hua, if London dares to approach us, we will destroy it. As soon as it comes in range – boom!"

"But that is what I'm trying to tell you!" cried Miss Fang impatiently. "London doesn't need to come within range of your guns. Crome will park his city a hundred miles away and burn your precious Wall to ashes! You have heard Hester's story. I believe that the machine Valentine stole from her mother was a fragment of an ancient weapon – and what happened to Panzerstadt-Bayreuth proves that the Guild of Engineers have managed to restore it to working order."

"Yes, yes," said an artillery officer, "so you say. But can we really believe that Crome has found a way to reactivate something that has been buried since the Sixty Minutes War? Perhaps Panzerstadt-Bayreuth was just destroyed by a freak accident."

"Yes!" Governor Khan clutched gratefully at the idea. "A meteorite, or some sort of gas-leak. . ." He stroked his long beard, reminding Tom of one of the dithery old Historians back at the London Museum. "Perhaps Crome's city will not even come here. . . Perhaps he has other prey in mind?"

But his other officers were more ready to believe the Wind-Flower's report. "He's coming here, all right," said one, an aviatrix from Kerala, not much older than Tom. "I took a scout-ship west the day before yesterday, Feng Hua," she explained, with an adoring look at Miss Fang. "The barbarian city was less than five hundred miles away, and approaching fast. By tomorrow night MEDUSA could be within range."

"And there have been sightings of a black airship in the mountains," put in Captain Khora. "The ships sent to intercept it never returned. My guess is that it was Valentine's *13th Floor Elevator*, sent to spy out our cities so that London can devour them."

Valentine! Tom felt a strange mix of pride and fear at the thought of the Head Historian on the loose here in the very heart of Shan Guo. Beside him, Hester tensed at the mention of the explorer's name. He looked at her, but she was staring past him, out through the open windows towards the mountains as if she half expected to see the *13th Floor Elevator* go flying past.

"No city can pass the Shield-Wall," said Governor Khan, loyal to his ancestors, but he did not sound convinced any more.

"You must launch the Air-Fleet, Governor," Miss Fang insisted, leaning forward in her seat. "Bomb London before they can bring MEDUSA into range. It's the only way to be sure."

"No!" shouted Tom, springing up so that his chair fell backwards with a clatter. He couldn't believe what she had said. "You said we were coming here to warn people! You can't attack London! People will get hurt! Innocent people!" He was thinking of Katherine, imagining League torpedoes crashing into Clio House and the Museum. "You promised!" he said weakly.

"Feng Hua does not make promises to savages," snapped the Keralan girl, but Miss Fang hushed her. "We will just hit the Gut and tracks, Tom," she said. "Then the Top Tier, where MEDUSA is housed. We do not seek to harm the innocent, but what else are we to do, if a barbarian city chooses to threaten us?"

"London's not a barbarian city!" shouted Tom. "It's you who are the barbarians! Why shouldn't London eat Batmunkh Gompa if it needs to? If you don't like the idea, you should have put your cities on wheels long ago, like civilized people!"

A few of the League officers were shouting angrily at him to be quiet, and the Keralan girl had drawn her sword, but Miss Fang calmed them with a few words and turned her patient smile to Tom. "Perhaps you should leave us, Thomas," she said firmly. "I will come and find you later."

Tom's eyes stung with stupid tears. He was sorry for these people, of course he was. He could see that they weren't savages, and he didn't really believe any more that they deserved to be eaten, but he couldn't just sit by and listen to them planning to attack his home.

He turned to Hester in the hope that she would take his side, but she was lost in her own thoughts, her fingers tracing and re-tracing the scars under her red veil. She felt guilty and stupid. Guilty because she had been happy in the air with Tom, and it was wrong to be happy while Valentine was wandering about unpunished. Stupid because, when he gave her the shawl, she had started to hope that Tom really liked her, and thinking of Valentine made her remember that *nobody* could like her, not in that way, not ever. When she saw him looking at her she just said, "They can kill everybody in London for all I care, so long as they save Valentine for me."

Tom turned his back on her and stalked out of the high chamber, and as the door rolled shut behind him he heard the Keralan girl hiss, "Barbarian!"

Alone, he mooched down to the terrace where the taxi-balloons waited and sat on a stone bench there, feeling angry and betrayed and thinking of things that he should have said to Miss Fang, if only he had thought of them in time. Below him the rooftops and terraces of Batmunkh Gompa stretched away into the shadows below the white shoulders of the mountains, and he found himself trying to imagine what it must be like to live here and wake up every day of your life to the same view. Didn't the people of the Shield-Wall long for movement and a change of scene? How did they dream, without the grumbling vibrations of a city's engines to rock them to sleep? Did they *love* this place? And suddenly he felt terribly sad that the whole bustling, colourful, ancient city might soon be rubble under London's tracks.

He wanted to see more. Going over to the nearest balloon-taxi, he made the pilot understand that he was Miss Fang's guest and wanted to go down into the city. The man grinned and started weighting his gondola with stones from a pile that stood nearby, and soon Tom found himself travelling down past the many levels of the city again until he stepped out on a sort of central square, where dozens of other taxis were coming and going and stairways branched off across the face of the Shield-Wall, going up towards the High Eyries and down to the shops and markets of the lower levels.

News of MEDUSA was spreading fast through Batmunkh Gompa, and already a lot of the houses and shops were shuttered, their owners fled to cities further south. The lower levels were still packed with people, though, and as the sun dipped behind the Wall Tom wandered the crowded bazaars and steep ladderways. There were fortune-tellers' booths at the street corners, and shrines to the sky-gods, dusty with the crumbly grey ash of incense sticks. Fierce-looking Uighur acrobats were performing in the central square, and everywhere he looked he saw soldiers and airmen of the League: blond giants from Spitzbergen and blue-black warriors from the Mountains of the Moon, the small dark people of the Andean statics and people the colour of firelight from jungle strongholds in Laos and Annam.

He tried to forget that some of these young men and women might soon be dropping rockets on London, and started to enjoy the flow of faces and the incomprehensible mish-mash of languages – and sometimes he heard someone say "Tom!" or "Thomasz!" or "Tao-mah!" as they pointed him out to their friends. The story of his battle with Shrike had spread through the mountains from trading-post to trading-post and had been waiting for him here in Batmunkh Gompa. He didn't mind. It felt like a different Thomas that they were talking about, someone brave and strong who understood what had to be done, and felt no doubts.

He was just wondering if he should go back to the Governor's palace and find Hester, when he noticed a tall figure climbing a nearby stairway. The man wore a ragged red robe with the hood pulled down over his face, and carried a staff in one hand and a pack slung over his shoulder. Tom had already seen dozens of these wandering holy men in Batmunkh Gompa; monks in the service of the mountain gods who travelled from city to city through the high passes. (Up at the mooring platform Anna Fang had stooped to kiss the feet of one, and given six bronze coins for him to bless the *Jenny Haniver*.) But this man was different; something about him snagged Tom's gaze and would not let it go.

He started following the red robe. He followed it through the spice market with its thousand astonishing scents, and down the narrow Street of Weavers where hundreds of baskets swung from low poles outside the shops like hanging nests, brushing against the top of his head as he passed underneath. What was it about the way the man moved, and that long brown hand clutching the staff?

And then, under a lantern in the central square, the monk was stopped by a street-girl asking for a blessing and Tom caught a glimpse of the bearded face inside the hood. He knew that hawk-like nose and those mariner's eyes; he knew that the amulet hanging between the black brows hid the familiar Guild-mark of a London Historian.

It was Valentine!

27

DR ARKENGARTH REMEMBERS

Katherine spent a lot of time in the Museum in those final days, as London went roaring towards the mountains. Safe in its dingy maze she could not hear the burr of the saws as they felled the last few trees in Circle Park to feed the engines, or the cheers of the noisy crowds who gathered each day in front of the public Goggle-screens where the details of Crome's great plan were being gradually revealed. She could even forget the Guild of Engineers' security people, who were everywhere now, not just the usual white-coated thugs, but a strange new breed in black coats and hoods, silent, stiff in their movements, with a faint greenish glow behind their tinted visors: Dr Twix's Resurrected Men.

But if she was honest with herself, it wasn't only the peace and quiet that kept calling her down to the Museum. Bevis was there, his borrowed bedding spread out on the floor of the old Transport gallery, under the dusty hanging shapes of model gliders and flying machines. She needed his company more and more as the city hauled itself eastward. She liked the fact that he was her secret. She liked his soft voice, and the strange laugh that always sounded as if he were trying it on for size, as if he had never had much call for laughter down in the Deep Gut. She liked the way he looked at her, his dark eyes always lingering on her face and especially her hair. "I've never really known anybody with hair before," he told her one day. "In the Guild they use chemicals on us when we're first apprenticed, so it never grows back."

Katherine thought about his pale, smooth scalp. She

liked that too. It sort of suited him. Was this what falling in love was like? Not something big and amazing that you knew about straight away, like in a story, but a slow thing that crept over you in waves until you woke up one day and found that you were head-over-heels with someone quite unexpected, like an Apprentice Engineer?

She wished that Father was here, so she could ask him.

In the afternoons Bevis would pull on a Historian's robe and hide his bald head under a cap and go down to help Dr Nancarrow, who was busy re-cataloguing the Museum's huge store of paintings and drawings and taking photographs in case the Lord Mayor decided to feed those to the furnaces as well. Then Katherine would wander the Museum with Dog at her heels, hunting for the things that her father had dug up. Washing machines, pieces of computer, the rusty ribcage of a Stalker, all had labels which read, *"Discovered by Mr T. Valentine, Archaeologist"*. She could imagine him lifting them gently out of the soil that had guarded them, cleaning them, wrapping them in scrim for transport back to London. *He must have done the same thing with the MEDUSA fragment when he discovered it*, she thought. She whispered prayers to Clio, sure that the goddess must be present in these time-soaked halls. *"London needs him! I need him! Please send him safely home, and soon. . ."*

But it was Dog, not Clio, who led her into the Natural History section that evening. He had glimpsed a display of stuffed animals from the far end of the corridor and gone prowling down to stare at them, a growl bubbling in the back of his throat. Old Dr Arkengarth, who was passing through the gallery on his way home, backed away nervously, but Kate said, "It's all right, Doctor! He's quite safe!" and knelt down at Dog's side, looking up at the sharks and dolphins that swung above her and the great looming shape of the whale, which had been taken off its hawsers and propped against the far wall before the vibrations could bring it crashing down.

"Impressive, isn't it?" said Arkengarth, who was always ready to begin a lecture. "A Blue Whale. Hunted to extinction in the first half of the 21st century. Or possibly the 20th: the records are unclear. We wouldn't even know what it looked like if Mrs Shaw hadn't discovered those fossilized bones. . ."

Katherine had been thinking about something else, but the name "Shaw" made her look round. The display case Arkengarth was pointing at housed a rack of brownish bones, and propped against a vertebra was a label that said, *"Bones of a Blue Whale, Discovered by Mrs P. Shaw, Freelance Archaeologist"*.

Pandora Shaw, thought Katherine, recalling the name she had seen in the Museum catalogue. *Not Hester. Of course not.* But just to get Dr Arkengarth out of lecture-mode she said, "Did you know her? Pandora Shaw?"

"Mrs Shaw, yes, yes," the old man nodded. "A lovely lady. She was an Out-Country archaeologist, a friend of your father's. Of course, her name was Rae in those days. . ."

"Pandora Rae?" Katherine knew that name. "Then she was Father's assistant on the trip to America! I've seen her picture in his book!"

"That's right," said Arkengarth, frowning slightly at the interruption. "An archaeologist, as I said. She specialized in Old Tech, of course, but she brought us other things when she found them – like these whale-bones.

Later she married this Shaw chappie and went to live on some grotty little island in the western ocean. Poor girl. A tragedy. Terrible. Terrible."

"She died, didn't she?" said Katherine.

"She was murdered!" Arkengarth waggled his eyebrows dramatically. "Six or seven years ago. We heard it from another archaeologist. Murdered in her own home, and her husband with her. Dreadful business. I say, my dear, are you all right? You look as if you've seen a ghost!"

But Katherine was not all right. In her mind, all the pieces of the puzzle were flying together. *Pandora Shaw was murdered, seven years ago, the same time that Father found the machine. . . Pandora the aviatrix, the archaeologist, the woman who had been with him in America when he found the plans of MEDUSA. And now a girl called Shaw who wants to kill Father. . .*

She could hardly manage to force the words out, but at last she asked, "Did she have a child?"

"I think she did, I think she did," the old man mused. "Yes, I remember Mrs Shaw showing me a picture once when she turned up with some ceramics for my department. Lovely pieces. A decorated vase from the Electric Empire Era, best of its kind in the collection. . ."

"Do you remember its name?"

"Ah, yes, let me see . . . EE27190, I believe."

"Not the vase! The baby!"

Katherine's impatient shout echoed through the gallery and out into the halls beyond, and Dr Arkengarth looked first startled, then offended. "Well, really, Miss Valentine, there's no need to snap! How should I remember the child's name? It was fifteen, sixteen years ago and I have never liked babies; nasty creatures, leak at both ends and have no respect for ceramics. But I believe this particular one was called Hattie or Holly or. . ."

"Hester!" sobbed Katherine, and turned and ran, ran with Dog at her heels, ran and ran without knowing where or why, since there was no way that she could outrun the dreadful truth. She knew how Father had come by the key to MEDUSA, and why he had never spoken of it. At last she knew why poor Hester Shaw had wanted to kill him.

28

A STRANGER IN THE MOUNTAINS
OF HEAVEN

Valentine's hand drew subtle, complicated shapes in the air above the girl's bowed head, and her face was calm and smiling, little suspecting that she was being blessed by the League's worst enemy.

Tom watched from behind a shrine to the sky goddess. His eyes had known who the red-robed monk was all along, and now his brain caught up with them in a flurry of understandings. Captain Khora had said that the *13th Floor Elevator* had been haunting the mountains. It must have dropped Valentine off in the crags near Batmunkh Gompa, and he had come the rest of the way on foot, creeping into the city like a thief. But why? What secret mission could have brought him here?

Tom didn't know what to feel. He was frightened, of course, to be so close to the man who had tried to murder him, but at the same time he was thrilled by Valentine's daring. What courage it must have taken, to sneak into the great stronghold of the League, under the very noses of London's enemies! It was the sort of adventure that Valentine had written about, in books that Tom had read again and again, huddled under the blankets in the Third-Class Apprentices' dorm with a torch, long after lights out.

Valentine finished his blessing and moved on. For a few moments Tom lost sight of him among the crowds in the square, but then he spotted the red robe climbing on up the broad central stairway. He followed at a safe distance, past beggars and guards and hot-food vendors, none of whom guessed that the red-robed figure was anything more than one of those crazy holy men. Valentine had his head bowed now and he climbed quickly, so Tom did not feel in any danger as he hurried along, twenty or thirty paces behind. But he still didn't know what he should do. Hester deserved to know that her parents' murderer was here. Should he find her? Tell her? But Valentine must be on some important mission for London, maybe gathering information so that the Engineers would know exactly where to aim MEDUSA. If Hester killed him, Tom would have betrayed his whole city. . .

He climbed onward, ignoring the pain of his broken ribs. Around him the terraces of Batmunkh Gompa were speckled with lamps and lanterns, and the envelopes of balloon-taxis glowed from within as they rose and fell, like strange sea-creatures swimming around a coral reef. And slowly he realized that he didn't want Valentine to succeed in whatever he was planning. London was no better than Tunbridge Wheels, and this place was old, and beautiful. He wouldn't let it be smashed!

"It's Valentine!" he shouted, charging up the stairs, trying to warn the passers-by of the danger. But they just stared at him without understanding, and when at last he reached the red-robed man and pulled his hood down he found the round, startled face of a pilgrim monk blinking back at him.

He looked around wildly and saw what had happened. Valentine had taken a different stairway out of the central square, leaving Tom following the wrong red robe. He went running down again. Valentine was barely visible, a red speck climbing through lantern-light towards the high places of the city – and the eyrie of the great air-destroyers. "It's Valentine!" shouted Tom, pointing, but none of the people around him spoke Anglish; some thought he was mad, others thought he meant that MEDUSA was about to strike. A wave of panic spread across the square, and soon he heard warning gongs sounding in the densely-packed terraces of shops and inns below.

His first thought was to find Hester, but he had no idea where to look. Then he ran to a balloon taxi and told the pilot, "Follow that monk!" but the woman smiled and shook her head, not understanding. "Feng Hua!" Tom shouted, remembering Anna Fang's League name, and the taxi-pilot nodded and smiled, casting off. He tried to calm himself as the balloon rose. He would find Miss Fang. Miss Fang would know what to do. He remembered how she had trusted him with the *Jenny* during the flight across the mountains, and felt ashamed for turning on her in the council meeting.

He was expecting the taxi to take him to the governor's palace, but instead it landed near the terrace where the *Jenny Haniver* was berthed. The pilot pointed towards an inn which clung to the underside of the terrace above like a house martin's nest. "Feng Hua!" she said helpfully. "Feng Hua!"

For a panic-stricken moment Tom thought that she had carried him to an inn with the same name as Miss Fang; then, on one of the establishment's many balconies, he caught sight of the aviatrix's blood-red coat. He thrust all the money he had at the pilot, shouting, "Keep the change!" and left her staring at the unfamiliar faces of Quirke and Crome as he raced away.

Miss Fang was sitting at a balcony table with Captain Khora and the stern young Keralan flier who had been so angry at Tom's outburst earlier. They were drinking tea and deep in discussion, but they all leaped up as Tom blundered out on to the balcony. "Where's Hester?" he demanded.

"Down on the mooring platforms, in one of her moods," said Miss Fang. "Why?"

"Valentine!" he gasped. "He's here! Dressed as a monk!"

The inn's musicians stopped playing, and the sound of the alarm-gongs in the lower city came drifting through the open windows.

"Valentine, here?" sneered the Keralan girl. "It's a lie! The barbarian thinks he can frighten us!"

"Be quiet, Sathya!" Miss Fang reached across and gripped Tom by the arm. "Is he alone?"

As quickly as he could, Tom told her what he had seen. She made a hissing sound through her clenched teeth. "He has come after our Air-Fleet! He means to cripple us!"

"One man cannot destroy an Air-Fleet!" protested Khora, smiling at the notion.

"You've never seen Valentine at work!" said the aviatrix. She was already on her feet, excited at the prospect of crossing swords with London's greatest agent. "Sathya, go and rouse the guard, tell them the High Eyries are in danger." She turned to Tom. "Thank you for warning us," she said gently, as if she understood the agonizing decision he had had to make.

"I've got to tell Hester!" he protested.

"Certainly not!" she told him. "She will only get herself killed, or kill Valentine, and I want him kept alive for questioning. Stay here until it is all over." A last ferocious smile and she was gone, down the steps and out of the panicked inn with Khora at her heels. She looked grim and dangerous and very beautiful, and Tom felt himself brushed by the same fierce love which he knew Khora and the Keralan girl and the rest of the League must feel for her.

But then he thought of Hester, and what she would say when she learned that he had seen Valentine and hadn't even told her. "Great Quirke!" he shouted suddenly. "I'm going to find her!" Sathya just stared at him, not stern any more, just frightened and very young, and as he ran towards the stairs he shouted back at her, "You heard what Miss Fang said! Raise the alarm!"

Out on to dark ladderways again, down to the mooring platform where the *Jenny Haniver* hung at anchor. "Hester! Hester!" he shouted, and there she was, coming towards him through the glow of the landing-lights, tugging the red shawl up across her face. He told her everything, and she took the news with the cold, silent glare he had expected. Then it was her turn to run, and he was following her up the endless stairs.

The Wall made its own weather. As Tom and Hester neared the top the air grew thin and chill and big fluttering snowflakes brushed their faces like butterfly wings. They could see lantern-light on a broad platform ahead where a gas tanker was lifting away empty from the High Eyries. Then there was an unbelievable gout of flame shooting out of the face of the Wall, and another and another, as if it were dragons, not airships, that were stabled there. Caught in the blast, the tanker's envelope exploded, white parachutes blossoming around it as it began to fall. Hester stopped for a moment and looked back, flames shining in her eye. "He's done it! We're too late! He's fired their Air-Fleet!"

They ran on. Tom's ribs hurt him at every breath and

the cold air scorched his throat, but he kept as close behind Hester as he could, crunching through snow along a narrow walkway to the platform outside the eyries. The bronze gates stood open and a crowd of men were pouring out, shielding their faces from the heat of the blaze within. Some of them were dragging wounded comrades, and near the main door Tom saw Khora being tended by two of the ground-crew.

The aviator looked up as Tom and Hester ran to him. "Valentine!" he groaned. "He bluffed his way past the sentries, saying he wanted to bless our airships. He was setting his explosives when Anna and I arrived. Oh, Tom, we never imagined that even a barbarian would try something like this! We weren't prepared! Our whole Air-Fleet. . . My poor *Mokele Mbembe*. . ." He broke off, coughing blood. Valentine's sword had pierced his lung.

"What about Miss Fang?" asked Tom.

Khora shook his head. He did not know. Hester was already stalking away into the searing heat of the hangars, ignoring the men who tried to call her back. Tom ran after her.

It was like running into an oven. He had an impression of a huge cavern, with smaller caverns opening off it, the hangars where the League's warships were housed. Valentine must have gone quickly from one ship to the next, placing phosphorus bombs. Now only their buckling ribs were visible in the white-hot heart of the blaze. "Hester!" shouted Tom, his voice lost in the roar of the flames, and saw her a little way ahead of him, hurrying down a narrow tunnel that led deeper into the Wall. *I'm not following her in there!* he thought. *If she wants to get herself trapped and roasted, that's her lookout. . .* But as he turned back towards the safety of the platform, the ammunition in the gondolas of the burning airships caught, and suddenly there were rockets and bullets flying everywhere, bursting against the stone walls and howling through the air around him. The tunnel was closer than the main entrance and he scrambled into it, whispering prayers to all the gods he could think of.

Fresh air was coming from somewhere in front of him, and he realized that the passage must lead right through the Wall to one of the gun-emplacements on the western face. "Hester?" he shouted. Only echoes replied, muddled with the echoing roar of the fires in the hangar. He pressed on. At a fork in the tunnel lay a huddled shape; a young airman cut down by Valentine's sword. Tom breathed a sigh of relief that it was not Hester or Miss Fang, and then felt guilty, because the poor man was dead.

He studied the branching tunnel. Which way should he go? "Hester?" he shouted nervously. Echoes. A stray bullet from the hangar came whining past and struck sparks off the stonework by his head. Choosing quickly, he ducked down the right-hand passage.

There was another sound now, closer and sharper than the dull roar of the fires, a thin, birdlike sound of metal on metal. Tom hurried down a slippery flight of steps, saw light ahead and ran towards it. He emerged into the cold and the fluttering snow on a broad platform where a rocket-battery gazed out towards the west. Flames flapped and tore in an iron brazier, lighting the ancient battlements, the sprawled bodies of the rocket crew and the wild shimmer of swords as Valentine and Miss Fang battled each other back and forth across the scrabbled snow.

Tom crouched in the shadows at the tunnel's mouth, clutching his aching ribs and staring. Valentine was fighting magnificently. He had torn off his monk's robes to reveal a white shirt, black breeches, long black boots, and he parried and thrust and ducked gracefully under the aviatrix's blows – but Tom could see that he had met his match. Holding her long sword two-handed, Miss Fang drove him back towards the rocket battery and the bodies of the men he had killed, anticipating every blow he made, feinting and swinging, jumping into the air to avoid a low back-stroke, until at last she smashed the sword from his hand. He went down on his knees to reach for it, but her blade was already at his throat and Tom saw a dark rill of blood start down to stain the collar of his shirt.

"Well done!" he said, and smiled the smile that Tom remembered from that night in the Gut, a kind, amused, utterly sincere smile. "Well done, Feng Hua!"

"Quiet!" she snapped. "This isn't a game. . ."

Valentine laughed. "On the contrary, my dear Wind-Flower, it's the greatest game of all, and my team appears to be winning. Haven't you noticed that your Air-Fleet is on fire? You really should have tightened up your security arrangements. I suppose because the League has had things its own way for a thousand years, you think you can rest on your laurels. But the world is changing. . ."

He's playing for time, thought Tom. But he could not see why. Cornered on this high platform, unarmed, with no chance of escape, what did Valentine hope to gain by taunting the aviatrix? He wondered if he should go forward and pick up the fallen sword and stand by Miss Fang until help arrived, but there was something so powerful and dangerous about Valentine, even in defeat, that he dared not show himself. He listened, hoping to catch the sounds of soldiers coming down the tunnel, and wondering what had become of Hester. All he could hear was the distant clamour of gongs and fire-bells from the far side of the Wall, and Valentine's flirtatious, half-mocking voice.

"You should come and work for London, my dear. After all, this time tomorrow the Shield-Wall will be rubble. You will need a new employer. Your League is finished. . ."

And light burst down from above; the harsh beam of an airship's searchlight raking across the snow. The aviatrix reeled blindly backwards, and Valentine leaped up, snatching his sword, pulling her hard against him as he drove it home. For a moment the two of them stumbled together like drunken dancers at the end of a party, close enough to Tom's hiding place for him to see the bright blade push out through the back of Miss Fang's neck and hear her desperate, choking whisper: "Hester Shaw will find you. She will find you and –" Then Valentine wrenched his sword free and let her fall, turning away, leaping up on to the battlements as the *13th Floor Elevator* came looming down out of the searchlight's glare.

29

GOING HOME

The black airship had been drifting in silence, riding the wind to this high rendezvous while the defenders of Batmunkh Gompa were busy with fires and explosions. Now her engines burst into life, churning the drifting snowflakes and drowning out Tom's cry of horror.

Valentine walked out along the barrel of a rocket launcher as nimbly as an athlete on a bar and sprang, spread-eagling himself for an instant on the naked air before his hands found the rope ladder that Pewsey and Gench had lowered for him. Catching it, he swung himself up into the gondola.

Tom ran forward, and was plunged into sudden darkness as the searchlight snapped off. Rockets from higher batteries came sparkling down to burst against the *Elevator*'s thick hide. One shattered some glass in the gondola, but the black airship was already powering away from the Wall. The backwash from its propellers slammed into Tom's face as he knelt over Anna Fang, shaking her in the dim hope that she might wake.

"It's not fair!" he sobbed. "He waited till you were dazzled! You beat him!" The aviatrix said nothing, but stared past him with a look of stupid surprise, her eyes as dull as dry pebbles.

Tom sat down beside her in the reddening snow and tried to think. He supposed he would have to leave Batmunkh Gompa now, get out fast before London came, but the very thought of moving on again made him weary. He was sick of being swept to and fro across the world by other people's plans. A thin, hot anger started rising in him as he thought about Valentine, flying home to a hero's welcome. Valentine was the cause of all this! It was Valentine who had ruined his life, and Hester's, and put an end to so many more. It was Valentine who had given the Guild of Engineers MEDUSA. Hester had been right; he should have let her kill him when she had the chance. . .

There was a noise at the far end of the platform and he looked up and saw a black mass of arms and legs and coat hurriedly untangling itself, like a big spider fallen from the ceiling. It was Hester, who had taken the wrong turning as she raced after Valentine and come out in an observation bunker high above. Now here she was, having scrambled down thirty feet of snowy wall and dropped the final ten. Her eye rested for a moment on the fallen aviatrix, then she turned and went to the battlements and stared out at the dark and the dancing snow. "It should have been me," Tom heard her say. "At least I would have made sure I took him with me."

Tom watched her. He felt tight and sick and trembly from the grief and rage inside him, and knew that this was how Hester must feel, how she had always felt, ever since Valentine killed her parents. It was a terrible feeling, and he could think of only one way to cure it.

He groped under the collar of Anna's coat and found the key on its thong and wrenched it free. Then he stood up and went to where Hester was and put his arms around her. It was like hugging a statue, she was so stiff and tense, but he needed to hold on to something so he hugged her anyway. Guns were still firing overhead in the vain hope of hitting the *13th Floor Elevator*. He put his face close to Hester's ear and shouted over the noise, "Let's go home!"

She looked round at that, puzzled and a little annoyed. "Have you gone funny?"

"Don't you see?" he shouted, laughing at the crazy idea that had just come creeping into his mind. "Someone's got to make him pay! You were right; I shouldn't have stopped you before, but I'm glad I did, because the Gut Police would have killed you and then we'd never have met. Now I can help you get to him, and help you get away afterwards. We'll go back to London! Now! Together!"

"You *have* gone funny," said Hester, but she came with him anyway, helping him find a way back through the Shield-Wall while soldiers came running past them, frightened, soot-stained and far too late, crying out in woe when they saw the bodies on the rocket-platform.

The night sky over Batmunkh Gompa was full of smoke and tatters of singed envelope fabric. Fires were still burning in the High Eyries, but already the roads in the valley were clogged with constellations of small lights, the lanterns of refugees, spilling away into the mountains like water bursting from a breached dam. With the death of the Air-Fleet the Shield-Wall was finished, and its people were fleeing as fast as their feet and mules and ox-carts and freight-balloons could take them.

Down at the mooring platform, ships were already lifting into the smoky sky and turning south. The Keralan girl, Sathya, was trying to rally some panic-stricken soldiers, sobbing, "Stay and hold the Wall! The Southern Air-Fleet will reinforce us! They can be here in less than a week!" But everyone knew that Batmunkh Gompa would be gone by then, and London would be pushing south towards the League's heartlands. "Stay and hold the Wall!" she begged, but the airships kept lifting past her, lifting past her.

The *Jenny Haniver* still hung at anchor, silent, dark. The key that Tom had taken from Anna Fang's body fitted snugly into the lock on the forward hatch, and soon he was standing on the flight-deck, staring at the controls. There were far more of them than he remembered.

"Are you sure we can do this?" asked Hester softly.

"Of course," said Tom. He tried a few switches. The hatch sprang open again, the cabin lights came on, the coffee machine started making a noise like a polite dog clearing its throat and a small inflatable dinghy dropped from the roof and knocked him over.

"Quite sure?" she asked, helping him up.

Tom nodded. "I used to build model airships when I was little, so I understand the principle. And Miss Fang showed me the controls when we were in the mountains. . . I just wish she'd labelled everything in Anglish."

He thought for a moment, then hauled on another lever, and this time the engines throbbed into life. Out on the mooring platform people turned to stare, and some made the sign against evil; they had heard of Feng Hua's death and wondered if it was her restless ghost aboard the *Jenny Haniver*. But Sathya saw Tom and Hester standing at the controls and came running towards them.

Frightened that she would stop him taking off, Tom hunted for the lever which moved the engine pods. Bearings grated as they swivelled into take-off position. He laughed, delighted at the way the airship responded to the touch of his hands on the controls, hearing the familiar creak and huff of the gas-valves somewhere overhead and the clang of the mooring-clamps disengaging. People waved their arms and shouted, and Sathya pulled out a gun, but at the last moment Captain Khora came stumbling out on to the platform, supported by one of his crewmen, and gently took it from her. He looked up at Tom, raising a hand to wish him luck, and the surprising pinkness of his palm and fingertips was what stuck in Tom's mind as the airship swayed uncertainly up into the sky and climbed through the smoke from the High Eyries. He took one last look down at Batmunkh Gompa, then swung her out over the Shield-Wall and turned her nose towards the west.

He was going home.

30

A HERO'S WELCOME

The clouds that had shed their snow on Batmunkh Gompa blew west to fall as yet more rain on London, and it was raining still when the *13th Floor Elevator* reached home, early the following afternoon. No crowds were waiting to welcome it. The sodden lawns of Circle Park were deserted, except for some workers from the Recycling Department who were cutting down the last of the trees, but the Guild of Engineers had been warned of Valentine's return, and as the great airship came nosing down into the wet flare of the landing beacons they ran out on to the apron with the rain beating on their bald heads and the lights making splashy reflections on their coats.

Katherine watched from her bedroom window as the ground-crew winched the airship down and the excited Engineers clustered closer. Now hatches were opening in the gondola; now Magnus Crome was going forward, with a servant holding a white rubber umbrella over him, and now, now Father was coming down the gangplank, easy to recognize even at this distance by his height and his confident stride and the way his all-weather cape filled and flapped in the rising breeze.

The sight of him gave Katherine a twisting feeling deep inside, as if her heart really was about to burst with grief and anger. She remembered how much she had been looking forward to being the first to greet him when he stepped back aboard the city. Now she was not sure that she could even bring herself to speak to him.

Through the wet glass she saw him talk to Crome, nodding, laughing. A surge of white coats hid him from her for a moment, and when she saw him again he had pulled himself away from the Lord Mayor and was hurrying across the soggy lawns towards Clio House, probably wondering why she hadn't been waiting for him at the quay.

She panicked for a moment and wanted to hide, but Dog was with her, and he gave her the strength she needed. She closed the tortoise-shell shutters and waited until she heard Father's feet on the stairs, Father's knock at the door.

"Kate?" came his muffled voice. "Kate, are you in there? I want to tell you all my adventures! I am fresh from the snows of Shan Guo, with all sorts of tales to bore you with! Kate? Are you all right?"

She opened the door just a crack. He stood on the landing outside, dripping with rain, his smile fading as he saw her tearful, sleep-starved face.

"Kate, it's all right! I'm back!"

"I know," she said. "And it's not all right. I wish you'd died in the mountains."

"What?"

"I know all about you," she told him. "I've worked out what you did to Hester Shaw."

She let him into the room and shut the door, calling sharply to Dog when he ran to greet him. It was dark with the shutters closed, but she saw Father look at the heap of books spilling from the corner table, then at her. There was a freshly-dressed wound on his neck, blood on his shirt. She twined a finger in her tangled hair and tried hard not to start crying again.

Valentine sat down on the unmade bed. All the way from Batmunkh Gompa, Anna Fang's last promise had been echoing in the corners of his mind: *Hester Shaw will find you.* To have the same name thrown at him here, by Katherine, was like a knife in the heart.

"Oh, you needn't worry," said Katherine bitterly. "No one else knows. I learned the girl's name, you see. And Dr Arkengarth told me how Pandora Shaw was murdered, and I'd already found out that she died seven years ago, around the time you got back from that expedition and the Lord Mayor was so pleased with you, so I just put it all together and. . ."

She shrugged. The trail had been easy to follow once she had all the clues. She picked up a book she had been reading and showed it to him. It was *Adventures on a Dead Continent*, his own account of his journey to America. She pointed to a face in a group photograph of the expedition; an aviatrix who stood beside him, smiling. "I didn't realize at first," she said, "because her name had changed. Did you kill her yourself? Or did you get Pewsey and Gench to do it?"

Valentine hung his head, angry, despairing, ashamed. A part of Katherine had been hoping against hope that she was wrong, that he would deny it and give her proof that he was not the Shaws' killer, but when she saw his head go down she knew that he could not and it was true.

He said, "You must understand, Kate, I did it for you. . ."

"For *me*?"

He looked up at last, but not at her. He stared at the wall near her elbow and said, "I wanted you to have everything. I wanted you to grow up as a lady, not as an Out-Country scavenger like I had been. I had to find something that Crome needed.

"Pandora was an old comrade, from the American

trip, just as you say. And yes, she was with me when I found the plans and access codes to MEDUSA. We never imagined it would be possible to reconstruct the thing. Later Pandora and I went our separate ways; she was an Anti-Tractionist and she married some clodhopping farmer and settled down on a place called Oak Island. I didn't know she was still thinking about MEDUSA. She must have made another trip to America, alone this time, and found her way into another part of the same old underground complex, a part we'd missed on the first dig. That's where she found—"

"A computer-brain," said Katherine impatiently. "The key to MEDUSA."

"Yes," murmured Valentine, astonished at how much she knew. "She sent me a letter, telling me she had it. She knew it was worthless without the plans and codes, you see, and those were in London. She thought we could sell it and share the proceeds. And I knew that if I could give Crome a prize like that it would make my fortune, and your future would be secure!"

"And so you killed her for it," said Katherine.

"She wouldn't agree to sell it to Crome," said her father. "She was an Anti-Tractionist, as I said. She wanted the League to have it. I *had* to kill her, Kate."

"But what about Hester?" said Katherine numbly. "Why did you have to hurt her?"

"I didn't mean to," he said miserably. "She must have woken up and heard something. She was a pretty child. She was about your age, and she looked so like you that she might have been your sister. Perhaps she *was* your sister. Pandora and I were very close at one time."

"My sister?" gasped Katherine. "Your own daughter!"

"When I looked up from her mother's body and saw

her staring at me. . .! I had to silence her. I struck wildly at her, and I made a mess of it. I thought she was dead, but I couldn't bring myself to make sure. She escaped, vanished in a boat. I thought she must have drowned, until she tried to stab me that night in the Gut."

"And Tom. . ." Katherine said. "He learned her name, and so you had to kill him too, because if he'd mentioned her to the Historians the truth might have come out."

Valentine looked helplessly at her. "You don't understand, Kate. If people discovered who she is and what I have done, not even Crome would be able to protect me. I would be finished, and you would be dragged down with me."

"But Crome knows, doesn't he?" asked Katherine. "That's why you're so loyal. Loyal as a dog, so long as you get paid and get to pretend that foreign daughter of yours is a High London lady."

Rain, rain on the windows and the whole room quivering as London dragged itself across the sodden earth. Dog lay with his head on his paws, his eyes darting from his mistress to Valentine and back. He had never seen them fight before, and he hated it.

"I used to think you were wonderful," said Katherine. "I used to think that you were the best, bravest, wisest person in the world. But you're not. You're not even very clever, are you? Didn't you realize what Crome would use the thing for?"

Valentine looked sharply at her. "Of course I did! This is a town eat town world, Kate. It's a shame Panzerstadt-Bayreuth had to be destroyed, of course, but the Shield-Wall *has* to be breached if London is to survive. We need a new hunting ground."

"But people live there!" wailed Katherine.

"Only Anti-Tractionists, Kate, and most of them will probably get away."

"They'll stop us. They've got airships. . ."

"No." In spite of everything, Valentine smiled, proud of himself. "Why do you think Crome sent me east? The League's Northern Air-Fleet is in ashes. Tonight MEDUSA will blast us a passage through their famous Wall." He stood up and reached for her, smiling, as if this victory that he was delivering would put right everything he had done. "Crome tells me that firing is scheduled for nine o'clock. There's to be a reception at the Guildhall beforehand; wine, nibbles and the dawn of a new era. Will you come with me, Kate? I'd like you to. . ."

Her last hope had been that he had not known Crome's mad plan. Now even that was gone. "You fool!" she screamed. "Don't you understand what he's doing is *wrong*? You've got to stop him! You've got to get rid of his horrible machine!"

"But that would leave London defenceless, in the middle of the Hunting Ground," her father pointed out.

"So? We will have to carry on as we always have, chasing and eating, and if we meet a bigger city and get eaten ourselves . . . well, even that would be better than being murderers!"

She couldn't bear to be in that room with him another second. She ran, and he did not try to stop her, or even call her back, just stood there looking pale and stunned. She left the house and ran sobbing through the rain-swept park with Dog at her heels, until the whole of High London was between her and Father. *I must do something!* was all she could think. *I must stop MEDUSA. . .*

She hurried towards the elevator station, while the Goggle-screen loops began to blare the good news of Valentine's return all over London.

31

THE EAVESDROPPER

ondon gathered speed, racing towards the mountains. Semi-static towns that had hidden for years on these high steppes were startled out of their torpor by its coming and went lumbering away, leaving behind them green patches of farmland and once a whole static suburb. The city paid no heed to any of them. The whole of London knew the Lord Mayor's plan by now. In spite of the cold, people gathered on the forward observation decks and peered through telescopes towards Shan Guo, eager for their first glimpse of the legendary Wall.

"Soon!" they told each other.

"This very night!"

"A whole new hunting ground!"

❂ ❂ ❂ ❂ ❂

Most people at the Museum were used to Katherine and Dog by now, and nobody paid very much attention as she hastened through the lower galleries with the white wolf trotting behind her. A few noticed the frantic look in her eyes and the tears on her face, but before they could ask her what was wrong or proffer a pocket handkerchief she had swept past, heading towards Mr Nancarrow's office at a near run.

There she found a smell of turpentine and the lingering scent of the art-historian's pipe tobacco, but no Nancarrow and no Bevis Pod. She ran back out into the hallway, where a fat Third-Class Apprentice was mopping the floors. "Mr Nancarrow's in the store-rooms,

Miss," he told her sullenly. "He's got that funny new bloke with him."

The funny new bloke was helping Mr Nancarrow drag a picture out of the storage racks when Katherine burst in. It was a huge, gilt-framed painting called *"Quirke oversees the rebuilding of London"*, by Walmart Strange, and when Bevis dropped the end he was holding it made a crash that echoed and re-echoed through the dusty store-room like a small explosion. "I say, Pod!" complained Nancarrow angrily, but then he too saw Katherine's face and quickly restrained himself. "You look as if you need a nice cup of tea, Miss Valentine," he muttered, hurrying away into the maze of racks.

"Kate?" Bevis Pod took a few uncertain steps towards her. "What's happened?" He wasn't used to comforting people; it was not the sort of thing an Apprentice Engineer was trained for. He held his arms out stiffly to touch her shoulders, and looked shocked when she flung herself against him. "Er . . ." he said, "there, there. . ."

"Bevis," she sniffled, "it's up to us now. We have to do something. Tonight. . ."

"Tonight?" He frowned, struggling to keep up with her rapid, half-sobbed explanations. "But do you mean just us alone? I thought your father was going to help us. . ."

"He's not my father any more," said Katherine bitterly, and realized that it was true. She clung to Bevis as tightly as she could, as if he were a raft that could carry her safe across this mire of misery and guilt. "Father's Crome's man. That's why I've got to get rid of MEDUSA, do you see? I have to make amends for the things he's done. . ."

Nancarrow came pottering back with two tin mugs of

tea. "Um! Oh! Ah!" he mumbled, embarrassed at finding his two young friends in one another's arms. "I mean . . . yes. Paperwork. Must dash. Back in an hour or two. Carry on, Pod. . ."

As he left, he almost fell over the fat Third-Class Apprentice, who had been mopping the passage just outside the store-room door. "For Quirke's sake, Melliphant!" they heard him snap. "Can't you keep out of the way?"

But Herbert Melliphant could not keep out of the way. Ever since his demotion he had been looking for a hand-hold that would help him claw his way back up to First Class. This Pod person had caught his eye a few days ago; this stranger who seemed so friendly with the old Guildsmen; who went about with the Head Historian's daughter; who dressed as an Apprentice but who didn't sleep with the others in the dormitory or join them for lessons. He had heard on the Goggle-screens that the Guild of Engineers were still hunting the people who had infiltrated their secret meeting, and he was starting to suspect that Dr Vambrace might be very interested in Nancarrow's little helper. As soon as the old man was out of sight he put down his mop and pail and stepped back to the door.

". . .the Anti-Traction League can't defend themselves," Katherine was saying. "That's what Father has been doing; spying out their cities and blowing up their Air-Fleet. That's why it's up to us."

"What about the Historians?" asked Bevis.

Katherine shrugged. "They're too scared to help us. But I can do it alone, I know I can. Father's invited me to the Lord Mayor's reception. I'm going to go. I'm going to find Father and tell him I've forgiven him, and we'll go to Crome's party like a happy little family; but while the others are all telling Crome how clever he's been and eating sausages on sticks I'll slip away and find MEDUSA and smash it. Do you think a hammer would do the trick? I know where Dr Arkengarth keeps the keys to the caretaker's stores. There's bound to be a hammer in there. Or a crowbar. Would a crowbar be better?"

She laughed, and saw Bevis flinch at the mad, brittle sound. For a moment she feared that he was about to say something like "Calm down," or "It can't possibly work. . ." She touched his face, his blushing ears, and felt the quick pulse beating in his throat and the muscles flexing as he swallowed.

"A bomb," he said.

"What?"

"MEDUSA must be huge – it probably fills half of St Paul's. If you really want to smash it you need explosives." He looked excited and scared. "The cleaning stuff the Museum caretakers use has nitrogen in it and if I mix it with some of Dr Nancarrow's picture-restoring fluids, and make a timer. . ."

"How do you know all this?" asked Katherine, shocked, because even she had not thought as far as bombs.

"Basic chemistry," said Bevis with a shrug. "I did a course, in the Learning Labs. . ."

"Is that all they think about, your lot?" she whispered. "Making bombs and blowing things up?"

"No, no!" he replied. "But science is like that. You can use it to do whatever you want. Kate, if you really want to do this I'll make you a bomb you can put in a satchel. If you can get to MEDUSA, leave it near the computer brain and set the timer and run away. Half an hour later. . ."

Outside, Melliphant's ear flattened itself against the wood of the door like a pale slug.

◊ ◊ ◊ ◊ ◊

Faster and faster and faster. It is as if the Lord Mayor's eagerness has infected the very fabric of his city; the pistons in the engine-rooms beat as eagerly as his heart, the wheels and tracks race like his thoughts, rushing towards the Wall and the next chapter in London's great story.

All afternoon Valentine has hunted for Katherine through the park, startling his friends from their suppers by suddenly looming up at the French windows, a dripping wraith in blood-stained clothes, demanding, *Is my daughter here? Have you seen her?*" Now he strides to and fro across the drawing room at Clio House, his boots dribbling water on to the muddy carpet as he tries to walk the wet cold of the park out of his bones, the fear out of his mind.

At last he hears footsteps on the gravel drive, footsteps in the entrance hall, and Pewsey bursts in, looking as wet and miserable as his master. "I tracked her down, Chief! She's at the Museum. Been spending a lot of time there lately, according to old Creaber on the front desk. . ."

"Take me there!" shouts Valentine.

"You sure, Chief?" Pewsey studies his own feet rather than look at his master's feverish, tear-streaked face. "I think it might be better if you let her alone for a bit. She's safe at the Museum, ain't she, and I reckon she needs a chance to think things over. She'll come back in her own time."

Valentine slumps down in a chair, and the old aviator moves quietly around the room, lighting the lamps. Outside, the daylight is fading. "I've polished your sword, and laid out your best robes in the dressing room," says Pewsey gently. "It's the Lord Mayor's reception, sir, remember? Wouldn't do to miss it."

Valentine nods, staring at his hands, his long fingers. "Why did I go along with his schemes, all these years, Pewsey? Why did I give him MEDUSA?"

"I couldn't rightly say, sir. . ."

He stands up with a sigh and heads for the dressing room. He wishes he had Kate's sharpness; to know so easily what's right, what's wrong. He wishes he had the courage to stand up to Crome the way she wants him to, but it is too late for that, too late, too late.

◊ ◊ ◊ ◊ ◊

And Crome himself looks up from his dinner (a puree of vegetables and meat-substitute, with just the right amounts of proteins, carbohydrates, vitamins, et cetera), looks up at the shivering Apprentice Historian whom Vambrace has just thrust into his office and says, "So, Apprentice Melliphant, I gather you have something to tell us?"

32
CHUDLEIGH POMEROY
PULLS IT OFF

She found that she could cope. Earlier she had wanted to curl up in a corner and die of grief, but now she was all right. It made her remember the way she had felt when her mother died; flattened by the great numb blow of it and faintly surprised at the way life kept going on. And at least this time she had Dog to help her, and Bevis.

"Kate, I need another bolt, like this one but longer. . ."

She had come to think of Bevis Pod as a sweet, clumsy, rather useless person, someone who needed her to look after him, and she suspected that that was how the Historians all thought of him as well. But that afternoon she had begun to understand that he was really much cleverer than her. She watched him work, hunched under a portable argon globe in a corner of the Transport gallery, carefully measuring out the right amounts of scrubbing powder and picture-cleaning fluid. Now he was building a timing mechanism out of lengths of copper picture wire and parts from the dashboard of a centuries-old bug, fitting it all into the satchel she had found for him.

"A bolt, Kate?"

"Oh, yes. . ." She ratched quickly through the pile of spare parts on the floor beside him and found what he wanted. Handed it to him. Checked her watch. It was eight o'clock. Soon she would have to go back to Clio House and fit a smile on to her face and say to Father, "I'm sorry I was so silly earlier – welcome home – please can I come with you to the Lord Mayor's party?"

"There," said Bevis, holding up the satchel. "It's done."

"It doesn't look like a bomb."

"That's the idea, silly! Look." He opened it up and showed her the package nestling inside, the red button that she had to push to arm it and the timing mechanism. "It won't make a very big bang," he admitted, "but if you can get it close enough to the computer-brain. . ."

"I'll find a way," she promised, taking it from him. "I'm Valentine's daughter. If anybody can get to MEDUSA, it's me." He looked rueful, she thought, and she wondered if he was thinking of all that wonderful old-world computing power, an Engineer's dream, about to be sacrificed. "I've got to do it," she said.

"I know. I wish I could come with you, though."

She hugged him, pressing her face against his face, her mouth against his mouth, feeling him shiver as his hands came up nervously to stroke and stroke her hair. Dog gave a soft growl, jealous perhaps, afraid that he was losing Katherine's love and would soon be abandoned, like the poor old soft toys on the shelves in her bedroom. "Oh Bevis," she whispered, pulling back, trembling. "What's to become of us?"

The sound of distant shouting reached them, echoing up the stairwell from the lower floors. It was too faint to make out any words, but they both knew at once that something must be wrong; nobody ever shouted in the Museum.

Dog's growl grew louder. He went running to the door and they both followed him, pushing their way quietly out on to the darkened landing. A cool breeze touched their faces as they peered over the handrail and down, the long spiral of stairs dwindling into darkness below with the bronze handrails gleaming. More shouts, then the bang and clatter of something dropped. Torch-beams stabbed a lower landing and they heard the shouting voice quite clear: Chudleigh Pomeroy's, saying, "This is an outrage! An outrage! You are trespassing on the property of the Guild of Historians!"

The Engineer security team came up the stairs in a slapping rush of rubber-soled boots, torchlight sliding over their coats and their shiny, complicated guns. They slowed as they reached the top and saw Dog's eyes flashing, his ears flattening backwards as he growled and growled and crouched to spring. Guns flicked towards him, and Katherine grabbed him by the collar and shouted, "He won't hurt you, he's just frightened. Don't shoot. . ."

But they shot him anyway, the guns giving sharp little cracks and the impact of the bullets wrenching Dog away from her and slamming him back against the wall with a yelp; then silence, and the whispering sound of the big body falling. In the dancing torchlight the blood looked black. Katherine gasped for breath. Her arms and legs were shaking with a quick, helpless shudder that she couldn't stop. She could not have moved if she had wanted to, but just in case a sharp voice barked, "Stay where you are, Miss Valentine."

"Dog. . ." she managed to whine.

"Stay where you are. The brute is dead."

Dr Vambrace came up the stairs through the thin, shifting smoke. "You too, Pod," he added, seeing the boy make a twitching move towards the body. He stood on the top step and smiled at them. "We've been looking everywhere for you, Apprentice. I hope you're ashamed of yourself. Give me that satchel."

Bevis held it out and the tall Engineer snatched it

from him and opened it. "Just as Melliphant warned us; a bomb."

Two of his men stepped forward and hauled the prisoners after him as he turned and started down the stairs. "No!" wailed Katherine, struggling to keep hold of Bevis's hand as they were dragged apart. "No!" Her voice bounced shrilly back at her from the ceiling and went echoing away down the stairwell, and she thought it sounded frail and helpless, like a child having a tantrum, a child caught playing some stupid, naughty trick and protesting at its punishment. She kicked at the shins of the man who held her, but he was a big man, and booted, and didn't even wince. "Where are you taking us?"

"You are coming with me to Top Tier, Miss Valentine," said Vambrace. "You will be quite the talking-point of the Lord Mayor's little party. As for your sweetheart here, he'll be taken to the Deep Gut." He grinned at the little noise Bevis made, a helpless gulped-back squeak of fear. "Oh yes, Apprentice Pod, some very interesting experiences await you in the Deep Gut."

"It wasn't his fault!" Katherine protested. She could feel things unravelling, her foolish plan running out of control and lashing backwards to entrap her and Bevis and poor Dog. "I *made* him help me!" she shrieked. "It's nothing to do with Bevis!" But Vambrace had already turned away, and her captor clamped a chemical-tasting hand across her mouth to stop her noise.

○ ○ ○ ○ ○

Valentine's bug pulls up outside the Guildhall, where the bugs of most of the Guild heads are already parked.

Gench gets out and holds the lid open for his master, then fusses over him like a mother sending her child off to school, brushing his hair off his face and straightening the collar of his best black robe, buffing the hilt of his sword.

Valentine looks absently up at the sky. High, feathery cloud, lit by the fast-sinking sun. The wind is still blowing from the east, and it brings a smell of snow that cuts through his thoughts of Katherine for a moment, making him think again of Shan Guo. *Hester Shaw will find you*, the Wind-Flower had whispered, dying. But how could she have known about Hester? She could not have met the girl, could she? Could she? Is Hester still alive? Has she made her way somehow to Batmunkh Gompa? And is she waiting in those mountains now, ready to climb back aboard London and try again to kill him – or, worse, to harm his daughter?

Pushing Gench's big hands away, he says, "If you don't mind missing the party, boys, it might be worth taking the *13th Floor Elevator* up for a spin tonight. Just in case those poor brave fools from the League try anything."

"Right you are, Chief!" The two old airmen have not been looking forward to the Lord Mayor's reception – all that finger-food and posh chat. Nothing could cheer them up better than the prospect of a good fight. Gench climbs in next to Pewsey and the bug veers away, startling Engineers and Beefeaters out of its path. Valentine straightens his own tie and walks quickly up the steps into the Guildhall.

The Engineers marched their prisoners through the lower galleries of the Museum to the Main Hall. There was nobody about. Katherine had never seen the Museum as empty as this. Where were the Historians? She knew they couldn't help her, but she wanted to see them, to know that somebody knew what had become of her. She kept listening for the pattering feet of Dog on the floor behind her, and being surprised when she couldn't hear them, and then remembering. Bevis was marching next to her, but he wouldn't look at her, just stared straight ahead as if he could already see the chambers of the Deep Gut and the things that would happen to him there.

Then, at the top of the steps that led down to the main entrance, the Engineers halted.

Down in the foyer, their backs to the big glass doors, the Historians were waiting. While Vambrace's men were busy upstairs they had raided the display cases in the Weapons & Warfare gallery, arming themselves with ancient pikes and muskets, rusty swords and tin helmets. Some had strapped breast-plates over their black robes, and others carried shields. They looked like a chorus of brigands in an amateur pantomime.

"What is the meaning of this?" barked Dr Vambrace.

Chudleigh Pomeroy stepped forward, holding a blunderbuss with a brass muzzle as broad as a tuba's. Katherine started to realize that other Historians were watching from the shadows at the edges of the hall, lurking behind display cases, pointing steam-powered rifles through the articulated ribs of dinosaurs.

"Gentlemen," said Pomeroy nervously, "you are on the property of the Guild of Historians. I suggest that you unhand those young people immediately."

"Immediately!" agreed Dr Karuna, training her dusty musket on the red wheel between Vambrace's eyebrows.

The Engineer began to laugh. "You old fools! Do you think you can defy us? Your Guild will be disbanded because of what you've done here today. Your silly trifles and trinkets will be fed to the furnaces, and your bodies will be broken on engines of pain in the Deep Gut. We'll make you history, since history is all you care about! We are the Guild of Engineers! We are the future!"

There is a heartbeat pause, near-silent, just the echo of Vambrace's voice hanging on the musty air and the faint sounds of men reaching for guns and arthritic fingers tightening on ancient triggers. Then the foyer vanishes into smoke and stabbing darts of fire, and the noise bounces from the high-domed roof and comes slamming down again, a ragged crackle split by the deep boom of Pomeroy's blunderbuss and the shrieking roar of an old cannon concealed in a niche behind the ticket office, which goes off with a great jet of flame as Dr Nancarrow sets his lighter to the touch-hole. Katherine sees Vambrace and the two men next to him swiped aside, sees Dr Arkengarth falling backwards with his arms windmilling, feels the man who holds her jerk and stumble and the thick slap as a musket-ball goes through his rubber coat.

He falls away from her, and she drops to her knees and wonders where to hide. Nothing remains of Vambrace but his smouldering boots, which would be cartoony and almost funny except that his feet are still inside them. Half his men are down, but the rest are rallying, and they have better weapons than the Historians. They spray the foyer with gunfire, striking sparks from the marble floor and flinging splinters of dinosaur bone high into the air. Display cases come apart in bright cataracts of powdered glass, and the Historians who are cowering behind them go scrambling back to other hiding places, or fall among the fallen exhibits and lie still. Above them, argon-globes smash and gutter until the hall is dark, stuttering like cine-film in the migraine flicker of gun-light, and the Engineers are pushing forward through it towards the doors.

Behind them, forgotten, Bevis Pod reaches for an abandoned gun and swings it up, his long hands feeling their way across the shiny metal for catches and triggers. Katherine watches him. The air around her is thick with wailing shot and whirling chips of marble and moaning battle-frisbees, but she cannot tear her eyes or her mind away from Bevis long enough to think about finding cover. She sees him unfold the gun's spindly arm-rest and wedge it into the crook of his elbow, and sees the small blue holes it makes in the backs of the Engineers' coats. They fling up their arms and drop their guns and spin about and fall, and Bevis Pod watches them through the bucking sights with a calm, serious look, not her gentle Bevis any more but someone who can kill quite coldly, as if the Engineer in him really does have no regard for human life, or maybe he has just seen so much death in the Deep Gut that he thinks it is a little thing and does not mind dealing it out.

And when he stops shooting it is very quiet, just the rubbery lisp of the corpses settling and a quick bony rattle that Katherine slowly recognizes as the sound of her own teeth chattering.

From the corners of the hall Historians came creeping. There were more of them than Katherine had feared. In the flicker of battle she had thought she saw all of them shot, but, although some were wounded, the only ones dead were a man called Weymouth, who she had never spoken to, and Dr Arkengarth. The old curator of ceramics lay near the door, looking indignant, as if death was a silly modern fad that he rather disapproved of.

Bevis Pod knelt staring at the gun in his hands, and his hands were shaking, and blue smoke unravelled from the mouth of the gun and drifted up in scrolls and curlicues towards the roof.

Pomeroy came stumping up the stairs. His wig had been blown off and he was nursing a wound on his arm where a splinter of bone had cut him. "Look at that!" he said. "I must be the first person to be harmed by a dinosaur for about seventy million years!" He blinked at Katherine and Bevis, then at the fallen Engineers. None of them were laughing at his little joke. "Well!" he said. "Well, eh? Gosh! We showed them! As soon as I told the others what was going on we all agreed it wouldn't do. Well, most of us did. The rest are locked in the canteen, along with any apprentices we thought might support Crome's men. You should have seen us, Kate! 'We won't let them take Miss Valentine!' we all said, and we didn't. It goes to show, you know. An Engineer is no match for a Historian with his dander up!"

"Or *her* dander, CP!" chirped Moira Plym, hurrying up the steps to stand beside him. "Oh, that'll teach them to fiddle with my furniture, all right! That'll show them what happens to—" The visor of the helmet she was wearing snapped shut, muffling the rest.

Katherine found the fallen satchel, lying in the muck and blood on the stairs. It seemed to be undamaged, except for some unpleasant stains. "I've got to go to Top

Tier. Stop MEDUSA. It's the only way. I'll go to the elevator station and. . ."

"No!" Clytie Potts came bounding up the steps from the front entrance. "A couple of Engineers who were stationed outside got away," she said. "They'll have raised the alarm. There'll be a guard on the elevators, and more security men here at any minute. Stalkers too, probably." She met Pomeroy's worried gaze and dipped her head as if it was all her fault. "Sorry, CP."

"That's all right, Miss Potts." Pomeroy slapped her kindly on the shoulder, almost knocking her over. "Don't worry, Katherine. We'll keep the devils busy here, and you can sneak up to Top Tier by the Cat's Creep."

"What's that?" asked Katherine.

"It's the sort of thing Historians know about and everybody else has forgotten," said Pomeroy, beaming. "An old stairway, left over from the first days of London when the elevator system couldn't always be relied on. It goes up from Tier Three to Top Tier, passing through the Museum on the way. Are you ready to travel?"

She wasn't, but she nodded.

"I'm going with her," said Bevis.

"No!"

"It's all right, Kate. I want to." He was turning dead Engineers over, looking for a coat without too many holes in. When he found one he began to fumble with the rubber buttons. "If the Engineers see you walking about alone up there they'll guess what happened," he explained. "But if I'm with you, they'll think you're a prisoner."

"He's right, Kate," said Pomeroy, nodding, as Clytie Potts helped the young Engineer into the coat and wiped away the worst of the blood with the hem of her robe.

He checked his watch. "Eight-thirty. MEDUSA goes off at nine, according to the Goggle-screens. That should give you plenty of time to do whatever you're planning to do. But we'd better start you on your way, before those Engineers get back with reinforcements."

33

WINE AND NIBBLES AND THE
DAWN OF A NEW ERA

The *Jenny Haniver* was filled with memories of Anna Fang; the mark of her mouth on a dirty mug, the print of her body on the unmade bunk, a half-read book on the flight deck, marked with a ribbon at page 205. In one of the lockers Hester found a chest full of money; not just bronze coins but silver taels and golden sovereigns, more money than she or Tom had ever seen in their lives.

"She was rich!" she whispered.

Tom turned round in the pilot's seat and stared at the money. All through their long flight from Shan Guo he had not thought twice about taking the airship; he felt as if they were just borrowing her to finish a job that Miss Fang would have wanted done. Now, watching Hester lift the tinkling handfuls of coin, he felt like a thief.

"Well," said Hester, snapping the treasure-chest shut, "It's no use to her where she's gone. And no use to us, since I expect we'll soon be joining her there." She glanced up at him. "Unless you've changed your mind?"

He shook his head, although the truth was that the anger he had felt earlier had drained away during his struggles to master the airship and steer it westwards through the fickle mountain weather. He was starting to feel afraid, and starting to remember Katherine and wonder what would become of her when her father was dead. But he still wanted to make Valentine pay for all the misery he had caused. He started scanning the radio frequencies for London's homing beacon, while Hester hunted through the lockers until she found what she needed; a heavy black pistol and a long, thin-bladed knife.

⚙ ⚙ ⚙ ⚙ ⚙

For one night only, London's great council chamber has been decked out with lights and banners and turned into a party venue. The heads of the greater and lesser Guilds mingle happily among the green leather benches and sit on the speaker's dais, chattering excitedly about the new hunting ground, glancing at their watches from time to time as the hour for firing MEDUSA draws closer. Apprentice Engineers tack to and fro among the revellers, handing out experimental snacks prepared by Supervisor Nimmo's department. The snacks are brown and taste rather peculiar, but at least they are cut into perfectly geometrical shapes.

Valentine pushes his way through the crowd until he finds Crome and his aides, a wedge of white rubber surrounded by the tall black shapes of Stalker security guards. He wants to ask the Lord Mayor what became of the agent he sent after Hester Shaw. He wades towards them, elbowing well-upholstered Councillors aside and catching quick snatches of their conversation: "There's Valentine, look, back from Shan Guo!"

"Blew up the League's whole Air-Fleet, so I heard!"

"What charming snacks!"

"Valentine!" cries the Lord Mayor when the explorer finally reaches him. "Just the man we've been waiting for!"

He sounds almost jolly. Beside him stand the geniuses who have made MEDUSA work again: Dr Chandra, Dr Chubb and Doctor Wismer Splay, along with Dr Twix, who simpers and bobs a curtsy, congratulating Valentine on his trip to Shan Guo. Behind her the black-clad guards stand still as statues, and Valentine nods at them. "I see you've been making good use of the old Stalker parts I brought you, Crome. . ."

"Indeed," agrees the Lord Mayor with a chilly smile. "A whole new race of Resurrected Men. They will be our servants and our soldiers in the new world that we are about to build. Some are in action even as we speak, down at the Museum."

"The Museum?"

"Yes." Crome watches him slyly, gauging his reactions. "Some of your Historians are traitors, Valentine. Armed traitors."

"You mean there is fighting? But Kate's there! I must go to her!"

"Impossible," the Lord Mayor snaps, gripping his arm as he turns to leave. "Tier Two is out of bounds. The Museum is surrounded by Stalkers and Security teams. But don't worry. They have strict instructions not to harm your daughter. She will be brought up to join us as soon as possible. I particularly want her to watch MEDUSA in action. And I want you here too, Valentine. Stay."

Valentine stares at him, past the frozen faces of the other party-goers, in the sudden silence.

"Where does your real loyalty lie, I wonder," muses Crome. "With London, or with your daughter? Stay."

"Stay." As if he's a dog. Valentine's hand curls for a moment on his sword-hilt but he knows he will not draw it. The truth is that he is afraid, and all his adventures and expeditions have only been attempts to hide himself from this truth: he is a coward.

He stretches a smile across his trembling face, and bows.

"Your obedient servant, Lord Mayor."

❁ ❁ ❁ ❁ ❁

There was a door in the wall near Natural History, a door that Katherine must have passed hundreds of times without even seeing it. Now, as Pomeroy unlocked it and heaved it open, they heard the strange, echoing moan of wind in a long shaft, mingled with the rumble of the city's engines. He handed Bevis the key and a torch. "Good luck, Mr Pod. Kate, good luck. . ."

From somewhere behind him came a great dull boom that set the glass rattling in the display cases. "They're here," said Pomeroy. "I'm needed at my post. . ."

"Come with us!" Katherine begged him. "You'll be safer on Top Tier, among the crowds. . ."

"This is my Museum, Miss Valentine," he reminded her, "and this is where I'll stay. I'd only get in your way up there."

She hugged him, pressing her face into his robe and savouring its smell of mothballs and pipe-tobacco. "Your poor Museum!"

Pomeroy shrugged. "I don't think the Engineers would have let us keep hold of our relics much longer. At least this way we'll go down fighting."

"And you might win. . ."

"Oh, yes," the old Historian gave a rueful chuckle. "We used to thrash them regularly in the inter-guild football cup, you know. Of course, they didn't have machine-guns and Stalkers to help them. . ." He lifted her face and looked into her eyes, very serious. "Stop them, Katherine. Stick a spanner in the works."

"I'll try," she promised.

"We'll meet again soon," said Pomeroy firmly, hefting his blunderbuss as he turned away. "You've got your father's gift, Kate: people follow you. Look at the way you stirred us up!"

They heard the cannon roar again as he closed the door on them, and then the clatter of small-arms, closer now and tangled with faint screams.

◊ ◊ ◊ ◊ ◊

"There!" said Tom.

They were flying high through thin drifts of cloud, and he was looking down at London, far ahead.

"There!"

It was bigger than he remembered, and much uglier. Strange, how when he lived there he had believed everything the Goggle-screens told him about the city's elegant lines, its perfect beauty. Now he saw that it was ugly; no better than any other town, just bigger; a storm-front of smoke and belching chimneys, a wave of darkness rolling towards the mountains with the white villas of High London surfing on its crest like some delicate ship. It didn't look like home.

"There. . ." he said again.

"I see it," said Hester, beside him. "Something's going on on Top Tier. It's lit up like a fairground. Tom, that's where Valentine will be! They must be getting ready to use MEDUSA!"

Tom nodded, feeling guilty at the mention of MEDUSA. He knew that if Miss Fang were here she would be coming up with a plan to stop the ancient weapon, but he did not see what he could do about it. It was too big, too terrible, too hard to think about. Better to concentrate on what mattered to him and Hester, and let the rest of the world look after itself.

"He's down there," whispered the girl. "I can feel him."

Tom didn't want to go too close, in case the Lord Mayor had set men to watch the skies, or sent up a screen of spotter-ships. He tugged on the controls and felt the big, slow movement as the airship responded. She rose, and London faded to a smudge of speeding light beneath the cloud as he steered her southward and began to circle round.

✿ ✿ ✿ ✿ ✿

They climbed out of darkness into darkness, Bevis Pod's torch flittering on stair after identical metal stair. Their big shadows slid up the walls of the shaft. They didn't speak much, but each listened to the other's steady breathing, glad of the company. Katherine kept looking back, expecting to see Dog at her heels.

"Five hundred steps," whispered Bevis, stopping on a narrow landing and shining his torch upward. The stairs spiralled up for ever. "This must be Tier One. Halfway."

Katherine nodded, too out-of-breath to speak, too on-edge to rest. Above them the Lord Mayor's reception must be in full swing. She climbed on, her knees growing stiff, each intake of breath a cold hard ache in the back of her throat, the too-heavy satchel banging against her hip.

❀ ❀ ❀ ❀ ❀

Through the windows of the airship Hester could see the Out-Country streaming past, only a hundred or so feet below, scarred with the same ruler-straight trenches that she and Tom had stumbled along on the days after they first met. And there was London, red tail-lights in the darkness, dimming as Tom brought the airship up into the thick poison-fog of the city's exhaust. He was good at this, she realized, and thought what a pity it was that his plan was not going to work.

The radio crackled into life; London Docks and Harbour Board, demanding their identity codes.

Tom looked back at her, scared, but she knew how to handle this. She went to the radio and flipped the "transmit" switch up and down quickly, garbling her message as if the communications system was shot. "London Airship GE47," she said, remembering the code name that had come crackling over the inn's loudspeakers in Airhaven all those weeks before. "We're taking Shrike back to the Engineerium."

The radio said something, but she snapped it off. Black smog pressed against the windows, and water droplets condensed on the glass and went quivering off this way and that, leaving wriggly trails.

"I'll circle the city for twenty minutes and then come in and pick you up," Tom was saying. "That should give you time to find Valentine and. . ."

"I'll be dead in twenty minutes, Tom," she said. "Just get yourself safe away. Forget about me."

"I'll circle back. . ."

"I'll be dead."

"I'll circle back anyway. . ."

"There's no point, Tom."

"I'll circle back and pick you up."

She looked at him and saw tears shining in his eyes. He was crying. He was crying for her, because she was going into danger and he would not see her again, and she thought it was strange that he cared about her that much, and very sweet. She said, "Tom, I wish. . ." and, "Tom, if I. . ." and other little broken bits of sentences that petered out in silence, because she didn't even know herself what she was trying to say, only that she wanted him to know that he was the best thing that had happened to her.

A light loomed out of the swirling dark, then another. They were rising past Tier Three, and very close. Tier Two slid by, with people staring up from an observation deck, and then Circle Park with lanterns strung between the trees. Tom fumbled with the controls and the *Jenny* went powering forward, low over the rooftops of Knightsbridge and up towards the aft edge of Top Tier. He glanced quickly at Hester. She wanted to hug him, kiss him, something, but there was no time now, and she just gasped, "Tom, don't get yourself killed," slammed the hatch-controls to "open" and ran to it and jumped as the airship swung in a shuddery arc over the rim of Top Tier.

She hit the deckplate hard and rolled over and over. The *Jenny Haniver* was pulling away fast, lit by the sparkling trails of rockets from an air-defence battery on the Engineerium. The rockets missed, darkness swallowed the airship, and she was alone, scrambling into the shadows.

✿ ✿ ✿ ✿ ✿

"A single airship, Lord Mayor." It is a nervous-looking Engineer, a shell-like radio clipped to his ear. "It has pulled clear, but we believe it may have landed a boarding party."

"Anti-Tractionists on Top Tier?" The Lord Mayor nods, as if this is the sort of little problem that crops up every day. "Well, well. Dr Twix, I think this might be a good opportunity to test your new models."

"Oh, goody!" trills the woman, dropping a plate of canapés in her excitement. "Come along, my chicks! Come along!"

Her Stalkers turn with a single movement and form up behind her, striding through thrilled party-goers to the exits.

"Bring me the boarders alive!" Crome calls after her. "It would be a pity if they missed the big event."

34
IDEA FOR A
FIREWORKS DISPLAY

Tom wiped at his eyes with the heel of one hand and concentrated on his flying, steering the *Jenny* away from London and up. He wasn't frightened now. It felt good to be doing something at last, and good to be in charge of this huge, wonderful machine. He turned her eastwards, pointing her nose towards the last faint gleam of day on the summit of Zhan Shan. He would circle for twenty minutes. It felt as if half that time had passed already, but when he checked the chronometers he saw that it was less than two minutes since Hester jumped down into London and—

A rushing, brilliant thing slammed into the gondola, and the blast plucked him out of his seat. He clung to a stanchion and saw papers and instrument panels and sputtering lengths of cable and the shrine with its photographs and ribbons and Miss Fang's half-read book all rushing out through a jagged hole in the fuselage, tumbling into the sky like ungainly birds. The big windows shattered and the air turned sharp and shimmery with flying glass.

He craned his neck, peering up through the empty windows, trying to see if the envelope was burning. There were no flames, but overhead a great dark shape slid past, moonlight slithering along its armoured envelope. It was the *13th Floor Elevator,* pulling past the *Jenny* and performing a lazy victory-roll far over the foothills of Shan Guo before it came sweeping back to finish him.

Magnus Crome watches his guests crowd out into the square, gazing up at the glare and flicker of the battle taking place above the clouds. He checks his wristwatch. "Dr Chandra, Dr Chubb, Dr Splay; it is time to deploy MEDUSA. Valentine, come with us. I'm sure you are keen to see what we've made of your machine."

"Crome," says the explorer, blocking his path, "there is something I must say. . ."

The Lord Mayor raises an eyebrow, intrigued.

Valentine hesitates. He has been planning this speech all evening, knowing that it is what Katherine would want him to say. Now, faced with the Lord Mayor's arctic eyes, he falters, stammering a moment. "Is it worth it, Crome?" he says at last. "Destroying the Shield-Wall will not destroy the League. There will be other strongholds to defeat, hundreds of fortresses, thousands of lives. Is it really worth so much, your new hunting ground?"

There is a ripple of amazement among the bystanders. Crome says calmly, "You have left it rather late to have doubts, Valentine. You worry too much. Dr Twix can build whole armies of Stalkers, more than enough to crush any resistance from Anti-Tractionist savages."

He starts to push past, but Valentine is in front of him again. "Think, Lord Mayor. How long will a new hunting ground support us? A thousand years? Two thousand? One day there will be no more prey left anywhere, and London will have to stop moving. Perhaps we should accept it; stop now, before any more innocent people are killed; take what you have learned from MEDUSA and use it for peaceful purposes. . ."

Crome smiles. "Do you really think I am so short-sighted?" he asks. "The Guild of Engineers plans further ahead than you suspect. London will never stop moving.

Movement is life. When we have devoured the last wandering city and demolished the last static settlement we will begin digging. We will build great engines, powered by the heat of the earth's core, and steer our planet from its orbit. We will devour Mars, Venus and the asteroids. We shall devour the sun itself, and then sail on across the gulf of space. A million years from now our city will still be travelling, no longer hunting towns to eat, but whole new worlds!"

Valentine follows him to the door and out across the square towards St Paul's. *Katherine is right*, he keeps thinking. *He's as mad as a spoon! Why didn't I put a stop to his schemes when I had the chance?* Above the clouds, the rockets flare and bang, and the light of an exploding airship washes across the upturned faces of the crowd, who murmur, "Ooooooooh!"

And Hester Shaw crouches at the Tier's edge as the Resurrected Men stalk by, green eyes sweeping the walls and deckplates, steel claws unsheathed and twitching.

The Cat's Creep ended in a small circular chamber with stencilled numbers on the sweaty walls and a single metal door. Bevis slipped the key into the lock, and Katherine heard it turn. A crack of light appeared around the door's edge, and she heard voices outside, a long, tremulous, "Ooooh!"

"We're in an alley off Paternoster Square," Bevis said. "I wonder why they sound so excited?"

Katherine pulled out her watch and held it in the thin sliver of light from the door. "Ten to nine," she said. "They're waiting for MEDUSA."

He hugged her one last time and whispered quickly, shyly, "I love you!" Then he pushed her past him through the door and stepped out after her, trying to look like her captor, not her friend, and wondering if any other Engineer had ever said what he had just said, or felt the way he felt when he was with Katherine.

◊ ◊ ◊ ◊ ◊

Tom scrambled through the debris in the listing wreck of the *Jenny*'s gondola. The lights were out and blood was streaming into his eyes from a cut on his forehead, blinding him. The pain of his broken ribs washed through him in sick, giddy waves and all he wanted to do was lie down and close his eyes and rest, but he knew he mustn't. He fumbled for the rocket controls, praying to all the gods he had ever heard of that they had not been blown away. And sure enough, at the flick of the right switch a viewing scope rose out of the main instrument panel, and he wiped his eyes and saw the dim upside-down ghost of the *13th Floor Elevator* framed in the cross-hairs, growing bigger every minute.

He heaved as hard as he could on the firing controls, and felt the deck shift under him as the rockets went shrieking out of their nests beneath the gondola. Dazzling light blossomed as they hit their target, but when he blinked the bright after-images away and peered out the black airship was still there, and he realized that he had barely dented the great armoured envelope, and that he was going to die.

But he had bought himself a few more moments, at least, for the *Elevator*'s starboard rocket projectors were damaged and she was pulling past him and turning to bring her port array to bear. He tried to calm himself. He tried to think of Katherine, so that the memory of her would be what he took down with him to the Sunless Country, but it was a long time since he had dreamed of her, and he couldn't really remember what she looked like any more. The only face that he could call to mind was Hester's, and so he thought of her and the things that they had gone through together, and how it had felt to hold her on the Shield-Wall last night, the smell of her hair and the warmth of her stiff, bony body through the ragged coat.

And from some corner of his memory came the echo of the League rockets that had battered at the *13th Floor Elevator* as she banked away from Batmunkh Gompa; the thick crump of the explosions and the small, bright, prickling noise of broken glass.

Her envelope was armoured, but the windows could be broken.

He lurched back to the rocket controls and re-targeted them so that the cross-hairs on the little screen were centred not on the *Elevator*'s looming gasbags, but on her windows. The gauge beside the viewscope told him he had three rockets left, and he fired them all together, the shattered gondola shivering and groaning as they sprang away towards their target.

For a fraction of a second he saw Pewsey and Gench on their flight-deck, staring at him, faces wide with silent terror. Then they vanished into brightness as the rockets tore in through their viewing windows and their gondola filled with fire. A geyser of flame went tearing up the companion-ladders between the gasbags and blew out the top of the envelope. By the time Tom could see again the huge wreck was veering away from him, fire in her ruined gondola and the hatches of her hold, fire flapping from her steering vanes, fire unravelling from shattered engine-pods, fire lapping inside her envelope until it looked like a vast Chinese lantern tumbling down towards the lights of London.

Katherine stepped out of the alley's mouth into a running crowd, people all around her looking up, some still clutching drinks and nibbles, their eyes and mouths wide open. She looked at St Paul's. The dome had not yet opened, so it couldn't be that that they were staring at. And what was this light, this swelling orange glow that outshone the argon-lamps and made the shadows dance?

At that moment the blazing wreckage of an airship came barrelling out of the sky and crashed against the façade of the Engineerium in a storm of fire and glass and out-flung scythes of blackened metal. A whole engine broke free of the wreck and came cartwheeling across the square towards her, red hot and spraying blazing fuel. Bevis pushed her aside and down. She saw him standing over her, his mouth open, shouting something, and saw a blue eye on the blistered engine cowling as it tore him away, a whirl of limbs, a flap of a torn white coat, his scream lost in the bellow of twisting metal as the wreckage smashed against the Top Tier elevator station.

A blue eye on the cowling. She knew it should mean something, but she could not think what.

She stood up slowly, shaking. There were small fires on the deck all round her, and one great fire in the Engineerium that cast Hallowe'en light across the whole tier. She stumbled to where the blazing engine lay, its huge propeller blades jutting out of the deck-plate like megaliths. Raising her hand to shield her face against the belching heat, she looked for Bevis.

He was lying broken in a steep angle of the debris, twisted in such impossible ways that Katherine knew at once there was no point even calling out his name. The flames were rising, making his coat bubble and drip like melting cheese, heat pressing against her face, turning her tears to puffs of steam, driving her backwards over wreckage and bodies and pieces of bodies.

"Miss Katherine?"

A blue eye on the engine cowling. She could still see the outline, the paint peeling under the tongues of the fire. Father's ship.

"Miss Katherine?"

She turned and found one of the men from the elevator station standing with her, trying to be kind. He took her by the arm and led her gently away, gesturing towards the main part of the wreck, the scorching firestorm in the Engineerium. "He wasn't in it, Miss."

She stared at his smile. She didn't understand. Of course he had been in it! She had seen him there, his dead, gaping face and the flames rising round him. Bevis, whom she had led here, who had loved her. What was there to smile about?

But the man kept smiling. "He wasn't aboard, Miss. Your dad, I mean. I saw him not five minutes ago, going into St Paul's with the Lord Mayor.

She felt the sinister weight of the satchel still hanging

from her shoulder, and remembered that she had a job to do.

"Come on, Miss," said the man. "You've had a nasty shock. Come and have a sit down and a nice cup of tea. . ."

"No," she said. "I have to find my father."

She left him there and turned away, stumbling across the square, through panicked crowds in smoke-stained robes and party-frocks, through the long, shivering bray of sirens to St Paul's.

◊ ◊ ◊ ◊ ◊

Hester was darting towards the Guildhall when the explosion lifted her off her feet and flung her out of the shadows and into the harsh spill of light from the blazing Engineerium. She rolled over and over on the quaking deckplate, stunned, her pistol skittering away, her veil torn off. There was a moment of silence, then noises came crowding in; screams, sirens. She shuffled through her memories of the moments before the blast, trying to put them in some sort of order. That light above the rooftops, that burning thing sliding down the sky, had been an airship. The *Jenny Haniver*. "Tom," she said, whispering his name to the hot pavement, and felt smaller and more alone than ever before.

She pushed herself up on all fours. Nearby, one of the new Stalkers had been caught by the blast and cut in half, and its legs were stamping aimlessly about and bumping into things. The shawl that Tom had given her blew past. She caught it, knotted it around her neck and turned to look for the fallen gun, only to find another squad of Stalkers, quite unharmed, closing in upon her from behind. Their claws were fire-coloured slashes in the darkness, and firelight lit their long, dead faces, and she realized with a hollow stab of disappointment that this was the end of her.

And above the black, silhouetted rooftops of the Guildhall, beyond the smoke and the dancing sparks, the dome of St Paul's was starting to open.

The *Jenny Haniver*'s shattered gondola moaned like a flute as the west wind blew through it, carrying it swiftly away from London.

Tom slumped exhausted at the controls, crumbs of broken glass clinging like grit to his face and hands. He tried to ignore the wild spinning of the pressure gauges as hydrogen leaked from the damaged envelope. He tried not to think about Pewsey and Gench, burning inside their burning gondola, but every time he closed his eyes he saw their screaming faces, as if the black zeroes of their open mouths were etched for ever on to his eyeballs.

When he raised his head he saw London, far to the east. Something was happening to the cathedral, and torrents of pink and green fire were gushing from the Engineerium. Slowly he started to understand what had happened. It was his fault! People must be dead down there, not just Pewsey and Gench but lots of people, and if he had not shot down the *13th Floor Elevator* they would still be alive. He wished he had never fired those rockets. It would be better to be dead himself than to sit here watching Top Tier burn and know that it was all his fault.

Then he thought, *Hester!*

He had promised her he would go back. She would be waiting, down there among the fires. He couldn't let her down. He took a deep breath and leaned on the controls. The engines choked back into life. The *Jenny Haniver* turned sluggishly into the wind and started inching back towards the city.

Katherine moved like a sleepwalker through Paternoster Square, drawn towards the transformed cathedral. Around her the fires were spreading, but she barely noticed. Her eyes were fixed on the terrible beauty above her; that white cowl unfolding against the night sky, turning towards the east. She no longer felt afraid. She knew Clio was watching over her, keeping her safe so that she could atone for the dreadful things Father had done.

The guards on the cathedral door were too distracted by the fires to pay much attention to a schoolgirl with a satchel. At first they told her to clear off, but when she insisted that her father was inside and flashed her crumpled gold pass at them they simply shrugged and let her through.

She had never been inside St Paul's before, but she had seen pictures. They hadn't looked anything like *this*.

The pillared aisles and the high, vaulted ceilings were still where they had always been, but the Guild of Engineers had sheathed the walls in white metal and hung argon globes in wire cages from the ceilings. Fat electric cables snaked up the nave, feeding power towards something at the heart of the cathedral.

Katherine walked slowly forward, keeping to the shadows under the pillars, out of the way of the scores of Engineers who were scurrying about checking power-linkages and making notes on clipboards. Ahead of her, the dais under the great dome was filled with strange machinery. A mass of girders and hydraulics supported the weight of the huge cobra-hood that towered up into the night, and around its base stood a forest of tall metal coils, all humming and crackling in a slowly rising surge of power. Engineers were hurrying between them, and going up and down the central tower on metal stairways, and many more were clustered around a nearby console like priests at the altar of a machine god, talking in hushed, excited voices. Among them she saw the Lord Mayor, and beside him, looking grim, was Father.

She froze, safe in the shadows. She could see his face quite clearly. He was watching Crome, and frowning, and she knew he would rather be outside helping with the rescue-work and only the Lord Mayor's orders kept him here. She forgot for a moment that he was a murderer; she wanted to rush over and hug him. But she was in Clio's hands now, the agent of History, and she had work to do.

She edged closer, until she was standing in the shelter of an old font at the bottom of the dais steps. From there she had a good view of what Crome and the others were doing. Their console was a cat's cradle of wires and flexes and rubberized ducts, and in the middle of it sat a little sphere no bigger than a football. Katherine could guess what that was. Pandora Shaw had found it in a deep laboratory of lost America and brought it back with her to Oak Island, and Father had stolen it the night he murdered her. The Engineers had cleaned and repaired it as best they could, replacing damaged circuits with primitive machines that they had cobbled together from Stalkers' brains. Now Dr Splay sat in front of it, his fingers spidering over an ivory keyboard, typing up green, glowing sequences of numbers on a portable Gogglescreen. A second screen showed a murky image of the view ahead of London, cross-hairs centred on the distant Shield-Wall.

"The accumulators are charged," somebody said.

"There, Valentine!" said Crome, resting a bony hand on her father's arm. "We are ready to make history."

"But the fires, Crome. . ."

"You can play at firemen later," snapped the Lord Mayor. "We must destroy the Shield-Wall *now*, in case MEDUSA is damaged by the blaze."

Splay's fingers kept clattering on the keyboard, but the other sounds of the cathedral faded away. The Engineers were staring in awe at the coil-forest, where weird, rippling wraiths of light were forming, drifting upwards towards the sky above the open dome with a faint, insectile buzz. Katherine began to suspect that they didn't really understand this technology that her father had dug up for them; they were almost as awed by it as she.

If she had run forward then, primed her bomb and flung it at the ancient computer, she might have changed everything. But how could she? Father was standing right beside the thing, and even when she told herself that he was *not* her father any more and tried to weigh his life against the thousands about to die in Batmunkh Gompa, she still could not bring herself to harm him. She had failed. She turned her face to the vaulted roof and asked, *What do you want me to do? Why have you brought me here?*

But Clio didn't answer.

Crome stepped towards the keyboard. "Give MEDUSA its target coordinates," he ordered.

Splay's fingers rattled over the keys, typing in the latitude and longitude of Batmunkh Gompa.

"*Target acquired*," announced a mechanical voice, booming from fluted speakers above Splay's station.

"Range: 130 miles and closing. Input clearance code Omega."

Dr Chubb produced a sheaf of thick plastic sheets, the laminated fragments of ancient documents. Faint lists of numerals showed through the plastic, like insects trapped in amber, as he flipped through the sheets until he found the one he wanted and held it up for Splay to read.

But before Splay could begin typing in the code-numbers there was a confused babble of voices down by the main entrance. Dr Twix was there, with some of her Stalkers close behind her. "Hello, everybody!" she chirped, hurrying up the aisle and beckoning for her creations to follow. "Just look what my clever babies have found for you, Lord Mayor! A real live Anti-Tractionist, just as you asked. Though I'm afraid she's rather ugly. . ."

"Input clearance code Omega," repeated MEDUSA. The mechanical voice had not really changed, but to Katherine it sounded slightly impatient.

"Shut up, Twix!" barked Magnus Crome, staring at his instruments, but the others all turned to look as one of the Stalkers lurched up on to the dais and dumped its burden at the Lord Mayor's feet.

It was Hester Shaw, her hands tied in front of her, helpless and sullen and still wondering why the Stalkers had not killed her straight away. At the sight of her ruined face the men on the dais froze, as if her gaze had turned them all to stone.

Oh, great Clio! whispered Katherine, seeing for the first time what Father's sword had done. And then she looked from Hester's face to his, and what she saw there shocked her even more. The expression had drained from his features, leaving a grey mask, less human and more horrible than the girl's. This was how he must have looked when he killed Pandora Shaw and turned round to find Hester watching him. She knew what would happen next, even before his sword came singing from its sheath.

"*No!*" she screamed, seeing what he meant to do, but her mouth was dry, her voice a whisper. Suddenly she understood why the goddess had brought her here, and knew what she must do to make amends for Father's crime. She dropped the useless satchel and ran up the steps. Hester was stumbling backwards, lifting her bound hands to ward off Father's blow, and Katherine flung herself between them so that suddenly it was *she* who was in his path, and his sword slid easily through her and she felt the hilt jar hard against her ribs.

The Engineers gasped. Dr Twix gave a frightened little squeak. Even Crome looked alarmed.

"*Input clearance code Omega,*" snapped MEDUSA, as if nothing at all had happened.

Valentine was saying "No!", shaking his head as if he couldn't understand how she came to be here with his sword through her. "Kate, no!" He stepped back, pulling the blade free.

Katherine watched it slither out of her. It looked ridiculous, like a practical joke. There was no pain at all, but bright blood was throbbing out of a hole in her tunic and splashing on the floor. She felt giddy. Hester Shaw clutched at her but Katherine shook her off. "Father, don't hurt her," she said, and took two faltering steps forward and fell against Dr Splay's keyboard. Meaningless green letters spattered the little Goggle-screen as her head hit the keys, and as Father lifted her and laid her gently down she heard the voice of MEDUSA boom, *"Incorrect code entered."*

New sequences of numbers spilled across the screens. Something exploded with a sharp crack among the looping webs of cable.

"What's happening?" whimpered Dr Chubb. "What's it doing?"

"It has rejected our target coordinates," gasped Dr Chandra. "But the power is still building. . ."

Engineers rushed back to their posts, stumbling over Katherine where she lay on the floor, her head on Father's lap. She ignored them, staring at Hester's face. It was like looking at her own reflection in a shattered mirror, and she smiled, pleased that she had met her half-sister at last, and wondering if they were going to be friends. She started to hiccup, and with each hiccup blood came up her throat into her mouth. A numb chill was spreading through her body, and she could feel herself beginning to drift away, the sounds of the cathedral growing fainter and fainter. *Am I going to die?* she thought. *I can't, not yet, I'm not ready!*

"Help me!" Valentine bellowed at the Engineers – but they were only interested in MEDUSA. It was the girl who came to his side and lifted Katherine while he ripped a strip from his robe and tried to staunch the bleeding. He looked up into her one grey eye and whispered, "Hester . . . thank you!"

Hester stared back at him. She had come all this way to kill him, through all these years, and now that he was at her mercy she felt nothing at all. His sword lay on the ground where he had dropped it. No one was watching her. Even with her wrists bound she could have snatched it up and stuck it through his heart. But it didn't seem to matter now. Dazed, she watched his tears fall, plopping into the astounding lake of blood that was spreading out from his daughter's body. Confused thoughts chased each other through her head. *He loves her! She saved my life! I can't let her die!*

She reached out and touched him, and said, "She needs a doctor, Valentine."

He looked at the Engineers, clustering around their machine in a frantic scrum. There would be no help from them. Outside the cathedral doors curtains of golden fire swung across Paternoster Square. He looked up, and saw something red catch the firelight beyond the high windows of the starboard transept.

"It's the *Jenny Haniver*!" shouted Hester, scrambling to her feet. "Oh, it's Tom! And there's a medical bay aboard. . ." But she knew the *Jenny* couldn't land amidst the flames of Top Tier. "Valentine, can we get on to the roof somehow?"

Valentine picked up his sword and cut the cords on her wrists. Then, flinging it aside, he lifted Katherine and started to carry her between the spitting coils to where the metal stairway zig-zagged up into the dome. Stalkers reached out for Hester as she scurried after him, but Valentine ordered them back. To a startled Beefeater he shouted, "Captain! That airship is not to be fired upon!"

Magnus Crome came running to clutch at his sleeve. "The machine has gone mad!" he wailed. "Quirke alone knows what commands your daughter fed it! We can't fire it and we can't stop the energy build-up! Do something, Valentine! You discovered the damned thing! Make it stop!"

Valentine shoved him aside and started up the steps,

through the rising veils of light, the crackling static, through air that smelled like burning tin.

"I only wanted to help London!" the old man sobbed. "I only wanted to make London *strong*!"

36

THE SHADOW OF BONES

Hester took the lead, climbing up through the open top of the dome into smoky firelight and the shadow of the great weapon. Off to her right, the charred skeleton of the *13th Floor Elevator* lay draped over the ruins of the Engineerium like a derelict rollercoaster. The fire had spread to the Guildhall, and the Planning Department and the Hall of Records were blazing, hurling out firefly-swarms of sparks and millions of pink and white official forms. St Paul's was an island in a sea of fire, with the *Jenny Haniver* swinging above it like a low-budget moon, scorched and listing, veering drunkenly in the updraughts from the burning buildings.

She climbed higher, out on to the cobra-hood of MEDUSA. Valentine came after her; she could hear him whispering to Katherine, his eyes fixed on the struggling airship.

"What idiot is flying that thing?" he shouted, working his way across the cowl to join her.

"It's Tom!" Hester called back, and stood up, waving both arms and shouting, "Tom! Tom!"

◎ ◎ ◎ ◎ ◎

It was the shawl that Tom saw first, the one he had bought for her in Peripatetiapolis. Knotted round her neck now, streaming on the wind, it made a sudden flash of red, and he saw it from the corner of his eye and looked down and saw her there, waving. Then a black wing of smoke came down over her and he wondered if he had only imagined that tiny figure inching out on to the cobra's hood, because it seemed impossible that anyone could survive in this huge fire that he had caused. He made the *Jenny Haniver* swoop closer. The smoke lifted, and there she was, flapping her arms, with her long black coat and her long-legged stride and her ugly, wonderful face.

❀ ❀ ❀ ❀ ❀

Katherine opened her eyes. The cold inside her was growing, spreading from the place where the sword had gone in. She was still hiccuping, and she thought how stupid it would be to die with hiccups, how undignified. She wished Dog was with her. "Tom! Tom!" somebody kept shouting. She turned her head and saw an airship coming down out of the smoke, closer and closer until the side of the gondola scraped against MEDUSA's cowl and she felt the down-draught from its battered engine pods. Father was carrying her towards it, and she could see Tom peering out at her through the broken windscreen, Tom who had been there when it all began, whom she had thought was dead. But here he was, alive, looking shocked and soot-stained, with a V-shaped wound on his forehead like the mark of some unknown Guild.

The gondola was much bigger inside than she expected. In fact, it was a lot like Clio House, and Dog and Bevis were both waiting for her there, and her hiccups had stopped, and her wound wasn't as bad as everyone had thought, it was just a scratch. Sunlight streamed in through the windows as Tom flew them all up and up into a sky of the most perfect crystal blue, and she relaxed gratefully into her father's arms.

Hester reached the airship first, hauling herself aboard through its shattered flank. But when she looked back, holding out her hand to Valentine, she saw that he had fallen to his knees, and realized Katherine was dead.

She stayed there, still with her hand outstretched, not quite knowing why. There was an electric shimmer in the air above the white metal hood. She shouted, "Valentine! Be quick!"

He lifted his eyes from his daughter's face just long enough to say, "Hester! Tom! Fly! Save yourselves!"

Behind her Tom was cupping his hands to his ears and shouting, "What did he say? Is that Katherine? What's happened?"

"Just go!" she yelled, and, clambering past him, started switching all the engines that still worked to full power. When she looked down again Valentine was dwindling away below, a dark shape cradled in his arms, a pale hand trailing. She felt like Katherine's ghost, rising into the sky. There was a terrible pain inside her and her breath came in sobs and something wet and hot was spilling down her cheek. She wondered if she could have been wounded without noticing it, but when she put her hands to her face her fingers came away wet, and she understood that she was crying, crying for her mum and dad, and Shrike, and Katherine, and even for Valentine as the crackling light around the cathedral grew brighter and Tom steered the *Jenny Haniver* away into the dark.

Down in the Gut, London's enormous motors suddenly cut out, without warning and all at once, doused by the strange radiations that were starting to sleet through the city's fabric. For the first time since it crossed the land-bridge the great Traction City started to slow.

In a hastily barricaded gallery in the London Museum, Chudleigh Pomeroy peered cautiously over the replica of the Blue Whale and saw that the squads of Stalkers advancing on his last redoubt had all stopped in their tracks, pale clouds of sparks coiling about their metal skulls like barbed wire. "Great Quirke!" he said, turning to his surviving handful of Historians. "We've won!"

Valentine watches the red airship fly away, lit by the flames of Top Tier and by the spitting forks of light that are beginning to flare around St Paul's. He can hear hopeless fire-bells jangling somewhere below, and the panic-stricken shouts of fleeing Engineers. A halo of St Elmo's fire flares around Katherine's face and her hair sparks and cracks as he strokes it. He gently moves a stray strand which has blown into her mouth, and holds her close, and waits – and the storm-light breaks over them and they are a knot of fire, a rush of blazing gas, and gone: the shadows of their bones scattering into the brilliant sky.

37
THE BIRD ROADS

L ondon wore a wreath of lightning. It was as if the ray that should have reached out across a hundred miles to sear the stones of Batmunkh Gompa had tangled around the upper tiers instead, sending cataracts of molten metal splashing down the city's flanks. Explosions surged through the Gut, heaving vast fragments of wreckage end-over-end into the sky like dead leaves in a gale. A few airships rose with them, seeking to escape, but their envelopes ignited and they shrivelled and fell, small bright flakes of fire amid the greater burning.

Only the *Jenny Haniver* survived, riding on the fringes of the storm, spinning and pitching as the shock waves battered her, streamers of rainbow light spilling from her rigging and rotor-blades. Her engines had all failed together in that first great pulse of energy, and nothing that Tom knew how to do would make them start again. He slumped down in what was left of the pilot's seat, weeping, watching helplessly as the night wind carried him further and further from his dying city.

"It's my fault," was all he could think to say. "It's all my fault. . ."

Hester was watching too, staring back at the place where St Paul's had been as if she could still see the after-images of Katherine and her father lost in the brightness there. "Oh, Tom, no," she said. "It was an accident. Something went wrong with their machine. It was Valentine's fault, and Crome's. It was the Engineers' fault for getting the thing to work and my mum's fault for digging it up in the first place. It was the Ancients' fault for inventing it. It was Pewsey's and Gench's fault for trying to kill you, and Katherine's for saving my life. . ."

She sat down beside him, wanting to comfort him but afraid to touch him, while her reflections sneered at her from fractured dials and blades of window-glass, more monstrous than ever in the fluttering glare of MEDUSA. Then she thought, *Silly, he came back, didn't he? He came back for you.* Trembling, she put her arms around him and pulled him close, nuzzling the top of his head, shyly kissing away the blood from the fresh wound between his eyebrows, hugging him tight until the dying weapon had spent itself and the first grey daylight crept across the plain.

"It's all right, Tom," she kept telling him. "It's all right. . ."

London was far away, motionless under banners of smoke. Tom found Miss Fang's old field glasses and focused them on the city. "*Someone* must have survived," he said, hoping that saying it would make it true. "I bet Mr Pomeroy and Clytie Potts are down there, organizing rescue parties and handing out cups of tea. . .. .." But through the smoke, the steam, the pall of hanging ash he could see nothing, nothing, nothing, and although he swung the binoculars to and fro, growing increasingly desperate, all they showed him were the bony shapes of blackened girders, and the scorched earth littered with torn-off wheels and blazing lakes of fuel and broken tracks lying tangled on themselves like the cast-off skins of enormous snakes.

"Tom?" Hester had been trying the controls, and had found to her surprise that the rudder-levers still worked. The *Jenny Haniver* responded to her touch, turning this way and that on the wind. She said gently, "Tom, we could try and reach Batmunkh Gompa. We'll be welcome there. They'll probably think you're a hero."

But Tom shook his head: behind his eyes the *13th Floor Elevator* was still spiralling towards Top Tier and Pewsey and Gench were riding their black, silent screams into the fire. He didn't know what he was, but he knew he was no hero.

"All right," said Hester, understanding. It took time to get over things sometimes, she knew that. She would be patient with him. She said, "We'll head for the Black Island. We can repair the *Jenny* at the air-caravanserai. And then we'll take the Bird Roads and go somewhere far away. The Hundred Islands, or the Tannhäuser Mountains, or the Southern Ice Waste. I don't mind where. As long as I can come too."

She knelt beside him, resting her arms on his knees and her head on her arms, and Tom found that he was smiling in spite of himself at her crooked smile. "You aren't a hero, and I'm not beautiful, and we probably won't live happily ever after," she said. "But we're alive, and together, and we're going to be all right."

ACKNOWLEDGEMENTS

I am gratefully indebted to Leon Robinson and Brian Mitchell, who provided me with inspiration, encouragement and good ideas, to Mike Grant, who published my early efforts in his late lamented small-press magazine *The Heliograph*, and to Liz Cross, Kirsten Skidmore and Holly Skeet, without whose patience, enthusiasm and sound advice this book would have ended its days in my fireplace as a lot of very neatly typed kindling.

Philip Reeve